Now You See Me

"Incredible! I could not put this book down. It caught me from page one and REFUSED to let me go until the very end. Author Tina Wainscott has the shining talent of being able to combine the genre of 'thriller' with the genre of 'romance' and somehow make it work! Once again Tina Wainscott delivers a heart-stopping story that will make many readers stay awake reading long into the night."

—*Huntress Reviews*

"Ms. Wainscott does a great job. Lots of tension and you're not sure who the killer is."

—*Old Book Barn Gazette*

"WOW! Ms. Wainscott is a suspense reader's dream author. The plot twist that develops halfway through threw me for a loop and I loved every minute of it. More twists and turns kept me turning the pages, cursing myself for not being able to read faster. Not only is the suspense at a fever pitch, but also the chemistry between Max and Olivia. . . . I'm on my way out to get more. I can't think of a higher recommendation than that."

—*Rendezvous*

Unforgivable

"*Unforgivable* is unforgettable, a rich, dark tapestry of good and evil—and the threads that bind them together. Excellent suspense; it literally kept me up all night reading."

—*Kay Hooper*, author of *Touching Evil*

"*Unforgivable* is a truly great read! Wainscott creates finely honed tension in a first-rate thriller where no one is who they seem and everyone is someone to fear. Don't miss it!"

—Lisa Gardner, *New York Times* bestselling author of *The Third Victim*

"Tina Wainscott kicks off her foray into the suspense genre in a very big way. *Unforgivable* is gripping, gritty, and quite terrifying."

—*Romantic Times* (Top Pick)

"How Mary Higgins Clark used to write . . . I will be keeping a sharp eye on this author!"

—Detra Fitch, *Huntress Reviews*

"Tina Wainscott delivers hard-hitting suspense with a touch of romance. With each turn of the page, the plot moves in surprising directions. The characters are finely crafted and complexly layered—nothing is as it seems. Be warned, this is not a story for the faint of heart; Wainscott's writing is often brutally direct and forthright. *Unforgivable* is unforgettable, romantic suspense of chilling intensity. Readers who appreciate well-written thrillers will enjoy this book."

—Megan Kopp, *Romance Reviews Today*

"Ms. Wainscott shows another side of her true talent as a writer . . . [The] suspense . . . grabs the reader from the very beginning and keeps the reader hooked until the very last page . . . I look forward to Ms. Wainscott's next mystery."

—*Interludes Reviews*

BACK IN BABY'S ARMS

"Ms. Wainscott sure knows how to add depth to her characters . . . The whiff-of-paranormal aspects, the passion, and the assorted conflicts within *Back in Baby's Arms* are what make Ms. Wainscott a favorite with both contemporary and paranormal fans."

—*Rendezvous*

"*Back in Baby's Arms* is a story of rebirth and renewal. . . . It is a tightly woven, very readable story . . . The suspense . . . makes this book a real page-turner."

—*HeartRate*

A Trick of the Light

"Tina Wainscott is back and in a big way. *A Trick of the Light* is suspenseful, poignant, and gripping. A great read."
—*Romantic Times*

"Wainscott delivers an unusual and satisfying romance with a supernatural twist."
—*Publishers Weekly*

"A five-star reading experience to savor . . . unforgettable!"
—*The Belles and Beaux of Romance*

"Ms. Wainscott has done a great job and has written one for your keeper shelf."
—*Old Book Barn Gazette*

"Fans of paranormal romances will feel they are on the way to heaven reading Tina Wainscott's latest winner . . . Wainscott makes the unbelievable feel real and right in such an exciting manner that her audience will want her next novel to be published tomorrow."
—*Affaire de Coeur*

"Quintessential romantic suspense. Wainscott, an award-winning author, knows how to keep her story moving and the sexual tension flowing . . . a book that will speak to both the primary fear of all parents and the hearts of all readers."
—*Once A Warrior Review*

"Remarkable . . . one of the most touching love stories I've read in a while . . . this is truly a 5-star!"
—*ADC's Five Star Reads*

IN A HEARTBEAT

"Contemporary romance with an intriguing twist. A pleasure for fans of romantic suspense."
— Deb Smith, *New York Times* bestselling author

"Wainscott . . . makes the impossible possible."
— Harriet Klausner

"Tina Wainscott has her finger firmly on the pulse of the romance genre, and with *In a Heartbeat* she catapults to the top of her peers . . . run, don't walk, to the nearest bookstore to buy this novel, which could possibly be the best contemporary of the year."
— *Under the Covers*

SECOND TIME AROUND

"Ms. Wainscott has a talent for making unusual situations believable . . . bravo!"
— *Rendezvous*

"A fabulous romantic suspense drama that melts readers' hearts . . . *Second Time Around* is worth reading the first time around, the second time around, and the nth time around."
— *Affaire de Coeur*

"A must-read . . . a well-written, romantic, feel-good story."
— *Gothic Journal*

ST. MARTIN'S PAPERBACKS TITLES
BY TINA WAINSCOTT

What She Doesn't Know

Now You See Me

A Trick of the Light

I'll Be Watching You

Second Time Around

Dreams of You

On the Way to Heaven

In a Heartbeat

Back in Baby's Arms

Unforgivable

IN
TOO
DEEP

Tina Wainscott

St. Martin's Paperbacks

IN TOO DEEP

Copyright © 2005 by Tina Wainscott.

Cover photo © Veer

ISBN: 0-312-93371-1
EAN: 9780312-93371-5

Printed in the United States of America

St. Martin's Paperbacks edition / October 2005

St. Martin's Paperbacks are published by St. Martin's Press, 175 Fifth Avenue, New York, NY 10010.

10 9 8 7 6 5 4 3 2 1

To Eva Rich . . . a woman who loved reading, loved life, and loved her family with the passion of a novel heroine. She will be missed, but she will never be forgotten.

And to Denise Simonds, Zoe's guardian angel.

ACKNOWLEDGMENTS

When you need help, you grab the nearest cop, right? Well, that's exactly what I did. (Okay, I didn't exactly *grab* him.) While in Miami doing research, I spotted an officer who was blissfully unaware that he was about to be assailed by something he'd never encountered before—an author. He graciously offered to answer some questions I had and was a wonderful help. My gratitude to Antonio "Tony" Sanchez, MSM, CLET, Commander, Investigative Services, Biscayne Park Police Department.

My appreciation also goes to David Kozad, retired police officer, for his answers to procedural questions.

Carol Glassman, journalist extraordinaire, helped with newspaper information.

Marty Ambrose, critique partner extraordinaire, gave me great feedback. My husband, Dave, was a big help with nailing down the plot on a drive to Miami.

As always, I found many wonderful books that helped to enrich my story. In particular, I wish to credit Ann Louise Bardach, author of *Cuba Confidential: Love and Vengeance in Miami and Havana.* Her book provided a fascinating subtext about Cubans living in Miami that I never knew about. Also helpful was *Cuban Miami,* by Robert M. Levine and Moisés Asís.

Another big help was Becky Mato, who gave me the particular phrases I needed in Spanish.

Also very appreciated was the Cuban deli around the corner that sated my constant craving for Cuban food during the writing of this book. Having grown up around Cubans, I have a deep admiration for them, their hardworking natures, and especially their fabulous food.

And finally, thanks to Tracy Jones for answering questions on magazine operations.

PROLOGUE

It was the greatest day ever, Elena Garcia thought, watching her uncle Luis cast his lure into the deep blue of Biscayne Bay. A little while ago he'd caught a young shark that had nearly tipped over their small boat. The disappearing sun splashed the sky with oranges and pinks. When she got home, she would take out her crayons and draw it for her *mami*, who hardly ever came out with them because of her journey from Cuba. She said only that the trip was long and hard, but Elena knew there was more to it from the shadows in her eyes the few times she talked about it.

Elena snuggled closer to her *pipa*, loving the sound of his laugh as Uncle Luis told a joke that she didn't understand. A boat engine drowned out the sound of their voices and laughter, though. When it kept getting louder, she lifted her head. Dusk played tricks on her eyes. It looked like a big, fancy speedboat was coming right at them. Then she realized it *was* coming at them.

Her father said a bad word. "Trying to play games with us," he muttered.

She could see two people on the boat, but they were in shadow. Any second it would veer away. Any second. But it didn't.

"Maybe it's not a game," Luis said. "Maybe they can't see us."

He and her father jumped up and waved their arms, shouting, "Hey! We're here!"

What was wrong with the two people on board? It was still light enough to see a boat on the water. *She* could see *them*. *Pipa*'s and Uncle Luis's voices suddenly faded. Why weren't they yelling? *Keep screaming and waving!* Then she saw: The boat kept coming, so loud, so fast, straight at them.

She couldn't move, even when *Pipa*'s scream returned in a way she'd never heard. She felt his hand shove her to the deck just before the boat crashed into theirs. Pieces flew through the air, stinging her arms and legs. The engine whined as the hull went over, and long seconds later it landed in the water on the other side.

Nothing seemed real in those minutes. Not the screaming nearby, the voice familiar, yet stretched thin in horror. Not the roar of the engine coming close once more. Was it going to hit them again? She waited for what seemed like forever, but her boat only moved up and down on the wake. The engine still filled the air with a choppy, hoarse noise and the smell of gas, but it was moving away.

Be brave, she told herself, making her eyes open. Blood. Everywhere, blood, dark red, shiny, on her arms and hands, dripping from the metal bench where she'd been sitting. She closed them again.

It's just paint, like the kind you used on the picture of the sun yesterday.

She forced her eyes open again. The bottom of the boat was filling with water, water mixed with red paint. She tried to sit up, but her arms hurt too much. Her fingers wouldn't work right. She used her hips to shift so she could see the rest of the boat. There, her *pipa,* lying on the other side of the bench, not moving! At least it looked like him. She could hardly see his face; it was covered in paint, too. Then she saw the deep cut across his chest, like the way Uncle Luis filleted the fish, the way you could see layers of muscle and bone.

But the fish were dead. *Pipa* couldn't be dead! She tried

to say his name, but her mouth wouldn't open. Though it hurt, she reached up and felt her face. At first she couldn't figure out what was wrong. All she knew was that something *was* very, very wrong. Her stomach lurched. *Her jaw was hanging from her face like a big lump of bread dough.* Her scream was only in her head, and even that was silenced as she fell into darkness.

1

Winslow Talbot relished her daily walk on the beach, especially with the snap of fall in the air. She looked at walking not as exercise but as a way to breathe, both physically and mentally. She loved living on the east coast of Florida, where she could watch the fireball rise out of the Atlantic Ocean every morning.

Winslow absently stepped around a clump of seaweed, her thoughts on the article she was working on for *Dazzle,* the society magazine where she was a feature writer. Her piece was on a young Nicaraguan artist, and Winslow was looking forward to seeing the exhibit and interviewing him that night. Writing challenged and fulfilled her, even before she knew what she wanted to do with her skills. Her stepfather, Grant, had gotten her the job at *Dazzle,* despite her assertion that she wanted to get it on her own merits.

Grant rarely asked permission; he just went ahead and did things for others. Of course she was grateful. He had been very good to her these past fourteen years.

The chirping of the cell phone clipped to her running shorts jarred her out of her thoughts.

"Winnie, it's me," Grant said when she answered. "You're at the beach, I presume?"

He was the only one she allowed to call her Winnie,

though she never let on just how reluctantly she did so. "You bet. What's up?"

"Can we switch our interview to this morning?"

Dazzle was doing a feature on Grant that was supposed to focus on him as a mover and shaker in Miami's real estate scene.

"I can come in about forty minutes if you don't mind a little sweat."

He chuckled. "You're beautiful, sweaty or not. See you soon."

Twenty minutes later she drank in one last look at the sun glinting off the cerulean ocean before walking to the parking lot. Her blue Volvo was another gift from Grant when he got embarrassed about her five-year-old car.

She could have probably bought ten Volvos for what the Ferrari he'd chosen would have cost. Sure, she liked nice cars, but flash wasn't her style. He'd been disappointed when she'd chosen the Volvo C70, a nice convertible in its own right. When she'd stood her ground, he had gone behind her back and ordered a flashy paint job—3-D silver cubes and spheres. She stood out whether she liked it or not. And she didn't.

At the light, she pulled the crossword puzzle magazine from the passenger seat and filled in an answer that Celine Dion's song reminded her of: *iceberg*. With the driving she did and the number of traffic lights she hit, she could usually finish a puzzle a day. A few minutes later she passed Haulover Park with the array of remarkable kites flying in the breeze. Her favorites were the ones that looked like swimming scuba divers. She crossed the bridge that led to Bal Harbour Village, a small, stylish community on the northern tip of the Miami Beach barrier islands. It was close enough to Miami Beach to feel the vibration of the excitement, the salsa beat, and the decadence, yet retain a subdued elegance.

Many a clever investor had racked up a shiny, new fortune

developing Miami. Her biological father had been one of those, risking everything on real estate schemes and riding the wave. Once, they had lived in a gated community: Paul; her mother, Georgina; and Winslow, one happy little family.

Until a reckless driver ended that one rainy Saturday night when Winslow was twelve. She'd gone with her dad to a meeting that had run past midnight. He was taking her for ice cream as he'd promised, making jokes to help her wake up. The truck had slammed into them from behind, sending them over the railing to the road below. Winslow crashed through the windshield when her restraints broke, ending up on the hood of the car.

She could still remember that moment of silence, so stunning after the sounds of crunching metal and shattering glass, then screeching brakes, people shouting, footsteps pounding on the pavement and splashing through puddles. She lifted herself and looked at her father. She would never forget the sight of him, his head cocked at an impossible angle, blood trickling from his mouth. She cried out, even though every movement sent excruciating pain through a face that felt as shattered as the windshield.

As terrible as that had been, what haunted her most was seeing the driver standing on the overpass looking down. She couldn't make out more than his height and thick, wavy hair. Then he ducked out of sight, leaving only the sound of burning rubber behind. She would never forget him standing there, doing nothing to help them.

Winslow had lost her father and then several months of her life while she recuperated in the hospital. In the aftermath the losses kept compounding. Nearly every bone in Winslow's face had been crushed. Paul had leveraged much of their assets on a development that couldn't survive without his guidance. All they had, once the debts had been paid off, was the house and the one life insurance policy he hadn't borrowed against. Even with health insurance, the costs were staggering.

Georgina's fierce pride kept her from telling anyone about their plight, much less asking for help. She sold off their valuables and pretended everything was fine for two years. She bought their clothing from sales racks. Winslow didn't mind the out of season clothing, but she hated the pretending, hated pushing her few remaining friends away so they wouldn't find out.

Grant, a business associate of Paul's, had checked in on them during those years. His and Georgina's marriage was one of convenience; he'd been a widower with a twelve-year-old daughter.

Grant had taken Winslow to a renowned plastic surgeon in Palm Beach and, without consulting her, had instructed him to make her doll perfect: altering her bone structure and giving her a sculpted chin and prominent cheekbones. Her first glimpse revealed the face of a stranger. Only her hazel eyes and dark brown hair were recognizable. Even now, as she glanced in the rearview mirror, she saw that stranger. A mask that she could never take off.

Winslow pulled around the curved road to the house. She parked in front of the three-car garage and clicked on her small recorder. "November second, interview with Grant Talbot, of the Connecticut Talbots. Angle is profile piece on one of the men responsible for creating Miami's skyline but just as well known for his charity works. Downplay political angle, though make it clear." Sebastian, her editor at *Dazzle,* wanted to feature Grant without having to interview the other candidates. That was the kind of loyalty Grant engendered.

She checked her jewelry, making sure that what little she wore were pieces Grant had given her. He chided her "simplistic" taste, at least compared to her stepsister Ashlyn's extravagance, but he'd finally accepted that one carat was preferable to five.

Winslow stepped out of the car and walked up the cascading steps to the entrance. Three years ago Grant had bought two adjoining lots in Bay Harbor Islands, west of Bal Harbor, with views of the Intracoastal and the Indian Creek Golf Course. The Mediterranean-style home boasted ornate columns, balconies, and arched windows with stone molding—an embarrassment of extravagance.

She let herself in and greeted the maid who usually answered the door. The rounded foyer had intricate inlaid marble floors and a ceiling that stretched thirty-eight feet high. A staircase curved to the second floor, adorned by a detailed iron and wood railing. Fresh flowers burst forth from Swarovski crystal vases as heavy as granite. Flowers were one of Georgina's lasting touches; Grant had never canceled the standing order. Winslow wondered if it was out of affection for Georgina's memory or because he never noticed the flowers—or the bill.

Winslow loved the textures of glass and the shell-stone wall, but she hated the coldness of the marble. At least her rubber beach shoes didn't echo as she walked to the right of the round, sunken living room.

Grant's office overlooked the terraced lanai and black pool with the infinity edge that seemed to drop into Indian Creek Lake. Through the open French doors she could see Grant on the ladder that reached the upper shelves of the built-in office furniture.

"Hi, Dad," she said.

He'd asked her to call him Dad even before he'd officially adopted her. She never called him Daddy. That's what Ashlyn called him in her possessive way, with a pointed look and lift of her chin, as though daring Winslow to try it.

He gave her the smile that was going to win him the governor's seat. "Be right with you, sweetheart." With book in hand, he climbed down the ladder. "Thanks for rescheduling."

"Anything for you," she said, meaning it.

Papers were scattered everywhere, flyers, forms, and publicity. She'd been too busy in the last few days to stop by and help get him organized, so she started sorting the papers on the coffee table while he flipped to a particular page and jotted something down.

"Ashlyn seemed to enjoy helping me out, but she hardly comes around anymore," he said, still writing. "When I mention it, she gets that pouty look and shrugs."

"I know that look. I've been careful not to usurp her place in your campaign. So have you. You haven't even asked for my advice in front of her."

Ashlyn had been threatened when she realized Grant sometimes asked Winslow's advice but never asked for Ashlyn's advice. For good reason, but no one would tell her that.

As Grant answered the ringing phone with an apologetic look, Jayce Bishop walked into the office carrying a sheaf of papers. His efficient smile disappeared when he saw Winslow organizing the files on the coffee table. "Don't do that. I had these exactly how I wanted them."

Jayce had fiercely dark blue eyes and feathery eyebrows as black as his hair. In his midtwenties, he still had a Cupid's bow mouth and a boyish face that oozed charm. If she'd spotted him as a stranger across the room, she might have thought his eyes alluring. It was the way he used them that negated the beauty and pushed them into unnerving.

"Didn't Grant tell you?" he said. "I'm his campaign manager."

Winslow looked at Grant. "I thought Pete was going to manage your campaign."

"He's about to embark on a nasty divorce. And Jayce here has experience."

Jayce said, "I worked with a family friend on his campaign for county commissioner. I've got it all under control. No need to worry your pretty head over anything." He went to work undoing what she'd just done, barely masking his annoyance.

She *was* worried. Jayce Bishop was a friend of one of the private country club's members. His family in Chicago was in the midst of a bitter inheritance battle, and he'd come to

Miami eight months ago to get away from the animosity. Though Winslow wasn't part of the country club crowd, she'd heard about his golf skills and his high-stakes betting. Members often bet five dollars a hole, but Jayce quickly garnered awe, ire, and respect by betting five thousand per hole. Grant had lost money, but he never seemed annoyed. Not only was Jayce a gracious winner, but he often gave his companions tips on their game as well.

Within two months he was being invited to dinner at the house, and within four months he and Ashlyn were engaged. Being a perfect son-in-law-to-be, he started helping out on Grant's campaign, talking him up at gatherings and benefits. Now Jayce was Grant's right-hand man. Jayce had shone his charm in Winslow's direction, too, saying he'd always wanted a sister. Something didn't feel right about him, though, and he'd picked up on her resistance. When he couldn't break past it, he backed off and merely treated her politely. She wondered if she was imagining the iciness in his eyes when he did look at her.

Grant slammed the phone down and pinched the bridge of his nose. "Winnie . . ."

"You have to reschedule," she said, coming to her feet and feeling some unexplainable relief to get away from Jayce. "It's all right. Let's do it tomorrow." She pulled out her Day Planner. "How's noon?"

Before he could reach for his schedule, Jayce answered. "We've got that charity golf scramble at nine, for cancer . . . or was it leukemia? One of those popular diseases. I think you're available in the afternoon."

Winslow couldn't help wrinkling her nose. "Three then, Dad?"

"That ought to do it," Jayce answered.

She said good-bye, vaguely including Jayce, before walking out to her car. Jayce's Ferrari Testarossa was blocking her. It was an older model, but he obviously spent as much time grooming the car as he did himself. The red paint perfectly reflected the palm trees swaying in the breeze. She blew out a breath and turned to walk back to the office. Jayce was already coming out the front door.

"I blocked you on purpose," he said, nearly floating down the steps in black shoes as shiny as his car. "Winnie, I wanted to talk to you before you left. Alone," he added.

She felt the muscles in her shoulders tighten. "Don't call me that."

He raised his eyebrows. "But Grant—"

"He's my dad; he can get away with it."

If she put Jayce off, she didn't care. He'd already taken over too many aspects of her family's life. He wasn't taking that.

He cocked his head. "You don't like that nickname, do you?"

"What did you want?"

He leaned against his car, forcing her to walk closer to hear his words over the sound of ruffling palm fronds. "Have you talked to Ashlyn in the last day or so?"

"Not since we all had dinner at Carpaccio's last Sunday, why?"

He looked like a little boy who'd been naughty. "We had a spat. You know how emotional Ashlyn can be, how flighty. She's been gone for two days now. I know she's just punishing me, making me worry, whatever. I *am* worried. She's not even answering her cell phone. I thought you might have an idea where she is. Maybe she's even staying with you."

Winslow wanted to laugh at that. They'd moved past their fighting days, but Winslow would be the last person Ashlyn would turn to in a crisis. That Ashlyn withheld her friendship used to hurt, but Winslow had long since gotten over it. Ashlyn would always consider her and Georgina intruders, but at least the two young women were civil. "Ashlyn has a habit of running off on a whim, whether to assist a friend in need or attend some event she just learned about. She doesn't always tell Dad until she's been gone for a day or two." Then she'd call and beg Winslow to water her precious bonsai collection given to her by Grant. Being a plant lover, Winslow complied, especially since Ashlyn's high-rise condo was only a few blocks away. "I have no idea where she'd be other than at Dallis's."

Dallis was Ashlyn's best friend, even though they couldn't have been more unalike. Dallis was a fashion nightmare that even Ashlyn couldn't fix. Winslow suspected their differences made the relationship work. The heavyset Dallis would never outshine Ashlyn and her fragile ego.

"They're not friends anymore," Jayce said, waving her off. "Is there anyplace where she could hide for a few days? Summer houses, seaside cottage?"

Dallis and Ashlyn not friends? That was new. "The house in Connecticut is closed up for the winter, and Ashlyn hates the cottage in England. I'd try her cousin in Greece or her aunt in Connecticut. One of her last-minute trips was to visit her aunt a couple of years ago when her pug died."

He was studying Winslow, as though weighing whether she was telling the truth. When he realized she was studying him back, he gave her a quick smile. "I'll check with them."

"I'm afraid you're asking the wrong person. She doesn't confide in me."

He nodded. "Hey, do me a favor and don't mention this to Grant. He's got enough on his plate without worrying about Ashlyn."

She reluctantly nodded, and Jayce hopped in his car and moved it. As she pulled out of the drive, she saw him taking the steps two at a time and walking into the house as though he owned it. For some reason, that gave her a shiver.

When Jayce returned, Grant was hanging up. "I realized I'd probably blocked her in."

"I feel bad making her reschedule again."

Jayce shrugged. "She seemed a bit put off, but she's got to understand you're an important man now. Until you win this election, things are going to take priority over her schedule. She'll get used to it."

Grant nodded. "But I want her to feel part of it." This election was taking its toll on everyone, and the campaigning had only just begun. Thank God he had Jayce to handle a lot of the incidental stuff. What would he do without him?

Jayce said, "Actually, Winslow told Ashlyn she was glad she didn't have to spend so much time helping you since I came aboard. She wouldn't want you to know that it was a burden, of course."

Grant frowned at that. He expected loyalty from his family and friends, but he didn't want to be perceived as a burden.

Jayce picked up a folder. "Now that I'm here no one has to do anything they don't want to."

"What happens when your inheritance comes through? You'll be too busy spending your money to help the underdog."

"Grant, I'm committed to your success. Heck, I'm going to be part of this family soon. Sure, you're up against an incumbent with a track record, but you're new, fresh, and you already showed them you're not full of bs when you were commissioner." The earnest business look left Jayce's face, and he smiled. "I have to admit, you're like the dad I never had. He was always too busy with his business to pay much attention to me. I wish he'd been a good father like you."

Jayce's words warmed Grant like a good whiskey. "I appreciate that. I feel as though you're the son I never had. I couldn't be happier with Ashlyn's choice of husband. As far as I'm concerned, you already are part of the family."

Jayce beamed at the words, but his expression changed to a more somber one. "Speaking of being part of the family . . . has Winslow said anything negative about me? Ever since I started dating Ashlyn, she's been as cool as ice to me. I've tried to be nice, to involve her in the wedding plans even. Just now I asked her for help in finding Ashlyn a wedding present. She said I was asking the wrong person. It . . . well, it kinda hurt. Not so much for me but for Ashlyn."

Grant didn't like the sound of that. Though the girls had never been close, they'd at least been friendly to each other. "I'll have a talk with her—"

"No, don't do that. She'll know I said something. It'll just take time, I guess. But it makes me wonder if she's jealous. Ashlyn's younger, but she's getting married first. Maybe it's a competition thing, or Winslow could feel threatened because I'm spending so much time with you. Sometimes it feels like she's got something against me personally. I just don't know what to make of it."

"I don't, either. Like you said, give her time. I'm sure you two will be the best of friends."

Winslow left the gallery at nine o'clock feeling jazzed about her interview with the Nicaraguan artist and his artwork. One of his paintings, depicting a lush courtyard, would look perfect on the wall behind her dining room table. The empty coffee mug and the hibiscus flower on the stone bench inspired thought-provoking questions. She was both journalist and photographer on these smaller events. Once in her car, she flipped through the pictures on her digital camera and liked what she saw.

As Nora Jones sang from Winslow's CD player, that nagging emptiness settled in the pit of her stomach. She enjoyed doing these articles, nothing too serious or deep. She did enjoy them. So why did she feel just a bit unsatisfied?

Because of Alex Díaz.

She made a sound of disgust and turned north onto A1A. Even at this time of night, traffic was a thick but steady flow. The air was warm and slightly muggy, but she'd taken down the roof anyway.

Neon pulsed in colors all around her, and so did the people who walked down the sidewalks and milled outside restaurants and bars. An ocean breeze sent everything into motion:

leaves, flowers, hair, and the silky dresses of three women walking toward a club. They didn't seem to mind how much thigh showed—or even a bit of derriere courtesy of the thong one of them wore.

The girls reminded her of Ashlyn. What had the fight been about that made her run away from the fiancé she seemed to adore? Ashlyn had dated on and off over the past several years, and Winslow couldn't remember her once running off *without* the current beau. None of those romances had lasted long, and none had become this serious.

A chilling thought assailed her. What if Jayce had done something to Ashlyn? As far-fetched as it sounded, it didn't *feel* that far off. After all, no one knew Jayce that well. Winslow acknowledged that her suspicions came from her dislike of him, but since she didn't know the source of that dislike, she wasn't going to dismiss it. She passed the road that led to Bay Harbor Islands and her condo and a few minutes later turned into Talbot Tower's lot. She would water the bonsais and take a look around.

When she couldn't quickly locate the card that allowed her access to the parking garage, she pulled into a spot in the lot. The doorman held the massive glass door for her as she entered. This was Grant's first solo project after forming Talbot Development four years earlier. The building was pure Ashlyn: designed by Walter Chatham, kitchens by Bulthaup, and bathrooms by Philippe Starck. All name brands.

The clicking of Winslow's heels bounced off marble and glass. The security guard nodded, recognizing her from other visits. Did he think it odd that she rarely came here when Ashlyn was in residence?

The elevator shushed to a stop at Ashlyn's floor; hers was the residence on the right. She liked to pretend that it was hers, and in truth, Grant *had* given it to her. But Winslow knew he still held the deed. She slipped out of her heels and walked through the rounded foyer to the living room. Rows of glass doors lined the rear wall. The view of the Atlantic

Ocean was breathtaking during the day; now it was just a huge black gulf.

The interior living room wall was curved, too, and along the upper wall snaked shelves for what must be a hundred champagne bottles, all emptied at some party or club. Ashlyn had affixed gold stars to the best. She'd chosen furniture to play off the curves: kidney-shaped sofas with low, contemporary profiles, lots of glass, all in pastel colors. Her bonsai collection took up a blue glass lacquer shelving unit.

Winslow picked up the crystal pitcher and poured water into each of the pots. "There you go, little guys. Aunt Winslow's here to take care of you." In the last two years she'd actually gotten attached to the miniature trees. They each had personalities, like prickly, smooth, or fuzzy. She didn't tell anyone, but she named all her plants at home.

Snippets from fashion magazines littered the surface of Ashlyn's glass coffee table. She clipped the tiniest details from outfits and glued them to other pictures. Then she'd buy the clothing and replicate what she'd created on paper. Sometimes the effect was stunning. At the least it was usually interesting.

Ashlyn's other trophies were clippings from society magazines. She hunted every local magazine searching for pictures of herself. Attached to the designer wallpaper in the dining room was a huge corkboard. Ashlyn pinned up the snapshot pages depicting the hip crowd at SkyBar, Crobar, and Rumi, at some fashion or awards show with Lil' Kim, a Calvin Klein briefs model, and even the latest *Survivor* winner. Ashlyn peered out from every page, hamming it up for the camera.

Looking at the pictures of young, beautiful people all having a fabulous time made Winslow feel like a fuddy-duddy. Not that she didn't enjoy a good party from time to time, but bars made her uneasy. And she was in bed before these people even got started.

The only sounds she heard as she walked to the master

bedroom were the soft squish of her feet on the plush beige carpet and a bass murmur from the condominium below. Ashlyn's desk and computer were in the bedroom sitting area. The computer was on, and Winslow fitted herself into the art deco chair and looked at the screen. The inbox was open. She had few personal e-mails; most were from Neiman Marcus announcing the new Juicy Couture or Anna Sui collection. The last five days' worth hadn't been read, while all of the previous e-mails had been opened—and thoroughly scanned, Winslow was sure.

As she was about to check the other open window on the computer, movement caught her eye. Her heart fluttered as she got up and peered into the living room. "Ashlyn?"

No answer. She wandered back through the foyer and looked in the kitchen, which was an enclosed room. She checked the other two bedrooms; one had a simple bed set for a guest, and the other held boxes and racks of out-of-season clothing. Something in the air felt different but she saw nothing out of place. A trick of the light then, or perhaps a bulb flickering in its death throes.

She returned to the computer and switched to the alternate window: the Internet browser. The history had been pulled up. As though someone had been looking for whatever Web pages Ashlyn had recently visited. Winslow's gaze kept sliding to the door just over her left shoulder.

None of the history pages looked promising, so she turned toward the red lacquer bed. It had been loosely made, though that was hard to tell beneath the piles of shopping bags and shoe boxes. Ashlyn clearly had gone on a shopping spree, but something had interrupted her enjoyment of the spoils. That worried Winslow. She picked up the receipt that went with the purple Manolo Blahnik boots with tassels around the tops. She couldn't help notice the price: $1600. The receipt was dated two days before, midmorning, as were the receipts for Ashlyn's other purchases.

Winslow walked through the master bathroom and into

the immaculate closet. Everything was as neat as ever: racks of shoes organized by casual, mules, dressy, and outrageous. Ashlyn had a shoe in every color, sometimes buying a "to die for" pair and then hunting for an outfit to match. Some shoes had never found their outfit and sat on the rack without more than the rub of the shop's rug on the sole. Prada bags hung on one rack, and Ashlyn's newest love, Gwen Stefani's designer bags, hung on their own rack.

Winslow liked quality clothing, too, but not to the extent that Ashlyn did. She occasionally splurged on a Dior gown for a charity ball she was covering. But those days of shopping the sales racks had stuck with her. She had a hard time paying several hundred or thousand dollars for one outfit. She marveled at how Ashlyn didn't even look at price tags before trotting to the dressing room.

Grant had given them each a credit card that he paid off every month. It seemed like taking too much to spend a lot on that card. Winslow already owed him so much. And in fact, she liked being able to take care of her own expenses. She charged just enough so that he wouldn't accuse her of being frugal. He seemed to take it personally when she didn't take what he offered.

Winslow looked behind her, not sure if she was imagining the shift of light. She'd been up here alone before, but had never gotten the willies like this. She looked at the top shelf and saw a large purple suitcase. Ashlyn had gone on and on about her new Prada luggage set. Two of the smaller pieces were gone. That was a good sign; it meant Ashlyn had left of her own volition.

Winslow turned off the lights and then leaned down to switch off the monitor. A wadded-up newspaper in the red trash can caught her eye. Ashlyn didn't read the paper; she only read society and fashion magazines. A bookcase alongside the far wall testified to her collection. Winslow smoothed the paper and sat on the slanted chair again. It was the front page of the *Miami Tribune*'s Saturday edition. Two stories dominated the headlines. One was a major drug bust off the coast. The other was a tragic boating accident on Biscayne Bay. Winslow had caught the story on the morning news, and she'd immediately changed the channel. Even though she chided herself for being a coward, her finger pressed the button on the remote anyway. The story had stirred too many memories about her accident.

She skimmed the article now, trying not to feel or imagine the scene. Luis García, his brother Jose García, and Jose's ten-year-old daughter, Elena, had been out fishing at dusk. A speedboat in the twenty-eight-to-thirty-foot range hit their boat at what the authorities speculated was full throttle, running completely over the boat. Jose had been killed instantly and was found in the boat along with his daughter, whose hands and face were severely lacerated by the boat's propeller. The girl was in critical condition. Luis ended up in the water where he'd succumbed to massive injuries. Authorities were seeking the operator of the boat that hit them and were putting out a call for witnesses seeing a boat with damage to the keel and bottom area, as well as to the outboard.

Winslow's throat had gone dry. This was why she never let herself get involved in news stories, why she cushioned herself from others' pain. She had a tenuous belief that there was justice in the world. She needed to believe that the man who had forced her father off the road was haunted by what he'd done. Stories about tragedies and people denying their sins broke down that belief. Her fears kept her from fully investing herself in life, and in moments of stark honesty she didn't like that about herself.

She turned the paper over and scanned the stories on the back side. Nothing seemed to relate to Ashlyn, and Winslow almost threw the newspaper back in the bin when something caught her eye: a hole in the top right corner surrounded by a faint square imprint. She walked to the bulletin board and matched the imprint to the square tacks etched with the words *Love* and *Peace*. Ashlyn had pinned the paper on the board. Which meant that it was important. Using the direction of the hole, Winslow could tell the front page had been facing out.

Before she could start contemplating which story Ashlyn had found fascinating and why, Winslow felt a compulsion to turn around. Goose pimples dotted her arms. She could see across the living room and into Ashlyn's bedroom from there but saw nothing that should cause the hairs on her arms to rise. She walked into the living room and looked toward the foyer. As she stood perfectly still and listened, she couldn't hear anything but the soothing murmur of the bass. She didn't recall hearing anything to alarm her.

When she turned toward the glass door next to her, she saw her eyes reflected back at her.

Only they weren't her eyes.

She felt soft prickles all over her scalp. It wasn't her face staring from the other side of the glass.

2

Winslow stumbled back as the glass door opened. Knowing the face didn't comfort her. Jayce reached out to steady her, but she shoved his hand away. "What in the hell are you doing? I don't know what kind of sick sense of humor you have—"

In a calm voice, he said, "I wasn't trying to scare you. I came in and heard someone prowling around, so I went onto the balcony to see who it was."

He started to close the door, but she reached past him and pushed it open again. "I need some fresh air," she said, though she wanted the possibility of someone hearing them, just in case. The sea-tainted breeze ruffled her hair and helped her to catch her breath. "So when you saw it was me, you thought you'd, what, just stand out there and spy?"

He didn't even look chagrined. "I wanted to see what you were doing."

"And what are you doing here, anyway? How'd you get in?"

He held up the key. "I am Ashlyn's fiancé, after all."

Those words slithered over her like cold, wet slime. But had Ashlyn given him the key, or had he taken it? The thought churned her stomach.

He said, "Did you find anything on the computer?"

He'd been watching her for that long. That was why she'd

had that eerie feeling, and he'd obviously been the flash of movement she'd seen. Her fists clenched at the thought. "Not anything more than you found, I imagine."

He didn't deny he'd already been looking. "How about the closet?"

"Her luggage is gone. That means she probably wasn't dragged out of here by her hair."

"By me," he said with a gritty smile. "Look, Winslow, as Grant said to me today, we're going to be family soon. You might as well drop this grudge you have and give in to my charm. Everyone else does."

Her stomach churned again. They'd be family. "I don't have a grudge against you," she said truthfully.

"Then why have you always given me the cold shoulder?"

She couldn't explain her aversion to him, not even to herself. It was something about his quick insinuation into her family's lives. She decided to downplay it. "Some people click, and some don't. It's a vibe thing."

This time his smile was patronizing. "You don't like my vibe. Cute. Well, let me tell you something: you'd better get used to my vibe. We're going to be in-laws. We're going to see each other all the time."

He was rubbing it in and enjoying it. Before she could think of a retort—she had to rein in her temper—he reached to the floor and grabbed the paper she'd dropped.

"What's this?"

"It's just a newspaper I found in the trash. I thought it might mean something."

"You walked over to her bulletin board." He did the same, obviously trying to figure out what she'd seen. "I hate this thing. It's going in the closet when I move in. So, Winslow, what were you looking for exactly?"

The friendly tone in his voice on that last sentence was so phony, a Gucci knockoff had more authenticity. She didn't want to tell him about the significance of the tack hole and how Ashlyn never read the paper. "I was trying to see if anyone in the articles matched the people in the pictures. But I couldn't tell, so I was going to throw it away."

He did that for her, crinkling it up into a tight ball, just as he probably had the first time, she realized. *Maybe you're just imagining all this menace. Maybe he reminds you of some kid who taunted you in school about your Frankenstein face.* The fact was, everyone else in their social circle liked Jayce. He'd won them all over, just as he'd said.

He walked into the bedroom. "There's got to be something here that will give us a clue."

Us. They were suddenly working together. Now *that* was cute. She noticed that he hadn't thrown the ball into the trash can. He held on to it, working it like one of those stress balls.

She followed him into the bedroom, looking for more subtle clues. "Did you talk to her cousin or aunt?"

"No. I don't want to alarm anyone. We know Ashlyn's flighty. She's trying to worry me, that's all. But there were no phone messages or e-mails from anyone, no plans being made. And *I* have her credit card." He flashed it triumphantly.

"You . . . what?"

He nodded toward the packages on the bed. "It was a challenge, that she could go a week without her charge card."

"And she let you take it?" Forget the silver spoon; Ashlyn grew up with a platinum card in her mouth. She probably didn't even know how to go into the bank and withdraw money. Now Winslow was sure Jayce had done something to her.

She walked to the other side of the bed and looked at the bookcase where Ashlyn kept her favorite magazines, including *Dazzle*. She started to feel between the magazines, but that sense of being watched made her turn around again.

Jayce continued to watch as she checked the drawers of the bookcase. He had probably already gone through these drawers. She was surer of that when he walked into the bathroom; he knew she wouldn't find anything. But she remembered something from the years they lived together as a family: Ashlyn sometimes hid things beneath her pillow, like love letters or special pictures.

Keeping an eye on the bathroom, Winslow slid her hand beneath the pillow. Her fingers jammed against the spine of a magazine and then pulled out last month's issue of *Dazzle*. Why would Ashlyn hide that?

She heard Jayce in the closet, moving boxes around from the sound of it. She flipped through the magazine looking for pieces of paper. The magazine opened to a section where several pages had been torn out. She turned to the contents page and matched up the missing pages' numbers—and was totally confused.

"Find anything?" Jayce asked, coming up behind her without making a sound.

She jumped, and luckily the magazine snapped closed. "Just more of her fashion page mutilation." She tossed the magazine on the bed as though it was of little importance. "What did you two fight about?"

"She wants a big fancy wedding; I want something small and private. Hell, I have no family to speak of. We've been at each other's throats so long, there's not a one I'd want at my wedding."

"That's sad," she said, not feeling particularly sorry for him. Over the years she'd heard about nasty inheritance battles with each party trying to grab as much money as they could. Dirty tidbits were dispensed with the enthusiasm of one sharing gold nuggets. At least Jayce didn't talk about it much.

"You wouldn't think so if you knew my family," he said, and from his expression, she believed him.

He picked up the magazine and fanned the pages. "She's going to have to put all these silly rags in one of the other bedrooms, too. Oh, sorry," he said, obviously remembering Winslow wrote for one of those "rags."

His insult was the least of her worries. She had to keep any expression from her face as her mind whirred through the possibility of where Ashlyn had gone. *Anywhere but there. Still, even there is better than some of the other possibilities.*

Jayce looked at the front cover. "This is the rag you write for, right?"

"Yes. Well, I don't see anything that's going to help . . . us. If she doesn't turn up tomorrow, we're going to have to start calling around."

Jayce followed her out of the bedroom, thankfully flinging the magazine back on the bed. "She's done this kind of thing before, right? And usually comes back or calls within a couple of days?"

"Usually." She didn't like the way he was watching her as she grabbed her purse and slid into her leather pumps.

His eyes narrowed. "You know where she is, don't you? Or you at least have an idea."

How could he know? She'd gotten good at lying during those two years of exile, as her mother had called it. Reasons why her friends couldn't come over, why she and Georgina hadn't been to the country club, oh, and Winslow's private tutor, too. She pasted on her most truthful expression and said, "Not a clue. Good night."

She almost expected him to join her in the elevator and keep questioning her, but he simply watched her as the door closed between them. She didn't like that he was staying there. Would he look through the magazine and put it together as she had?

"Ashlyn, if you're going to make me face Alex Díaz, you'd better damn well be there."

When the doors opened on the lobby level, she headed to the security guard at the desk. "Did Ashlyn authorize Jayce Bishop to get a key to her apartment?"

"Sure did," the burly black man said. "Couple of weeks ago. Maybe I should have called up, let you know he was coming. But seeing as he's going to be living there when they get married, I didn't think about it."

"That's all right." She started to turn away but paused. "He knew I was up there?"

"I mentioned it so he wouldn't startle you." His expression fell. "I hope that was all right, Miss Talbot."

She felt her face pale. "That was fine. Take care."

Jayce knew she was in the condo. But he'd said he didn't know and that's why he'd gone out to the balcony. That meant he'd lied. And she wanted to know why.

When Winslow walked into her second-floor condo, she relaxed for the first time in an hour. It hadn't helped that Jayce had been driving behind her until she turned onto her street. He could have been going to Grant's house, but it was pretty late for that. The luxury hotel where Jayce was staying, the Astonia, was in the opposite direction.

Chirpy meows preceded her two cats as they ran to greet her. Salt, the white shorthair, was flicking water from his paws. Winslow knelt down. "You've been playing in the fountain again, haven't you?" Salt had a fascination with water and was always prowling around the fountain in the corner of the living room. Pepper, the black shaggy cat, didn't care for water, but he did love the plants that surrounded the fountain and was always digging up the dirt in the big clay pots.

With the first order of business done, both cats trotted across the Mexican tile into the kitchen for their snack. Winslow followed and gave them their fish-flavored treat. Georgina had been mortified when Winslow told her she'd gotten her cats at the animal shelter. Goodness, they weren't even *pedigreed*! Who knew where they came from?

Giving a homeless kitten or two a home seemed the right thing to do, and the black and white siblings won Winslow's heart immediately. The strays had climbed up inside a car for warmth during a cold spell. The car's owner had no idea they were tucked inside until he heard a thump when he started the engine. A veterinarian had donated his services to fix Salt's broken pelvis and Pepper's broken leg. Most people wanted a cute kitten, not one with a crooked face or a white blind eye and torn ear. They were the only ones Winslow wanted. They'd been curled up in their cage, not even trying to catch her attention. Apparently they'd gotten used to being passed by. That thought had nearly broken her heart. Once she'd started talking to them, they'd wobbled over and started purring.

Georgina and Grant had clearly thought Winslow strange for taking damaged specimens. Neither considered the reason behind her need to save those particular cats. They'd obviously forgotten that she was as damaged physically as those kittens were.

They'd thought she was crazy to buy this condo, too. Didn't she want one in the Tower? Or in one of Grant's other buildings that overlooked the Atlantic Ocean? No, she didn't. Those slick places, umpteen stories tall, didn't appeal to her. She'd gone apartment shopping by herself, unwilling to be influenced. When she found Catalina Point, she'd fallen in love. It had been built in the seventies, but the new owner had refurbished the exterior, courtyard, and pool.

The two-story building was on a piece of land that overlooked the Intracoastal and the prestigious Bal Harbor gated community across the way. Winslow wanted something that was hers. Her taste, her choice, with her name on the deed. Grant had given her money for the down payment, but she intended to pay him back someday. He wouldn't like it, but she'd make him take the money. For now she made the payments and tucked a bit of money into safe investment accounts.

She went into the bathroom, dipped the small sponge into the jar of makeup remover, and rubbed it across her cheek. Porcelain-smooth skin disappeared in steaks, revealing the faint lines the accident and surgeries had left behind. Time and laser treatments had softened and lightened them to the approximate tone of her skin. When all of the

Dermablend makeup was removed, she stood back and looked at herself. Nobody had ever seen her without make-up. Even the two men she'd slept with hadn't seen her completely naked. She'd cleaned her skin after they'd gone to sleep and reapplied the makeup before they woke.

The makeup ritual had started as soon as her skin had healed. Her mother had always hidden ugliness from others. She covered her moles and imperfections, turned away from disaster or deformities. After the accident she'd hidden Winslow from concerned friends, and later she slathered on makeup to hide her scars. *People will stare; they'll ask questions. It's a fact that people judge you by your looks. That's why I have to work so hard to stay young and beautiful.*

Georgina had died attaining that beauty two years ago when the helicopter taking her to an exclusive Swedish spa crashed. Winslow couldn't shake the chill whenever she remembered how her mother had harangued her to accompany her. Not for mother-daughter bonding, but to "refresh her looks."

The more acquaintances and the men she dated raved about her supposed perfection and beauty, the harder it was to reveal her imperfections. *This is not really me. I'm just a plain Jane beneath this mask with too little chin and too much forehead. Would you like that girl? Would you treat her the same?*

She was afraid she knew the answer, and it made her feel like an impostor. People accepted her at face value. What no one knew was, she had trouble accepting her own face.

She turned away from her reflection and walked to the wicker shelving unit that held the last few years of *Dazzle*. "Hi, Fred," she said as she settled on the flowery couch. Of course, the rubber plant didn't greet her back, but she didn't mind. She knew her words kept his leaves shiny and new shoots sprouting up all the time. All of the plants in her condo looked healthy and happy. Her balcony was crammed with foliage. She wondered what her neighbors thought when they overheard her talking to her plants.

Salt and Pepper jumped on the couch and tried to dominate her lap space. She absently stroked them with one hand while flipping to the article in the last issue—the one Ashlyn had torn out. Winslow had covered the black-tie event honoring jazz musician Armando Tamargo as a Cuban cultural icon. The Miami Cultural Society had cosponsored the event with FREE, a political organization. Grant was there to schmooze the Latino vote. FREE's founder, Lazaro Díaz, had been charismatic and gracious. Her gaze slid over the pictures of Lazaro and Grant posing for the camera and then a big picture featuring Gloria Estefan crooning alongside Tamargo.

Winslow reluctantly looked at the picture of Alex Díaz, Lazaro's son. Alex had both impressed and intimidated her at first. He was about her age and he *owned* a newspaper. *Mojo* was aimed at the young Cuban-American crowd, and he was covering the event, too. At the time, Alex had struck her as charming and sexy. His olive skin was tan, his hair jet-black, and his soulful eyes were nearly as dark. He had a full, sexy mouth that made a woman think of hot kisses on a sultry summer night.

Ashlyn had spent quite a bit of time with him, as Winslow recalled. She and Jayce were newly engaged then, but he'd had to fly home on business, so he wasn't pinned to her side as usual. Ashlyn and Alex seemed to have a rather deep discussion, until his father called him over for pictures. Winslow had found it odd that they'd talked so long. He was as far from Ashlyn's crowd as anyone could be. Whatever he'd been saying to her, though, had brought out the compassion in his eyes. Winslow had realized she'd spent a lot of time watching the two of them and forced herself to focus on her job.

She had probably traded no more than twenty words with him the entire evening. So when he called after her article ran in *Dazzle,* she was surprised at the champagne bubbles his voice produced in her stomach. Until he'd criticized her article.

"Your writing was fine," he began, barely a compliment. "It's the article itself that I have a problem with. You didn't even hint at the major political significance of who was there. My father cajoled, begged, and blackmailed some of the most hard-line exile leadership in Miami to attend this event. Groups who have clashed over politics—and I'm talking bombs, death threats—were in one room, talking together. Laughing, singing. Arguing. But talking. All you wrote about was Gloria Estefan, and what she and the politicians' wives were wearing. You gave us good coverage of the food. But you missed the whole point!"

Thinking back, she knew there were plenty of things she could have told him. Like, *Stuff it,* for starters. But he'd taken her off-guard. "Cuban politics? Bomb threats? It was a *cultural* event."

Not the right answer, she realized, when he made a sound of disgust. She hung up. He'd made her feel dumb and out of touch. She would have questioned whether they were at the same event, but unfortunately, she remembered him clearly.

She hated to admit how much his criticism bothered her. Until then she'd never had much input on her writing, other than gentle suggestions from Sebastian, her editor. Then to have someone imply that her writing was inadequate—that it was *fluff*! She'd tried not to let it bother her, but darn it, it did.

She scanned the article and saw that a lot had been written about Gloria and what people wore. That's what Winslow's job was, to cover the celebrities, the society people, and their designer clothing. She'd been embarrassed to admit she knew nothing about what groups some of those people represented.

When she reached the end of the article, she tried to figure out what significance it could have to Ashlyn. She wasn't pictured in the article, something that had thrown her into a tizzy. Luckily Winslow hadn't taken the photographs and had had no say in which ones were chosen. Her gaze went back to Alex. Ashlyn had made some connection with him.

She'd heard her talking to Grant later about the plight of Cuban rafters and how he should help FREE to assist them. Grant had explained the wet foot/dry foot policy, according to which Cubans had to get to the shore without assistance to be considered for citizenship. And in the way she briefly embraced some cause or another, Ashlyn had complained about how unfair that was.

Winslow felt vaguely ashamed that she knew very little about Cuba other than it was run by a Communist dictator and how everyone had been up in arms over the Elian Gonzales affair. She had told herself she would try to learn more about the Cubans she shared Miami with, but she hadn't gotten around to it yet.

Now, as she stared at Alex's picture, she wondered again if Ashlyn had gone there. She hoped Ashlyn had. It was better than worrying that Jayce had done something to her. But Winslow also hoped she'd gone anywhere but there. She set the magazine down with a sigh. Either way, she was going to have to face Alex Díaz again.

3

Winslow got in a quick walk on the beach the next morning, did a last read-through on her article, and headed to *Dazzle*. She walked into Sebastian's offices where his secretary, Amelia, sat at an oak desk that dwarfed her. She was fresh out of high school, a perky blonde who wanted to move up to photographer someday.

"He's on a conference call," Amelia said, grimacing as though the news would break Winslow's heart. "He's going to be a while."

Winslow wondered if Amelia had picked up on the way her professional relationship with Sebastian was becoming a little less professional and a little more personal. Yeah, Winslow knew that getting involved with her boss was a really bad idea. Especially when he was fifteen years older and a friend of her father's. Still, at twenty-eight, she hadn't met many men who made her think of the future. Sebastian was a comfortable fit, and he didn't focus on her looks.

"No problem," she said. "Just give this to him when he's done."

Winslow was happy with the piece, but as she handed it to Amelia, she didn't feel quite satisfied with it. Had she gone deep enough?

Damn that Alex Díaz. It was his fault she was questioning her writing. She didn't want to go too deep, didn't want to find pain or suffering beneath the surface. Like wondering what had caused the scars on the hands of the artist and what now caused the shadows in his eyes? It made her think that the woman in the painting who'd left behind her coffee mug and the flower hadn't gone in to call her lover and make amends. Maybe there had been a darker reason for her hasty exit.

"You all right?" Amelia said, and Winslow realized she was still holding on to the hard copy of her article while Amelia was trying to take it from her.

"Sorry, just distracted. Please tell Sebastian that I've got some personal business to take care of, but I'll be in this afternoon."

"I hope everything's okay." She looked genuinely concerned, which made Winslow pause.

"Thanks, I'm sure it will be."

"I love that blouse. Can I have it when you get tired of it?"

The sheer yellow blouse with green circles, worn over a yellow shell, was one of Winslow's favorites. Wearing it paired with black dress pants, she felt confident, something she would need. "You got it."

Amelia sighed. "I want to grow up to be you."

Winslow's smile faded as she walked out of the room. *But you don't even know me. All you see is the outer me.* It was disturbing that someone envied her for things she wasn't even sure she wanted.

Winslow walked out to her car, unfolded the Miami map she kept in her glove compartment, and located *Mojo*'s offices. She hoped Alex wouldn't be there. *If he is, please don't let him say anything more about my article.* She knew why her writing was her tender spot; it was her identity, apart from her face and her family, neither of which was really her own. She had her job because of Grant. She drove this car because of Grant. Her writing, though, that was hers. The things that were most important in her life sometimes felt so tenuous.

She took AIA all the way down and crossed the Mac Arthur Causeway. Only one cruise ship sat at the Port of Miami across the channel. The air, plumped by seawater, had a hazy quality.

Brickell was one block off the beach, and the ocean breeze pummeled the palms. Dirt devils swirled out of the side street where another chrome and glass building was going up. She turned onto Miracle Mile, leaving behind the well-dressed businesspeople and upscale restaurants to enter an older section of town. The quaint shopping district obviously catered to ethnic groups. Cuban, Portuguese, and Argentinean restaurants were interspersed between chain stores in one- and two-story buildings. Banyan trees grew over the divided road, and she pulled off her shades to look for the address. The paper and the organization shared the same building; the signs for both were nondescript and nearly hidden in the overgrown shrubbery flanking the entrance. She searched for a parking spot alongside the curb. Finding nothing, she pulled down the side street and found a lot for FREE and *Mojo*'s offices.

The next challenge was finding a spot in the fenced-in lot, which took her five more minutes of circling waiting for someone to leave. That, however, paid off when she saw the yellow Porsche Boxster. Ashlyn had passed on the Ferrari, too, but only because she didn't like the stiff ride. She'd made up for it by getting not only the Boxster S but every option as well. The vanity plate on the back, *Ashlyn1,* said it all. But Winslow was too relieved to roll her eyes as she usually did. She'd found her stepsister, and she was likely all right. Now Winslow needed to find out why she was here.

The two-story art deco building was probably built in the eighties, with large glass doors at the entrance and a round window above that revealed stairs going up to the second level. She wasn't sure what she expected, but that didn't stop her from being surprised. The first floor was divided into several offices with one large open space near the front. The men and women were of varying ages, though all, she guessed, were Cuban. One man was on the phone, his voice explosive and his arm gesturing as he talked about something that obviously excited him. Two women traded rapid-fire Spanish, hardly letting each other finish her sentence before barreling on. And surprisingly, neither seemed to mind. It was a different world, and Winslow couldn't have felt more out of place. Could Ashlyn really be here somewhere?

Unfortunately, she wasn't one of the people in view. Winslow's stomach tightened a little more. Just as one woman noticed her, a voice boomed from her right.

"Ah, the daughter of Mr. Grant! Bienvenido! Welcome!"

She turned to find Lazaro coming down the stairs, his hands extended toward her. He was stocky, with graying wavy hair and brown eyes that sparkled. He covered her hand in his and squeezed in greeting.

"I'm surprised you remember me," she said, feeling a little relieved.

He tapped his finger to his head. "I remember everyone. But such a beautiful woman, who could forget?"

She smiled. "Thank you. It's good to see you again."

"You are looking for your sister, no? Come; she's working on the magazine."

Working? That unlikely scenario confused Winslow as she followed Lazaro up the stairs. He moved fast and a ring of keys jingled at his hips. Now she only hoped she could find Ashlyn and drag her out of there before seeing Alex.

That, of course, was not to be. He was at the top of the stairs looking over papers in a green folder.

"Alejandro, *mira,* look who's here!" his father shouted.

When Alex looked up she felt an odd jolt. All right, so what if he was strikingly handsome in an exotic sort of way? He also recognized her immediately, and he at least had the decency to give her a rather sheepish smile.

Lazaro grasped his shoulder and said something in Spanish before nodding at her and zipping back down the stairs.

Alex's black T-shirt was so worn it appeared gray and butter-soft. Even dressed down, he looked good, especially the way the fabric molded the curves of his muscles.

"Good to see you again," he said, tucking the folder beneath his arm and extending his hand to her. When their fingers slid against one another, she felt that annoying jolt again. She became aware of the Latin music coming from somewhere, a sensual song with words she couldn't understand. She realized she'd held on to his hand too long and jerked back.

The side of his mouth quirked. "I don't suppose you're here to see me."

"Uh, no. I'm here to see Ashlyn."

He nodded. "Again, I'm sorry I jumped on you about the article. That's what your magazine is about, high society and their clothing, but I didn't realize that until it was too late."

His apology took her off-guard. She rarely heard a man admit he was wrong, but something else struck her about his words. "What do you mean, *again*?"

"Didn't you get my card? I sent it after our call. After you hung up on me," he added with a lift of his thick, arched eyebrow. "I would have called to apologize, but I figured you'd just hang up on me again."

She felt her cheeks flush. "Sorry about that. I . . . I just didn't know what to say."

He laughed. "You probably did, but you were too much of a lady to say it." He held out his hand again. "Apology accepted?"

She shook his hand. "Of course, but . . . I never got your card."

"I sent it to your office. I figured you fed it to the shredder."

Lazaro came up the stairs again and shoved a folder at Alex, giving him instructions in that rapid Spanish. Even if Winslow knew Spanish, she wouldn't have been able to follow the conversation. He turned to her. "Did my hot-headed son apologize yet?"

"Papí, I'm a grown man now. I can handle my own apologies."

Lazaro playfully ruffled Alex's hair as he looked at her. "He has his father's—how you say?—*pasión*. Passion. Gets a man into trouble sometimes."

Alex waved his father on, obviously embarrassed. "Go on, save Cuba, why don't you?"

Lazaro laughed as he shot down the stairs again, amazing her how he wasn't even short of breath.

Despite his irritation, Alex was smiling as he shook his head. "The price of working with your family."

"There are more of you here?" she asked.

He nodded toward the young man in the back corner office. "My cousin Alberto manages accounting. My brother Enrique is an editor. My other brother helps out in between his fishing charters. My assistant editor is another cousin, though she just had a baby."

It did seem like one big family, Winslow thought as she looked at the open space in the center of the room where people chatted and laughed as they worked. It even smelled homey, of coffee and something sweet. A long table held both a coffee and espresso machine along with the various condiments. White bakery boxes contained an assortment of pastries. A beat-up radio with a wire hanger for an antenna spouted Latino music.

A young woman in high heels and too much makeup walked up to the small desk at the front and looked chagrined at not being at her post. The girl was probably apologizing and Alex was probably telling her it was all right. Winslow liked the cadence of their language, especially the smooth way words came out of Alex's mouth.

She turned away from that mouth and looked around, still not seeing Ashlyn. This place couldn't have been more different from *Dazzle*'s serene, well-decorated offices. Visitors never saw the workings of the magazine, and the music would never tempt them to tap a foot or, as she observed here, move their whole body to the beat.

Alex startled her by drawing her aside with a touch of his hand on her elbow. His voice was low, intimate, and flavored with a slight Latin accent. "Ashlyn's in the back, working—trying to work—the layout software. She called me Saturday, sounded upset. Said she wanted to help out at the organization, but later admitted she needed to get away for a few days. I knew it was more than that, so I told her to come to my house. I finally got out of her that she was fleeing an abusive boyfriend, though she wouldn't talk about it. I saw bruises on her collarbone, but she wouldn't discuss those, either. She didn't want to go to the police. The suggestion terrified her."

"An abusive boyfriend? Did she mention the name Jayce?"

"Wouldn't say. Does she have more than one boyfriend?"

Winslow leaned against the railing around the stairwell. "No, just the one. They're engaged. I can't believe he'd be stupid enough to hit her, though."

"Something is going on with her. When I met her at the benefit, she was full of life and energy. Now . . . she's subdued. When she doesn't know I'm looking, she frowns and draws herself into a tight ball."

"She's staying with you?"

"In the guest room," he clarified. "I told her she was welcome to stay as long as she needed." He smiled. "Don't look so worried. I'd never take advantage of a woman in need."

That wasn't what she was worried about. No, she just didn't like that Ashlyn was staying with him. She didn't want to explore why. "I believe you."

"Come; I'll take you to her." He guided Winslow to a doorway that led into a large room with cubicles in three of the corners. A large monitor sat on each desk. The tips of his fingers felt soft against her elbow; she wondered if he even realized he was doing it.

No one could have looked more out of place than Ashlyn, and not only because she was pale skinned among a group of olive-skinned Cubans. She wore a vivid pink top and hip-hugging white pants covered with splotches that matched the top. Her pink earrings were one single splotch, also matching, and her neck was circled with them on a thick gold chain. Even on the run, she accessorized.

She was fully focused on the monitor at one of the desks, her expression a pained grimace. It startled Winslow to see her fingers curled into her palms and her shoulders hunched. The Ashlyn in all those society pictures was not the Ashlyn of the last month or so. She *was* more subdued, quieter, and even more insecure than she usually was. It shamed Winslow to admit that she hadn't noticed, when Alex, who hardly knew Ashlyn, had.

Ashlyn's head jerked up, and her red eyes first took in Alex and then blinked in disbelief at Winslow. "What are *you* doing here?"

"Long story. We need to talk."

Her gaze slid to the computer screen but quickly returned to Winslow. "I'm working."

"Go ahead," Alex said. "Take a break."

She didn't want to; that was clear. Winslow crossed her arms and waited stubbornly until Ashlyn relented. She dragged herself up from the chair, tucked her arms around her waist, and walked toward the stairs. Winslow felt a twinge deep inside her: dread. After the engagement announcement at dinner, Winslow had taken Ashlyn aside and asked if it wasn't a little fast. As usual, Ashlyn had brushed her off with an accusation of jealousy.

Every now and then Winslow felt a tug of affection for her stepsister, but it was usually crushed by some careless comment. Winslow understood the lack of faith in the world that one has when one loses a parent. Ashlyn had no female role model, either, and often sought her identity in friends and boyfriends.

Ashlyn walked quickly down the stairs, as though she could lose Winslow. She was small framed, with a delicate bone structure and pale skin that burned with ten minutes of sun exposure. Her strawberry blond hair was fine, and she often cursed her fly-aways. Her complexion was sometimes blotchy, tinged pink by tiny blood vessels broken by champagne indulgences. Winslow knew Ashlyn's blotchy skin embarrassed her. The topic was off-limits.

Ashlyn pushed open the front door and walked through without even looking to see if Winslow was behind her. She stopped just outside, though, tightened her arms beneath her chest, and turned to face Winslow. "Why did you follow me here? Does Grant know? Oh, jeez, what am I going to tell him?"

Winslow grasped her shoulders. "Grant doesn't know. Jayce asked if I knew where you were, and I got worried. Ashlyn, is he hitting you?" She started to reach for the high neckline of her shirt, but the girl shifted away. "You told Alex you're hiding from an abusive boyfriend. Is it true?"

"No. Alex kinda jumped to that conclusion and I let him believe it so he'd help me. Jayce and I had a fight, and I got out of control. He pressed me against the wall a little too hard to calm me down. I can't blame him for that."

"Yes, you can. If he left bruises on you, that's abuse." Seeing that Ashlyn wasn't going to acknowledge that, Winslow went on. "What were you fighting about? You're in some kind of trouble, aren't you?"

Ashlyn looked at her, tears filling her eyes, her lower lip lodged between her teeth. To keep it from trembling, Winslow realized. Before she could say anything, a male voice broke the moment.

"Baby, thank God you're all right."

Winslow could hardly believe it. Jayce stepped between them and pulled Ashlyn into his arms. "Do you realize how worried I've been?"

Ashlyn's surprise evaporated and she clung to him. "I'm

sorry. I just needed some time away . . . alone. To think."

Jayce looked up at the building. He obviously had no idea what it even was. Which meant . . .

"You followed me," Winslow said, hardly believing it.

He turned Ashlyn so that he was facing Winslow. "I could tell you had an idea where she was. I needed to find my girl, and you weren't cooperating."

It gave her the creeps to think that he'd been following her. "What about your golf scramble?"

"I found Grant another partner. I told him Ashlyn was feeling overwhelmed by wedding plans and I needed to be with her. He understood. In fact, he thought a lot of me for putting his daughter first."

Ashlyn was crying softly, and Winslow couldn't tell if she was afraid or relieved that he'd found her. She was still clinging to him, though.

"Ashlyn, can we talk alone?" Winslow said, tapping her back. "We need to finish our conversation."

Jayce pulled back, though he still held Ashlyn's shoulders. "Do you need to finish your conversation, sweetheart? Or are you ready to come home?" The way his gaze held hers, Winslow thought he was hypnotizing her.

"I'm ready to go home," she said, and he rewarded her with a kiss.

"Good girl. We don't need to drag Winslow into our personal problems, do we?"

Ashlyn shook her head without even thinking about it.

Winslow said, "I'm always here if you need me, Ashlyn."

Jayce turned to her with an almost injured expression. "You've never been a sister to her. Why would she turn to you now?"

Winslow could hardly believe the statement. He acted as though *she* were the one who'd snubbed Ashlyn, who'd ignored her, who'd been jealous and insecure. She couldn't even come up with a reply.

Jayce pressed his forehead to Ashlyn's. "Ready to go?"

She nodded. "Oh, my purse is still upstairs." She rubbed at her eyes and runny nose. "I can't go back there looking like this."

Just as Winslow was going to suggest that Jayce get it, to give her a few seconds alone with Ashlyn, he beat her to the punch. "Would you be a good sister and get it for her?"

Beat her *and* pinned her with that simple request. "What about your other things?"

"Everything's in my car. Thanks for getting my purse. And tell Alex thank you for everything. And sorry for leaving him like this. I don't think I was much help anyway."

What else could she do but get her purse? Winslow watched them as she walked inside and up the stairs. Jayce was cuddling Ashlyn, and she certainly didn't look afraid. She was telling him something, though, confiding in him the way Winslow wished she'd confided in her.

Alex was standing by the desk Ashlyn had been working at. The concern in his eyes touched Winslow, and it even, in an odd way, made her feel a little jealous.

"She says that her fiancé, Jayce, pushed her against the wall when she had a tizzy. She claims he's not abusing her, that she let you believe that so you'd help her. And then he showed up."

Alex's shoulders stiffened. "He's here?"

"Hold your horses. He's all cuddly now, and she's not afraid of him. I don't know what to make of it. He's going to take her home, or likely, he'll follow her car home. She said she's sorry for leaving like this and thanks you for your help."

"I was only giving her token work so she'd feel like she was helping." He nodded to the screen. "She's been working on this for an hour, and I don't see anything done. She looked awfully upset, though. Are you sure it's safe to let her go?"

Winslow leaned across the empty chair and grabbed the purse she'd seen on the floor. "Ashlyn's got her father to talk to if she really needs help. We're not all that close. We're only stepsisters."

"Ah, that explains it. The difference," he said in response to her questioning look. "You're nothing alike." Perhaps fearing she might ask for details, he went on. "Tell Ashlyn if she needs help, I'm here, too."

"That's good of you," Winslow said, meaning it.

He gave her a smile that set off the whiteness of his teeth. "See, I'm not such a bad guy. I just occasionally jump to conclusions without checking the facts."

She really didn't like the way his smile tickled her stomach. Thankfully, the man he'd identified as Alberto called out, "Alejandro!" followed by something in Spanish.

"I've got to take that call." He paused, as though he wanted to say something else. *Call me sometime. Can I call you sometime?* Some part of her wanted to hear those words, but his cousin yelled again impatiently, and Alex gave Winslow an apologetic look and grabbed the nearest phone.

Are you crazy? A hotheaded, hot-blooded Cuban? Get out while you can.

She paused, though, when her gaze caught the story on the large monitor. She recognized the layout software, a sort of paint-by-numbers process where you filled in the blanks. The words in the article were in Spanish, of course, but she recognized the picture of the wrecked boat. It was a story about the hit-and-run boating accident. The victims were Cuban, she remembered from the article at Ashlyn's. This story showed pictures of the family and the little girl in the hospital, her face almost completely bandaged. Winslow felt a sinking feeling in her stomach. Ashlyn had been upset, staring at the screen. She did get impassioned about causes at times, but they usually either were personal or involved some animal.

The sinking feeling turned into a full-fledged drop. The newspaper article that had been tacked up on the bulletin board. Her reaction to this story. Jayce had a speedboat. He'd wanted Ashlyn back under his control so badly he'd followed Winslow. *Oh, God, it was Jayce's boat that hit the Cubans' boat and fled the scene.*

She turned so quickly she didn't see that Alex had returned. He put his hands on her shoulders out of instinct. "Are you all right?" he asked.

"I've got to go."

She rushed down the stairs, Ashlyn's pink purse swinging out of control.

Jayce stood alone outside the front doors. He reached for the purse, which Winslow reluctantly gave him. "She's in her car. Look, she's just getting freaked about the wedding, that's all. I keep telling her that a simple ceremony would be a lot easier. There's nothing for you to worry about." He was trying that hypnotizing thing, his eyes on hers this time, his voice low and soothing.

She blinked. "You put bruises on her."

"I didn't realize she bruised that easily. I promise I won't do it again. There's nothing for you to worry about," he repeated in that slow, deliberate way.

She started to ask him if he was the captain of the hit-and-run boat but held back the words. He'd never tell her, and he was too cool to give it away in his expression.

"I'm sorry about the comment on not being a sister to Ashlyn," he said, surprising her. "I didn't want you to upset her."

She was surprised, but she didn't buy the sincerity of his apology. Since she had just heard a real apology, Jayce's sounded flat.

He held out his hand. "Friends?"

She didn't take it. "We may not be as close as blood sisters, but if you do anything to hurt her, I'll make you more trouble than you can imagine."

She'd definitely taken *him* by surprise. Actually, her protective feelings for Ashlyn had surprised her, too. His hand remained suspended for a few seconds and then he snatched it out of the air. He laughed in the way one does when he's unsure of the situation. "Is that a threat?"

She gave him a twenty-four-carat smile; no, make that a cubic zirconia smile. "You have nothing to worry about if you never hurt her."

His voice was low and soft when he said, "Then I guess I have nothing to worry about. I don't plan on hurting *her*."

He turned and walked away, Ashlyn's purse hanging from his finger. Winslow had to wonder: had she imagined the slight emphasis on the word *her*?

4

Ashlyn almost found reason to smile at the sight of Jayce walking her way with her pink purse swinging at his side. He got into the car and closed the door with a thud, then handed her the purse.

"Thanks," she said in a thick voice.

"You want to tell me what's going on?"

"I needed time to think things over, and you were putting too much pressure on me."

"What did you need to think over, Ashlyn? Going to the police?"

She shook her head. "I won't do that, Jayce. I promise."

Her phone rang in the tune of the latest Gwen Stefani song. She looked at the screen. "It's Winslow."

"That woman is not your friend. She'll pretend to be because she wants to know what's going on. Nosy bitch. She's only going to cause trouble." He leaned closer and poked her collarbone. "*You* have to convince her that I'm not beating you. I won't tolerate anyone thinking I'm a thug."

Ashlyn nodded. "I said you didn't mean to. But I'll make sure she knows."

"She likes when things aren't going right for you; you know that, don't you? She enjoys your conflicts. She'd love to think I'm hitting you. Can you imagine how she feels right now, her younger sister getting married before she even has a prospect? She's probably wishing she'd caught my eye instead of you."

"She didn't, did she?"

He rubbed her cheek. "No, baby, not at all. I've never seen a more beautiful woman than you."

"More beautiful than Winslow? I mean, she's, like, perfect."

She loved the way he was shaking his head, no way, not even close. She hated how beautiful Winslow was, hated that her daddy's money had made her that way. If she'd had the guts, she could get her nose trimmed and her cheekbones lifted. Oh, and bigger boobs. The thought of going under the knife petrified her and kept her the homely little sister with bad skin.

"I know Winslow's trying to take your place in your dad's life."

She nodded, still stung by Jayce's confession of last week. Grant had admitted that Winslow was much more helpful than Ashlyn. Oh, Ashlyn tried, the dear heart, but she really made more of a mess of things than anything else. She thought back over the last day and a half working for Alex and realized her daddy was right. She just wasn't good at that kind of thing. She knew Grant asked Winslow for advice. It stuck her like a knife when she realized he'd never asked her for advice, other than on which tie to wear.

Jayce reached over and turned her chin toward him. "Grant didn't know I was listening, but I heard him tell someone on the phone that—I don't know; maybe I shouldn't say anything."

She clutched his arm. "No, tell me. What did you hear?"

He took her hand in his. "That he considered Winslow as much of a flesh and blood daughter as you. You know they have their little routine, their father-daughter breakfast together, and then she comes back to the office and helps him for a couple of hours. Does he do that with you?"

She pushed out her lower lip. "No."

"If it makes you feel any better, I'm pushing her out, making her unnecessary."

The phone rang and Winslow's cell phone number appeared in the screen again.

Jayce took the phone and turned it off. "You have to stay away from her. If she finds out what happened she'll tell Grant, and what would he think of us then? It's too late to go to the police now."

No, Grant could never know.

"She's going to hound you night and day, try to break you down. I know how women like that are. She smells a story, smells the destruction of Ashlyn. She sees her opportunity to completely take over." He kissed her. "No one will ever take your place with me, I promise you that. I will do everything I can to protect you. Let me move in with you. That way if Winslow shows up, I'll be there. And let's move up the wedding. Planning a big wedding is going to be too stressful on you. Let's just do a small ceremony next month . . . this month . . . this weekend!"

She had to laugh at his proposal. His promise soothed her ragged heart and almost made her forget how he sometimes subtly threatened to leave town if she didn't do what he wanted. God, she'd already announced their engagement and had a small party at their favorite restaurant to celebrate. He couldn't leave her now. She stroked his dark hair. He was so beautiful, and he loved her, and he thought she was prettier than Winslow. She couldn't lose him.

"Move in," she said. "Let me think about the wedding."

He let out a whoop and kissed her again. He kissed her fingertips and the small engagement ring he'd given her—until his money came in, and then he was buying her a huge pink diamond. He held on to her fingers, though, his expression somber all of a sudden. She was almost used to his sudden mood swings.

"I want you to promise me something."

"Anything."

"That you won't ever tell anyone—including Winslow—what happened last weekend. If the police started investigating . . . I'd have to disappear. I can't take that chance, not with the inheritance issue."

In just a few seconds, his assurances of everlasting love evaporated. But she could control this and keep him forever. "I promise. I'll never tell a soul."

At quarter till three, Winslow walked into Grant's office for their interview. She only had an hour before the editorial meeting. She was hoping they'd be alone so she could ask if he'd noticed a change in Ashlyn's behavior. She was startled to find Jayce sitting at Grant's desk, his feet propped on the edge, talking on the phone.

"He did a damn fine job when he was a commissioner. The only reason he wasn't reelected was because he didn't run. The only reason he didn't run was because he was going to run for governor. He's a champion for the Jewish community. In fact, back in Connecticut he grew up in a Jewish neighborhood."

Winslow's eyebrows lifted at that bald-faced lie. The gated community had only admitted Jews when they had been legally forced to.

Jayce merely smiled at her and continued. "He wants to work on getting funding for a Holocaust exhibit. . . . Yeah, but this one will be different. It'll feature artwork by survivors. We'll even try to find artwork children might have done while in camp. No big names, just real people expressing themselves. Can I set up a time for him to speak to your group? . . . Great." He flipped through the schedule book. "The morning of December twelfth works for us." He pulled his feet from the desk and used Grant's Mont Blanc to write in the date. "I'll be in touch in a week or so to gather a list of topics you'd like Grant to address. Thank you."

Winslow once again felt unnerved at the way Jayce had taken over. She'd never seen him at Grant's desk before, yet he looked comfortable—and not the least bit embarrassed at being caught there.

"Just got Dad in big with the Jews."

The way he'd tossed out that last word seemed disrespectful. Then something else occurred to her. "*Dad?*"

He finished writing the note and only then looked up at her. "I'm trying it out. He told me I'm like the son he never had, and after all, I will be family soon."

"Next year," Winslow said.

"Maybe sooner." He looked at the equipment she was pulling out of her bag: recorder, camera, and notepad. "What are you doing?"

"What do you mean, maybe sooner?" she answered, ignoring the way he'd asked her as though she were the one who had taken over.

He leaned back in the leather chair and put his feet up again. "I'm thinking that Ashlyn doesn't handle stress well and a big wedding might be too much to take on. The only reason we were putting it off until next fall was because of the time needed to pull it together."

"Does Grant know?"

"I'm going to tell him tonight. The three of us are having a wedding planning dinner and Ashlyn's supposed to make a decision by then. Won't he be happy?"

He'd thrown so much at her at once she could hardly get her mind around it. All of it subtle and none that settled well. They weren't including her in the dinner. They were moving up the wedding. Jayce was already calling Grant *Dad.*

"Why would he be happy?" she asked.

"No big wedding to pay for. And Ashlyn won't be driving him crazy with all the details. You should be happy, too. She'd be driving you crazy."

Ashlyn had talked about having a big fairy-tale wedding since Winslow had known her. She'd sketched a dozen dress designs, planning to buy a dress and then modify it. Winslow was hoping that Ashlyn would ask her to accompany her dress shopping, had even suggested it.

When she focused on Jayce, he was watching her with a hard expression. "So, what are you doing here? I hope you're not going to mess with my files again."

Her fingers clenched. "I'm here to interview Dad. We have an appointment at three."

"He's not here," Jayce said, dropping his feet to look at the schedule book. "He's at a charity tea wooing the University Women's Club. Says here his appointment with you is at four."

"You're the one who scheduled it for three." She walked over and looked at the book. It did say *Interview with Winslow* in the four o'clock slot. She knew it was for three. Didn't she?

He merely shrugged. "Grant will be here at four, if he doesn't get hung up."

"I can't stay that long." She started packing up her things.

"Now, now, don't get mad. Grant can't be at your beck and call right now. Besides, you're the one who wrote down the wrong time." He tilted his head. "Or maybe you're just mad at yourself."

She shot him a look and jerked the zipper closed.

His feet were on the desk again, and he was pressing the tips of his fingers together. "Winnie, I don't want you to have the wrong idea. Ashlyn is as safe as a nun in a convent with me. I'd never hurt her or let anyone else hurt her. We had a fight, she was getting on my nerves about wedding this and that, and I said to forget the big wedding. She thought I meant to forget the wedding itself and that's when she went off. I shook her shoulders to get her to listen to me. She punished me by running off. That's all there is to it. I don't want you talking to Grant about this, because that'll only upset Ashlyn more when he asks her about it. I love your sister, so stop looking at me like I'm some ogre. I'd like to be a real brother figure to you." He tilted his head and gave her a charming smile.

Only that smile never quite lit his eyes, and it left her cold. She slung her bag strap over her shoulder. "Tell Grant I'll call him to reschedule." That polite, womanly part of her whispered demurely that she should say something in response to Jayce's most generous offer. But the rebellious side of her, the one had that exasperated her mother, had other ideas. Maybe she *had* written down the wrong time. She compromised and said, "Have a good dinner," before turning to leave. "And don't call me Winnie."

She hated that she didn't feel comfortable in Grant's office anymore. She couldn't move anything or file something. Jayce had taken over the office, her sister, and even Grant. Their exchanges often left her feeling . . . icky. She couldn't pinpoint what it was exactly that made her feel that way. Maybe she was just feeling threatened, usurped in her position of helping Grant. Maybe she was misinterpreting things.

As she walked across the marble foyer, she glanced back. She could see him still sitting in the chair, tip of the pen in his mouth. He was watching her. He waved, and she turned and walked out the front door.

Her arms were covered in goose bumps.

Grant rushed into the office at two minutes before four, removing one tie and starting to retie another more casual version. He looked around even though he knew her car hadn't been out front. "Where's Winnie?"

His future son-in-law said, "Do you know she hates that nickname?"

Grant came to a stop. "She said that?"

Jayce grabbed a stack of messages and stood up from his makeshift desk. "Yep, though I doubt she'd say it to your face. She's already been here and gone. She thought your appointment was at three."

"But you said it was four, right?" Grant had so many appointments that the times swirled around in his head. Thankfully Jayce kept him on track. But hearing that Winslow didn't like the name he'd been calling her for years hurt. Especially since she'd told Jayce and not him.

Jayce nodded to the calendar where the notation was clearly written. "She was annoyed, like it was your fault or something. She said she'd reschedule."

"We have our weekly breakfast tomorrow. Maybe we can do the interview then."

Jayce, ever efficient, flipped the schedule to the following day. "Uh . . . no, you don't. Your breakfast date wasn't in the calendar. I scheduled you as guest speaker at nine at the Miami Gay Rights Association's breakfast meeting. Didn't I mention that yesterday? I'm sure I did. They had a last-minute cancellation, and I grabbed the spot for you."

Grant chewed the tip of his thumb, a habit he'd had trouble breaking. "Well, I appreciate that, but—"

Jayce pointed to his laptop computer. "I've already written down your salient points, and you're great at winging the rest. The gay vote is very important here, you know. Wear your pink tie. Unless you have one in rainbow colors. I told them you have a gay cousin and several gay friends, so you understand their issues."

"You told them *what*?"

"Surely you know someone who's gay?"

"Well, sure, but—"

"Sometimes a little white lie goes a long way, and what does it hurt? Don't make me look bad."

Grant released a sigh. "I don't suppose I can cancel now; I'll just have to make amends with Winnie—Winslow. But no more lies, Jayce, white or otherwise."

"Sorry, just trying to schmooze the key groups. We'll talk about your Jewish background later." He gave a soft laugh.

"You *are* kidding, I hope."

"Sort of." He grimaced. "Okay, not really. I got a little carried away in all the excitement. I want you to win, really, really bad."

With the passion in that last sentence, Grant couldn't bring himself to belabor the issue. "We'll discuss this later. But I mean it. No more lies."

"I don't suppose you could dig up a Hispanic relative." He held up a hand at Grant's expression of disbelief. "No, no, I haven't committed to your having one. Just wondered if anyone had dallied with the maid a generation or so back." Jayce glanced at his gold watch. "You've got the hour open; I say we get a martini at the country club and then we can pick up Ashlyn for dinner. Give Winslow a call from the club. Besides, I've got some wedding plans to discuss with you."

Grant winced and then immediately felt guilty. He should be happy for his younger daughter, but a big wedding and a political campaign were too much to handle at once. The fuss she'd made her eighteenth birthday party into would be nothing compared to this. He'd been hearing about her Cinderella wedding since she was five years old.

Jayce slapped him on the back. "I know what you're thinking, Dad. Can I call you Dad now?" Jayce led him toward the door. "But you're going to like this idea. Ashlyn's *already* stressing over the wedding. I'm trying to talk her into making it a small ceremony, moving it up, and then having a big bash for friends and family afterward. Come on; let's figure out how we can convince her over a martini."

Grant looked at Jayce. "You never fail to amaze me."

Jayce's smile twitched at the compliment. "Just you wait, Dad. I've only just begun."

Winslow had had a hard time getting to sleep. Her mind kept questioning what she suspected and what she should do about it. On top of that, she felt disconnected from her father. He'd called from the country club, sounding a little tipsy, and canceled their weekly breakfast date. For the last few years they'd had breakfast, caught up on things, and then she would help him out at his office. He'd always told her he wanted her up-to-speed on his business, just in case.

Sure, he'd sounded apologetic about having to cancel. But what really bothered her was he'd called her *Winslow*. He'd started to say "Winnie" and then corrected himself.

She rolled over with a sigh and forced negative thoughts from her mind. A cool breeze washed in through the open French door that led to the balcony. She concentrated on the sound of water lapping against the seawall as the tide came in: *one, two, three, four, five, six . . .*

It felt like she'd just dropped off to sleep when she heard something that jerked her back to consciousness and jump-started her heartbeat. Her eyes opened wide, taking in the wall of her bedroom. She reminded herself that the dark, looming shadow in the corner was Corky, her ficus tree. The water still lapped at the seawall. She'd been sleeping with the door open during the cool winter nights ever since she'd moved in. So did two of her second floor neighbors, and they'd never had a problem. It was probably just someone putting out the garb—

Before she could even complete the thought, Salt shot off the bed and, by the sound of his feet thundering on the tile, ran into the bushes around the fountain. Pepper, lying some-where on the bed, started growling. Winslow could see the eerie glow of his golden eye as he looked behind her. What was out there? She started to turn around when movement caught her eye. One of the shadows on the wall moved. *Someone was behind her, at the open door.*

Oh, God, oh, God, what do I do? Scream? Unable to breathe, she slid off the back side of the bed. She heard movement and swung around, ready to fend off an attacker. It was Pepper taking off into the darkness. Winslow took in the room as she grabbed the black iron lamp from the night-stand. Books tumbled to the floor along with a plastic glass filled with water. Her frantic gaze took in her surroundings, her lungs readying to shatter the air with a scream.

Nothing moved but the curtain on the door that floated in the breeze. She unplugged the lamp and moved toward the balcony. As she approached, light and shadow shifted again on the tile floor. She held the lamp like a baseball bat, inching toward the balcony. Still ready to scream. Darkness could play tricks on her eyes. She wanted to be sure before she woke the neighbors. She spared two fingers to switch on the balcony lights and leaned out the doorway.

The scream evaporated in her throat. Two chairs, a small wrought-iron table, and twenty-odd plants. Only then did she think to look over the railing to the strip of grass below. If someone had been here, he'd had plenty of time to jump over the railing and disappear around the corner.

She checked the doors that led to the living room and her office. They were locked. She slipped back through the bedroom and out to the living room. She ran through each room, flicking on switch after switch, chasing away shadows. And cats. Pepper, at least, was startled again at the barrage of lights and urgent activity and scampered behind the fountain where Salt probably cowered.

The front door was still bolted. Winslow peered between the wooden blinds. No one lurked there or around the pool. The wall clock surrounded by palm fronds read two o'clock. In the glaring light with fear still pounding inside her, the whimsical clock seemed strangely out of place. She realized she'd left the door to the balcony open in her rushed scan of the place.

Her gaze darted all over as she made her way back to the bedroom and locked the door. Feeling weak in the legs, she dropped onto the bed and caught her breath. Had someone actually been in here? The cats had either seen or heard something. Their reaction was too dramatic. She was still in flight or fight mode, adrenaline shooting through her veins, heart pounding.

Something had woken her, and something had scared the cats. She'd seen the shadows move, though that could have been her imagination. She thought about calling her dad or even the police, but she hadn't really *seen* anything.

The police would chide her for keeping her balcony door open; burglars could climb up the ornate design of the railing. And heck, she'd probably just dreamed it all. She'd been asleep, hadn't she? Grant would insist she sell and move into the guarded safety of one of his condominiums.

Slowly, she pushed up from the bed and went to the living room to coax her cats from the fountain foliage. Salt crept out and rubbed against her leg. His tail was still fluffed, proof of his fright. Pepper was having none of it. His eye shone from the shadows.

"All right, stay there." She picked up Salt and carried him to the bedroom, locking the door after her. The lights stayed on. And for a long time, she listened to every sound. Her mind told her it had been nothing.

Her gut, however, told her something different.

5

Winslow expected to have dreams of thieves creeping into her bedroom, of shadows coming to life beside her bed. And perhaps she had, in those first hours of sleep. When she woke, though, it was the last dream that echoed in her mind. The screech of metal was familiar, the jarring of the car and the shattering of the windshield in her face. The sight of her father's broken neck. Except that it was Grant in the driver's seat, not Paul. When she lifted her head, she didn't see the driver standing there watching. Instead, shrouded by a thin fog, a boat idled in the near distance. One shadowy figure stood at the helm.

It was her voice screaming for help. But it wasn't her accident.

She woke with a start ten minutes before her alarm was set to go off. The room was a dull gray, the first inkling of dawn creeping in. Salt, sensing Winslow's wakefulness, scampered over from his corner of her bed and demanded some affection. He seemed to suffer no residual effects from the night before. She might have suspected it had all been a bad dream, except that Pepper wasn't in bed and both doors were closed. Light peeped from beneath the door leading to the living room. Pepper's paw also peeped from beneath the door in a plea to be let in.

She left the bed long enough to open the door. The whole

episode of the night before now seemed silly. The cats probably *had* heard something out back, perhaps a raccoon scavenging for crabs along the seawall. Maybe one had even climbed up on the balcony.

As soon as she pushed that from her mind, the dream edged back in. "I hate that dream," she said to the cats as she stroked their backs. "The helplessness and shock and anger; it's like I'm there all over again. This is why I didn't want to learn too much about that boating accident." She tried to rub the grit from her eyes. "But that's not why I had the dream. It's my subconscious telling me that Jayce and Ashlyn were involved in that accident." The question was what was she going to do about it?

She climbed out of bed, took care of bathroom business, and made her way to the guest bedroom on the other side of the living room. It doubled as her office, since she rarely had guests. The desk faced Indian Creek and the exclusive, gated community across the way. Seeing the rising sun reminded her that she was skipping her beach walk. She stretched her foot beneath the desk and pressed the power strip button with her toe. The cats, sensing that she was about to sit down for an hour or two *before* they were fed, meowed fiercely.

"Don't worry, you wee beasts. I'm going to feed you first."

In pajamas with red cats all over them, she shoved her feet into red fuzzy slippers and trudged into the kitchen. Pajamas and silly slippers were an indulgence nobody but her cats knew about, and they were sworn to secrecy. She fed them, poured a large glass of orange juice, and settled in front of the computer.

The *Miami Tribune*'s Web page still held the initial article in their archives. She took a deep breath before she read the first paragraph. The very stories she avoided, and now she had to carefully read each word. The hit-and-run had happened last Friday at 5:30 PM. The story was brief. More space was given to pictures of the once happy family and the wreckage of the boat. Pictures that would reach for your heart. She couldn't help looking at the girl, only two years younger than Winslow was when she'd been in her accident.

Her finger rubbed the picture on the screen, the smiling olive-skinned face with chubby cheeks. Even with their differences, it was hard not to see herself. She looked at the pictures on the wall. Another brown-haired girl, with her mother and father, and on a boat ironically. Two months later that smile would vanish forever. She'd gone from ordinary, to scarred, to beautiful in the space of a few years.

Elena García had also suffered cuts to the face and hands, the article had said. How badly? And who would pay for the surgeries it would take to fix her? Jayce, if he'd caused the accident. He had a lot of money coming to him when his inheritance came through. He owed her.

This little girl needed justice. She needed the person who killed her father and uncle to pay for his actions. Winslow knew how hard Elena's life would be, how she would nearly lose faith in the world, in justice. In the human heart.

Winslow looked further on the Web site but didn't find any follow-up articles. No news. Good, that meant the girl was holding her own. Or even out of the danger zone. Papers didn't waste much space on good news.

She was far from an investigative journalist, but she grabbed her notepad and jotted down what she knew and what she needed to know, like which marina the Garcías launched their boat from and if they kept their boat there. She would find out where Jayce kept his boat, too. She needed a peek at her father's schedule to see what he was doing last Friday. Then she could find out if Jayce was with him. She wanted to know everything about the Garcías, the timing of their trip, and exactly where the accident happened.

She wasn't ready for the police yet, not until she had something substantial. Especially since the suspect wasn't some stranger or distant acquaintance.

She did a global search on the Internet but came up with nothing else pertaining to the accident. What now?

Alex Díaz. The name popped into her head almost before she'd asked the question. He was doing a story on the Garcías. He might even know them. Could she fool him into thinking she was doing a story for her magazine? She was willing to try.

She jumped in the shower and dressed in an outfit that was as simple and elegant as the one she'd worn yesterday. She needed to feel confident and professional while she lied through her pearly whites. The prospect of facing Alex rattled her just as it had the day before. She wasn't sure if it was the lying part or simply seeing him again. Either way, she had no choice. She needed to find the truth. If Jayce had recklessly destroyed lives and was too much of a coward to face the consequences, she sure as heck wasn't letting him marry into her family.

Toby Meyers scampered across the spongy grass to the seawall behind his grandma's apartment, his fishing pole already rigged with a lure. The tackle box rattled with each step; he loved all the bright lures tucked into their little slots. His grandma was watching him, even though she'd already warned him about falling into the water. Sheesh, he was ten years old already and he knew how to swim. The only way he'd end up in the water was if he caught a really big fish and it pulled him in. Since his worrywart grandma made him wear a stupid life vest, he wouldn't drown anyway.

Something shiny in the grass diverted him from his course, and he wandered over to check it out. "Wow." He picked up the brass piece fashioned into four connecting rings. "Cool, brass knuckles." He tried them on, just like one of the thugs in the action movies he and his friend Bobby liked to watch. Bobby would be totally jealous when he saw these! Toby made punching motions, pretending to smash some mean guy's face. These had raised stars designed to inflict even more damage. *Pow!*

He wondered where they came from. He looked around and then up. Not from the pretty lady who lived upstairs, that was for sure. Unless she had a brute for a boyfriend. He glanced back at his grandma, who was still watching, and slipped them into his pocket. Then, with a cheerful whistle, he walked over to the seawall and readied his rod.

Winslow timed her stop at Grant's office so he would be at the breakfast meeting. She was hoping Jayce had gone with him but wasn't surprised to find him there. At least he wasn't sitting at Grant's desk.

"Winslow, what brings you by?" he asked as though she were a client.

She waved him away in a *don't bother to get up on my account* way and went to the schedule book on Grant's desk. "I just need to look something up."

Jayce didn't get the message; he was peering around her shoulder before she'd even opened the book. "Can I help?"

"No." She shifted away from him as she flipped to the previous Friday. Grant had a three-hour meeting penciled in at the Fountainbleau with Trigon, his former development partners. Grant had set aside his solo aspirations to run for governor, but he wasn't opposed to joining his former team for a project. She had, in fact, agreed that he should keep his fingers in the pie, just in case. She'd never actually said the words *in case you lose,* but he'd known what she meant.

Jayce was perched on the corner of the desk watching her. His citrus cologne tickled her nose.

She turned to him. "I see that Dad had the meeting with Trigon. Do you know how it went?"

"He didn't say. I only deal with his political business, at least for now."

She tried to ignore the implication of the last phrase. "Be glad he doesn't drag you to every meeting. That'd be boring." She was scrambling for some obtuse way to pin him down. "I sure hope you didn't hang around here waiting for him on a beautiful Friday evening. You and Ashlyn probably went out on the town."

"Something like that," he said.

Darn, he was looking at her suspiciously. Had she given herself away? Well, she knew she wasn't good at this kind of thing. Obviously she was going to have to get better.

She flipped to that day's schedule. "I'm penciling myself in for three o'clock today. I'll call Dad to confirm it."

She walked out of the office and this time didn't look back. All right, Jayce had the opportunity to leave the office by three o'clock last Friday. Grant probably wouldn't know if he was there or not.

She made the drive down to the FREE/*Mojo* building and went upstairs to the newspaper's offices. She spotted Alex near the back talking to one of his employees. He had a nice voice, she thought, and a nicer laugh. As though he sensed her there, he turned and smiled. She realized just how genuine her return smile was, at least until she remembered why she was there.

"Hey," he said when he approached, drawing out the word. He had a tall mug in his hand that smelled of strong coffee.

"Hey yourself. I have a favor to ask. I want to do an article on the García family for *Dazzle*. There's probably a fund for her hospital bills, right?"

"Yeah, and friends of the family are doing a benefit. That's what the article was about that your sister was working on."

"Maybe I can cover that, too, as part of my piece."

He blinked, and his glossy eyebrows narrowed. "Wait a minute. Your magazine is doing an article on a middle-class Cuban family?"

She rushed in before he could ask more. "I think the magazine should expand its focus. Look at real people, real situations."

"But there won't be any Gloria Estefan or politicians. Or fancy clothing. Just regular people, and to be honest, it's really geared toward Cubans. We're going to have black beans and rice, roast pork, yucca. Paper plates and plastic forks."

"Yucca?"

He laughed softly. "I'll bet you've never even had Cuban food, have you?"

"I've had the chicken at Pollo Tropical."

"Didn't you try any of the food at the Tamargo event?"

"I was working, not a guest."

"Working." He said it as though the concept of her working was hard to believe.

"You think my magazine is snobbish," she said, not a question.

"Yes, I do," he answered, without a hint of apology. "That was my mistake before, not realizing that *Dazzle* is about high society, flash, and celebrity. After I called you . . . well, I felt bad. Then I looked through the rest of the magazine, and I got it. Which is why I'm confused about why your editor would even consider covering this story."

She shored up her shoulders. Who said lying was easy? "As I said, it's a new direction. We'd like to include a piece every now and then about real people. What I need is more information about the Garcías, the accident, anything I can get hold of. I couldn't find much in the paper about it."

He rolled his eyes at that. "Politics. It's complicated," he added at her questioning look. "An article on the García family," he repeated, as though he just wasn't sure. "All right, I'll help you."

"Great. Maybe one of our readers will have seen something. You never know."

"Yeah, sure. We can get together tonight and talk about it over dinner."

That took her by surprise. "Dinner?"

"I know a great Cuban restaurant in Coconut Grove. If you're going to write about Cubans, you have to eat the food. Should I pick you up?"

"I'm way north of here. I'll meet you here at, what, six thirty?"

"You got it. See you then."

She'd gotten conflicting signals from him, she thought as she went down the stairs. He'd seemed happy to see her until she told him why she was there. She wasn't sure he'd bought her story until the dinner invitation. Maybe he thought she was using the article as an excuse to get close to him.

Well, dinner with a sexy Cuban was a small price to pay for information. She could probably handle that.

Alex gave Winslow a wave before she exited the building. Through the front window, he watched her walk to a fine-looking convertible with the most interesting paint job he'd ever seen. She was fine looking, too, even more so than the car. The sun caught on her warm brown hair and her creamy pale skin.

His brother Enrique slid up next to him at the railing. "Forget that one, Romeo. That *Americana* is way out of your league."

"Who are you calling Romeo, *mujeriego*?"

"At least I *have* skirts to chase. You're becoming a workaholic like Papí."

"I haven't met the woman who means more to me than *Mojo* yet." He watched Winslow's car pull out of the parking lot, getting blinded momentarily when the sun reflected off the glass.

"And you still haven't," Enrique said, making Alex realize he'd watched her car for as far as he could see it. "She's *intocable*."

"I know." Untouchable. Except he did want to touch her.

"So was the one who was here helping. They're sisters, right?"

"Stepsisters."

He wasn't sure what Ashlyn's story was, either. He pushed away from the railing and headed back to work. He wasn't going to mention that he was having dinner with that untouchable woman. No way was she writing an article about the Garcías. She was either making up an excuse to get to know him better or . . . he didn't know. Couldn't even imagine. While his ego jumped on the former part of that supposition, Winslow didn't seem like the type of woman who would lie to get a date. Or need to.

So he'd play along with her—and find out exactly what she was up to.

"Hi, stranger," Candy said as Winslow walked into *Dazzle*'s luxury offices. The bubbly, petite receptionist was in her fifties but dressed like a twenty-year-old. Beneath her suit jacket her skirt only came to midthigh. The colors were bright enough to burn the retinas.

"Yeah, I know. I've been working on a story." True, even though guilt still pricked at her. She dumped her purse and briefcase on her desk. "Is Sebastian in?"

"Funny, he was asking about *you* a few minutes ago."

The differences between the offices here and Alex's digs struck Winslow again. The Muzak version of a Bee Gees song drifted from speakers built into the ceilings instead of loud Latin music from a well-worn radio sitting on a table. That music, though, lent the place energy, and as Winslow made her way to Sebastian's office, she felt no energy buzzing here, heard no excited conversations from a distant desk.

She walked into the secretary's office. "Hi, Amelia, is—"

Sebastian walked out of his office at that moment. "There you are."

He stepped back, a gesture meant as an invitation to enter. His office was done in the same beige and butterscotch hues as the rest of the place. Instead of Muzak, Puccini's *La Bohème* filled the air. Grant had tried to convince her that she liked opera, but she couldn't find a taste for it.

Sebastian closed the door and gave her an affection peck on the cheek. He was in his midforties, classically handsome, and, well, just classic altogether. The way he parted his thick blond hair on the side reminded her of Ricky Nelson. They'd had lunch a few times and dinner twice. He was moving slowly, and she was in no hurry, either. She was still weighing the wisdom of crossing the line. She was attracted to him, not in a Space Mountain roller-coaster way, but more like the Jungle Cruise: a slow ride with occasional surprises to look forward to.

She sat in the leather chair in front of his neat-as-a-pin desk, and he leaned against the edge in front of her. At work they kept a strictly professional demeanor. Here in the privacy of his office, he was a little more personal.

He'd never been married but had made it clear he was ready to devote some time to finding a wife. "Amelia said you had personal matters to take care of. Is everything all right?"

"Yes, thank you. How did you like my article on the Nicaraguan artist?"

Sensing that she was moving on to business, he reached for the marked-up copy on his desk and handed it to her. "I could tell you liked his work. It really came through in the writing."

She rolled his compliment around in her thoughts even as she thanked him. Did that mean when she wrote about something that didn't fascinate her it showed, too? That her work heretofore was substandard?

She pushed the doubts from her mind. "I'd like to propose a human-interest piece, something a bit different for us. Did you hear about the two Cuban men and the little girl who were rammed by a speedboat last Friday? The girl, Elena, is still in the hospital in critical condition. There's going to be a benefit to help with the hospital bills, a real down-to-earth Cuban affair. Black beans and rice and something called yucky. We really should be more culturally diverse. The article I did on the Cuban cultural award was a good start. I spoke with Alex Díaz yesterday."

Again, that pinprick of guilt stabbed her at mentioning Alex's name. "I'm going to get more information about the family. Alex said there are political complications; maybe I could look into that as well."

Sebastian was already shaking his head. "*Dazzle* doesn't take on causes; we cover the people who take them on. I'm sorry, but your proposal just isn't suitable."

She knew that. And by the way he was studying her, he was wondering if she was off her nut.

"What if somebody prominent, like Grant for instance, sponsored a benefit?"

"Why would he do that? Benefits and charity balls are for big causes. They're about glitz and glamour and the rich and well placed. That's what people want to read, what they want to support. Not black beans and rice under tents in a *parking lot*." He tilted his head. "Why are you so interested in this?"

She couldn't reveal her suspicions about the hit-and-run, and she didn't want to get into her past and the accident that took her father's life. She couldn't explain the need that was a knot in her stomach. "The story touched me. I'd like to delve into deeper issues, go behind the glitz and glamour." That was exactly what she didn't want to do all these years, and yet the words coming out of her mouth felt true. "Like interviewing someone who has been helped by the Cancer Society to go along with coverage of the ball, for example."

"How can you write deep articles when you aren't the type of person to open up? You keep yourself closed pretty tight, Winslow. With you, everything's on the surface."

She could hardly swallow. "Are you saying . . . I'm shallow?"

He chuckled and took her hand. "No. All I'm saying is that you keep your feelings hidden, and to write about suffering and courage requires tapping into those feelings. I've never seen that come through in your writing. You skim over the negative. I'd love to know why. I've even thought about asking Grant, just to help me understand. But that seemed like cheating, and to be honest, I like your lack of drama. You're smooth water, and I've had enough passionate, demanding women in my life to appreciate someone who glides on the surface. Besides, passionate women are often unsatisfied with one man."

She slid her hand free of his, feeling as though he'd just slapped her face. Was this how people saw her? Closed, smooth water—dispassionate? She surged to her feet.

Sebastian put his hands on her shoulders. "Winslow, I'm not criticizing you, honestly. I like your qualities—and I do see them as qualities. That's why we get along so well, why I think we'd be a good team down the road. Don't be mad. If you think it through, you'll see that I'm right and that it's okay."

He was trying to placate her, but he was only making it worse. To be called dispassionate as a compliment was too much. He was saying that all he wanted to know was the beautiful mask she wore and not the scarred girl beneath. She'd never shared that girl with anyone. She locked her away along with all the other bad memories. He was right; she had never let anyone in, hadn't opened herself to pain and passion. In the way that her mother had hidden her from her friends, Winslow had hidden herself, too.

"Forget this Cuban thing," he said, having watched her ruminations. "How is the article on your dad coming?"

She had to refocus. "I've had to reschedule the interview a couple of times, but we're on for three today. I'll have it to you by tomorrow afternoon." She walked to the door, but something she remembered made her turn back. "Did I receive a note from Alex Díaz a few weeks ago?"

She'd never seen Sebastian taken off-guard, and it looked odd on him. His face flushed, and he blinked rapidly. "Why do you ask?"

"He said he sent me a card." She was too embarrassed to go into the reason why. "I never got it."

"You're already peeved at me. Can we talk about this later? At dinner maybe?"

"Let's talk about it now."

"I saw the card in the stack of mail, before Amelia had a

chance to go through it. I noticed the return address, but
didn't realize it was addressed to you specifically until I
opened the envelope. He was apologizing for something
he'd said about your article."

She didn't believe for a moment that he'd accidentally
opened her mail. "And you didn't pass it on once you realized it was for me?"

He pulled her away from the door, where Amelia might
overhear. "I'm not exactly in a secure place in our . . . well,
our growing relationship. He invited you out for a drink or
dinner, and to be honest, I didn't like the idea. A young, hot
Latin guy . . . who knows? He might press your buttons. So I
tossed it."

He'd left his fingers on her arm, and she pulled away
from him.

"That was wrong, unethical, and . . . it just plain pisses
me off."

"It *was* wrong, but didn't I do it for romantic reasons?
Really, Winslow, you should be flattered."

She walked back to the door. "Do I look like I'm swoon-
ing?" And then she walked out.

This was why she shouldn't think of pursuing anything
personal with her boss. She'd just jeopardized her job, but
she wasn't going to be cowed by that prospect. If he fired
her, then she didn't want the job anyway.

For the next hour she tweaked the article Sebastian had
edited and printed a final, clean copy. She would leave it
with Amelia and head out to interview her father. She tore
through half of a crossword puzzle while she ate a cup of instant soup. The words *serene, dilemma,* and *boring* (even
though it referred to drilling) made her stomach sour. She
began to wonder if this puzzle had karmic significance when
the next answer was *propeller.* As she spooned up the last
noodles, she hoped the last clue wasn't an omen.

She wrote the word *Titanic.*

6

Winslow sensed a distance between her and Grant during their interview out by the pool that afternoon. Once Jayce vacated the premises, after she'd twice asked him to give them privacy, she thought their easy exchanges would resume. She was keenly aware that Grant hadn't called her Winnie once.

She'd already assured him it was all right that he'd missed their breakfast, and she'd apologized for getting the time wrong the day before. Still, an awkwardness hung between them she couldn't understand or get past.

"Okay, I think that covers everything," she said, shutting off her recorder. "Let's get pictures, some with the water behind you and some with the house."

They were sitting on the plush wooden chairs with a light breeze washing away the heat. Today represented the reason that so many people flocked to South Florida during the winter. She cursed the increased traffic even as she relished the dry, balmy breeze.

As she took the last few pictures, she asked, "Dad, have you noticed any difference in Ashlyn's behavior in the last month or so? Tilt your head up just a little . . . there, that's it." After capturing the shots, she set the camera down and sank into the chair opposite him.

"I haven't seen her much lately. She's been too busy with

her wedding plans to help me, and I've been too busy to talk to her. We've been out of touch." Winslow could tell that bothered him. "I feel out of touch with both of you."

"You're busy with the campaign. I understand."

"Now that you mention it, though, I have noticed . . ."

"What?" she asked, anxious for an opening.

"She is different. She's been calm lately. Not as prone to her histrionics."

"Since she's been seeing Jayce, you think?"

"Yeah, I'd say that. That's what she needed, obviously, someone to take control of her. I'm afraid I let her get away with too much. I felt I owed her, after she lost her mother so young and all. For the first time in years, she's . . . well, I hate to use the word, but I think it's apt: she's tame."

"Wouldn't you say, though, that's she's almost subdued? I haven't even seen her wearing any outlandish outfits lately. That's always been her thing, you know, altering her clothing and showing it off."

"I'm not sure that's an altogether bad thing. I just think she's happy, settled in her life, and busy planning her wedding."

It made sense and yet didn't feel quite right. "Which she's moving up, I understand."

"They're talking about it. Jayce seems to think that the wedding is stressing her out, and that a small ceremony would be better. I agree. And he wants to move it up since there isn't going to be as much planning. That boy is head over heels in love. I'm really happy for her." He tilted his head. "Are you all right about Ashlyn getting married before you?"

"Oh, sure. It's just . . ." Movement near the house drew her attention to Jayce, who was looking exactly as though he were going to interrupt them—again. "I'm fine. One last question, Dad. Last Friday, when you met with Trigon, do you know if Jayce and Ashlyn went out on his boat?"

"Last Friday . . . I told him to take the afternoon off. He's been putting in almost as many hours as I have." That last was said with a pride that grated on Winslow, though she wasn't sure why. "I'm not sure what he did, but he was gone by the time I returned. Why?"

"Someone thought they saw them out on the water. I was just wondering. Do you know where he keeps his boat?"

Answer, quickly, she thought as Jayce neared.

Grant did much worse. He looked up at Jayce. "Where do you keep your boat?"

Winslow could have sunk into the thick cushion.

"Boone's Marina over by Miami River, why?" He sat down as though the question were an invitation to join them.

Grant nodded toward her. "Someone thought they saw you out with Ashlyn last Friday."

Jayce looked at her, and his eyes narrowed slightly. "Nope, wasn't us. Who thought they saw us, Winslow?"

He was challenging her or more like cornering her.

She waved away his question. "You wouldn't know her. She lives on Biscayne Bay. She asked me, and I knew you had a speedboat, so I thought it could be you."

"Well, she was wrong," he said in an amiable manner. He gave Grant a smile that would charm money from a tight-wad. "Dad's going to extend the dock so I can park *In Too Deep* right here at the house." He turned to her. "That's the name of the boat, *In Too Deep.*"

Winslow was too busy watching Grant's expression to respond to Jayce; he obviously didn't mind or wasn't surprised by Jayce's calling him Dad. Why did it irritate her so much?

"It's a long haul to the marina," Jayce continued, "so I haven't been taking her out as much as I should. When Ash and I get married, we'll be able to go out all the time."

Jayce was beginning to make Winslow feel claustrophobic. She put everything back into her bag and stood. "Gotta run, Dad." She gave him a hug when he got to his feet. "Love you."

"You, too, Win."

Well, it was better than her full name. She couldn't help wondering why he had stopped calling her Winnie. As much as she didn't like the nickname, she missed it. She gave Jayce a cursory good-bye and headed off to charm Alex.

Winslow was sure that she was nervous only because of the lie. She hated lying, though she wasn't strictly opposed to it when it was necessary. After she'd parked, she walked through the half-empty lot. Lights still blazed inside the building, and she could see movement on both floors. Alex stepped outside and greeted her with a warm smile. Apparently he didn't always wear soft-but-worn T-shirts. His long-sleeved burgundy shirt and black pants set off his eyes and tanned skin perfectly. That he'd dressed for her sent a thrill through her while she tried to forget that she'd dressed nice for him, too. It wasn't a date, she reminded herself. She hadn't, after all, worn a dress and panty hose.

He took her in as she neared him, an admiring gaze that respectfully didn't linger on any one area. "You look great."

The compliment also took her off-guard and she smiled a *thank you* and then felt silly for not saying it. *Come on, Winslow; get a grip here.* At least she didn't say that he looked nice, too; then it would have really felt like a date.

He held out his arm to the right. "We'll take my car down to Coconut Grove. Your car will be fine here. We usually lock the lot after six."

He led the way to a vintage black Camaro and held the door for her. The dashboard and leather seats gleamed. Just as she got in, she heard a man calling, "Alejandro," and a stream of Spanish that sounded like a mixture of annoyance and taunting.

Alex had a chagrined smile as he glanced at her and then answered. She had a feeling the conversation was about her. She suspected, in fact, that he'd looked at her to see if she understood. She'd long ago lost the Spanish she'd learned in school. She'd gotten some practice while attending the

University of Miami, but since graduating with a communications major she had rarely spoken to anyone who didn't speak English.

Alex closed the door and walked around to his side. As soon as he got in, she said, "That was your brother Enrique, right?"

Alex nodded. "He lusts after your car."

She sensed that the conversation hadn't exactly been about her car. Not that she would call him on that.

Alex turned south on Brickell Avenue a few minutes later. The windows were open, the breeze swirling her hair. When she glanced at him, she found that he was looking at her.

"I can close the windows and turn on the air if you want."

She picked the strands from her lips. "I like fresh air." That reminded her of leaving her bedroom door open and the strange shadows she thought she'd seen the night before.

"How's your sister doing? I didn't get a chance to ask you earlier. You took me by surprise."

"I haven't seen her since yesterday, but she, Jayce, and my father went out to dinner last night. I have to believe he's not physically abusing her, not when he works so closely with my father. But . . ."

"But what?" He glanced at her as he weaved through traffic.

She shook her head. "I don't know. There's something about him I don't trust. I told him he'd better not hurt Ashlyn or I'd cause him all kinds of trouble. He laughed."

Alex seemed to appraise her threat capability. "I'd take you seriously."

She held her hair back with her hand and tried not to let him see how much she liked that. "So, I took you by surprise, hm?"

"I didn't think I'd see you again. Then you tell me you're doing a story on the Garcías."

"You didn't bring anything on the accident," she said, realizing she hadn't noticed until now. She didn't see a folder in the car, either.

He tapped his temple. "It's all up here. I used to take my car to the García brothers' repair shop. Before they got big mouths." When she raised her eyebrows, he said, "Politics," and left it at that.

Sunset colors splashed all over the western horizon. The eastern sky was darkening to a vivid indigo blue studded with stars. She noticed that his hair didn't move in the wind and doubted it was due to hairspray. She imagined his hair felt thick and coarse, the waves holding the strands together. At their lapse into comfortable silence, he leaned over and turned on a stereo that was definitely not the vintage of the car. The CD kicked in with what *did* sound like vintage Cuban music. He started to switch to something else, and she touched his arm.

"I like it. Who is it?"

That clearly surprised him, probably as much as her visit. It surprised her, too, that she was slouched into the seat and comfortable enough to touch him.

"Did you see *The Buena Vista Social Club*? It was a movie about guitar legend Ry Cooder, who brought together the greatest musicians in the history of Cuba. This was the album they produced."

She heard flavors of salsa, mambo, and even jazz as one song passed to another. The first had made her feel languid; this one made her feel like stripping off her clothes and swaying her hips. Passion. Yes, she could feel the passion of the music. Damn Sebastian, anyway, for creeping into her thoughts at just that moment, calling her shallow and dispassionate. That wasn't the way she felt then. Uh-uh, no way.

They drove into Coconut Grove, a trendy upscale shopping and dining district. Winslow had come a few times with friends for an afternoon of shopping.

Platános was located at the corner of one of the open-air malls. On one side an ornate railing surrounded several tables. Though the evening air was cooling down, every table was occupied. He pulled up to the front entrance, and a young man came running out and caught the keys Alex tossed him. Alex then opened the car door for her and led her to the arched wooden doors.

"Plátanos isn't the kind of restaurant you're used to dining in," he said, though not apologetically.

She had to smile as a young woman opened the door and greeted them, Alex by name. Though people waited inside, the hostess took them directly to a table near the back corner by a large terra-cotta fountain. She didn't hand them menus. Addressing Alex as Alejandro like the others, the waiter greeted them in the same warm way, and before he left another waiter set two drinks on their table.

The air smelled of roasted meats and fresh garlic. Though most of the waitstaff looked to be Spanish, about half of the clientele were not. Winslow eased into the cushiony chair Alex held for her.

"What are you smiling about?" he asked, settling into his chair.

"You're right; I'm not used to eating out in a place like this. I'm used to *living* in a place like this." She took in the Mexican tile floors interspersed with small triangles of floral tiles and the various fountains and plants everywhere. "This is exactly what my apartment looks like."

That made him smile. He picked up his glass. "Salud."

A caramel-colored liquid filled the glass. Leaves clung to the ice cubes, and a white stick served as a stirrer.

"What is it?" she asked.

"A Mojito. Dark rum, limes, sugar, and a splash of club soda, garnished with a stalk of sugarcane."

"And parsley?"

He laughed. "Mint."

She tipped her glass against his and took a sip. It was strong and different from anything she'd ever had. The mint was a refreshing touch. "I've heard of them but never had one. Interesting."

The waiter brought a basket of sliced bread that had been buttered and pan seared. Still no menu.

Alex seemed to read her mind. "Since you've only had fast food Cuban, we're going to have the classics to initiate you."

"You must be a regular here." The music playing in the background had the same effect as the drink, making her feel warm and languid.

"You could say that."

She picked up on his vagueness and also realized that what she saw in the employees' manner was respect. "Do you own this place?"

He placed a finger over his mouth and gave her a conspiratorial smile.

She leaned forward. "Wait; don't tell me. Politics."

"Very good." He looked genuinely pleased, though she hadn't a clue how it applied to the restaurant.

"When you called to criticize my lack of coverage about the political implications . . . is this all related, even to the Garcías?" When he nodded, she said, "How? If you're going to criticize me, then you're obligated to enlighten me."

He looked chagrined about that call, but he'd already apologized. "I suppose I am. But all this is off-the-record, journalist to journalist." She was surprised when he leaned forward, too; his voice was already low and sultry. "How much do you know about Castro?"

"Just what I read in history classes. He was a rebel leader who took Cuba back from one dictator only to become one himself."

Alex nodded. "My grandfather fought with Castro; he thought he was fighting for freedom. At least he died believing he had made a difference. He was killed in battle, and Castro considered him a war hero. The irony is that my grandfather would have hated what Castro did once he took power: taking away people's businesses, their freedom. When my grandmother refused the honor and denounced Castro, she was imprisoned. She died of pneumonia eight months later. My father was thirteen at the time. His uncle took him in, and ten years later they came to Miami."

Talk about putting a personal spin on textbook history. "Wow, that's so noble. And sad."

"I never knew them, but I wish I had." He grew quiet for a moment and then took a drink. "My father is considered an *exiliado*, an exile of Cuba. He walks the edge of hard-line exiles—*duros*—who believe that being anti-Castro is the only way. The irony is, what the *exiliados* condemned and left Cuba for they advocate here. If people speak out for lifting the Embargo, they'll be threatened at the least, killed at the worst. They could be castigated on Miami radio stations, which can lead to their businesses being boycotted, physical assaults, even death threats. If a club hosts a Cuban entertainer who doesn't want to defect, the building could be bombed. Those who don't forcefully disagree with Castro are pointed out as *traidores*. Traitors. Even the *Americano* politicians bow to the exiles. The exile leadership is more powerful than you can imagine."

"It sounds like you don't agree with them."

He gave her a lopsided smile. "Not exactly. I'm more interested in reuniting families than the political aspects. The Cuban Revolution split families the same way the U.S. Civil War did. Families are torn apart, divided by loyalties and beliefs. Daughters, sons, and nieces are disowned, for both leaving and staying. Every day charters take Miami Cubans to see their relatives in Cuba. The exiles denounce this as well as those who send money to their families. Over a billion dollars a year was sent from the U.S. to Cuban families. Exiles lobbied for the limits put in place last year. Now we can only visit Cuba every three years and send money only to close relatives."

"And your father supports this?" It was hard to see the charming Lazaro fighting for this cause.

"He believes that the only way to undermine Castro is to hurt the economy. It's a viable strategy, but it's hard to take when it hurts our families. My father sees both sides, too, but he believes hard times now will mean freedom later."

"He doesn't condone bombings and threats, does he?"

"FREE walks the fine line of Miami Cuban politics. It doesn't advocate violence, but it can't condemn it; otherwise, it wouldn't be around for long. My father's goal is to get the next generation ready for when Castro dies."

"So what was the significance of the event honoring Tamargo?"

"Tamargo lives in Cuba. He's come here to perform twice before, and when he didn't defect, the exiles denounced him. Because of that, ten years ago somebody threw a Molotov cocktail into the nightclub he was to perform in and nearly burned it down. He had the guts to speak out against the exiles, saying that he had the freedom to do as he chose and that no one should be punished for that.

"The Miami Cultural Society has always stayed out of politics. They honor musical legends and celebrate Cuban heritage, regardless of where that person lives. Amazingly enough, my father chose to stand with them when they honored Tamargo. One of the most outspoken exile leaders was there, as well as some of the softer exiles. But of course, you wouldn't have known that, and as I said, it was wrong to have expected you to report that."

He paused as the waiter brought two large plates of steaming roast pork, white rice, and stalks that looked like potatoes. Two bowls of black beans, a bowl of some kind of liquid, and a plate of plantains were set to the side. The waiter spoke for the first time. "Is everything all right?"

Alex deferred to her, and she nodded. "It smells great. Better than the chicken, and that was pretty good for fast food."

The waiter bowed slightly and then left.

"The proper way to eat black beans is to pour them over the rice." Alex demonstrated. "The pork is self-explanatory. This is yucca." He pointed to the potato-like stalks. "It's a root and, like the pork, it's marinated in *mojita,* a garlic-and-sour-orange marinade. There's more of it here in this bowl. Some people call it *mojo,* which is where I got the name for my newspaper. You can add more if you like." He drizzled it on both the pork and the yucca.

She took a bite of pork, and it nearly melted in her mouth. "Mmmm." She caught herself rolling her eyes. The black beans and rice were wonderful, though she had to get used to the thick-slimy texture of the yucca.

"Cuban food isn't exactly healthy. Here they offer low-fat and low-carb choices, too."

"They," she repeated.

He lifted his shoulders. "I'm a silent partner. I came up with the concept and most of the financing, but someone else is the owner of record. I want to keep this place separate so any fallout wouldn't hurt anyone here. *Mojo* is for my generation, U.S.-born Cuban Americans who don't harbor so much rage. Who want to know more about their heritage. My paper tells them when Cuban entertainers are coming, and it reports on the events afterward. We don't judge; we let our readers choose whether they want to attend. Of course, there are always protesters, and I let each party have its say, even if it's anonymous. People are afraid to speak out."

"But if your father is one of the exiles, why are you worried?"

"I'm not so worried about the paper. My father insisted we share the building, to protect my employees and me. Sometimes the extreme hard-liners make threats, but they wouldn't dare damage the FREE building. That protection wouldn't extend to the restaurant."

"I'm surprised your dad supports you so much."

He smiled. "He protects me because I'm his son. He doesn't always agree with me. We've argued; we've yelled and thrown things. But we promised before I started *Mojo* that we wouldn't let politics fracture our family."

She ate one of the sweet panfried plantains and washed it

down with a sip of Mojito. "I never knew about any of this. How do the Garcías fit in?"

He actually glanced around to make sure no one was listening. "They were *dialogueros,* a dirty word among Cubans in Miami. They advocated resumed relations with Cuba, lifting the Embargo."

"So they weren't popular."

"That's putting it lightly. Once the Garcías started speaking out, they were denounced. People stopped taking their cars to their shop. Even I did. If someone vandalized or bombed their shop while my Camaro was there . . ." He couldn't even imagine it, obviously.

She would have smiled but for the rest of the implication.

"That's why I'm curious as to why you want to do a story on the family. No one has claimed responsibility for the hit-and-run, but . . ." He shrugged, letting her put the rest together.

Up to then, she'd realized why Ashlyn had been so comfortable talking to Alex at the dinner. Now he'd turned the conversation back to the reason they were dining together. She was on.

"The magazine is going to start featuring human-interest stories, and I want to do an article on Elena García."

He was shaking his head. "I don't think that's a good idea. Based on what I just told you, do you?"

But she knew that it probably wasn't politics at all; she just couldn't tell him that. "*You're* doing an article on the benefit for Elena."

"I'm prepared to take those risks. If a few hard-line exiles did have something to do with this, they need to see the innocent victims of their violence. If someone took exception to you taking up the cause of *dialogueros,* could your pretty offices withstand bomb threats? More than that, I'm concerned for your safety."

"Ah, you didn't bring me here to give me information. Your goal is to talk me out of writing the article."

"That's because you haven't told me everything."

Thankfully, the waiter came, giving her time to think about her response to that. "Are you finished?" he asked, and again Alex deferred to her. She nodded, and a busboy cleared their plates. The moment the crumbs were cleared from the cloth, their waiter brought them coffee and something that looked like custard drizzled with caramel and artfully topped with coconut.

"Flan and *café con leche,* Cuban coffee with steamed milk. My favorite," Alex said, and took a bite of his flan.

"Thank you for sharing your culture with me." The flan melted in her mouth, leaving only the bits of sweet coconut to chew. The coffee was good, even though she wasn't much of a coffee drinker.

"My pleasure," he said, spending more time watching her than eating.

He was being a perfect host, letting her enjoy dessert before he pressed for answers. He was old-fashioned, chivalrous, and willing to go out on a limb for his convictions. She admired that. It made perfect sense that he would be concerned for her safety but also would expect more information when she decided to pursue the story despite his warnings.

She didn't want to lie to him, and yet she couldn't reveal her suspicions. Even though he'd trusted her with the secret of his restaurant ownership and Cuban-American politics, she couldn't reveal her secret. Alex was an admitted hothead, and she wasn't sure what he'd do.

She could tell him something she'd never told anyone, though. And it *was* the driving force behind her need to investigate the accident. It was also a test for herself; could she open up and share a piece of her soul?

Just as he had done, she leaned forward and spoke in a low voice. "Elena is the reason I'm writing the article," she began. "I feel a special connection to her because . . . when I was twelve, my father and I were involved in a hit-and-run, too. A car accident. My father was also killed, and . . ." She ran her fingers over her face, feeling the lines even though they weren't raised anymore. "I was left with severe cuts on my face, just like her. For two years we couldn't afford to get the plastic surgery I needed, and, well, life was hard." *Frankenstein, Frankenstein!* the children's taunts echoed. She was surprised that Alex didn't search her face for scars.

"Thankfully, I was able to get the surgeries I needed. I can't imagine my life without them. But Elena may not get those surgeries unless the boat operator is caught." Her throat was getting thick with emotion; it felt strange swirling inside her, prickling her eyes. All those long-buried feelings had risen to the surface. The little girl she had been would never get justice, but if Winslow had anything to do with it, Elena would.

Alex reached over and covered the hands gripping her coffee mug. "I'm sorry. That's a horrible thing to have happen, especially at that age."

It had helped that this place reminded her of home, but the wellspring of emotion was beginning to scare her. This was why she kept the world's pain at a distance. And why Sebastian thought she was shallow, probably why she *was* shallow. She felt naked, exposing her feelings to Alex. He had made her feel passionate and put her at ease, but he was still a virtual stranger. *Do this for the information, for Elena.* It was ironic that Winslow had to open herself up to keep her secret.

"For years after the accident, I had dreams about it. The man who hit us, he was standing there looking at our smashed car. Then he left. I couldn't believe he could just run away. Since I read the article, the dreams have come back. Only . . ." She was mortified to discover she'd twined her fingers with his on the mug. "Now I see someone on a boat watching the wreckage, watching *and not doing anything.*" She freed her hands from his and took a sip of her coffee.

Alex's brown eyes were filled with understanding and something she couldn't identify. "I want you to keep the political aspects in mind." When she nodded, he said, "What do you need to know?"

She let out a silent sigh of relief as she reached into her bag and took out a small notepad. "Which marina did the Garcías keep their boat at?"

"I doubt they had a slip. I remember seeing their boat on a trailer parked next to their shop. My boat's twenty-four feet, so theirs was about seventeen. I've seen them launch at Boone's Marina a few times. That's where I keep my boat." He smiled wistfully. "Every now and then they'd all go, Lidia, her daughter, Elena, and the two brothers. I didn't think they had room for any fish." His smile faded. "They left around four o'clock, Lidia said. She went to the docks to see them off. She blames herself for letting Elena go."

Winslow's heart had jumped at the mention of Boone's Marina. She'd jotted that down, focusing on the facts and not the images of a family out having fun. "The accident happened at five-thirty PM."

"Yeah, and they were found by another boater at five-fifty PM. I can't imagine coming upon that scene." He rubbed his eyes. "No one reported the accident, either, so the bastard not only didn't have the guts to stay and help the people he'd hit, he didn't even call it in."

She could see Alex's temper rising in the flare of his nostrils and the way he tapped his fork against his plate. All that energy excited her in some strange way, maybe because it was so foreign to her.

He asked, "Did the guy who hit you and your father at least call for help?"

"He didn't need to. There were cars in the vicinity. But no one came forward to identify the car." She looked at her notes, wishing she knew more about investigating. "The article said the police thought it was a speedboat in the twenty-eight-to-thirty-foot range going full throttle."

"They could tell from the damage."

"Do you really think the exiles had something to do with this? Couldn't it just as easily be someone not paying attention, maybe even drunk?"

"Sure. So far there haven't been any murmurings in the exile community, other than rejoicing. The Garcías have been outspoken *dialogueros* for a few years. They haven't done anything lately to instigate repercussions, though. Something like this would usually follow a protest or some other public effort to change policy. The question would be why now? But these things don't always make sense. Grudges can last a long time. Once you're a *dialoguero* you're denounced forever."

It was possible, though unlikely, that the exiles had run down the Garcías on purpose. That left Jayce with plenty of room to be the culprit. No doubt Ashlyn was upset about the accident, and he was probably bullying her into keeping quiet.

"One more question," Winslow asked, wanting to lighten the mood before they left. "I've heard people calling you Alu . . . Alehandro. I thought your name was Alex."

He gave her his crooked grin. "My formal name is Alejandro Ángel Aznar Díaz." When she blinked at the long list, he said, "Cuban names usually include our mother's maiden name. Aznar is my mother's last name. Ángel is my middle name. Yeah," he said with a laugh when he saw her eyes crinkle with humor. "Angel, figure that. Most *Americanos*—non-Cubans—butcher my first name, so I just go by Alex."

She grimaced. "Kind of like what I just did." She set her napkin on the table. "Thanks so much for dinner. And for your help."

"Good luck with your article. And Winslow . . . be careful."

His words echoed in her mind long after he'd driven her back to the office building and she'd pulled back onto the highway. But she wasn't thinking of *duros;* she was thinking of the expression on Jayce's face when he found out she was asking Grant about his boat.

She drove to Talbot Tower and parked in the garage. Ashlyn was obviously upset about the accident. She was Jayce's weak link, and Winslow figured she could break her down. Ashlyn might be flighty and self-absorbed, but she did have compassion hidden deep beneath the layers of D&G and Hale Bob.

As Winslow got out of her car, she felt a sinking in her stomach when she saw Jayce getting out of his Ferrari one row over.

"Evening," he said, giving her a nod. "You here to see Ashlyn?"

"I thought I'd check in on her, see how she's doing."

"Not good." He held up a drugstore bag. "She's got her period, and she's miserable. I got her some ibuprofen. She's not going to be up to seeing you, I can tell you that. When I left a few minutes ago, she was curled up in a ball moaning."

Winslow paused. He was probably telling the truth; Ashlyn had always had monster periods. Besides, she wasn't going to get anywhere with Jayce apparently doting on Ashlyn.

He laughed, as though sharing a joke with her. "Hell, she's probably not going to even let sleep in our bed tonight. Every time I move, she screams that I'm shaking the bed."

"Have you . . . moved in?"

"She figured why should I pay rent at the hotel when we're going to be married soon anyway?" He lifted two fingers, scout's honor. "I'm a perfect gentleman."

He was goading her. The thought of it made her grit her teeth and hold back the reaction he was looking for. Part of that reaction was alarm, though. He was moving too fast. Dating, engaged, and now living together in lightning speed.

Though Jayce was looking toward the entrance, he unerringly reached out and grabbed her wrist. His expression was pleasant, but his words were deadly serious. "I don't like people snooping around in my business. If you want to know something, just ask me, got it?"

She yanked her arm free. "Did you run over that small boat last Friday?"

"No," he answered, obviously not taken by surprise at her blunt question. "End of story. Snooping doesn't look good on a pretty woman like you, Winslow. Remember that."

He walked away without looking back. She rubbed her wrist, though he hadn't gripped her hard. Just the imprint of his fingers on her skin made her want to rub him away. She would talk to Ashlyn. She was just going to have to be sneaky about it.

7

Alex had vivid dreams all night, too, but they weren't about accidents. They were about Winslow Talbot. He'd intended to maneuver the truth out of her and then found himself explaining Cuban politics to her. He owed her that much, he figured, for jumping on her lack of knowledge. He liked the way she'd listened, really listened, to what he was saying. And he liked the way she opened herself to him. It wasn't easy, and that made it all the more beautiful. Even her pain was beautiful; it showed that she was human and not the perfect doll he'd thought her to be that first night he'd met her.

He could tell that the music, the restaurant, and the food had drawn her in. He'd told himself he wasn't trying to impress her; he'd never live up to her standards anyway. Then she'd surprised him by not being anything like the high-society women he'd known.

He rolled out of bed, used the bathroom, and changed into shorts and a tank top. Two miles every morning, rain or shine. He jogged around the neighborhood of upper-class Spanish-style homes, an amiable mix of Cuban and white people. Not once had he availed himself of the golf course that was within walking distance. He'd bought his house from an elderly cousin who wanted a condo.

After Alex had returned and showered, he called Lidia

García to check on Elena. He told Lidia about the woman who was doing an article on the accident and smoothed the way for Winslow to see her.

After steaming milk into his *café con leche,* he called the offices of *Dazzle.*

"I'm sorry, but Winslow is out for the day," the receptionist said in a chirpy voice. "Hold, and I'll connect you to the editor."

Damn, voice mail would have been fine. He'd already ascertained that Winslow's private number was unlisted, and he hadn't thought to get it from her last night.

"This is Sebastian Bentley; may I help you?" The man's voice dripped with superiority.

"I was looking for Winslow Talbot. The receptionist said she was out. I can leave a message—"

"She may be out for a couple of days. I can get a message to her if you'd like."

Alex knew that asking for her home number would be pointless, and he'd be annoyed if the man gave it to him. "Sure. This is Alex Díaz. I wanted to give Winslow some information for an article she's doing on Elena García, the girl hurt in the boating hit-and-run."

There was a moment of silence before Sebastian said, "She's not writing anything on the García family for our magazine. Of course it was a terrible accident, but that kind of article just isn't appropriate for *Dazzle.* I already told her that. Thank you for calling."

Alex was still staring at the phone after the man hung up. There was no article. Everything Alex had felt for her hardened to a knot in his stomach. She was lying, just as he'd first suspected. He'd been stupid enough—heck, dazzled enough—to believe her.

He dropped the phone into the cradle. "You're not the first bozo to fall for a wily *Americana*'s charms."

He was back to step one: finding out what Winslow Talbot was up to.

• • •

Winslow walked the beach, returned to her condo, and got ready for the day. But it wasn't a day of work. She slipped into linen pants and a yellow sweater and headed to Boone's Marina. A weak cold front had moved through the night before and dropped the temperature by fifteen degrees. It left a clear morning with a nip in the air.

She walked confidently into the marina office and sidled up to the counter. "I'm looking for Jayce Bishop's boat, *In Too Deep*. I left my watch in the cabin. He only brought me here the one time, last Friday, and I don't remember where the boat was docked." She gave the skinny red-haired man at the counter a wink. "We'd already had a bit of wine, you see." She held up keys that were supposedly given to her by Jayce, though they actually belonged to Grant's yacht.

She didn't really consider herself a sexual person, but she did know how to use her wiles when necessary. The man wasn't subtle about checking out the cleavage she was showing as she leaned against the counter.

"Well, let me see. Bishop, you said?"

"Yep. You know him?"

He shook his head as he looked at a big chart that represented the docks. Each slip was labeled with a last name, and she spotted "Bishop" before he did. Still, she let him find it and then turn around to say, "It's in Eleven-B."

She gave him a perky, "Thanks," and headed out, following the signs to row 11. The marina was situated on a river that led out to Biscayne Bay. Twenty rows of docks stuck out like fingers into the river, and vessels of all sizes and styles bobbed in the gentle wake of a passing boat. Alex's boat was here, too, though she pushed that thought from her mind.

She'd never seen Jayce's boat; thus far he'd only taken out Ashlyn. Twice he'd invited them all out, apologizing for having such a small boat, nothing like Grant's yacht. Grant then offered to take everyone out on *The First Million* instead.

Those were the only times Ashlyn hadn't perched in the seat next to Grant's captain seat almost the entire time.

If Jayce's boat was here and Winslow could ascertain that it had been here all week, it probably wasn't involved in the collision. That's what she was hoping for. As much as she didn't like Jayce, she didn't want her sister dragged into his recklessness.

She stopped in front of the empty slip at 11-B and uttered the words, "The boat . . ."

"It's still not back," a man said beside her, and she swung around to see a short Hispanic man eyeing the keys in her hand. "You Jayce's girlfriend, right?"

She blinked. "Yes. Yes, I am."

He nodded toward the office. "I heard you asking about it. Something about a watch."

The boat wasn't back. She was trying to work through those words and play along with this man at the same time. "Yeah, it's my favorite watch, too. Daddy gave it to me for my birthday. I just know I left it on the boat the last time we were out. Friday, wasn't it?"

"How could you forget?"

She shrugged. "I'm bad with days."

The sudden splash of water hitting fiberglass startled her, and she saw a scrawny-looking guy on the boat across from Jayce's slip. He was hosing off his deck but watching them.

The Hispanic man led her away from the spray of water. "It's still gonna be a few more days. It's out of my way, but I can go take a look for you." He seemed to be waiting for more than an answer.

She belatedly realized he was hinting for money. For his trouble, of course. "I could give you something for your time." She handed him a twenty.

"I've got to finish up something here; then I'll go look for it. You'll be here?"

"Yes. Thank you. Oh, what's your name, anyway?"

"Manny."

She watched Manny walk over to a large boat at the end of row 12, where another man waited with a frown and crossed arms. She wanted to inconspicuously keep an eye on Manny. She turned back to the scrawny man who obviously cleaned his boat more than he cleaned himself, and forced a smile. "Hi. You live on your boat?"

"Uh-huh," he answered, taken off-guard that she'd deigned to talk to him, probably.

Those who lived aboard usually made friends with other boaters. She knew from summer trips on *The First Million* that the boating crowd was a social community that kept an eye out for their neighbors' property.

"Do you know Jayce, the guy who keeps his boat here?"

"Seen him a time or two. With a redhead once." He looked her up and down. "Not you."

She supposed Ashlyn could be called a redhead, though she'd be mortified. *Strawberry blonde,* she'd correct anyone who dared.

"Do you know if his boat went out on Friday afternoon?"

"Didn't pay much attention." He gave a piercing whistle, and an even scrawnier guy on the boat next to his gave a nod. He was sitting on the back deck with a beer in hand. "Lady here wants to know if that boat was gone Friday."

The guy got to his feet and looked at her. "Why d'ya wanna know?"

"She thinks her boyfriend's two-timing her," the first guy said with a rough laugh.

"I think he may have hit another boat that day," she said, hoping for a reaction, maybe for more cooperation than an insecure girlfriend might engender.

"The *Cubans,*" the second guy said with obvious disdain. "Why do you care?" He looked at her, as though she were too . . . well, too something to care about a family of Cubans.

"Because two men died and a little girl's life hangs in the balance, that's why."

Both men quieted and looked behind her. She turned to

find Manny walking up. How much had he heard? Had she just spoiled her own story?

"I'm going now," he said. "Be right back."

As soon as he turned the corner, she left, too. She glanced back at the men who were both watching her. "Thanks," she called, though they hadn't been much help.

The guy in the office opened the door when he saw her coming. "Did you find what you wanted?"

"Yes, thank you."

Manny had paused by her car, looking at that damned paint job. He leaned around the back and then walked around the front. Curiosity sated, he climbed into a beat-up truck with big tubs of adhesive and rolls of fiberglass in the back. She jumped into her car and followed him.

A man dialed the phone, and a voice answered, "Hello," in his usual cranky way.

"Hey, it's me. There was a woman down here asking questions about Cubans. And who was out on Friday afternoon. Know what I mean?"

"Find out who she is."

"I've got her car make and license plate. I'll get my friend to run it and let you know."

Winslow followed the truck into a rather seedy part of the city. It was once industrial, though several of the buildings looked abandoned. She kept her distance, since her car would stand out. Manny pulled into a fenced-in dirt lot, parked next to another truck, and disappeared inside an old steel building. There were no business signs indicating just what was done here. She had an idea when she saw a boat inside the open door. She parked just past the building, next to an overgrown pepper bush.

Her canvas sandals crunched on the coarse gravel as she walked toward the open gate. Manny was inside; she saw no

one outside. Heart thumping, she stepped through the opening and crouched behind two wheel-less cars as she inched
closer to the building. All of this subterfuge seemed so odd
and yet natural at the same time.

She heard two men talking, their voices bouncing off the
tall metal walls.

"She said she left a watch on the boat. She gave me a
twenty to look for it. If it's worth a bunch, I'll tell her it
wasn't here. If it turns up at a pawnshop and she finds out,
she won't be able to identify me. 'Some Spanish guy,' that's
what she'd say."

No, that wasn't true. *Scumbag, short,* and *paunchy* would
be in there, too.

Another voice sounded harsher, but not Spanish. "Are
you sure it's his girlfriend? You ever see her?"

"No, but this dame's classy, Corky. A real looker. Who
else could it be? She knew the boat was being repaired and
that it had been out on Friday. It's her."

"Well, hurry up and get rid of her. I don't want any
trouble."

Get rid of her? She didn't like the sound of that. She took
one more step and saw what she needed to see. The material
they used to repair fiberglass partially obscured the words *In
Too Deep* on the front hull. It looked less damaged than
she'd expected.

She crept to her car and returned to the marina, just in
case Manny did. She didn't want to raise any flags, especially considering the other guy's attitude. Manny did return
a few minutes later, shrugging his shoulders.

"Sorry, ma'am, but I din't see no watch. Maybe you left it
somewhere else? Or up on the deck and it got washed overboard."

She sighed. "I'll go home and look again. I was sure I'd
left it on the boat. Thanks so much for checking." She tried to
forget what he'd said and gave him as near a genuine smile as

she could manage. He ambled to the big boat at the end of the next dock. The guy was asking him questions, looking at her.

She could feel something in the air that hadn't been there before. Something malevolent. It made her uneasy, and she quickly walked to the car. Time to bring in the police. Surely they could connect the damaged areas on Jayce's boat to the accident. These weren't people she wanted to tangle with.

First, though, she needed to talk to Grant. She owed him that much, if she was going to report his future son-in-law to the police. Ashlyn would be questioned, too, and possibly be implicated for failing to report the hit-and-run. Hopefully her cooperation would help.

Elena, we're going to get justice for you. You won't have to live your life wondering who stole so much from you.

Winslow sat in the formal living room and did half of a crossword puzzle while Grant finished a strategy meeting with Jayce and two other men who would become important to his campaign when they got closer. The election was still a year away.

She wasn't going to help matters. Grant with his single-focus mind wasn't going to like being involved in an investigation. She filled in another clue: *Perfect Storm.* Half of the words seemed significant, even if some were a stretch.

"Sorry you had to wait," Grant said, startling her out of her thoughts. "We've now studied all the special interest groups and come up with angles on approaching them."

"Do you know you have a Jewish background of sorts?"

Grant looked chagrined. "And several gay friends, apparently. I guess I could include Scott Roberts, though he's more of an acquaintance than a friend."

"You don't mind that Jayce is lying?"

"Of course I do, and I've asked him to stop. He's just a bit misguided and too enthusiastic, that's all."

She held her tongue, but inside she raged at Grant dismissing Jayce's faults so easily.

Grant said, "Sounds like you've got something important on your mind."

She tucked her puzzle book into her bag. "Can we talk outside?"

They stepped into a balmy breeze. Cloud shadows chased across the lawn and lanai as they made small talk on the way to the boat dock. The pilings and boards had been painted brown, and pointy black caps on the pilings kept the birds from perching and leaving a mess. *The First Million* hardly moved in the light chop on the water.

The breeze would ensure that even if Jayce was lingering nearby, their words would be blown away. They sat on the dock bench.

"Dad, I know this is the last thing you need right now, and I'm sorry to dump this on you, but you'll understand." She told him about the hit-and-run and her suspicions. "I've got to do something."

He was chewing the tip of his thumb, a habit that was endearing in a boyish way. Her mother had constantly reminded him how childish it was, but she'd failed to eradicate it. "Sneaking around old buildings, consorting with lowlifes. Winslow, this isn't like you. I don't understand why you're doing this."

They rarely talked about the car accident or surgeries. Grant had thought that by erasing most of the damage from her face he'd also wiped away the inner scars. She now regretted letting him believe that.

"Because that man who ran us off the road was never caught. He never paid for his actions. I think about him, about the fact that he walked away without even seeing if we were dead or alive. I believe Jayce did the same thing to the Garcías. I don't want Elena living with the agony of injustice. She needs the same kind of surgeries I had. I know those surgeries must have cost you so much. I want the same thing for her."

He didn't address any of that. "All you know is that Jayce

could have been out on the boat that afternoon. You don't know for sure that he was."

"No, but the police could determine if the damage to his boat was due to an accident."

"But would they be able to prove that his boat was the one? Could they prove he was driving?"

"Let them worry about that. They can do amazing things by matching paint and fibers. Don't you watch *CSI: Miami*? As for who was driving, Ashlyn could attest to that. She'd have to cooperate."

He was still working it through. "Do you really think Jayce is capable of doing something like that? That's what you're accusing him of, leaving people to die. That's a horrible allegation."

"I do think Jayce is capable of it."

Grant made a scoffing sound. "You don't even know him."

"You don't, either. He's only been around for four months. It's kind of creepy the way he's infiltrated our family . . . calling you *Dad*."

"Creepy? Come on, Winslow. I'm surprised you don't see the reason he's become so close to us. He has virtually lost his family over this inheritance dispute. His beloved grandfather is dead, and the rest of the family are at each other's throats. He sees us as a surrogate family. He told me he'd like to be a brother to you."

Yes, that sounded so nice and sweet and cozy. "Oh, so I misinterpreted it when he told me to butt out of his life."

"Does he know what you suspect?"

"He wasn't referring to the hit-and-run. Well, I don't think he was. He knows I was asking you where he keeps his boat, and if he was out Friday. Actually, if he's guilty, he may suspect I'm checking into it. He won't let me talk to Ashlyn, either."

"I think I know what this is about. Jayce confided that he feels animosity from you and he's bewildered as to its cause. Frankly, so am I. The fact is, I feel as though do I know Jayce well. He's never given me reason to suspect him of being capable of doing something so heinous. And he's been worried about you doing just this kind of thing."

Grant had never seen what she saw in Jayce, and she could tell he wouldn't believe her observations. Whatever she told him would only make her look like she was imagining things, picking on poor Jayce, who was so concerned about what Winslow thought of him. What scared her more than anything was how Jayce had completely won over Grant. That Jayce had gone to Grant about her made her even more suspicious.

"Dad, he put bruises on Ashlyn. She was probably panicked about the accident and he squeezed her shoulders too hard. He told me she was freaking about the wedding and I know she does tend to get into tizzies over the slightest thing, but come on, to freak out so much he had to grip her that hard? She ran away from him on Saturday and hid out for a few days. Hid from *him*. Maybe if you talk to her, she'll tell you everything."

He was shaking his head. "Ashlyn would have told me if he'd hit her. And you should have seen them at dinner a few nights ago. They're talking about moving up the wedding— she brought it up—and he positively dotes on her. She didn't look like a woman who'd been bruised by her fiancé."

Winslow started to argue further, but he held up his hand. "I know you don't like Jayce, though I don't understand why. Maybe you're a little jealous that Ashlyn found someone and you haven't yet. Maybe you feel threatened because he's working with me now. I don't know, but Jayce is right; you do seem to have something against him. I like him, and he's been a big help to me already. He enjoys being my campaign manager; he doesn't look at it as an obligation, like you and Ashlyn do."

"Dad, I've never looked at helping you as an obligation. You know I'd do anything you ask to help out, and gladly so."

"Then you know how important this is to me. Do you

realize what it would do to me if you started accusing my campaign manager and my daughter of leaving the scene of a fatal accident? After all I've done for you, I can't believe you'd let some Cubans threaten the one thing I want most."

Some Cubans. He'd flung the words out there, as though their heritage made them insignificant. "Those Cubans died, Dad. The girl will be scarred forever, inside and out."

He put his hand on her arm. "Sometimes there isn't justice in this world. Sometimes, like with your accident, the bad guy gets away. Do you understand what I'm saying?"

She did. He didn't want her to pursue this. *After all he'd done for her.* He was calling in all those gifts and favors. He'd done it before, subtly used his kindnesses to twist her arm, to get her to attend something when she had other plans.

He stood and waited for her to come to her feet. "You're wrong about Jayce, and I think you're wrong about this hit-and-run. Let it go."

She watched him walk toward the office. She was sure Jayce was observing them, and in fact, spotted him inside the bay windows. He didn't move away when he saw her looking at him. She walked around the side to her car instead of through the house. The truth was, she didn't feel welcome there just now.

All those years of playing stoic about her accident had backfired. Grant couldn't realize how it had impacted her life. She knew Grant would be reluctant to buy her theory, but she hadn't expected him to be a staunch supporter of Jayce. She thought he'd at least consider it and then let her make the right choice. He'd tried to take the choice away from her.

She got into the car and pulled out of the driveway. Her subconscious knew where she was going before she did.

Before Grant returned to the office, he pulled out his cell phone and called Ashlyn. She answered on the second ring.

"Hi, sweetheart. I'm just checking in, making sure everything's all right."

"Sure, Daddy, everything's fine."

Except . . . he could hear it in her voice. "Are you sure?"

After a slight pause, she said, "Not really. I . . . I shouldn't bother you with it. Never mind."

"Bother me," he said, maybe a little too firmly.

She seemed to consider it and then said, "The three clubs I called about the reception are already booked."

Nothing serious, he thought with relief. "How about we have it by the pool at Talbot Tower? We can have L'Auberge cater it, hire a band, make it special."

"That's a great idea! I'll call Mr. Wegman and see when it's available."

"I think a smaller wedding is the smart way to go. Less stress on you." He paused. "Winslow's got some idea that Jayce is abusing you. That he bruised your shoulders."

He could picture his daughter rolling her eyes to go with the sound she made. "I told her it was nothing, but because she doesn't like Jayce, she has to make a big floofing deal about it. Yes, he put two tiny bruises on me, because I had a tizzy. He felt just awful about it. He's been a doll ever since."

"You ran away from him, she said."

Again she made the sound. "I should have figured she'd go to you about this. It's really none of her business. We had a fight, that's all. Just a normal fight."

"Nothing else?" He wasn't sure he wanted to even bring up Winslow's weightier allegations. "You know you can talk to me about anything, right?"

"Of course. Everything's fine, Daddy. No need for you to worry."

No, he didn't need to question her about the accident. He could tell in her voice that things were, indeed, all right. "Good. I'll talk to you soon."

When Grant walked back into his office, Jayce looked up from his papers. "Looked like Winslow had some serious business to discuss. She all right?"

If Winslow could see the concern on Jayce's face she'd

forget her crazy suspicions. "Nothing for you to worry about."

Jayce relaxed. "Good. You don't need any problems right now. None of us do."

More relief rushed through him. "You're right about that." Winslow would drop this silly investigation and hopefully warm up to Jayce soon. She probably did feel threatened by his presence in her family, but that would pass. And Grant had an idea that might distract her long enough to allow her feelings to fade.

"How about we grab some lunch, son?"

8

W hen Winslow looked up at the hospital, it felt as though she'd swallowed a baseball. It had been sixteen years since she'd been in a hospital—not even this one—but she could still smell the antiseptics and hear the sounds of footsteps coming and going down the hallways, could still feel her muscles tightening, wondering if those steps were coming to her room, were from a doctor, a nurse, or her mother. Wishing they were her father.

After taking a deep breath and walking inside, she was happy to learn that Elena had been moved to a regular room. The smells and sounds were the same, Winslow noticed, as she took the elevator up ten floors and walked down the hallway.

She heard people talking in Spanish when she neared the room and continued past the open doorway. Two women and a man were leaving, calling good-bye in the tone of voice one used with children. Before stepping into the room Winslow waited for them to leave. A blue curtain separated two beds. Bears and elephants decorated the walls in a vain effort to lift the fear and despair of being here.

The first bed was unoccupied. Elena's mother, Lidia, sat by the second bed. She looked up, a questioning expression on her haggard face.

Winslow stepped forward. "Hi, I'm Winslow Talbot. I—"

Lidia stood. "Yes, Alejandro said you might talk to me, about your article, right? I'm very happy to hear this."

Winslow felt bad for her lie, especially since Alex had initiated contact with Lidia. But her lie was for a good cause, especially where Elena was concerned. Lidia pulled one of the extra chairs closer and gestured for Winslow to sit on it.

Winslow's gaze went to the bed before she even sat down. Her stomach clenched at the sight of the bandages, since that was all she could see of the girl. Brown eyes tried to focus on the new visitor, but Elena drifted into sleep despite her fight. Winslow felt her heart open, felt the connection between them tighten like a silk cord.

Lidia was looking at her daughter, her mouth drawn in a tight frown. When she turned to Winslow, her eyes were wet with unshed tears. "She cannot talk. Her jaw was sliced across like this." She drew the edge of her hand across her mouth.

Winslow couldn't help cringing. "How terrible." Her hands went to her face, thankful her cuts hadn't gone so deep. "I'm so sorry for you both."

Tears fell down Lidia's cheeks, and she wiped them away. "I shouldn't have let her go. I had one of those bad feelings. Jose, my husband . . ." She seemed to realize that he wasn't her husband anymore and took a stilted breath. "He said, 'Why not? We won't be late. Besides, it's Friday. No school tomorrow.' Luis, his brother, teased me about being a worry—how do you say?—wart. She was fussing, wanting to go. And this white man waiting to launch his boat behind us was impatient and started arguing with Jose, calling us 'spics.' I told Jose to go, take her. I'll never forgive myself for that. I should have listened to my feeling."

Winslow didn't know what to do, but she reached out to touch Lidia's arm. "I know it's easier to say than do, but don't blame yourself. Out of the thousand choices we make every day, we have no idea which one might hurt us. At least she's still here. She's going to be all right, isn't she?"

Lidia started to nod, but she shook her head. "She will be alive, yes, but how will she live with"—she lowered her voice to a whisper, and Winslow had to lean forward to hear the rest—"scars all over her face, with part of her jawbone gone? We have no insurance. My husband and his brother were self-employed. I only work part-time. We came here ten years ago, risking our lives for a new start. We'd heard how well Cubans were doing here. But even our own people don't accept us. We are considered *balseros*—rafters. Because we had no sponsor, we spent almost a year in detention. After we were released, we discovered that the earlier immigrants look at us with suspicion. They keep their distance. And Jose and Luis, they made it harder by speaking out. Jose, he used to say, 'We came to America so we could speak what we believe. But it's all a lie.' "

Winslow didn't let on that she knew about that. She could only nod in sympathy. Her gaze, however, locked onto Elena. She looked so helpless, so lost in all the bandages. Even her hands were swaddled. Winslow's face only looked as smooth as it did because of the expertise of the best plastic surgeons. They had rebuilt the cheek crushed in the accident. They could rebuild Elena's jaw, too, but only with the right funds.

Lidia had wiped her face and blown her nose. "Alejandro said you wanted to ask me things, for your article. What do you want to know?"

Her article. She hadn't come to interview anyone, only to see Elena, to look at her and ask herself whether she could walk away from the truth.

"Does she remember anything about the accident?" Winslow asked after pulling out her small notepad. She didn't think Lidia would be comfortable talking with a tape recorder rolling.

"Not much. She cannot speak or write. The police, they asked many questions, and she would blink once yes and twice no. She remembers the boat coming at them. And she remembers *dos*—two people on the boat. She couldn't tell if they were man or woman."

Two people. Jayce and Ashlyn? How could they not have seen the Garcías' boat? If Jayce had left Grant's office at three o'clock, could he have been drunk by five thirty? Winslow supposed it was possible that they were doing more than drinking.

Lidia spoke about her family, their hardships, and how they had been thinking of moving to New York, where their views would be tolerated more. Winslow felt Lidia's words, her pain, and the disappointment of broken dreams. Her pen furiously scratched across the paper.

When they reached the end of the interview, Winslow was surprised to feel a connection with this woman who was so different from her. She touched Lidia's arm again. "Thank you for sharing this with me. I'll do my best to present your story with all the emotion that it deserves, so that others will be as touched as I am. There's a fund set up for Elena's medical bills, right?"

Lidia nodded and then pulled out a wrinkled slip of paper and recited the name and bank account number. It was the same bank Winslow used. "There is a benefit, too," Lidia said.

"Yes, Alex told me. Um, Alejandro," she added when Lidia didn't seem to know whom she was referring to. Yes, she'd butchered the name, but Lidia knew what she meant. "He said it was for the Cuban people, and our readership is primarily white."

"Rich white people," Lidia said, obviously repeating what Alex had told her. "Will they care about some poor Cuban girl?"

Winslow couldn't lie, so she shrugged. "I'm willing to take that chance."

It wasn't until she'd exchanged good-byes with Lidia and was waiting for the elevator that Winslow remembered there was no article. And that she was there to make a decision about whether to drop her suspicions. During their conversation, her heart had made up her mind. She rubbed the leather surface of her notepad holder. She would write the article.

When Lidia called Alex, he was in the middle of four different things at *Mojo*. But he took her call, hoping it wasn't bad news.

"Your lady friend came by the hospital," she said.

"Winslow Talbot?"

"Yes. She was very nice. I could see that she cared, that her heart was in her eyes, as they say."

He hadn't sent her. So she'd gone on her own, for whatever reason that she was pretending to write this article. He didn't want to tell Lidia that, though, so he simply said, "Good. I hope her heart is in the right place."

Lidia told him that Elena was doing better and thanked him for his help.

"The article about the benefit will run in this week's edition," he told her.

"Are you sure you should do that? I don't want you to get any trouble for us."

"People need to know what's going on. That's what my newspaper is all about. It's a risk that needs to be taken. Some of my readers will care, Lidia. And some will help."

She thanked him and hung up. He wished he knew how to get hold of Winslow. He wanted to confront her with her lie. She was definitely going through the motions of researching an article about the accident. He couldn't imagine what her motive was. He knew she wasn't working with the *duros*. But he had an idea where she'd be looking next.

He called a friend and, after they exchanged greetings, said, "Do me a favor. If you see a classy brunette, beautiful, drives a blue Volvo with a cool paint job, asking questions, call me."

Winslow drove past the warehouse that contained Jayce's boat. It was closed up tight, surrounded by a tall fence topped with barbed wire. Grant was right; she didn't have enough proof, and what if the police couldn't figure out if Jayce's boat had hit another boat? The repairs were probably almost finished. She needed to make absolutely sure, as sure as she could, that his boat could have been in an accident. If she could study it, look at the GPS, if it had one, maybe she could see where he'd been.

She drove home and, after giving Salt and Pepper a little loving, started going through the last year's worth of *Dazzle* magazines. She typically had one or two pieces in every issue, along with a column. She flipped to each article and read the headlines. Several were about charity balls. One was about a prominent local author who had prattled on about how much he was making. Two more were about twins who'd gone to New York and become successful at modeling and a father-and-son development company making a difference in Miami by designing their buildings to fit the landscape.

She tossed the last one over her shoulder. "Drivel!" Not one article on something that mattered. Not one piece that made a difference in anyone's life other than the subject who was getting his or her flash of the spotlight.

It was exactly what she'd suspected. She sat down at her computer and pressed the power button with her toe. She didn't want to think about structure, angles, or openings, middles, and endings; she was going to let herself write without any censuring. To do the article justice, she would have to open herself again to the feelings she'd endured after her accident.

After doing so with Alex, she found it wasn't quite as hard this time. She started the article in Elena's point of view, one that was familiar. And most effective. Then she moved into Lidia's point of view briefly before reverting to reporter again. The slant was about justice, how the world lacked it, and how people could make a difference by stepping up to help. She also wrote about taking responsibility for one's actions, no matter how painful or embarrassing. She was nearly breathless as she put the final touches on it.

"Wow." She'd never felt this way after finishing an article. Sure, she'd been pleased, happy to get it done on time, but she'd never . . . *felt something*. Now she felt angry and outraged and overflowing with sympathy.

She called Sebastian, and when he answered, she said, "I'm coming in." She didn't even give him a chance to respond.

She wasn't sure how to interpret the expression on his face when she walked into his office twenty minutes later. Curious, of course, and wary would be part of it. At least he smiled, but he didn't stand and come around to the front of the desk. For that she was relieved. She handed him the printed pages with a flourish.

"What's this?" he said without even looking at it.

"My article on the hit-and-run boating accident. Before you pooh-pooh it, read it. You've never seen anything like that from me before. And you'll never consider me shallow again."

He winced. "Winslow, I didn't mean that the way it came out."

"Yes, you did. And you know what? You were right. I just told a stranger things about myself that I've never told anyone."

"Alex Díaz," he guessed.

"How did you know?"

He didn't answer but glanced at the pages she'd handed him. At least he was curious, but he set them down after reading no more than a few sentences. "I already told you, we don't cover human rights; we cover society."

"You're not even going to read it?"

He disappointed her by handing it back. She hadn't even tempted him. "I'm glad you're here, though. I've got an interesting assignment for you."

Now it was her turn to look wary. "And that would be?"

"The Truffle Festival in Umbria." He handed her a paper with travel dates and information.

She blinked. "In *Italy*?"

"It starts this weekend, so you'll need to work with our travel agent right away to arrange your flights and accommodations. Amelia's already given them the preliminaries, so they're expecting your call. The following week is the Bonfire Festival in Abruzzi. While you're there, cover that as well. We'll run them in consecutive months, give our readers a little international flavor."

She could only stare at him. "A truffle festival."

He gave her a dazzling smile. "One of the world's finest delicacies."

"Why isn't Marcia covering these? She does all of the travel pieces."

"She's working on her article on Barbados. This came up at the last minute, so I'm pulling you in."

The prospect of covering a festival in honor of truffles deflated her after finishing the piece on Elena. "I'm in the middle of something personal right now. I can't leave the country."

He gave her the stern look she'd seen him use with the other writers but never her. "It's not an optional assignment, Winslow."

She felt a flush of anger as she pushed to her feet. She couldn't leave now. She needed to go back to the warehouse and look at the GPS. She had to . . . oh, wait a minute. "Grant put you up to this, didn't he?"

Sebastian did a bad job of looking ingenuous. His flushed face gave him away again. "Of course not."

"Be a man and admit it. Grant told you to get rid of me

for a while." She shook the piece of paper he'd given her. "And this was all you could come up with, a *truffle* festival? Come on, Sebastian."

His mouth tightened. "Take the assignment or pack up your office." He then forced a smile to soften those words when her eyes widened. "I need you to cover these events. It's that simple. You've taken the last few days off, you've wasted time on articles that will never appear in our magazine, and you even lied about that."

"Lied about what?"

He had the look of someone who'd let the cat out of the bag. "Just take the assignment. Don't put me in a tight spot."

The anger surging through her made her feel like a volcano about to erupt. "Oh, I see," she said in a strained voice. "Because you were kind enough to give me some emergency personal time off, I should repay you by leaving the country. As a favor to my father."

"I told you—"

"I didn't realize that all kindnesses were like deposits in the bank that had to be available for withdrawal. But I'm damn well learning!"

She stalked past Amelia, who'd heard her last angry words. She went to her office and closed the door. Several deep breaths helped to ease the pressure in her chest. She'd never blown up like that. She'd never been this angry before, except at Ashlyn's selfish behavior at times. So that was it; either go to Italy or lose her job. Grant had pulled in some favors of his own apparently.

This had been her dream job: plush offices, her own space where she could set her plants and hang her paintings of beach scenes. A window. But it wasn't worth compromising her values. Since tapping into that place to write Elena's article, Winslow wasn't sure she could go back to writing about fashion and . . . truffles.

She took the box in which her new printer had come and

placed her personal things inside. Sebastian came in as she
set her second plant in the box.

"You're quitting."

"You made it clear that I have only two choices."

He looked pained, but she went back to filling the box. She
took down her two paintings, slung her purse over her shoulder, and hefted the box. He was still standing in the doorway.

"You're in my way," she said.

"Winslow—"

"Look, I know you're in a jam. You promised Grant you'd
get rid of me, and it didn't work. Now you can't back down.
So tell him you did your best, and I'm sure he'll be as proud
as pie of you. I'm not interested in staying anyway, so don't
agonize over it. I can't work for someone who has no in-
tegrity. You're a sellout, and you're a mail stealer, which is a
federal offense, by the way.

"I know my article isn't suitable for this magazine. I had
to write it. I can't explain why, but I did. All I asked was that
you read it. When I wrote that piece, I felt something I've
never felt before. I realized that's what I want to write. So if
it makes you feel any better, I would have left eventually."

She wished Candy a good life and walked out the front
door. Losing her job at *Dazzle* wasn't a big deal, and losing
her potential relationship with Sebastian was an even smaller
deal. The only thing she was worried about was what Grant
would say. That meant she had to get proof to satisfy him that
she was right about Jayce being the kind of person who could
leave the scene of a fatal accident. Then Grant would have to
go along with turning him in.

She sat in her car for a few minutes, trying to figure out
what to do next. If she was going to have a look at the GPS
on Jayce's boat, she needed the location of the accident.
Once again, Alex was going to be her best bet for that, and
after their lovely dinner the night before she was sure he'd
help. She started her car and headed to his offices,

On the way, she called Grant. More than the nickname

Winnie, she felt the absence of his warmth when she identified herself. Maybe Sebastian had already told him what had happened.

"Dad, I need to ask you a question, and I need an honest answer. Did you ask Sebastian to send me to Italy?"

He was silent for a moment, perhaps weighing how much to admit. Finally he said, "He told me you quit."

At least he had given her some credit. Still, her disenchantment in him was a sinking feeling in her stomach. "Dad—"

"Win, it's for your own damn good. I didn't expect you to quit. I know how much that job means to you. If you grovel, I'm sure Sebastian will let you come back."

"I can't go back. I've lost respect for him."

"What about for me? You've obviously lost any loyalty you felt for me. Have you also lost respect, too?"

She couldn't answer right away. She had hoped Grant would vehemently deny manipulating her life. "I am loyal to you, Dad. But I owe Jayce nothing. How can I respect myself if I let him get away with this?"

Grant let out a sigh filled with disappointment and pain. "Jayce didn't run anyone down. You have to trust me on this."

"Trust you? How can I trust you when you seem so taken in by him? I always told you that you were too trusting. It scares me how he's got you wrapped around his finger."

"You're just threatened by him. It's a natural reaction. You want to believe the worst of him. And apparently of your sister."

She could hardly talk. Feelings of isolation and betrayal tightened her throat like a fist.

"Did you hear me?" he asked.

Why did you stop calling me Winnie? Why are you taking his side? Why have you all turned against me? She couldn't answer him without those questions coming out, too. Finally, she said, "I have to go. I'm in traffic." Her thick voice gave her away, she was sure, and she swiped at the moisture gathering in her eyes. Grant had always been a hero to her. He wasn't perfect; that she knew. But now she wasn't sure she knew him at all.

The sun was setting as she reached FREE's parking lot. She remembered they locked the lot at six o'clock and was relieved to find the gate still open at five till six. Enrique, the brother who had called out to Alex when they'd left, came out the door just as she reached the entrance. He stopped short and took her in, not quite in the gently appraising way Alex had done.

Enrique's smile spread into a shark's grin, and he said something in Spanish, the only word of which she understood was *Americana*. "You're looking for Alejandro, yes?"

"Is he still here?"

"He's getting the weekend edition ready, so they're all going crazy. You'll find him in the editing room."

Winslow parked, walked inside, and started up the stairs. She peered into the large room that Ashlyn had been in. Alex and another employee were in the back corner looking at a computer with a huge monitor. Winslow stood there a moment, not sure whether to approach or wait for Alex to see her. He looked up before she could give it much more thought. She'd actually looked forward to that smile of his, but he didn't give it to her. He nodded toward the open area and lifted a finger to let her know he'd be right there.

He was preoccupied with the deadline, something she could understand. She'd keep it short. She meant to only stand by the doorway of his office, though she couldn't resist looking around. Several cartoons hung on the wall, though they were in Spanish. Three coffee mugs sat on the cluttered desk, empty but for a layer of sugar at the bottom. She liked the pictures on his shelves that showed casual family scenes.

She smiled, inching in farther. He wasn't a pencil chewer; she hated that. He wasn't neat, either. The desk held just enough clutter to indicate that he was busy but not sloppy.

That's when she saw the folder on his desk with the words *García, Lidia, Elena* on the tab. Before thinking better of it, she walked over and flipped the folder open. Most of the clippings and notes were in Spanish. She spotted the police report and her heartbeat skipped like a stone across the water. Some of the abbreviations she didn't understand, but she knew a GPS position number when she saw one. She wrote it down and was slipping the paper into her bag when Alex's voice startled her.

"What are you doing?"

She jumped, feeling guilty at snooping. "Hi. I was looking at your pictures and then I saw the folder on your desk and didn't think you'd mind—"

He snapped the folder closed. "When you're lying, I do mind."

She felt the flush of her cheeks give her away. "What do you mean?"

"I called your office to tell you that Lidia García would talk to you, and your editor told me about the article you're *not* doing for his magazine."

"All right, I might have left out that he wasn't amenable to publishing the article. But I did write it and I turned it in to him today. He rejected it." She pulled the printed sheets of paper from her purse. "Read it." She figured she owed him that much.

"Truffle festival?"

"Oh, not that." She snatched the top page and crinkled it up. "The rest is my article. I wrote it after my interview with Lidia."

He didn't read it, either, but he did hold on to it. "Who is this article for, Winslow?"

"I . . . don't know. Right now it's for me. It was something I needed to do."

He clearly didn't know what to make of her. She hated that, but she deserved it.

"I have to go," she said. "I'm sorry to have bothered you."

She heard him call her name but quickly made her way down the stairs. Luckily Enrique was talking to someone coming into the lot and hadn't closed the gates. She had alienated two editors in one afternoon. She didn't want to risk anything else. As she pulled out of the parking lot, though, she had a feeling she was going to risk a lot more before this was over. And more than anything, she was terrified that Grant would only be one of those things.

9

S neaking around really wasn't her thing, Winslow thought as she pulled just past the metal warehouse the following morning. At least she'd thought to program the number for the Miami police into her cell phone. She'd called Ashlyn's apartment, but no one answered. Then she'd called Ashlyn's cell number and been surprised when she'd answered.

"Hi, it's Winslow. Where are you?"

"I'm shopping for a wedding dress."

The thought of her doing that, presumably alone, jagged at Winslow's heart. "Want some company?"

"No, thanks. You'll just ask me questions and make accusations against Jayce."

Grant had said they were moving up the wedding. When would it be? Instead of asking, Winslow said, "I won't ask anything," but Ashlyn was talking to someone nearby.

"Not that one. I need this one in a size six."

They had gone shopping together a few times when they both needed something for the same event. Winslow had never seen anyone so passionate about the act of buying clothing. Ashlyn had accused her of laughing at that passion, but Winslow had just been enjoying it.

"Look, I'm busy. I have to go."

And she was gone, just like that. Winslow had considered

trying to find her. There were only so many bridal places in this area, after all. But then she'd be proving Ashlyn's suspicions by hunting her down.

So she'd returned to the warehouse and watched the two men for an hour and a half. The doors were wide open, and from this angle she could barely see Jayce's boat inside. The white guy—Corky, she remembered from the conversation she'd overheard—periodically walked out to his truck to get a can from a cooler. He'd lean against the back of the truck and savor his beer, his face lifted to the sun.

At nearly twelve, Manny got into his junker of a truck and left. Winslow hunkered down while he passed, and then got out of her car. She'd brought her digital camera and the scrap of paper on which she'd written the GPS coordinates of the accident. She had dressed down as much as her wardrobe allowed: jeans and a blue silk shirt. Her hair was tucked beneath a beach hat.

She walked down the crumbling asphalt road as though she were heading past the fenced lot. Then she slipped inside the open gate and to the left where clumps of pepper bushes concealed her. Did private investigators feel so much adrenaline pumping through them as they sneaked around? Did their hearts pulse in both fear and triumph?

Seventies rock and roll pounded from the warehouse, along with the sound of an intermittent sander. When her legs started aching from standing, she sat down. Her plan was to get behind the old cars when Corky broke for lunch, which she hoped would be soon. She'd take pictures, get on the boat and see if it had a GPS, and if so, check out the recent trips. She had watched Grant check coordinates on the GPS, and she'd actually operated one on an old boyfriend's boat. She figured she could muddle her way through.

The radio's volume jumped even higher, and the guy finally sauntered out. He pulled off a breathing mask and wiped sweat from his brow with it. He climbed onto the back of his truck and flopped down in the bed with a groan. She knew he could sit up at any moment, but she had to take the chance and make a move. The old car was only a few yards away from her hiding place. She skirted between branches and crab-walked to the car just as the guy sat up.

"Hey!"

His voice shot fear into her. *What do I do? Stay hidden? Crawl under the car? Surrender?*

"Where's the rest of the beer? . . . Yeah, pick up a six-pack on your way back. . . . Yes, it sure is your turn to buy, you cheapola son of a bitch."

Relief turned her into a puddle for a moment. He was talking on the phone, probably to Manny. She forced her muscles to de-puddle and peered around the front bumper. The chrome was peeling away, leaving a dull gray metal beneath. She could see part of the truck from here but not the man. Which hopefully meant he couldn't see her, either.

She crossed the gap and paused behind the second car, listening for any movement. When she heard the pop of a can being opened, she moved to the back of the car. The open doorway was only a few yards away, but that space was wide open. That was going to be the tricky part. And she didn't have much time. This guy would be finished with lunch soon, and it sounded like Manny would be returning.

She peered around the back of the car. She wasn't in his direct line of sight, but he would see any quick movement in the corner of his eye. His head cocked to an angle, and he slid off the back of the truck and walked to the front gate.

She took the opportunity to duck inside the warehouse. When she took a cautionary peek around the edge, he was still looking at something—oh no, he was looking at her car. She'd parked in the corner of the lot across the street, tucking her car in a spot closest to the road, next to an array of dusty vehicles. Darn paint job!

No time to fret about it. Except that Manny might recognize it. Hopefully this guy's curiosity will have passed by then.

She turned on the camera and faced the boat. Damn. The

name was completely obliterated now and the damage was fixed, too. Still, she snapped several pictures and then walked around the other side. Luckily the name was still on that side. There was no damage on this side, but the police would be able to verify that it was the same boat pictured in the other photographs.

The rest of the boat must have been repaired already; she saw no sign of damage underneath the hull. She'd take a look at the propellers before she left.

The building gave the impression of impermanence. No calendars adorned the walls; there was no desk to process invoices. What kind of repair shop was this, without any signs promoting their business?

Hurry up and get rid of her. I don't want any trouble.

Not the kind of business she wanted to be caught sneaking around in. She climbed up on the back platform of the boat and over the small door. Ah, a GPS. She had to be quick about it. After flipping the power switch for the electronics, she turned on the GPS. It seemed to take five minutes to warm up, though it was probably a few seconds. She clumsily maneuvered around the different menus. Thin blue lines indicated the many paths he'd taken the boat.

The hit-and-run had occurred in Biscayne Bay, which narrowed down her search. She found one meandering line that went around Claughton Island and south. When she moved the cursor over a particular point, a box in the right corner showed the global position numbers. She remembered seeing a notation in the report that the position was approximate, since the boat had had time to float before being found.

Her heart started thrumming as she moved the cursor over the line, watching the numbers draw closer and closer to the ones on her paper. Bingo. Jayce had been in the area. Still not solid proof, but she was sure there was a way to find out when these trips had occurred. She'd let the police sort through that. She now had enough evidence for an investigation.

They'd probably be interested in these two guys as well.

She took pictures of the screen, pressed the power button, and waited for the screen to go blank before replacing the rubber cover. When she turned around, she had only a second to form a vague impression of someone standing behind her—before the lights went out.

Corky pressed the grimy buttons on his cell phone. "Jayce?" he confirmed before saying anything else. "It's Corky. We got a problem here."

"Hold on a sec." A few seconds passed before Jayce said, "What's up?"

"We've got a woman here. She was at the marina yesterday, and Manny . . . well, the idiot assumed it was your girlfriend. Said she'd left a watch on the boat. Manny came to the warehouse to look, and I'm figuring she followed him. I just now caught her on the boat, looking at the GPS. I found a slip of paper on her with some coordinates."

Jayce cursed. "Does she have brown hair, beautiful face, greenish eyes?"

Corky laughed. "Her eyes are closed, and I didn't get much of a look at them before I conked her on the head. But yeah, that sounds like her." He held up a set of car keys. "She drives a convertible Volvo with a three-D paint job. Manny recognized it from the marina; she was doing a stakeout, this chick. Who is she?"

"My future sister-in-law, about to cause me a lot of trouble."

"And us, too. She a cop?"

"Not even close. She's a rich debutante who's been snooping around in my business."

"Manny said he saw her talking to a couple of guys on the boats near your slip. Heard her saying something about Cubans."

Jayce asked, "You said her eyes were closed. Is she dead?"

Corky thought he heard a trace of eagerness in Jayce's

voice. "No, man, just knocked out. Manny brought her car here. We put her in the trunk." He looked over at the woman tied up with boat lines and stuffed into a very small space. She stirred, and he saw her eyes move beneath her closed lids. He nodded to Manny, who closed the lid.

"Look, we gotta close up shop. Getting caught fixing your boat ain't gonna do us any good business-wise."

"All right, here's what you're going to do. Dump the boat. Take it out and sink it. I'm going to report it stolen, so don't screw around. If you try to sell it, you'll get caught with a stolen boat and I've never seen you two in my life; got it?"

The man's superiority rankled. And Corky didn't appreciate the jerk insinuating that he would double-cross him. 'Course, he hadn't had time to think about keeping the boat. "It's gonna cost you."

"Of course it is. I'll give you five grand. And you never heard of me, either."

"How do we get our money?"

"I'll call you tonight. Just get the hell out of there."

"Hey, what about the wo—" Damn, he'd hung up. He turned to Manny. "We've got to dump the boat. We'll figure out what to do with her later."

Ashlyn had never felt so out of sorts in her life. Everything should have been going wonderfully for her. She'd finally found a man who loved and cherished her, a man who thought she was beautiful. She'd never once caught him staring at Winslow as she had with some of the guys she'd dated. Knowing she'd never be able to trust the guy, she always broke things off. Once Winslow had the nerve to ask why her relationships never seemed to last long, like she really cared or something.

It was the first time she'd ever come home from shopping with less than four bags or boxes. She'd always loved the feel of juggling all the bags and packages, needing the assistance of the doorman all the way to her apartment. Now she had one large bag and a dress covered in plastic. She hung it in the closet, staring at it for a moment before putting the bag of accessories on the shelf. Her wedding dress. Shouldn't she feel more excited? Too bad Winslow had only offered to accompany her for her own selfish reasons. Having company would have been nice. Somehow her friends had drifted off over the years, and even Dallis had turned away when she started dating Jayce. Of course, Dallis had no fashion sense at all, so she wouldn't have been much help.

Jayce had talked her out of the fairy-tale wedding that she'd always wanted. He was right; she'd be overwhelmed by all the details, even with a wedding planner. She knew that she wouldn't give up control anyway. Daddy didn't need the distraction of a big wedding in conjunction with his campaign, either. And poor Jayce, he didn't have any close family to invite. She'd gotten the impression that he'd be embarrassed by the lack of people on his side of the church.

So now they were getting married out by the pool by Judge Camilla Winston, a friend of the family's. And suddenly the ceremony was planned for next week. Ashlyn wasn't even sure how that had happened. It had gone from next year to a few months from now, since they didn't have all the plans to make, and then, *What are we waiting for? Let's do it now.* That was Jayce talking, and the fact that he was so eager to make her his wife filled her with unimaginable joy. He would be hers forever.

When she turned, she was startled to find the object of her thoughts walking into the closet. "God! You scared me."

Instead of apologizing, he said, "We've got a problem. Winslow found the boat."

"What?"

He led her back out to the bedroom and indicated that she sit on the bed. "Winslow has a bug up her ass about this boat thing. She's been to Grant, she's been to the marina asking questions, and now, believe it or not, she found the damn boat."

Panic curled around Ashlyn's throat. She'd been trying so hard not to think about this. "Where is she now? She'll go to the police, won't she? And we'll have to make up a story, and, oh my God, they'll know I'm lying, and—"

"Ashlyn, calm down." He gripped her arms but was careful not to leave marks. "I've got it all figured out, but you have to pull yourself together. Otherwise everything comes out. You *will* pull yourself together. You will be my little actress, won't you?"

She nodded. She loved how he always knew what to do.

He said, "I know what Winslow's doing. She thinks she's going to finger us for that accident, and won't she look like a big hero? She thinks it'll make Grant love her more than you."

"He already does," she whined.

"We're going out on the boat. Get ready; pack the cooler with a bottle of wine and some caviar and crackers. Go."

"But we don't—"

"We don't know that we don't. Move it."

He returned a few minutes later dressed in white pants and a blue shirt. She was scrambling to put everything together. He watched her snug the wine into the ice and close the lid.

She gestured to her outfit. "Will this work?"

"No, change. It's going to get cool, so wear pants. You look like a Neiman Marcus ad."

She wasn't sure that last statement was a compliment. He teased her about her addiction to shopping so much she felt silly even reading her daily e-mails. She didn't show him her clippings, either. Whenever she was about to get mad at him, he'd pull her close and tell her how much he loved her. She'd swallow the words in her gratitude.

"How's this?" she asked, lifting her arms a few minutes later.

"Perfect. Let's go put on a show."

Winslow came to in complete darkness. She became aware of a throbbing pain at the back of her head, made worse because she was partially lying on it. When she tried to shift, fear slammed her into full consciousness. She couldn't move. Couldn't see. And she was curled into an awkward ball. Her mouth was numb, but she couldn't even move her lips. She'd been gagged! The tip of her tongue felt the weave of a thick rope that tasted both moldy and salty.

It came back to her, but she couldn't fit the pieces together. She'd been looking at the boat, found the GPS coordinates, yes, and then she'd turned it off and was ready to leave, and . . . that was all.

Noise came from outside whatever she'd been locked in, but she couldn't identify it. The men had caught her. That was the only explanation. And they'd put her in . . . She felt the floor beneath her. New carpet. She was in a trunk. Both men had trucks, so that meant . . . she was in *her* trunk. They'd thrown her into the trunk of her own car!

10

Jayce tutored Ashlyn on the skills of lying, so by the time they walked to his slip and discovered the boat missing she was able to act completely shocked and upset. He asked some of the nearby boaters if they'd seen anything. One had possibly seen two guys taking his boat over to the launch area at night over a week ago. Others hadn't been to the marina in a couple of weeks.

Ashlyn, per his orders, sat on top of the cooler with her chin in her hands looking despondent while he gave the responding officers information about his boat. The officers would put out an alert, notify the Coast Guard, and be in touch if they found anything.

Jayce carried the cooler as they walked back to her Porsche.

"It's over," she said. "Will those guys have the boat gone in time?"

"If they know what's good for them."

"How do you even know people like that? You knew who to call when we came back so they'd meet us out on the water and take the boat." It was something she'd been wondering but been too timid to ask.

He tweaked her chin. "I didn't know these guys. One of the caddies at the club has connections. He told me he could get anything. We've got one more thing to do," he said when he'd closed the door after getting in. "This part's easy."

Was she still in the parking lot? Winslow wondered as she quelled the panic. No, they wouldn't have risked carrying her across the street.

So they must have driven the car into the warehouse. It helped to reason everything out and took her mind off the grinding noises she heard. She was sure they'd called Jayce to let him know a woman had been snooping around on his boat. He would know exactly who that woman was.

What now? Would they kill her? The thought struck a sharp fear into her. She posed a threat to these men as well. She struggled against her bonds. They had some give, and she kept working them.

She heard more noises: an engine, the screech of metal, and then the engine moved away. They were leaving. She'd rather have them leave her for dead than open the trunk and kill her. Perhaps they were hoping she'd suffocate. Or drown in her own sweat.

She started working on the bonds again but heard footsteps scraping across the concrete floor. Then a swishing sound and more noises she couldn't identify. She was careful not to make a sound in case they were hoping she'd die without their help. She even kept her movements minimal so the car wouldn't rock.

It seemed like an hour had passed since the first truck left. Finally things went quiet again. But she hadn't heard the other vehicle leave. Several more minutes passed before footsteps sounded again. They moved closer.

She heard car keys jangling and then someone fumbling to insert the key into the trunk lock. Light flooded her senses just before the shadow of a man leaned down toward her. Through the hair plastered to her damp skin she searched for signs of a knife, for any kind of weapon, before her gaze settled on Manny's face.

"You a bad girl," he said, looming over her. "What am I going to do with you?"

She could only think her suggestions since she couldn't speak. Waves of trembles washed over her. She shook her head at whatever heinous thought was making his mouth curl into a smile.

Luckily, the thought didn't last long. "I hate stupid white bitches that stick their nose into other people's business. Now we got to go somewhere else for a while, lose work. You're not gonna find us. We broke in here to use this place for one job. We move around a lot, see. This was a perfect place, but you ruined it." He clenched his fist, as though he was going to hit her. She flinched, and he laughed.

"I'd like to hit you, lady. I'd like to do more than hit you. Corky said it's not worth it. But you're gonna spend some time here in this trunk of your pretty little car. *If* you get out, we'll be long gone."

If. No, she wouldn't think *if,* only when.

He slammed the trunk shut, and both the pressure and the sound popped her ears. She could barely hear the metal doors being closed and then a distant engine starting and fading away.

Okay, she told herself, taking deep breaths to calm down. *This is what you wanted. You're going to get out of here. There's probably a release latch somewhere. All you have to do is get loose and find it. You can only do that if you stay nice and calm.*

She didn't remain calm the whole time, but she relentlessly worked the rope until she'd loosened it enough around her wrists to slip free. It was when she twisted to search for the lever that she got an idea of how long she'd been curled up. Her back wouldn't move, and her body screamed in pain. She had to work her muscles loose the same way she'd worked the rope, a little at a time.

She found the lever and popped the trunk. Shards of

sunlight sliced through the darkness where the seams didn't meet.

Numb, clumsy fingers worked the gag and then the bonds at her ankles. It took several more minutes to maneuver out of the trunk, and then she stumbled to the cold, hard floor when her legs wouldn't hold her. Pain shattered her knees at the impact, and she rolled into a ball. It took a lot longer to gather the bravery and energy to try it again, but she straightened her body and stretched her limbs. The darkness played tricks on her eyes, making amorphous shapes swoop down at her and causing the slices of sun to wiggle. She stretched again, ignoring everything but the sensations in her body.

The light didn't penetrate the darkness enough to illuminate any part of the warehouse. She found her car only because she knew it was nearby. She felt along the floor until her head made contact with the tire. Even that relatively soft surface caused the pain in her head to explode again, and she had to catch her breath while on all fours. After carefully exploring the surface of her scalp, she found evidence of the injury that had rendered her unconscious: a big lump.

She patted the side of the car until she located the door latch. Thankfully it opened, and she crawled into the car. Light burned her retinas, and she had to squeeze her eyes shut for a few seconds. She cracked one open, then the other, and slowly opened them again. Her car. She laid her head down on the seat and felt such gratitude that she'd been right and that her car was here. Her keys and purse were lying on the driver's seat. When she reached out, she noticed her rings were gone. So was her necklace. Manny couldn't resist. She reached into her purse and, after digging around for a minute, found her cell phone. Dialing 911 was the easiest thing she'd done in the last forty minutes.

The police and an ambulance found Winslow fifteen minutes later. By the time they arrived, she had found her way out of the building and was able to wave them down. The sun was on its downward trek, giving her a clue as to how late it was. Manny had taken her watch, too, of course.

Paramedics looked her over at the ambulance while two detectives asked questions. "She really needs to go to the hospital. This is a nasty bump," the female medic said.

"I'm fine," Winslow assured them. She wasn't going to mention that she was still a little woozy if she turned her head too fast. "If you find these two guys, they'll give you Jayce."

She'd told them everything, describing the two men as best as she could. They'd cleaned out the warehouse, even sweeping the floor. ID techs were going over the space and her car for evidence.

One of the detectives said, "Okay, tell us again why you were sneaking around some warehouse occupied by men you suspected were doing shady business."

They thought she was nuts. "I wanted proof before I went to the police. And I had it before those creeps jumped me. I took pictures of the boat and even the PGS—I mean the GPS. But they took my camera, too."

The medic shook her head. "See, you need to go to the hospital."

"No, I need to go with you when you question Jayce Bishop. I tried Ashlyn's apartment, and there was no answer. I'll bet they're at my father's house."

The police were going to have to take her home, anyway. Her car would be kept until they were finished investigating.

She got into the back of their unmarked car and directed them to Grant's home. It was dark now, and as soon as she walked into the foyer, she could see the lit torches out on the loggia. Grant, Jayce, and Ashlyn were sitting at a table having drinks. The only thing that would have made the sight more painful would have been the sound of their laughter, but they looked to be having a rather serious discussion.

Esme, the maid, peered in from the direction of the

kitchen. She'd obviously heard the door close. She started to smile at Winslow but stopped when she saw the two men. Even though they were in plainclothes, she clearly identified them as cops.

"Everything's fine," Winslow said, but that didn't convince Esme. Her brown eyes still looked alarmed, and when Winslow caught her reflection in the huge bevel-cut mirror she understood why. She looked like a harridan, with her hair in disarray, dirt smudging her face and clothing, and her eyes blazing with both pain and anger. She combed her fingers through her hair as she led the two men through the round living room and out to the loggia.

Grant stood immediately, either at the sight of her or because he also knew these men were the police. Ashlyn stared at them with a deer-in-the-headlights look. This was going to be over, Winslow thought. She hoped Ashlyn would break down or Jayce would confess and the wheels of justice would turn for Elena.

The two detectives introduced themselves to Grant, both uttering that it was a pleasure to meet him. Jayce stood, too, and went through the motions, and then Ashlyn was introduced.

Detective Ramey, the older of the men, said, "Sorry to disturb your evening, sir. Your daughter Winslow was falsely imprisoned in the trunk of her car by two men allegedly associated with Mr. Bishop. These men were allegedly repairing a boat belonging to Mr. Bishop that was involved in a recent hit-and-run accident. The men and the boat are gone, but we're looking for them. Sir." He said this to Jayce. "Were you involved in the hit-and-run boating accident of November fourth of this year at approximately five thirty in the afternoon?"

"No, sir."

"Do you have knowledge of any such accident?"

"Only through the news reports. It was terrible. I hope they find the guy who did it."

If she didn't know better, *she* would believe him. Ramey asked the same questions of Ashlyn, and she coolly replied in the negative.

Grant said, "November fourth? Let me check my schedule, gentlemen. Jayce here is my campaign manager, and he's been working night and day for the last few weeks trying to get things in motion. He doesn't usually leave until after five."

Good. Grant would tell them he'd been in a meeting and let Jayce leave early. Why didn't Jayce look worried? He, in fact, turned to her. "Winslow, I don't understand why you're doing this." He addressed the detectives. "I'm marrying her sister. Her younger sister. She's had it in for me since day one, though I've been nothing but nice to her. Haven't I, honey?"

Ashlyn was now narrowing her eyes at Winslow; her mouth was tight. At Jayce's question, she nodded. "He really has been. She's just trying to spoil things for me. I'm getting married next week and she's jealous."

"Wait a minute. You said you were moving up the wedding, but—*next week*?" Winslow said, sidetracked completely.

Ashlyn covered her mouth, as though she'd let out a secret. But of course they weren't going to invite Winslow.

Jayce said, "In deference to your father's campaign, we decided to forgo the big wedding. And since we weren't doing that, there was no reason to put it off so long." He made a show of hugging Ashlyn and kissing her cheek. "We're in love. Why wait?" This he directed to the detectives, just as Grant came back with his leather schedule book.

He showed the two men last Friday's schedule. "I had a meeting with my development group at three. Jayce was with me. We'd been running errands and I ran late, so he dropped me off and finished his running, then picked me up. The meeting went longer than I anticipated, and poor Jayce ended up sitting in the car for about an hour."

Winslow stumbled and caught hold of one of the chairs at the table.

Jayce shrugged. "I did a couple of crossword puzzles. Wasn't a big deal."

Crossword puzzles! The other part was harder to believe. Grant was lying for Jayce. Winslow started to accuse him of that but shut her mouth. How could she do that to the man who had done so much for her? But how could he do this to her?

The detectives were looking at the book.

She said, "Jayce, if that's true, why didn't you just tell me that when I asked you about the hit-and-run?"

"Come on, Winslow; how was I to take you seriously? You've become"—he looked at her as though her appearance were the norm for her lately—"crazy about this."

Grant took the book back from the men. "Winslow was in a hit-and-run accident when she was twelve. The driver was never found. I didn't realize how deeply that accident had affected her until she became caught up in this story. She told me about the men and the boat that she thought was Jayce's—"

"I saw the name *In Too Deep* on the side."

Grant patiently tolerated her outburst, as though he had to do that a lot. "She was sure it was Jayce's boat, though she'd only seen it from the road. It was inside a warehouse."

"I saw it clearly enough. It *was* Jayce's boat."

"Maybe it was." Jayce's shaped eyebrows lifted. "It makes sense." He turned to the detectives. "Ashlyn and I went to the marina to go out for a sunset cruise tonight and discovered the boat had been stolen. We reported it, though it didn't sound like there was much hope of getting it back. That's why we came here, to tell Grant about it."

Fury engulfed Winslow that Jayce was able to turn everything around to his benefit. "That's a lie! They only pretended to go out so they could *discover* the boat missing. They knew it was gone all along. They just reported it stolen to cover his . . . well, his butt."

Jayce still had a look of wonderment on his face.

"Winslow probably did see my boat and the two guys who'd stolen it. They were stripping it so they could sell it, I bet."

Winslow made a sound of frustration. "That's not it at all. Manny, the guy I talked to at the marina, thought I was Jayce's girlfriend. He said Jayce's name. The other guy told Manny he didn't want any trouble."

"They never said that," Jayce said. "And they didn't want trouble because they'd stolen my damn boat."

She thought of suggesting that the police talk to the men on the boats near Jayce's slip, but she doubted they'd cooperate.

Grant said, "Think about it, Winslow. Two unsavory men were working on—let's say it was Jayce's boat—even though it wasn't an actual repair shop. They're boat thieves, not murderers, so when you find their hiding spot, they tuck you away until they can clean house and get away. You just ended up in a bad situation, and no wonder." He turned to the detectives. "I told her it was dangerous to sneak around in that part of town, and I also told her that I knew Jayce and Ashlyn would never have left those people like that."

He put his hand on Jayce's shoulder, and the action stabbed Winslow like a knife. "I haven't known Jayce a long time, but in the few months that he's been part of our lives, I have never observed him being anything but courteous and thoughtful. You know how you get a gut feeling about someone right away? I got that kind of feeling about Jayce. And he's proven it out."

Winslow had had one of those feelings, too, and so far he'd proven it out to her, too. But Grant's betrayal—and portrayal of her as an unbalanced woman turning unresolved feelings into paranoia—was even worse. To prove her point, she'd have to call Grant a liar. And as much as she wanted to do that, she couldn't.

She had a thought. "Check Jayce's cell phone. I'll bet those two men called to let him know I was there."

Jayce handed over the cell phone clipped to his pants. "Have at it if you'd like."

The detectives shook their heads. "That won't be necessary. Ms. Talbot, you've had quite a knock on your head. I wish you'd go to the hospital," Ramey said. When she said no, he added, "All we have is a woman getting caught sneaking around on private property on the wrong side of town. If we find the two men who assaulted you, hopefully we'll get answers about the boat."

"If you find them, check the numbers they've dialed on their cell phones. I know you'll find Jayce's number."

"Oh, Winslow," Grant said in a disappointed tone she'd never heard before.

Detective Ramey said, "Ms. Talbot, perhaps you should let us take you home if you won't go to the hospital. You need to rest. You're still on an adrenaline high, but when that drops, so will you."

Ashlyn said, "Resting shouldn't be a problem. She just quit her job. She had a great job at *Dazzle* writing stories about the balls and benefits and she blew it. She's crazy with this boating accident. She wanted to write about it, and when her boss wouldn't let her put a story about a poor Cuban family in his high-society magazine, go figure, she quit."

Oh, jeez, it did sound bad. Ramey slanted a look at her. Winslow hadn't missed the use of the word *crazy* more than once. She decided to keep her mouth shut for now and walked back into the living room. The detectives thanked everyone for their time.

As soon as they reached the foyer, she said, "I'm not crazy. Yes, my accident is why it's so important to me that justice be served for that girl. But I'm not imagining things. Jayce was off that afternoon, at least in time to be out on Biscayne Bay at five o'clock. That was his boat in the warehouse. And they were repairing damage on the sly for Jayce."

Both men looked at her skeptically. Ramey said, "Get some sleep and maybe things will make sense in the morning."

"They already do make sense." She tried to rein in her

temper. Getting emotional would get her exactly nowhere. "I just need proof. That's what I was trying to find. I had pictures; I had the coordinates of the hit-and-run and a picture of Jayce's GPS showing he'd been in the vicinity."

They opened the door for her, and she slid into the backseat of the car. "Ms. Talbot, we'll do everything we can to find the two men who assaulted you, and perhaps they can shed some light on this whole thing. Until then, I suggest—no, I insist— that you stay out of police business and keep yourself safe."

As soon as they got into the car, she said, "I thought someone was in my condo the other night. I had the balcony door open—I'm on the second floor—and I saw shadows moving on the wall opposite the door."

Ramey put the car into gear and pulled away, and the other detective, Capperson, turned around to look at her. "Did you report this to the police?"

"No. At the time I wasn't sure. I didn't have any proof that someone had been there," she finished, her voice growing softer. This wasn't helping her case.

"All I can say is that when you start putting yourself in precarious situations, you have to expect some trouble. What's the expression? You mix with the element, and the element mixes with you. You're a . . ." He took her in and amended, "I'm sure you're a beautiful woman with a lot going for you. Go back to your magazine and write about balls. Leave the investigative work to us."

Ramey snorted, probably at the balls reference. They dropped her off a few minutes later. Capperson offered to come up and look her apartment over just in case. *Just in case the bogeyman comes back,* he didn't say. Still, he did his duty, scaring her cats into hiding by his very presence and bidding her a good night.

She stripped off her clothes, stuffed them into the trash can, and went to turn on the shower. She told herself that she wouldn't look in the mirror, but inevitably her gaze went right to it. Her eyes were bloodshot; her hair, despite the finger combing, was still a mass of brown tangles. Dirt and fuzz and other things clung to the tangles.

While she massaged conditioner into the tangles, she looked at the rest of her face. A good deal of her makeup had been smeared, revealing the lines left from her surgeries. For a moment she felt a sick twist in her stomach at Grant, Jayce, and Ashlyn seeing her *real* face. Then she realized that the lighting out on the loggia was too dim to see much.

She stepped beneath the steaming hot water while her aching muscles sighed in relief and the throbbing in her head kept some out-of-tune beat. Alone, the betrayal of Grant's phony alibi sank its claws into her. Her father, pillar of society, had lied to protect a coldhearted killer. A killer who was about to marry his daughter, and with his blessings. He'd talked up Jayce and talked her down. Made her sound unbalanced. The worst part was, she'd made herself sound unbalanced.

Well, the *little lady, keep your pretty nose out of police business* routine wasn't going to stop her. In fact, it made her even more determined to find proof that a killer was about to marry into her family. And above all, she had to show a girl that there was justice in the world.

She had a feeling that that girl might also be herself.

Grant sank back into his chair and covered his mouth with his hand. That was the hardest thing he'd ever done. Seeing the accusation of betrayal in his daughter's eyes had nearly torn him apart. But seeing her gleam of determination had kept him going. She'd gone too far.

"I'm sorry about that," Jayce said, obviously seeing Grant's conflict. "I didn't want to drag you into this. It couldn't be helped." He placed his hand on Ashlyn's. "It's only Ashlyn that I'm thinking of. You know that, don't you?"

Grant nodded, jamming the tip of his thumb into his mouth and chewing on the short nail. "Maybe this will knock some sense into Winslow. Maybe we can go on from here."

But he wasn't sure they could go on. Something had broken between him and Winslow. He had broken it. It scared him to think that he couldn't fix it.

Ashlyn's laugh sounded contradictory to his dark thoughts. "Did you see the look on her face when she heard the wedding was next week? I'm glad we didn't involve her in it. I am kinda sorry that she won't be there, only for your sake. But you can see how awkward it would be, especially now. I used to consider her so sensible and smart. She always had it together. Now, I don't know what to think. Maybe my getting married and that accident bringing back her past was just too much for her."

Jayce looked oddly relaxed, leaning back in the chair, one leg propped up on the other. "She puts on this confident air, but inside she's obviously very insecure. Now that Grant has moved into the actual campaign mode, he doesn't have time to dote on her. Her little sister is getting married, while she will probably be an old maid." Obviously feeling he had stepped over the boundaries, he quickly added, "I mean, she doesn't seem to date much."

"I don't know what to think, what to do."

Jayce asked, "Has she ever taken drugs? That you know of?"

"No," he answered. "I can't even imagine her doing something like that. She's always taken care of herself."

"Just a thought. The look in her eyes . . ." Jayce shuddered. "It scared me, to be honest. I've seen that look before. In Chicago, whenever we had to go through the rough side of town, we'd see these heroin addicts walking around like zombies. The scary thing was that some of those people were once professional, normal members of society."

Grant shook his head, but the memory of a frazzled, unbalanced Winslow returned. When was the last time they'd had a good talk? He wished he had had breakfast with her last Wednesday. Maybe he would have seen this coming.

Jayce stood, giving his hand to Ashlyn, who also came to

her feet. "Dad, I'm sorry this happened, but we appreciate the alibi. Makes us sound like criminals, doesn't it?" he asked Ashlyn.

She gave Grant a hug. "I know it was hard to lie to the police. I hope it won't ever have to happen again."

Jayce said, "Well, Winslow's going to either bounce back from this or go even deeper."

Grant hated that last thought. "I'll check on her tomorrow. Try to find out what's really going on."

They bid him good night, but he remained on the softly lit loggia listening to the water falling from the hot tub into the pool. He'd chewed his nail to the quick, and he pressed a napkin to the tender, bleeding line. Ashlyn had always been his problem child, but she'd never gone off the deep end like this. Her fits passed quickly, and even when they argued, she was curled up in his lap the following day asking for forgiveness.

Winslow wouldn't be asking for forgiveness. And he couldn't ask her for forgiveness without opening himself up to accusations. She'd be right, but he didn't want to defend himself. He didn't want to see her disappointment, didn't want to feel that sharp pain when her eyes glinted with tears of betrayal. And mostly, he didn't want to contemplate what might happen if she continued to press for justice.

Corky's cell phone rang later that night, rattling his keys on the nightstand. Late-night calls meant one of two things: a job or trouble. That he didn't recognize the number on the display could go either way. "Hello?"

"Corky? It's Jayce."

Trouble, he thought, coming to a sitting position. *And money.* "Yeah."

"Winslow went to the cops, and they're looking for you. How clean did you leave the warehouse?"

"Very. We wiped the car, took one of those minivacs to the carpets and seats. The warehouse, well, it's not like we could do the same. But our fingerprints aren't anywhere."

"Good. The cops think you stole my boat and were stripping it. They think the woman's one hole short of a round of golf, so that'll help. You have one of those disposable cell phones, right?"

"Yep."

"Trash it. Winslow's smart. She told the cops to look at my cell phone and trace the numbers. Feasibly, they could do that, if you had a regular phone. Then she'd ID you and it'd be all over. The cops weren't interested, but I don't want to take any chances. Get rid of the phone and get the hell out of Miami for a while."

"Not before we get our money. You should add extra for our trouble. We're gonna lose business, leaving town."

"She wouldn't have found you if it weren't for your incompetent associate. Five thousand, and two more for travel expenses. That's it."

"Deal. The regular place?"

"I'll be there at eleven."

The phone disconnected and Corky tossed it on the floor. He should have haggled for more, but he held back. He'd been dealing with a lot of types of people over the years. He always got a sense right away what sort they were. Some were just scared and needed help in a sticky situation. Some were career criminals who needed a helping hand once in a while. Corky had spread the word that he was available for all kinds of services.

Jayce had been a little scared when he'd called. He'd gotten himself into a tight situation. But Corky couldn't quite get a bead on the kind of person Jayce was. Cold was about all he could get. A real haggler. And something else, something he couldn't put his finger on. He had a feeling that if he was drowning and Jayce was standing by the shore, he wouldn't jump in after him. That he would, in fact, enjoy watching as Corky took his last dying gasps.

11

When Winslow finally woke and was ready to face the day, she found an envelope on the floor in front of her door; it contained a note written by Grant and a key:

> *Win,*
> *I'm sorry things got out of control. I've left the*
> *Mercedes for your use until your car is released.*
> *Just be careful where you drive it. And be careful*
> *anyway.*

Damn, she'd missed him. The feeling of loss that had permeated her sleep spiked again. She read on.

> *Don't forget the dinner party tonight. I know*
> *you're not very happy with me, but I need you*
> *there with your prettiest dress and smile. Senator*
> *Wiggins will be there, and you know how much he*
> *likes you. We can talk about everything afterward.*
> *   Grant*

Double damn. She'd forgotten about the dinner party. The last thing she needed to do just then. She would go, though, out of that long-bred obligation. The car loan was a guilt present. He couldn't stand that she knew he was lying. But why would he lie to protect Jayce? Jayce must have convinced Grant it was to protect Ashlyn. Leave it to Jayce to use Ashlyn to cover his own sorry ass.

Winslow showered again, letting the hot water pound her achy body, washing off the violation of being handled by two strangers while she was unconscious. She'd carefully kept the what-ifs at bay, thankful that the men hadn't been murderers or rapists. Or that Jayce hadn't come to do the job.

Was he capable of murder? She shivered at the question. Maybe not, but he was after something. It wasn't money, unless he thought he'd be cut from the family inheritance. And Ashlyn, oh, had she loved last night! The chance to one-up Winslow, and boy, had she done that. It all hurt so bad Winslow nearly doubled over in the shower.

"No, you can't let them beat you down. You know Jayce was involved in that hit-and-run. Once you have hard proof, no one can call you crazy."

Energized, she downed a yogurt and drove to the beach to clear her head and work her muscles. She was halfway back when she had an idea. Two ideas, actually. And neither would take her to the wrong side of town. Well, at least not to the really wrong side of town.

She went back home and dug through the photographs on her computer that she'd taken over the last few months. When she found the one she wanted, she printed it out. Glancing down at herself, she rolled her eyes and took yet another shower, washing off the sweat and salty mist from her skin. Then she dressed professionally and drove to the Astonia, an elegant high-rise hotel that, like Talbot Tower, was right on the beach. It was located south of Bal Harbour Village. If Jayce had gone out on the boat that evening, he would have probably come back to his room and changed beforehand.

Jayce had stayed here for a few months, so the doorman should remember seeing his comings and goings. The man on duty today was in his fifties and reminded her of Fred Flintstone with his square frame and black hair.

She gave him a charming smile. "Hi, I was wondering if you could help me." She slipped him a hundred-dollar bill. "I have a quick question. Off-the-record." Before he could tell her no she showed him the photograph of Jayce and Ashlyn during a dinner party last month. "Does this man look familiar?"

The man was conflicted, glancing at the picture before quickly turning away. "He's your boyfriend, right? Cheating?"

It only took her a second to adopt that story. "We're getting married in a month, and I think he's seeing my sister. That's the girl in the picture. You understand how I need to know this before we exchange vows, don't you?"

He looked pained, but finally relented and studied the picture.

She said, "I think they went out on his boat last Friday night. Can you remember seeing him walking in and out that afternoon, around three or even as late as four?"

He finally looked up at her. "You say he was staying here?"

"Yes, since April."

"No, ma'am, not here. I've worked full-time since July, all shifts, and I haven't seen this guy. And I see everybody."

"You're sure?"

"Positive."

She felt a thrum in her chest. Jayce had lied about staying here. But why? He was in town, so he had to stay somewhere. With a woman? No, he spent so much time with Ashlyn and Grant he couldn't possibly be seeing someone else.

Winslow was stymied by this revelation. She walked back to her car, making sure she had the right hotel. No, she was sure he'd said Astonia more than once. They'd talked about the figure-eight pool with the islands in the middle.

She looked at her watch when she got into her car. Four o'clock. She still had time for her second task of the day. She committed a cardinal health sin by going to the McDonald's

drive-through for a cheeseburger and fries and then headed to
Boone's Marina.

Ashlyn couldn't believe her eyes. As she passed the Astonia,
she saw Winslow walking out. She felt compelled to call
Jayce.

"Hi, sweetheart," her dad said, warming her.

Something good had come out of this ordeal. She'd
grown closer to her father. Or more precisely, she'd nudged
into Winslow's spot. "Hi, Daddy. I'm looking forward to
dinner tonight. Is Winslow going to be there?"

"I hope so. You know how Senator Wiggins likes her.
And . . . I want this smoothed over. I don't feel right about
the way we left things."

"I know, but we had to do it. And if Winslow doesn't
show, I'll be extra nice to the senator." Maybe she could take
Winslow's place there, too. Except that she couldn't fend off
his grubby hands with such grace. No, she couldn't be like
her sister at all. "Could I talk to Jayce please?"

"What's up, babe?" he said a few seconds later, sounding
as though he was in the middle of something. Of course,
they had to make preparations for the dinner that night.
Esme couldn't handle a six-course dinner for twenty-five
people. A catering staff was coming in, but Ashlyn was sure
Jayce was overseeing the details.

"I was coming back from Marla's Boutique with shoes to
match my wedding dress and I saw Winslow walking out of
the Astonia."

"When?"

"Like two minutes ago."

He was silent for a moment, and just when she was about
to ask if he'd heard her, he said, "You didn't mention this
to . . ."

"Daddy? You said not to."

She heard the background noise change to the murmur of
the waterfall and the squawk of a seagull as Jayce walked

outside. "We've already dragged him in too much. You understand that, don't you?"

"Yes." She didn't like keeping things from her daddy. Jayce sometimes told her to keep things from him, but he always had a good reason for doing so. Daddy had so much on his mind these days, after all. She also suspected that if her daddy knew that Winslow was still digging up trouble, he'd probably ask her not to come tonight. But she wasn't that mean. Was she?

"Should I follow her?" She pulled into the turn-around lane.

"Yeah, you do that, but not too closely."

Ashlyn turned around and headed back toward the Astonia. She saw Winslow's car—Daddy's cool Mercedes SLK32 Roadster, she was annoyed to note—pulling out and heading south in front of her. Ashlyn kept her in her sights.

Winslow pulled into the Boone's Marina parking lot and cut the engine. She tucked her purse on the floor and pocketed the keys. It was near the time when the Garcías had launched their boat. That might have been close to the time that Jayce and Ashlyn left, too. Photograph in hand, Winslow walked toward the docks.

The sun should have been hovering above land, but an incoming cold front blanketed the sky in thick clouds. Wind swirled dirt and debris on the asphalt, making her blink the sand out of her eyes. Grant wasn't going to get the patio-side cocktail hour he'd envisioned tonight. No torches, soft music, or waiters gliding among the tables with trays of ornate treats. He had claimed no motive for the party, though he'd invited some of the most politically influential people he knew. All friends and all supportive of his ambitions. *It never hurt to stoke the fire,* that's what he'd said. Winslow thought she'd be organizing the details for him. That was before Jayce took over.

The words *took over* reverberated inside her, but she

pushed them away as she rounded the office building. She walked along the docks showing the picture of Jayce and Ashlyn to everyone she saw. Most people only gave it a cursory look, others studied it, but either way, they didn't remember ever seeing the couple.

She saw one of the men she'd talked to before and decided not to bother him. A heavyset woman was helping her elderly golden retriever off the houseboat she obviously lived on. A potted palm sat in the back corner of her deck, and she'd put in a ramp for the stiff-gaited dog. Winslow liked her on sight.

"Hi, fella," Winslow said, kneeling down and stroking the dog's tan and white hair. She looked up at the woman. "I was wondering if you've ever seen these two people. She's my sister."

The woman took the photograph, cocked her head, and then recognition lit her face. "Yes." She frowned. "I remember them."

Winslow's heart rate jumped. "Were they here last Friday? Around this time of day?"

"No, it was a couple of weeks ago." She tapped the picture. "I remember because of the girl. Your sister. She was the one carrying the cooler and her boyfriend carried nothing, which I thought was rude. A bag dropped off the top and fell into the water. He said, 'Dammit, Ashley, you're a g-d klutz.' I won't even say that word, but he did. She set the cooler down and meekly said she'd get it. And he let her. She had to lie down on these dirty boards and reach for it. I guess they had sandwiches in there, because he got mad that they were all wet and flung them in the trash can. He said, 'You're lucky I put up with your sh—well, you know—'cause I don't know who else would.'"

Winslow didn't like the sound of that at all. "I've never seen him act that harshly with her." And she was sure her father hadn't, either.

"I know it was these two. He's slick looking, got that

pouty mouth and screams metrosexual. You know, when guys get all primpy and pretty. And he had this superior posture. But it was her I remember most. I work in an abused women's shelter. I know the posture: slumped shoulders, the way they cower, their expressions. He might not be hitting her yet, but he's working up to it. Right now he's breaking her down, eroding her self-esteem, making her feel as though he's the only guy who could ever see something valuable in her. That's the beginning. Only the beginning." The dog whined, having held it in for long enough, apparently. "Get her help now."

Those words prickled down Winslow's arms. Jayce an abuser? Yes, she could believe that. But how could Ashlyn put up with it? Her insecurity, her need for male attention, and her desire for love. Ashlyn wasn't a beautiful woman, but she was pretty. Sometimes Winslow had envied Ashlyn for her lack of scars, even when she would snidely comment on Winslow's perfection. Supposed perfection.

It was also possible that this woman *saw* abuse everywhere. She seemed to have a chip the size of a rock on her shoulder. Winslow tried to imagine Ashlyn's posture of late. She hadn't noticed cowed shoulders, meek gestures, or flinching. But she had noticed Ashlyn's lack of passion for her fashion redesigns. In fact, Winslow hadn't seen much enthusiasm at all, even with her wedding coming up.

Get her help now. Of all people, Winslow was the last person who could reach out to Ashlyn. Dallis would be a good choice to intervene, but they weren't friends anymore. That had struck her as odd. Maybe that was something to check out, too. Grant was the one person Ashlyn would listen to, but he wouldn't listen to Winslow.

And that was a problem she wasn't sure she could solve.

When the person on the other end picked up, he said, "Winslow Talbot is here snooping around the marina again. She's asking questions, showing people a picture."

"A picture of what?"

"I don't know, but I'm sure it has something to do with the accident. I heard her say 'last Friday.' "

"What in the hell is she doing? Keep an eye on her. See if you can warn her off. Scare her. You still have Charlie?"

He smiled. "Yep, sure do." He felt the hard lump in his pocket. "Ready and waiting."

"Good. Go to it, but don't leave any evidence. Don't let her see you, either. Last thing I need is for her to identify you which could then lead the cops to me."

"I'll give her a good jolt."

"Make sure she gets the message. Otherwise I'll have to take care of her myself."

Ashlyn called Jayce again, and Grant answered again. "Hi, honey. Hey, you're our best customer today. Don't tell me you need Jayce's advice as to what to wear tonight." He said it with a laugh, but she realized that she had been asking for his advice.

No, you've been asking for his approval.

She pushed the stern voice from her mind. So what if he wanted some say in her wardrobe? He'd get bored of that soon and leave her to her own devices. And soon she'd get back to her special Ashlyn tweaking. She just hadn't been in the mood lately.

"No, Daddy, but I need to talk to him for just a minute."

"He's finishing up a call on the other line. I'll tell him you're holding. See you tonight."

"Yep," she said, sounding so falsely cheerful it made her sick.

After a few moments Jayce got on the line. "Yeah?"

"She's at Boone's Marina."

"All right, good job. Are you still there?"

"I'm in the parking lot."

"Okay. Go on home now. That's not a place for a woman

like you to be at near dark. I'll see you here in an hour."

But Winslow was there, wandering around asking who knew what? Winslow was braver than she would ever be. Just another thing to hate about her.

A fine mist started falling as Ashlyn put the car in gear and pulled away. Great, the stupid cold front had to come in tonight. Poor Daddy would have to keep everyone inside. She wondered if Winslow would make it in time for dinner. What would she do if Winslow never made it at all?

Winslow was glad she'd worn flat shoes as she walked around the two storage buildings where the crane pulled in the boats. The wind was getting cooler, and she wished she'd worn long sleeves. Florida winters were strange that way. Air-conditioning during the day, heat at night. Tank tops to sweatshirts. She glanced at her watch. She still had enough time to get ready and make it to Grant's soiree if she left in less than twenty minutes. Around the back of the second four-story building was the boat launch. No one was launching or bringing in boats at the time. On the other side of the launch were two more sets of boat storage buildings. The parking lot was empty. No one to question.

But she hadn't only come here to question people, she realized. She'd come to see the last place that Elena knew a happy life. The last place that her dad and uncle were alive. Winslow walked down to where the water lapped against the pebbly concrete. That was what she hated about life, that one arbitrary choice could change everything.

"Lady, I hear you're asking about someone taking a boat out last Friday in connection with that accident."

She turned around to find a skinny guy with his cap pulled way down over his face. Her instincts told her not to trust him, but she wanted to hear him out. "Yes, I am."

He took a step closer. "Well, I'm here to tell you to mind your own damned business, you nosy-assed bitch."

When he reached out, she was prepared to see a knife.
She saw nothing but the back of his hand coming at her. Before she could move, he touched her.

It felt as though he'd set her arm on fire. Pain traveled up
and exploded in her head. She didn't have thoughts of getting away; she couldn't think at all. Her body twitched in
some ghastly effort to escape, but she had no control as she
dropped to the ground.

12

Alex told himself it was probably shameful to be alone on a Saturday night, but he didn't feel that way. The whole house was opened to the incoming front; he was sitting outside by the pool. He'd gotten in some fishing that morning and was now ready to panfry the two snapper he'd caught. The Mojito was going down nice and smooth, despite the fact that it reminded him of Winslow.

She had him all tied up in knots. When she'd gone to his office two nights before, she looked upset. Her face was pale, her eyes troubled. Then she'd snooped in his file, even written something down. He didn't know what. When he'd called her on her lie, she had looked sorry but not sneaky. After she'd left, he'd wanted to write her off as a woman he didn't want to get involved with. Or think about.

Then he'd had to go and read her article. He picked up the pages from the glass table on his lanai. Truthfully, he thought it would be a cover, something she'd scribbled just in case he wanted to see it. He'd been blown away. The language, the flow of words, the sense of emotion, had been completely different from her other articles in the issue of *Dazzle* he'd read. This story had really touched her. She'd captured Lidia's guilt and put Elena's pain and her uncertain future into words so exquisite he felt Elena's blood flowing through him.

Yesterday he'd called Winslow's magazine's offices to get in touch with her. He couldn't believe that she wasn't working there anymore. When charmed, the receptionist confided that Winslow had quit unexpectedly.

He didn't know what to make of the woman. She was beautiful and rich, but she didn't act like either. She'd told him about her accident, and he knew it hadn't been easy. They'd connected. He'd felt it on a gut level, and she had, too. He understood why she was drawn to Elena's story, but he still couldn't figure out what she was up to. She had put her heart into an article that she suspected would never be published.

He narrowed his eyes. Or maybe it could. He could publish it in *Mojo* as a commentary. It would have to be translated, of course, but that was easy. He'd have to get Winslow's consent. It would give him a reason to contact her—if he knew how to do so.

His phone rang at that moment, and he had the odd notion that it was her. She had no way of finding him, either, not his home number. It was unlisted, just as hers was.

The voice that greeted him in Spanish was decidedly male. "Hey, it's Orlando. You asked me to let you know if an *Americana* was asking questions at the marina. There's a woman here doing just that. She asked me if I'd ever seen this couple she had a picture of. She was trying to find out if they'd taken out their boat last Friday. I don't know if it has any connection to what you—"

He sat up straight in the chair. "What does she look like?"

"Very nice, brown hair just past her shoulders, pale skin—"

"Great body?"

"Hey, man, stop interrupting me. Tall, just curvy enough—"

Alex hung up and ran inside.

Pain ricocheted through Winslow's body as she climbed from the depths of a dark, deep well toward consciousness.

Pebbles pressed into her back while a cold mist settled onto her clothes and skin. She heard her name, dimly at first, but becoming more insistent. She liked that voice, she thought lazily, finding it hard to pull her thoughts together.

A hand tapped her cheeks. "Winslow, wake up."

She slowly opened her eyes, then closed them when mist touched the surface. She smacked her lips and tasted rain.

Arms went around her and propped her up. She attempted to open her eyes again, and the first thing she saw was Alex looking very worried. She couldn't suppress the giggle that erupted, though it made her head hurt.

"Winslow, are you all right? What happened?" He was running his hands over her, so gently it almost tickled. "Ow," they both said when he touched the bump on the back of her head. "Did someone hit you?"

"That's from yesterday when the repair guys locked me in my trunk," she said, hearing her words slur.

He blinked. "What?"

Her thoughts started congealing. She was lying on the wet ground near the boat launch. It was misting. She'd been out for who knew how long. Someone had done something to her that had knocked her unconscious. And . . . what was Alex doing here? She pushed him away and tried to get to her feet. She was wobbly, and he held out his hands to help her. She didn't want his help and she wasn't ready to stand, so she sat down again.

"What are you doing here?" she said with fewer slurs this time.

"This is where I launch my boat," he said, not quite answering her.

"No one's doing any boating right now. A cold front is coming in."

"I know. That's why we need to get you out of the rain. Tell me what happened."

"Not until you tell me why you're here."

He let out a soft sigh, and she caught the scent of rum and

mint. She couldn't remember the name of the drink. "When I found out you were lying about writing the article for your magazine, and then Lidia said you had gone to the hospital, I knew you were investigating the accident. But I couldn't figure out why. Nothing about you made sense." He took her in. "Still doesn't. But I did guess you'd come here, so I asked a second cousin to keep an eye out for you. I had planned to confront you . . . Well, that was before I read your article. Then I just wanted to talk to you. Now I find you passed out here. *Me asusto casi a morirme!* Scared me half to death."

For some reason, that made her smile, for a second anyway. "You had someone spying on me?"

"Keeping an eye out *for* you. You can understand why I wanted to know what you were up to. If you'd told me the truth, it might have been a lot easier on me."

She lifted her hands, and he helped her to her feet. "A guy came up to me, said he heard I was asking about the boating accident, and then he reached out and I saw something black in his hand and"—she looked at her arm where he'd touched her; there was a red mark—"it was the strangest thing I've ever experienced. It was like a jolt of electricity shooting through my body. I felt dizzy and weak and, oh my God, so much pain, and then everything went black."

He examined the mark. "A stun gun maybe. Shocks you. My aunt has one, to protect herself with. Hers is called a Monster, packs over six hundred thousand volts."

"You can assure her it works. I don't know how long I've been out." That thought scared her, that she'd been lying there helpless.

"It depends on the voltage and whether he just touched you or actually shot you with it. Some can put you out for twenty minutes or more."

She couldn't help shuddering at that. He put his arm along her shoulders and guided her to the parking lot. She didn't argue when he steered her toward his Camaro.

"I should call the police," he said.

"I don't think it'll do much good."

"Winslow, you were attacked."

"Because I was snooping around."

She slid in and was grateful when he started the engine and put on the heat. He turned down the music, though she could hear strains of a salsa beat.

She rubbed her arms for a few seconds, gathering her thoughts. Something he'd said came back to her, and she gave him a sideways look. "You read my article."

"Yep. You were kind of like Cinderella, running off and leaving me only a clue."

This time she allowed herself the smile. "I felt bad about lying to you. I didn't know what to say."

She let a few seconds lapse and realized he was going to make her ask. So she did. "What did you think?"

"I'll tell you when you tell me what's going on."

The heat warmed her cheeks, and she leaned into it for a moment and closed her eyes. "I don't suppose you'll believe me any more than anyone else does, but I probably owe you an explanation."

"Damn straight," he said, looking relieved.

So she told him everything and watched his expressions change with the story: suspicious when she told him about the things Jayce had said to her, scared when she relayed getting knocked out and thrown in her trunk. "So basically, my dad thinks I'm nuts, the police agree, and my sister and her fiancé hate me. I've lost my job and"—she gave him a soft smile—"I probably just lost you, too."

She realized what she'd said. Not that she'd ever had him.

Instead of looking confused or horrified, though, he smiled. "You haven't lost me." That smile didn't last long, though. "Winslow, you've put yourself in danger trying to find out if Jayce is behind this."

"Do you think he is?"

"The question is how will you prove it? The boat's probably long gone."

She smiled again at that and felt such an overwhelming relief. "Thank you," she said, and in shock realized she was about to cry.

"For what?" he said softly.

"Believing me. Or at least not dismissing me."

He reached out and cupped her chin, obviously picking up on her impending tears. She squeezed them back and cleared her throat. "It's been a long, lonely struggle. My cats are the only ones who believe me."

"You've got to stop your investigation. You could have gotten killed—twice. It was probably the same guys both times, and you suspect they work for Jayce. How long do you think he'll play nice before he gets serious?"

Locking her in a trunk and stunning her was playing nice? But that was his point, and she felt anger replace all that softness and relief. She pushed his hand away. "You're telling me to let it go?"

"Not for your father's political career. For your own safety."

She shook her head. "Oh, great. You, the man who puts himself on the line to let the downtrodden have a voice, who advocates freedom against tyranny, telling me to back down? *You* are a hypocrite!"

He backed away, holding up his hands to ward her off. "I'm only—"

"You're the one who lit into me because I wasn't passionate—no, that was Sebastian. *You* said I was shallow, that I didn't look deep, didn't look past the gloss. Well, you know what? You were right. I didn't look because I didn't want to see pain. I have lived with pain and anger at injustice, but I've also lived afraid to tell people what I really felt. I didn't want to lose my place in my world. Between that and living with a face that feels like a mask, I already feel like an impostor."

The tears were coming again, and she realized she'd let out too much. Maybe the jolt had shaken her emotions loose.

He clearly didn't understand the last part, and she hoped he'd focus on the rest instead.

"Winslow, I'm sorry I did that to you. I didn't mean to make you—"

"I'm glad you did. You made me see what I was burying inside."

"But I didn't say anything about you not being passionate. Sebastian, your editor . . . he said that?"

She looked out the side window. "We were sort of dating. He liked that I wasn't passionate. I'm not passionate, but I—"

He leaned forward and kissed her. His hands slid up into her damp hair, cradling her face. She liked that, liked the feel of his thumbs rubbing at her jawline, liked the taste of rum and mint and the feel of his tongue against hers.

"You're passionate," he said simply after he'd finished the kiss. "I read that article. Your passion and outrage saturate each word. I reread the article you did on Tamargo. They're totally different."

"I'm a different writer now." Her fingers had come up to touch her lips, and she felt them stretch into a smile. "You liked the article."

"I loved it. I want to run it in my paper, if it's all right with you."

She nodded. "Yes, of course."

"Anonymously. I'm not putting you at risk. And yes, maybe I am a hypocrite, but I don't want you putting yourself at risk, either. What happened to Lidia's family was a terrible thing. If you keep digging, it sounds like another terrible thing will happen to you."

She settled back in the seat, her emotions roiling: anger, outrage, passion, and yes, even lust. Lord, he could kiss.

When she didn't answer, he said, "What did you mean, you've felt like an impostor?"

Damn. He'd picked up on that. "I have to go. My dad is giving a party and he expects me there. It's the price I pay to be his daughter, and for his generosity. If I don't go, Senator Wiggins will grope my sister instead."

She opened the door as he started to protest. She turned back to him. "I think Jayce may be abusing my sister. Maybe just emotionally at this point, but it could become more. It's not only about a little girl I don't know. It's about my sister, whom I don't even talk to anymore. I think she's in trouble. I'm the last person she'll listen to. And I'm the only one who can help her."

Winslow had just enough time to pretty up, grab something suitable from her closet, and get to Grant's fashionably late. Several cars were already parked in the drive. A valet had been hired to juggle the parking situation.

The young man wearing a clear rain poncho over his suit approached on her side. "Good evening, ma'am."

"Evening." She wasn't going to start the lying yet. It was *not* a good evening, though Alex's kiss had made up for some of it. The mist was now a light downpour. She was still achy, from either the Taser or yesterday's assault. She hoped a glass of champagne would ease both her aches and her nerves. She got out of the car and walked toward the house. Time to pretend again. She now had to pretend not only that things were still warm and cozy with her family but also that she felt at home here.

For the first time, she felt like an invited guest herself. Or maybe even the hired help, there for a purpose. Otherwise, she was sure she would have been uninvited, under the pretense of her absence being easier on the family at this time.

Before she reached the top of the steps, a butler opened the door and welcomed her. She wasn't wearing a wrap or coat, so she passed by him without pausing to surrender it. She only shook away the raindrops and felt vaguely like a dog shaking off the rain.

The music was a pleasing blend of Celtic and classical. The round stone table in the center of the foyer, which usually held a spectacular floral arrangement, now held a tall, cylindrical one that left room for the assortment of food. A few people hovered over the trays, deciding which delicacy they wanted. Three more guests were seated at the round bar. Senator Wiggins was admiring the wine room situated beneath the curving staircase, and Winslow ducked into Grant's office and set her purse on the desk. She then took the long way into the kitchen, not quite ready for him.

Esme was overseeing the hired help. Winslow knew that Esme was Spanish, though she realized that she had no idea if she was Cuban, Puerto Rican, or some other nationality. She would make a point to find out.

Esme, in her accented English, directed a woman in a tuxedo shirt and black pants to take a tray of champagne glasses out to the guests. Then Esme smiled at Winslow and said, "Some of the guests are being given a guided tour. Your father and sister are with them."

"Good. I mean, good to know, thank you." That gave her time to get a glass of champagne, and she took one from the tray as the woman passed.

It had been tempting to don dress pants tonight. Dealing with panty hose was a pain even when she had plenty of time. She'd grabbed an indigo dress from the closet and rifled through her packets of panty hose to find something suitable. She had pinned her hair up with a gold and diamond clip and almost forgotten to add earrings. The front of the dress was adorned with colorful glass beads, making a necklace superfluous. Salt and Pepper had swirled around her legs, begging for attention. She'd felt guilty giving them only a quick rub before departing again.

She started to greet the guests. Judge Camilla Winston exchanged cheek brushes, air kisses, and compliments with her. "You must be so excited, your sister getting married next Saturday and all." Camilla leaned in conspiratorially. "Did she choose a perfectly dreadful maid-of-honor dress for you?"

"I, uh, haven't seen it yet," Winslow stuttered. "She's moved this wedding up so suddenly, I'm not sure what she's doing anymore." She knew she'd never be the choice for maid of honor, though Ashlyn had asked her to be a bridesmaid when she'd first gotten engaged. Now Winslow probably wouldn't even be invited.

"I was surprised when Grant called and asked me to officiate." Camilla waved her hand and rolled her eyes. "Oh, the passion of young love!"

Can't you see that it isn't right? That he's in too much of a hurry? Winslow merely smiled.

She felt a hand slide around her waist and settle just below the small of her back. *Senator Wiggins,* she thought with a grimace, and pasted a smile on her face as she turned around.

"There's my favorite Talbot, though don't tell your father and sister." He gave her a squeeze and she knew he was trying to see if she was wearing panties. He'd once commented on that when he couldn't feel panty lines. She'd worn the all-in-one panty hose again.

"Thanks, Senator."

She could almost mouth his response by now. "Call me Charlie, my silly girl." He was tall, good-looking, and probably somewhere in his sixties. "We're much too close for titles."

She knew she'd be sitting next to him at the dinner table, at his request. She glanced up and saw Grant, Ashlyn, and two other guests in the upstairs loft/library. Winslow could see the shadow of guilt on Grant's face when he spotted her, but he covered it with a smile. "Hi, hon!"

Ashlyn didn't even look at her. She purposely turned to the guests and pointed out the faux painting inside the individual squares in the coffered ceiling.

"Uh-oh," Camilla whispered in that same conspiratorial tone. "Looks like Sis is mad at you."

Winslow waved it away. "Just the usual stepsister thing."

Didn't most stepsisters accuse the other of leaving the scene of a fatal accident? For a moment she was tempted to pull the judge aside and tell her everything. She nixed the idea. Bad time, bad place, wrong judge.

Thankfully, Charlie was whisked away by another of the single women to try some aged whiskey that was "tremendous!"

Sensing someone watching her, Winslow scanned the area and found Jayce carrying on a conversation with Mr. and Mrs. Cutler in the living room. Jayce's gaze had slid to her just as she'd looked over, and he let it linger before turning back to the couple. The arrogant iciness in his eyes complemented the sound of rain growing heavier. He knew that she'd found his boat; he probably knew she'd been looking at the GPS. More important, he knew that she was threatening his cozy little situation. But the arrogant glint told her that he also knew she would never be taken seriously.

When Ashlyn reached the bottom of the stairs, Mrs. Cutler called her over. "Congratulations, sweetheart! I was telling Jayce here that he should take you to Grand Cayman or the Australian reef for your honeymoon if you're going scuba diving. The Keys are lovely, but so much of the coral has been damaged by careless divers. Such a pity."

Winslow had no idea they were even taking a honeymoon, much less where. She took one of the crackers topped with pâté and pretended to give her next choice of delicacy a great deal of concentration. The tall floral arrangement in the center of the table gave her some camouflage, so she could observe surreptitiously.

Ashlyn's voice sounded quivery. "The Keys is just fine for me. I've never scuba dived before."

Mr. Cutler said, "You'll love it."

Ashlyn's laugh sounded quivery, too. "That's what Jayce says. I have to take courses first. He's already certified. Then we're going to rent a boat for the week." She had wrapped her arms around herself as she spoke, and her shoulders were slumped. She did not want to scuba dive. Winslow was sure Ashlyn imagined all the terrible things that could happen.

Jayce put his arm around her shoulders. "She keeps wanting to change her mind, but I'm not letting her."

Ashlyn's smile was more of a wince. "I'm a fraidy cat; that's what he keeps calling me. But it can be dangerous, can't it?"

Both Cutlers nodded, and she said, "But if you're careful and you know what you're doing, you'll be fine. Once you're under the water looking at the coral reefs and all the fish, you'll forget about the danger. Most accidents happen because someone isn't paying attention to their air gauges or they're goofing around. A friend's son thought it would be *cool*, as he put it, to try to ride a nurse shark. They're not aggressive, but they don't like being molested. The shark bit him in the leg. Nothing serious," Mrs. Cutler added at Ashlyn's horrified expression. "A few dozen stitches. Still, it only happened because he was playing recklessly."

"There *are* sharks out there," she said, turning to Jayce.

Mr. Cutler said, "Well, sure; it's the open ocean."

Ashlyn's face had gone pale, her eyebrows pulled up to the creases on her forehead. "Jayce, I don't—"

He squeezed her tight against him. "You'll be fine. Stop being a baby."

A guest next to Winslow commented on the exotic tray of sushi, and she had to look away. By the time she was done explaining what some of the odd-looking pieces were, the foursome had wandered off to mingle with other guests.

Winslow watched Ashlyn carefully, remembering what the woman at the marina had said. She wasn't sure she had ever seen an abused woman. That wasn't the kind of thing one talked about. Ashlyn did seem withdrawn. Her dress was nothing special, not altered in the Ashlyn way. She wasn't animated and, in fact, didn't partake in many conversations. Jayce seemed to do all the talking, and what disturbed

Winslow was that even when a question was directed at Ashlyn she deferred to Jayce for the answer.

Alex was right; the changes in the girl were clear now that she was looking for them. Grant would just reiterate that Ashlyn was tamed if Winslow pointed it out. She suspected he was glad that his flighty, anxious daughter was now someone else's responsibility.

How long had Ashlyn been like this? Winslow was ashamed to realize she didn't pay much attention to her stepsister. Now she was paying attention, and she didn't like what she saw. Jayce seemed to be the doting fiancé here, always touching Ashlyn in some way with affection—and control? Winslow wondered.

Even though Winslow carried on conversations with others, her gaze followed the happy couple as they socialized. That's how she noticed the signal. When Jayce was ready to move on, he tapped whatever part of Ashlyn his hand was on. Two taps, pause, two taps. Within a minute, Ashlyn would make an excuse and they'd move on. The creepiest part was that Jayce's face betrayed nothing of whatever made him want to move on. He was charming and animated, the way Ashlyn used to be, and then gracious as *she* made the excuse to leave. Winslow felt irritation scrabble up her spine.

As the dinner bell rang, so did a distant cell phone. Almost everyone made some kind of motion to check their phones before realizing they weren't wearing them. The ringing was coming from Grant's office, and Jayce excused himself with apologies. Conversation resumed with everyone joking about how anytime a cell phone rang a whole room's worth of people would go searching for their phones.

Winslow casually wandered to the far side of the living room as though looking for a misplaced drink. The edge of the couch was near the door to the office, and she strained to hear Jayce's soft voice in the darkened room.

"I'm glad to hear that, but that's not why I called you

earlier. I might need you. I have a problem developing, so be ready. I have to go."

Winslow nearly tripped over her own feet to move away from the doorway. It didn't matter; he walked straight to the dinner table, where guests were still finding their assigned places at the long table. She pretended to give up on finding her drink and made her way to the dining room, finding her place next to good old Charlie.

She'd noticed that Jayce had left his phone in the office. As she thought about how she'd get in there, Charlie set his hand on her thigh. "Goodness, honey, you must have boyfriend troubles."

She blinked, bringing herself to the situation. "Why do you say that?"

"You've been in another world. Saw you over there looking for your glass of champagne." He lifted the half-full glass. "I told you I'd take it to the table."

"Oh." She felt her face flush, particularly since people nearby were listening. "No, I don't have boyfriend trouble." She thought of Alex and felt her face warm further.

"Yes, she does," Mrs. Cutler said from across the table. "Look at that blush!"

Winslow spent the rest of dinner dodging questions about her love life and heck, wasn't it time to settle down? She actually considered telling them about her Cuban boyfriend and watching their dumbfounded reactions but decided against it. Some of the people here looked at the influx of Latinos as a nuisance; some saw it as an invasion. There had been occasional heated conversations about how the country was catering to people who couldn't bother to learn the language, and often political guests were asked why every form was bilingual now. Winslow wasn't about to open that can of worms.

"You still working for that little magazine?" Charlie asked. He had the habit of putting his hand on her thigh

every time he asked her a question, though thankfully he removed it once she'd answered.

"No, I quit."

Mrs. Cutler nodded in approval. "Why tie yourself down?
You could always write a book."

Like that was easy. Thankfully, no one asked why she'd
quit. No, it wasn't to loll around thinking of nothing more
than tomorrow's tennis date or the weekend's social gathering. She caught Grant's gaze as he looked at her, but he
quickly turned away. It hurt, and she hoped he'd only
looked away so as not to reveal his guilt. She couldn't see
Ashlyn and Jayce, since they sat on the same side of the
table as she.

She was distracted but managed to make small talk
throughout the long meal. After dinner, drinks were served
in the living room. The rain was coming down in torrents
now, sending foliage banging against the windows. She was
glad to have something benign like the weather to discuss.

Smokers wandered out to the covered loggia to indulge
their vice, and Winslow drifted with them. The mist blew in
from the bay, cool and refreshing but sending the less dedicated smokers inside. She could see Jayce talking with Grant
and Charlie, though Ashlyn was nowhere in sight.

The office was still dark but for the red and green lights
of the various machines. Winslow walked to the other side,
where French doors led outside. As she had hoped, they
were unlocked, and she slipped inside. Her purse was on the
desk, and she took out her cell phone and turned it on so
she'd have a little light. Jayce's phone was the same type as
hers, so she knew the layout of the buttons. She went through
the menu and found the number for the last incoming call.
Feeling around in her purse, she found her small recorder
and said the number. She started to scroll down the list, intending to recite them all and later call them, hoping to identify the men who had stuffed her into her trunk.

Lights blinded her, and she was startled to find Jayce walking toward her. Her finger pressed the clear button on the phone as she tried to hide her guilt. *Look annoyed at being disturbed; that shouldn't be hard to do.*

"I was making a call. Do you mind?"

"I do when it's my phone."

She thought she did surprised well as she looked at the phone. "No, it's not. I left it right—"

He picked up her phone and shoved it at her. "Here." Not for a second was he falling for her innocent routine. *That's my story and I'm sticking to it.*

"Oh." She looked at the phone in her hand, which he promptly snatched. "Sorry, I thought it was mine."

"You're not going to find what you're looking for, you sneaky little *bitch*." That last word he bit out with a poisonous tone.

"So this is where the political machine turns!" Mrs. Cutler said from the doorway. "May I?"

Jayce waved her in, though his expression was stiff with tension. Had she heard him? Winslow hoped so, but he'd said it in a low growl, and Mrs. Cutler looked too taken in by the built-in units to have heard anything.

Jayce played the charming host, showing her the charts he'd devised and the state-of-the-art machinery. Winslow walked out—and right into Grant. He held her hands in his, at first from reflex and then on purpose. "I want to talk to you before you leave."

She nodded and then smiled falsely at the others who also wanted to see the office. If only Grant had heard Jayce's vicious words.

Within the hour guests started dribbling out into the rain. The weight of pretending was dragging her down, and Jayce's hostile stares were tearing holes in her placid facade. She stood by the door and wished everyone a good night.

Grant followed her into his office after the last guest had departed. He closed the door, and she only then noticed that he looked fatigued as well. Maybe his lies were wearing him down, too.

"Thank you for the use of the car," she said first, because that was the polite thing to do.

His smile was painted with pain. "It's the least I could do. Winslow . . ." He seemed at a loss for words, and she was tempted to jump in and scream, *Why did you lie for them? Why did you make me look like an idiot?* She held her tongue and let him gather his thoughts. "I know why you feel so strongly about this, but you need to trust me. The truth would only cause a lot of problems for all of us."

"The truth," she said, her words flat.

"I know what happened, and it's not what you think."

"What did happen?" She was prepared to hear some outlandish story or pathetic excuses about lack of visibility or maybe they thought they hit a log.

"I can't say." He squeezed her hands. "I'm asking you to trust me." It was said in that *after all I've done for you* tone she knew so well. "Have I ever done anything unethical? As unethical as lying to the police, for God's sake?"

She shook her head. He'd never done more than the average person, she supposed.

"Then you have to trust that I have good reason to do so."

His expression was earnest; she couldn't deny that. *He* believed whatever Jayce and Ashlyn had told him before Winslow and the detectives arrived. "Are you sure they're telling you the truth? Jayce is a liar, Dad. He never stayed at the Astonia for instance. If he lied about that, he could be lying about anything."

Grant ran his hand through his hair as he ducked his head. "What is it that you have against Jayce? I don't understand this vendetta."

"I don't trust him. Maybe you got a good feeling about him, but I got just the opposite. I don't like the way he controls Ashlyn, and I don't like the way he's rushing her into marriage. It doesn't feel right; none of it does."

"She's happy. The Astonia, well, that's probably a misunderstanding. Why would he lie about that? This has got to stop, Winslow. Everything is going to look bad to you. I want you to stop this snooping, come back to our family, and be happy for Ashlyn. I want things smoothed out so you can come to the wedding. But only if you can be truly happy for them . . . if you can accept Jayce. Can you do that?"

He looked into her eyes, pleading with her to do as he asked. No matter how much she owed him, she couldn't say yes. And so she walked out with a gaping hole in her heart.

13

When Winslow got home that night, she changed into her cat pajamas, washed her face, and sat down at the computer. The pajamas and her cats made her feel safe and comfortable again. She knew it was only temporary. Salt and Pepper twined around her feet, thanking her for the treat she'd given them a few minutes ago. She absently petted them as she waited for the computer to boot up.

She played back the number from Jayce's cell phone and wrote it down. The area code wasn't familiar. If only she'd had more time, she could have found those repair creeps' number. Jayce had obviously been watching her; he knew exactly what she'd been doing. It had probably taken him a few seconds to extricate himself from a conversation to follow her.

She went to the online white pages and tried several options, including reverse number lookup. When nothing turned up, she went the old-fashioned way and called the operator, who told her that the area code belonged to San Francisco and that it was likely a cell number. There was no way to find out who owned the number.

San Francisco? Jayce was from Chicago. She tried to remember what he'd said. He had a problem developing, and the person on the other end should be ready. Was she that problem? And what would this person do about it? Since the number belonged to a cell phone, he or she could be anywhere. Even in Miami.

On a lark, Winslow went back to the Internet and asked for listings for Jayce Bishop in Chicago. There were two listings for J. Bishops. After calling both numbers, she eliminated them as possibilities. Jayce could have sold his house or condo, she supposed. On another lark, she looked up San Francisco, too. There were six viable listings, and she made her way down the list. She eliminated four by asking for Jayce, but the other two couldn't be discounted. "This is probably a dead end. Even if he did have a residence in San Francisco, what does it prove? That he had enough money for two residences."

As she was about to log off, she had another idea and did a global search on *heir, dispute,* and *Bishop*. Several articles appeared, and she read them. The Chicago Bishops were indeed mired in a bitter dispute. An excess of $1.4 billion hung in the balance, plus properties and other assets. The press was having a field day with each round of accusations and litigation. Some family members were mentioned, but none of the grandchildren were named. Maybe Jayce was telling the truth about that, and maybe he didn't have the money to stay at the Astonia and had been too ashamed to admit to staying at a Holiday Inn.

With that bit of reassurance, she went to sleep. The balcony doors remained tightly shut.

The following morning, Winslow woke with a panicky feeling in her stomach. "God, the wedding is next week." She imagined barging into the church objecting to the marriage. But there wasn't going to be a church. The wedding would probably be held at the house.

She pushed herself out of bed, giving the cats some quality time after they'd been fed. She couldn't afford to be denounced by her babies, too. As she sat on the floor and watched Salt wriggle on his back, Winslow tickled his tummy and said, "I've got to find proof that Jayce is abusing Ashlyn emotionally. Or proof that he rammed the Garcías' boat. Either way, it'll disrupt the wedding. I need to talk to Ashlyn. I know—well, I think—I could get through to her if I could only get her alone."

She tilted her head at Pepper, who was pawing at a wrinkle on her pajamas. "Dallis. Something happened between her and Ashlyn. I'm going to find out what it was."

An hour later, Winslow was on her way to the Snake Pit. Dallis's father was Johnny Slither, from the popular eighties band Snake Pit. He'd tried to regain some popularity à la Ozzie Osbourne by appearing in a season of *The Surreal Life*, a reality show that moved a group of has-been stars and sort-of celebrities into one tacky house.

Dallis and her father lived in SoBe, land of thong bikinis, bars, and decadence. The two-story structure was painted a combination of sea foam green and pink. Nothing unusual in Miami, though it was a bit gaudier than the surrounding homes. While Johnny had blown some of his money on drugs and women, he'd also invested in a vineyard in Chile that was doing well for him. Word was he was trying to revive the band now that rock and roll was coming back into vogue.

Dallis had elected to keep her father's original last name, Jordan, which had made her easy to find in the phone book. Dallis had invited Winslow to stop by but had warned that her father had hosted one of his parties the night before. Winslow was to open the front door and walk up the stairs, ignoring anything unpleasant she might see on the way.

She had never been to any of Johnny's parties, but Ashlyn had told wild stories about them as part of dinner conversation. Now Winslow walked up to the double doors, feeling strange about walking into someone's house without knocking. It was eerily quiet inside. The interior felt like a cave, with the black tile floors and thick drapes covering the windows.

She could see, however, people sprawled on the dark furniture and even on the fur rug in front of the green marble fireplace. As she moved farther into the house, she picked up the soft sound of snoring in stereo, coming from different directions.

She walked up the curving staircase and followed Dallis's directions to the room at the end of the hallway. When she knocked, a hoarse voice invited her in. Dallis had sounded asleep when Winslow called earlier. Sitting in her huge, rumpled bed, she looked like she'd still been sleeping.

"Hi," Winslow said, stepping inside. "Did I wake you again?"

"I've been dozing on and off. Stayed up too late last night. Come in." She reached over, without completely leaving the bed, and shoved a laundry basket's worth of clothing from the black fur chair onto the floor. The scent of cigarettes lingered in the air.

She was a big, square girl with striking features. Her short black hair was sticking out in all directions, and she didn't help matters by rubbing her fingers through the thick strands. "I'm glad you called me about Ashlyn. I've been worried about her."

Winslow reluctantly settled into the chair, feeling as though she were stepping into a bear's embrace. "I'm worried, too. I thought you could shed some light on her relationship with Jayce, and why you're not friends anymore."

Dallis twisted her mouth. "Because of Jayce. He's a supreme butthead." She scratched her nails against her scalp, and the sound grated on Winslow's nerves.

The walls in the bedroom were painted a flat black with what looked like splatters of pink blood randomly dripping down the walls. On one wall the "blood" spelled out Dallis's name.

Winslow averted her attention to Dallis. "What did he do that made you think that?"

Again without quite leaving the bed, she leaned over and

took a three-foot python out of an aquarium. Winslow stiffened, but Dallis didn't seem to notice her discomfort. In fact, she lifted the snake and said, "Winslow, this is Bob-the-snake. Bob-the-snake, Winslow."

"Bob . . . ?" Had she actually been introduced to a *snake*?

Dallis shrugged. "I named him something benign hoping that Ashlyn wouldn't be so freaked by him. She still was, but by then the name had stuck. I know, you're wondering how we could have been such good friends, being so different and all."

It had crossed her mind, so she gave a loose shrug.

"Our differences made our friendship more interesting and, I thought, more durable. She enjoyed trying to change my fashion sense, and truthfully, I liked that she cared. I even bought some of the bright outfits she suggested." The loss of that friendship hurt; that was clear. "I tried to get her to loosen up a bit, and she tried to refine me. It was futile, but it gave us purpose." She shrugged. "You wanted to know about Jayce."

Bob worked through her fingers and kept trying to escape. Without even looking, Dallis kept bringing him back to her. "Well, he broke up our friendship for one thing. He controlled her, everything she did. He didn't like me; I could tell right off the bat. Now I know that's not surprising in and of itself. But I got the impression he didn't like me in her life."

Winslow leaned forward in interest, saw the snake slithering toward her side of the bed, and sat back again. "Like he wanted her all to himself?"

"Yeah, exactly. I told Ashlyn it annoyed me, but she was so, 'Oh, I'm in love with him, and isn't it sweet how he wants me all to himself,' that she wasn't listening. She's one of those people who needs a lover in her life to feel complete, you know? Well, you probably do know."

Winslow didn't know that, but it made sense, so she nodded.

Dallis started to light up a cigarette but stopped before the tip ignited. "Ashlyn used to give me hell about smoking, even though she smoked when she drank." She eyed her cigarette and then set it on the nightstand. "The guys she dated were twinkies, but they were cool with Ashlyn and me being friends. Not Jayce. He made up his mind that he didn't want me around, and Ashlyn gave in. He took me out on his boat with them once, and then never again. I saw them a few weeks back when we were out on my dad's boat. I'd called her earlier to see what she was doing, and she said she was busy. It hurt, you know? She got all embarrassed when she saw me. I left a message for her later saying I wasn't mad. She never called me back."

"Did you ever see Jayce hurt Ashlyn? Grab her arm or pinch her?"

"Nothing like that. But he always had his hands on her. Not in a lusty way, just a . . . possessive way. That's how I saw it."

"Did Jayce ever say anything threatening to you?"

She thought back on that. "No, but I got a vibe from him, you know? An icky vibe." Bob had lifted his head and was looking at Winslow, his tongue flicking in her direction. For Dallis to get an icky vibe was really saying something.

"I did, too."

"But the thing that bothered me most about him was the way he changed Ashlyn. It was like she became codependent with him. Couldn't make a decision, not even what she wanted to drink, without getting his opinion or approval."

"Yes!" The snake backed up at her outburst, and his tongue started moving rapidly. Winslow had to agree with Ashlyn; naming him Bob didn't make him more benign. She lowered her voice. "That's exactly what I noticed. Even someone who didn't know her very well noticed." Alex's face popped into her mind at that thought, but she pushed him away so he didn't distract her. "She looks cowed."

"Ashlyn's got a rich daddy. I always worried that her wobbly self-esteem would get her into trouble someday. I saw a gold digger try to work his charms on her once, but he was too slick. She saw right through him. I guess Jayce has money of his own, or is getting it, but I got the same feeling. He was working her."

The words chilled Winslow. She thought of the signal he'd given Ashlyn when it was time to move to the next person at the party. "Was there anything specific you can remember that really bothered you? Everything I've seen is so subtle. Grant is about as in love with Jayce as Ashlyn is."

"He didn't even try to charm me. He just wanted me out. And he won. I redecorated my room to reflect my angst and abandonment. Ashlyn had made it all girlie." The snake coiled around Dallis's thick wrist, and her fingers began to get red from lack of circulation. She didn't seem bothered. "No, I can't think of anything specific. Like you said, subtle stuff. I questioned a couple of things early on, and she pooh-poohed me. So he wanted her all to himself. So he never talked about his family or his past. He was mysterious, maybe even the black sheep of the family. It was all romantic to her."

Winslow was glad to find someone who saw Jayce the way she did. Unfortunately, Dallis didn't have anything else to offer that might knock off the rose-colored glasses Grant wore where Jayce was concerned. "Did Jayce ever mention California? San Francisco, to be precise?"

"Nope. He was from the Midwest somewhere. He talked about that sometimes, but not a lot." Dallis's fingers were now getting purple.

The sight made Winslow's fingers ache. She climbed out of the chair with no small amount of effort. "I'd better go. Thanks for your input."

Dallis was finally unwinding the snake from her wrist. "Anything I can do to help, let me know."

Winslow handed her a business card. "If you remember something specific, call me at the home number. Right now that's what I need."

When Winslow left, she felt even more afraid for Ashlyn. And more helpless to do anything about it.

Winslow drove back toward home. She now had two people who had noticed a big difference in Ashlyn since Jayce came into her life. Not enough to bring to Grant's attention, unfortunately. He still saw the change as positive. He probably saw her severed friendship with Dallis as positive, too.

Winslow found herself at her favorite beach, where she usually thought about upcoming assignments at the magazine. Now she came to think, to pray, and to keep her fears at bay. Usually Sundays were crowded, but it was in the sixties, too cool for most beachgoers. She bundled up in her jacket and slid into her beach shoes.

A small, cowardly part of her whispered, *Just let this go, beg for your job, and return to the way things were.*

Another, more sinister voice said, *What if you're imagining all this about Jayce? Maybe you are threatened by his presence, by Grant's affection toward him. Maybe you secretly don't want Ashlyn to be happy.*

No, it wasn't true!

Letting go would be the easiest path. Even Alex didn't want her to proceed. And with good reason. Look what had already happened to her.

"Alejandro," she said, wanting the name to roll off her tongue. It stumbled instead.

As she walked, the cool wind brisk on her face and the sand gritty in her eyes, she examined her motives and, indeed, her very self. She prayed that God guide her in making the right decision.

What she came up with was that she couldn't walk away from what her instincts were telling her: that Jayce was a danger to Ashlyn. Running over that boat and walking away from his responsibility made him a terrible person. But his control over Ashlyn had a sinister feel to it. Justice was important to Winslow, but protecting her sister was more important. Both of those meant she had to move forward.

Finding proof to connect Jayce to the hit-and-run was a near impossibility at this point. Ashlyn was her only hope. If Ashlyn told the authorities the truth, that might be the wedge Winslow would need to get her away from Jayce's influence for a while. Winslow had to remind Ashlyn of how she was before Jayce and get her to see how she'd changed.

So Winslow made a plan. Because it was Sunday, she couldn't implement it until the following day. As she headed to the Mercedes, she wondered if Grant would love her enough to loan her his car when this was over.

"Ms. Talbot, it's been a while," Tiffany, the saleswoman at Neiman Marcus, said to Winslow Monday morning. It was almost, but not quite, an accusation. Tiffany was a walking mannequin, dressed in a shiny black linen pantsuit, her hair perfectly coiffed, makeup just so. She even moved like a mannequin, her hands in a graceful pose, her arms akimbo.

"I'm not the shopper my sister is."

Tiffany was already eyeing Winslow's outfit, and she could see their inventory going through her mind.

Winslow jumped ahead. "I'm not here to shop, actually. My sister was in a week ago Saturday doing some heavy-duty shopping. Frenzy shopping, I'd say. Were you the one who helped her?"

"Last Saturday, last Saturday . . . yes, that was me. She always asks for me when I'm here. Something I appreciate very much."

"Did she seem . . . . distracted? Different than usual?"

Tiffany considered that, tapping her red fingernail to her chin. "Yes, now that you mention it, she was. But she can be, well, distracted at times." Tiffany was too polite and wise to say "flaky".

"I understand, but was she more so on that day?"

"Yes, I'd say she was. Is she all right? You almost sound as though she's missing and you're investigating."

In a sense that was true. "I'm just a little worried about her."

Tiffany wasn't about to pry into her customers' private lives, so she said, "Our session was normal, in that she picked an assortment of outfits and had her cappuccino with extra foam while she tried them on. But she usually gets a gleam in her eyes. I know she alters clothing, and I can see her mind working. She's very talented."

She *was* talented, Winslow thought. Maybe more so than she'd ever given her credit for. "But this time she wasn't gleaming?"

"Not really. She was on the phone a lot, too." Tiffany's picture-perfect face scrunched up in a frown. "Asking for advice. That was strange. She'd never done that before, even when she used to come in with her heavyset friend."

"Advice from a guy?"

"I think so. She never said who it was, but it sounded like a man. And they were . . . well, I guess you could call it arguing."

"Over what?"

"I couldn't tell, and I didn't try to listen."

Probably about the hit-and-run.

"And then she went to the men's department and purchased several items there. I went to check on her and she was on the phone asking questions about size and colors."

She was buying Jayce clothing. "How much did she buy in the men's department?"

"Probably half a wardrobe's worth. I'd rather it didn't get back to her that I'm telling you this."

"It'll be our secret. You've been a big help; thanks."

It was nearly eleven o'clock. Jayce would be at work, which meant Winslow had an opportunity to get Ashlyn alone and, she hoped, get the truth.

Fifteen minutes later Winslow took the elevator up to Ashlyn's floor and knocked. Ashlyn opened the door, and her expression drooped at the sight of Winslow.

Winslow's expression probably drooped at the sight of the phone tucked between Ashlyn's ear and shoulder. When she said, "It's Winslow," in a derogatory voice, Winslow knew who was on the other end. Especially when she heard a voice say, "Close the door on her."

Winslow stepped inside to make sure that couldn't happen. "I just want to talk," she said softly, hoping Jayce wouldn't hear. "No arguing."

"She's inside," Ashlyn reported in a stiff voice, as though Winslow were some intruder with nefarious intentions. "All right. Bye."

Winslow knew Jayce was on his way over. He was only a few minutes away. Damn, she wished she'd talked to Ashlyn alone right after the accident. Jayce had had a week to work her, and after the scene at Grant's with the detectives Winslow wasn't sure Ashlyn could be swayed to reveal the truth now. In seeming proof of that, Ashlyn crossed her arms over her chest in a defiant gesture.

"I'm here as your sister," Winslow started. "Not about the accident."

"You went to the marina," Ashlyn blurted out. "So don't lie about why you're here." At Winslow's dumbfounded look, she added, "I saw you leaving the Astonia and followed you."

Jayce knew she'd been there. That made it more likely that he was behind her attack. "Okay, I was there. I was asking about Jayce at the Astonia, and you know what the doorman told me? Jayce never stayed there. He lied. I'm not here about the hit-and-run." A small lie. "I'm concerned about you. Jayce has pushed up the wedding, and you've only been dating a few months. He was making a call to someone in California at Dad's party. But Jayce isn't from there. Do you know who he'd be calling?"

Ashlyn looked pained. "No, but I don't know all of his acquaintances."

"That's my point. We don't know much about him at all.

Yes, you're in love with him, and he's charmed Dad, too. Come here and look at who you used to be." Winslow walked into the dining room. "Where's your clipping board?"

"In the front bedroom."

As Winslow walked to the room, she said, "Jayce made you put it in here, didn't he?"

"Well, why should he look at me partying with other guys while he eats?"

"Sounds like something Jayce would say. And then you volunteered to move it, I bet."

Ashlyn looked stung, giving Winslow the answer. That's what scared her, how Jayce manipulated her, how he was probably manipulating Grant the same way. The bulletin board even faced the wall. "He made you turn this around, didn't he? He wants to cut you off, from your friends, from your past, from who you are. I haven't seen you smile like this in the last month. Have you?"

She wouldn't even look at the pictures. "I'm a different person now. I'm going to be a married woman. That party girl is in my past."

"But are you a happy person? Your fashion tweaking used to make you passionate. And you're good at it. Have you been doing that since you've been engaged to Jayce?"

With her arms still crossed over her chest, she walked back to the foyer. "That was a silly pastime. Even you used to say—"

"I was wrong." And in that moment, Winslow realized it was true. "I admit that I thought the way you altered things was . . . well, I thought you were a vapid fashionista. But now"—that she'd been snooping around in Ashlyn's life—"I realize it was much more than that. You're talented in design and accessorizing."

"You're just saying that to try to win me over so I'll tell you . . ."

"The truth? I do want the truth, about how Jayce is treating you. Ashlyn, you're asking his advice on what to wear. You, the expert on fashion, asking his advice. Think about it. He controls you. I think he's emotionally abusing you, and he may even be physically abusing you. I saw those bruises. That's only a start."

"When you're in a relationship, that's what you do, ask for input, for advice. Oh, but you wouldn't know that, would you? You've never been in a relationship! You're just jealous of my happiness. If you can't be happy for me, and it's obvious that you can't, I want you to leave."

Her words about not having been in a real relationship bit into Winslow. Those were the kinds of things Ashlyn would say to create strife between them, and Winslow would walk away. She couldn't walk now.

"I do want you to be happy. I don't think you are." Ashlyn hadn't negated that Jayce was hurting her physically. "Is he hitting you, Ashlyn?"

"No! Why are you trying to act like a big sister now? You never cared about me before, and I never cared about you, either. So why start now?"

Because I never saw you as anything more than a selfish spoiled brat. Because I was afraid to open myself up to you and have you hurt me with your snide rejection. "Because you were never in danger before. I wish we were closer; I really do. But I do care about you. We are sisters, even if not by blood. I don't want you hurt, Ashlyn."

"You're breaking my heart," she said.

"No, you're breaking *my* heart. Even Alex Díaz noticed the change in your attitude from the dinner to honor the musician to the time you worked for him. You ran away for a reason. Because Jayce hurt you."

Ashlyn was shaking her head, her chin tucked low. Winslow wasn't getting through. Jayce had brainwashed her. If there were bruises, something that Winslow could tell Grant to look for, maybe he would at least listen to her. But she was running out of time; Jayce would be there any minute.

"Then show me you have no bruises. Show me that he's not hurting you." When Ashlyn again shook her head, Winslow reached for her. Ashlyn wore a pink top with a design on the sheer sleeves that would camouflage any bruises. "What are you hiding?"

Winslow tried to push the sleeves up to reveal the pale skin of Ashlyn's arms. She let out a yelp and pulled away, tearing the delicate fabric. The more she struggled, the more desperation fueled Winslow. She tugged at the collar of the shirt, finding no new bruises on Ashlyn's neck or shoulders.

"If you've got nothing to hide, why are you fighting me?" Winslow said, holding on tight to Ashlyn's arm to keep her from moving away.

"*You're* going to put bruises on me!" Ashlyn screeched.

Winslow wasn't expecting the arm that came from behind and wrenched her off-balance. In that flash of surprise, she saw Ashlyn's relief as she looked behind Winslow, and felt breath at her ear and the arm tighten around her chest.

"She's crazy!" Ashlyn said, looking down at the ripped sleeve. "She tried to rip my clothes off!"

"I was only trying to see if he's bruising you," she said, trying to wriggle free of Jayce.

He held her fast with both arms now. "If you don't calm down I'm going to call security."

"Let go of me," she said, hating the feel of his arms around her. He was treating her as though she were some lunatic. The way Ashlyn was looking at her . . . all right, she'd gotten a bit overexuberant.

"Not until you stop fighting. Not until I think you're ready to be let go."

He was in control, and he liked it. She stomped on his foot, and he shoved her against the wall. "Ash, call security," he said.

Ashlyn's look of triumph morphed to one of horror and indecision.

Winslow stopped struggling. "Ashlyn, it's all right; I'll leave."

"You're damn right you will," he said, and finally let her go.

She moved quickly away from him. "Ashlyn, if you need someone to talk to . . . I'm here. I'm sorry I got rough. I only wanted to make sure you were all right."

Jayce escorted her to the door, blocking her view of Ashlyn. "Bye," he said, giving Winslow a shove and closing the door in her face.

She had little hope of her offer being taken up on, she realized as she headed for the elevator doors. She had completely alienated her sister and given Jayce more ammunition in convincing Grant that she was off her nut.

This visit had been a mistake, but it was a chance she'd had to take. When she stepped inside the elevator she was startled to see Jayce standing at the open doorway watching her. His expression was fierce as the doors slid shut.

There's something else you're forgetting. Now that Jayce knows how serious you are, you've just become a bigger threat to him. And you don't know what he'll do to stop you.

14

Jayce gathered Ashlyn in his arms. After watching him strong-arm Winslow, Ashlyn wasn't quite ready to accept his embrace. Eventually she softened against him.

"I'm sorry you to had endure that," he said. "I couldn't let her attack you."

"Why does she think you're a horrible person? Why does she think you're beating me?"

"I think she's on something. You saw the look in her eyes, didn't you?" When she didn't answer right away, he tilted her chin so she had to look at him. "You did see that crazy glint, right? You even used the word *crazy*."

Crazy, yes, but drugged? She nodded, though, because he was expecting her agreement.

He tilted her chin up again. "Are you all right?"

"I've never seen her like that. It was disturbing."

"I'm sure it was. That boating accident really knocked her off-balance." He studied Ashlyn. "Something else is bothering you, isn't it? What did she say?"

"That you control me, that I'm not really happy. She said you didn't stay at the Astonia, that the doorman had never seen you."

"Yeah, and I'm sure he remembers everyone that comes and goes."

Well, sure, he wouldn't remember everyone. "She's desperate to find something on you." Concerned. And willing to go to extreme lengths to prove her point. Ashlyn had never seen her look like that before. "She also said something about you calling someone in California."

He pinched the bridge of his nose. "She was on my cell phone Saturday night, at the party. I caught her in Dad's office. She pretended she thought it was her own. I'm sure she was looking for the number of the repairmen, but I've already erased it. See, she's not concerned about you. She wants to prove we hit that boat. That's all she cares about."

She rubbed her temples. This was giving her a headache. "Who are you calling in California?" He looked a bit taken aback at her question, and she quickly added, "Not that I suspect you of anything. But she's right; I don't know a lot about you."

"It's my cousin, the one who keeps me abreast of the situation in Chicago. Didn't I mention that he's in San Francisco?" He kissed the top of her head. "I'd better get back to work. You going to be all right?"

"Yes."

"I'll tell the security guard not to let her in anymore. You don't need this kind of harassment."

This was out of hand. She understood when Jayce had suggested changing the locks so Winslow couldn't walk in on them. But barring her from the building? That seemed extreme.

She said, "All right. At least until she comes to her senses."

His expression darkened. "I don't know that she will come to her senses. Dad's about had it with her. I wouldn't be surprised if she doesn't just fade out of our lives. You wouldn't mind that, would you?"

She could only lift a shoulder. For years after Georgina and Winslow had joined their family, she'd wished they weren't around. Still, letting Winslow drift from the family seemed wrong somehow.

Jayce continued, "And our lives will be much better. And

speaking of, did you get a chance to talk to Dad about giving us this condo?"

She shook her head. "But I will." Jayce had been surprised to learn that the condo wasn't in her name.

He pulled her into his arms, though she could only think of how he'd detained Winslow so tightly. "I'm just thinking of your financial security, baby doll. I'll leave it up to you as to whether you want my name on it or not. Of course, I'll feel more at home if I'm on the deed. Otherwise I might want to move."

She pulled away. "Move?"

"I want a home of our own. With this place in Dad's name, it doesn't feel that way. It's like we're borrowing it. Talk to him; see what he says."

He kissed her good-bye and left. She wandered into the front bedroom and looked at the board full of clippings. She hardly remembered that girl anymore. Daddy and Jayce said that was a good thing. She'd been on the verge of a melt-down, drinking and partying too much. Her life was now getting settled. She was happier, right? And she hated her stepsister and didn't care if she was excommunicated from the family. Right?

Right. Jayce had shown her more affection and caring than Winslow had ever shown. And no matter what, Ashlyn wasn't going to lose him. She'd do anything to prevent that from happening.

Grant had just wrapped up a call when Jayce returned. The expression on his face spoke of conflict and concern. "Is Ashlyn all right?"

Jayce sat in the chair near his desk. "I debated whether to tell you this. But you should know. It's your daughter af-ter all."

Not problems with Ashlyn. Since Jayce had come into her life, the crises had been reduced greatly. When they did occur, Jayce was the one handling them.

"It's Winslow again," Jayce continued. "When I got to the condo, she was assaulting Ashlyn. Tore her clothes and everything."

Grant couldn't even fathom that scene. "There had to be some misunderstanding."

"I think it's drugs. I'm sorry to say it, but I really do. She had a wild look in her eyes. Ashlyn was terrified. I had to bodily hold Winslow to calm her down, and then I ordered her to leave the premises. I told security that she wasn't to be allowed back in. It was an awful scene, Dad. I'm glad you weren't there to see it. She even went to the Astonia and got some doorman who's probably only been working a week to say that he'd never seen me there. She's still trying to prove we were on the boat that hit the Cubans. And she's not going to give up. She's going to get hurt."

Grant stuck the tip of his thumb in his mouth, feeling the sting of his previous chewing episodes.

"Dad, I know you don't want to hear this, but you've lost control of her. She's even worse than Ashlyn was before I came along. The only way you're going to be able to get her back under control is to threaten her: If she doesn't curtail her activities, you'll cut her off financially. Cut her out of the will. Whatever will shock sense into her."

The pain radiating from the tip of Grant's thumb helped keep the panic at bay. "I don't know. That seems so drastic."

"Drastic is the only way to get through. Remember, it's for her own safety."

"I'll talk to her."

Jayce nodded. Sometimes it seemed to Grant as though Jayce were in charge. At times it bothered him; now he was grateful for Jayce's guidance. He had lost control of his daughter. And he wasn't sure how to get it back.

Alex was chastising himself for once again not getting Winslow's phone number when he had an idea. He dialed a number.

"May I speak with Grant Talbot, please?" he asked when a man answered. "This is Alex Díaz from *Mojo*, a newspaper that covered an event he attended recently."

There was a pause, and the man's voice chilled considerably. "Mr. Talbot isn't available. I can leave him a message."

This had to be Jayce. He obviously knew Alex was the man Ashlyn had run to. No way was Jayce going to take a message for Grant Talbot, nor would he give a message to Winslow.

"No thanks," Alex said, frustrated as he hung up.

Winslow was like Cinderella: she always left before he could get her number. Instead of leaving a glass shoe, she left him with questions, concerns, and a desire that was keeping him up at night.

It was time to talk to his resources.

Winslow was surprised to find Grant at her door that evening. From the pained look on his face, he knew about the incident at Ashlyn's apartment. She invited him in and offered him a drink.

He didn't sit, nor did he acknowledge her offer. He stood there and asked, "Are you taking drugs?"

She blinked, unable to even comprehend the question.

"Just be honest with me, Winslow. I can handle anything but lies."

"I've never taken drugs, not even a sleeping pill. You think I'm on drugs because I'm concerned that Jayce is emotionally abusing Ashlyn. Jayce told you how I—wait; he'd say that I attacked her. Yes, I went a little overboard, but only because I wanted answers and I knew that Jayce was hightailing it over so I wouldn't get those answers. He's got her brainwashed, and he's got you brainwashed, too." She didn't like the calculated way Grant was studying her, without love or emotion at all.

"I've already asked you to stop this groundless investigation of yours. I asked you to trust me."

"About the hit-and-run. But this is more than that. This is

about Ashlyn's safety. A woman at the marina said Ashlyn looked like an abused woman. She works in a woman's shelter, so she recognized the body language. I realized that she's right. Ashlyn isn't tamed, Dad. She's cowed. He's got her under his thumb."

Now she saw disappointment in Grant's expression. "You went to the marina, the one where the Cubans' boat was launched. Looking for witnesses, I presume, who could place Ashlyn and Jayce there at the time of the accident."

Emotion prickled her eyes and the back of her throat. "I went to the hospital and saw that little girl, the one who survived the hit-and-run. And no, I couldn't let it go. But it's not only about that girl anymore. It's about your daughter. Look at what Jayce is capable of. Leaving the scene of an accident knowing that people were seriously injured. He had me locked in the trunk of my car." Now the emotion was breaking through, and she didn't want to tamp it down. "And at the marina, Jayce had me shot with a stun gun. I lay there for several minutes, unconscious on the boat ramp. That's the man who's marrying your daughter, whom you see as a son. Dad, open your eyes. Look at what's going on, what he's doing."

She swiped at her eyes, realizing the toll all this had taken on her. "Jayce suggested that I was doing drugs, right? He probably said I'm nuts. That's what he wants you to think. He wants me out of the picture."

"Paranoia is one of the side effects of drugs."

"I'm not taking drugs."

"If you don't get help . . ."

She searched his eyes, seeing his emotions now. "How can I get help for something I'm not doing?"

"See a psychologist. Get some kind of help, Winslow. You can't keep going on like this. I can't keep going on like this. I feel torn between my two daughters."

"I'm just trying to get the truth. I don't want Ashlyn hurt."

"If you don't get help, I'm . . . going to have to cut you off . . . financially."

It had taken a great deal of effort to say those words, but he had said them, and they stuck her right in the chest. And not because she wouldn't have his money.

"I suppose Jayce suggested that ultimatum, too," she said quietly, and could see it was true.

He only took her accusation as one more piece of evidence of her overwrought paranoia. "It doesn't matter who suggested it. I don't see any other way to force you to get help."

She walked to her purse and removed the credit card he had made her take in the first place. She handed him the keys to the Mercedes as well as to her Volvo. "The car is at the police station. I'll have them contact you when it's ready."

He had clearly thought she'd crumble at the thought of losing his support. She had money in her accounts. Not a lot, but enough to get her by until she could get another job.

He stared at the keys in his hand and then handed them back. "The car is yours. It's in your name. When you get it back, return the Mercedes."

That was as much as he'd relent. He kept the card and walked out the door. Grant didn't like losing control of his daughters. But Winslow couldn't back down, not now. She went to the window and watched him pull away in his Jaguar through the opening into the courtyard. She might not have crumbled, but her heart was falling to pieces. Why did it hurt so much?

Because giving her money was his way of giving her love. He might have lost his affection for her, but she had lost something, too. She'd lost respect for her father.

When her doorbell rang later that evening, she hoped it would be Grant, ready to stumble over himself with apologies. Ready to believe her. "Hold on!" she called, racing to the bathroom to smooth on her Dermablend cover makeup. *Her mask.* The small container of thick makeup felt heavier than usual. She covered the lines, ran to the door—and found Alex standing there.

He walked right in. "I'm not leaving until you give me your phone number. That's number one. Number two, two days ago you get yourself shot by a stun gun, you tell me you suspect your sister's fiancé of doing it, and then you disappear to leave me wondering if you're dead, alive, or somewhere in between." His face was infused with ire, but it faded a little when he took her in.

She was wearing blue pajamas with cows jumping over moons. On her feet were the pink slippers that reminded her of her grandmother who had died years ago. Her hair was in pigtails. She was too surprised and too annoyed to be embarrassed. Well, mostly. "Somehow I missed the part about having to check in with you."

"You ran off before I could outline it for you."

"What?" Now her face flushed with anger. "Okay, let me outline it for you. I didn't ask you to come to the marina to save me and I don't have to check in with you."

"If you're going to put yourself in dangerous places, then yes, you do. Maybe this guy is behind the hit-and-run, or maybe it's political, but if you're snooping around you're going to get hurt. The least you can do is let me know you're alive once in a while. And tell me what you're up to *before* you're up to it." He took her in again, from head to toe, and the corner of his mouth twitched.

She leaned against the back of the overstuffed chair in front of the fountain, crossed her arms in front of her chest, and narrowed her eyes at him. "You can't come barging in here demanding things from me. We're not even friends technically. Or anything more."

He stood just inches in front of her and crossed his arms, too. "You used me for information. That gives me the right. And against my better judgment, I care about you. That gives me the right. Because you're blinded by this mission, and you need someone who can tell you that you're out of your head for sneaking around marinas at dusk. Because you need someone to accompany you. And because I have a feeling you don't have anyone right now to do that . . . and to pull you up when you've been knocked down. And maybe because you also need someone who can kiss you senseless once in a while, just to balance things out."

Those words, along with the desire crackling in his dark eyes, had an effect similar to that of the stun gun. Her muscles contracted, she could hardly think, and she felt a jolt run along her veins. She told herself the jolt was annoyance at his arrogance, nothing to do with remembering his kiss way too clearly. Or that he'd loved her article, had seen passion in it. Maybe she did have passion somewhere deep inside her. Or maybe she had that passion for Alex. And that was a bad idea.

"This particular arrogance you have . . . is it something that runs in your family or is it part of being a Latino?"

"Probably a little of both. Cuban men, at least the ones in my family, are known to be loyal, fiercely protective"—he leaned closer with every word—"passionate . . ."

"Hotheaded," she supplied.

"Not where you're concerned, not anymore."

That stopped her. "Why not?" She'd gotten more passionate because of him, and he was less passionate because of her?

"You taught me a valuable lesson in jumping to conclusions. I've been wrong about you more than once."

She tilted her head. "Wrong how?"

"When we met that first night, I thought you were cool, rich, beautiful, yes, maybe a little shallow, and the type of woman who thought she was too good for anyone but her social class." He gave a soft laugh. "I would have never pegged you for someone who would sneak around old warehouses and marinas, who would reveal her own pain to write so beautifully about a little Cuban girl."

"I didn't know about that woman, either." She loosened her crossed arms. "So am I still cool?"

"On the outside." He moved his hands around her, barely

skimming her hair and shoulders. It made her want him to touch her. "You have a force field around you. I think you've had it for a long time."

She didn't like hearing that, even though she knew it was true. "I'm not rich anymore. Grant gave me an ultimatum: drop my investigation or I'm cut off. I'm sure Jayce was behind it. I've learned that if someone doesn't like him, he wants her cut out. He did that to Ashlyn's best friend too."

Alex dropped his hands to his sides. "See how you moved that conversation to someone else? Very smooth."

"I don't like talking about myself. All right, so you don't think I'm shallow anymore. Right?"

"Right. But you're still beautiful."

She tried to hide her frown at that. "Is that important to you? Beauty?"

He ran his fingers down her face. "Yes, very. But I'm talking about inner beauty."

She wanted to believe that, but to prove it she would have to show him her real face. The imperfect one. The thought seized her insides.

His voice was soft. "You said you feel like you wear a mask."

She had opened up to Alex more than anyone else in her life, but she just couldn't reveal that part of her. "I don't know what I was saying. I'd just been shocked."

He knew she was lying; she could tell by the slow way he nodded. "I wish I didn't like you so much. You're the first woman I've ever met who made me cautious. I don't know that it's a bad thing necessarily. It's just . . . different."

A meow made them both turn to the fountain, and Salt wandered out from beneath the foliage. He was wary, having decided to brave the stranger in order to rub against Winslow's leg.

Alex knelt down and offered his hand. "Hey there. What's your name?"

Winslow felt odd answering for the cat, but she said Salt's

name. He slowly approached, his whiskers twitching. Obviously approving of Alex, Salt rubbed against his hand, putting his scent on Alex. Winslow watched Alex's face as he realized that Salt's face was warped.

He cupped the cat's face. "What happened to you, big guy?"

"He and his brother were stray kittens when they climbed into a car engine to get warm. Someone started the car. His face became permanently schmooshed."

"Schmooshed, huh?" He turned back to the cat. "Poor guy."

Pepper inched his way out, two steps forward, one step back. Alex did the same thing with him, holding out his hand and letting Pepper approach him at his own pace. He did, but he didn't rub Alex's hand. Pepper was more comfortable staying a few inches away. Alex slowly reached out and touched the torn ear. The white blind eye blinked at the gentle touch.

Alex looked at Pepper with a tilted head and thoughtful expression. Then he looked at her. "You got these two from a shelter?"

"Sure."

"And these weren't the only cats there, right?"

"They had lots of kittens. What's the big deal?"

There was a deal; she could see it in his eyes. She couldn't tell what he thought of that, and it drove her crazy to wonder. To make matters worse, he stood and took in her apartment. She felt as though he were looking at her naked body, assessing each curve, the three moles on her stomach, and the too-large space between her big toe and the rest.

"What?" she asked when she couldn't stand it anymore.

"You're right; it does look like my restaurant."

That's not what he was thinking. By the spark in his eyes, he liked what he saw, at least.

Salt surprised her by stretching up the length of Alex's leg, begging for more petting. He obliged, scratching the cat beneath his chin. When Salt ambled off a minute later, Alex pulled out his cell phone. "Give me your phone number."

"Wait a minute. How did you find me?"

"I'm a newspaper man. I have my resources."

"Uh-huh. You have my address but not my number?"

"My source couldn't get that."

She recited the number and then her cell number. He pulled out a card on which he'd written his cell number and home information on the back. "If you have some crazy idea about sneaking around, call me. I don't think my heart could handle finding you passed out somewhere again. Or worse."

Those words warmed her from the inside out, even though it sounded as though he was going to leave. She wanted to ask him to stay, and she knew she should let him go. The apartment felt different with him in it. Charged with a spicy sensuality. Warmer. His tight white pants and black cotton shirt didn't hurt.

He lingered at the door, and she wanted to think he was torn between leaving and asking to stay. He was cautious around her. Only around her. He probably wouldn't ask to stay.

His gaze lingered on Salt for a few moments before rising to her. "Your dad gave you an ultimatum. You didn't cave in?"

"What he took away wasn't just money. I realized money is his way of giving love. Since he came into my life, he's done so much for me. I've always felt that I owed him for that. But he asked me to let go of something that is very important to me. He asked me to stop looking into a man who I believe is a danger to his daughter. I couldn't do it. He told my editor at *Dazzle* to force me to go to Italy to cover a stupid truffle festival. Sebastian gave me an ultimatum, too."

"And you quit."

She nodded. It felt so good to see admiration in his face over her choices that tears tickled the back of her throat. She'd become so emotional since opening that valve.

"And this was the guy who said you didn't have passion?"

She nodded again.

He shook his head, obviously disagreeing with Sebastian.

He touched her chin. "You have plenty of passion. You just have to learn what to do with it."

She felt that tingle in her veins again. "Yes, I do."

He cleared his throat and seemed to shake away whatever thought had jumped to mind. "Are you all right money-wise?"

"I'm fine, thanks. I was planning on paying Grant back for the down payment he put on this place. I can live off that while I . . . well, until I figure all this out."

"So what's next? Where are you going to look now? The boat's probably gone."

She pulled her pigtails loose. "Maybe ask around at the marina some more." At his quick inhalation, she added, "I'll bring you along, Mr. Macho Cuban Male, all right?" She gave him a smile, but it quickly faded. "The truth is, I just don't know. But I'll think of something."

"I'm sure." He pointed to the card. "Call me."

It was an order, but she couldn't blame him. He cared about her. At the moment, he was the only person who did. "Yes, sir."

He paused, as though he wanted to say—or do—more. His gaze swept over her face, resting on her mouth long enough to make her lick her lips in an automatic gesture, long enough to warm the pit of her stomach.

"I'd better go," he said, as though something inside was arguing in the other direction. He opened the door and stepped out.

She walked to the door. "Thanks. For caring."

The look he gave her said it wasn't his choice. As he started to turn away, she said, "Oh, and I don't."

He stopped. "Don't what?"

"Your last supposition of me from that first night we met. I don't."

She closed the door and leaned against it, her mouth curled into a smile. Maybe he'd figure it out, or at the least he'd go crazy trying to remember what he'd said. He'd considered her a woman who thought she was too good for anyone but her social class. She'd never met many people outside her social class. And now that she had . . .

She dared a peek between the wooden blinds. He was standing just outside the glow of light by her door trying to remember.

And then he did. With a pained expression, he rubbed his hand through his hair and reluctantly walked toward the stairs. She hoped he didn't hear her chirp of a laugh.

"Alejandro," she whispered, pushing away from the window. She sat down on the floor and let her cats climb on her. "Alejandro," she said again and again until the word rolled off her tongue.

"Alejandro, what am I going to do with you?"

She had ideas that involved Cuban music and a soft bed or maybe the couch or, heck, just about anywhere. She realized, though, that his admission about her making him cautious had made it harder. She couldn't just make love with him and keep her soul hidden. He wouldn't accept that. And she wasn't sure she could open herself up and show him everything.

He was sitting in his car across the street from Winslow's apartment. When the spic walked out, he blinked twice. The guy from the marina. After he'd zapped her with the stun gun, he heard footsteps coming around the storage building. He'd walked to the other side in time to keep out of sight. The guy had leaned over her. He knew her name, so they were acquaintances.

He hoped that was all there was to it. She was a pain in the ass all by herself. He had given her a final warning and hoped she'd take it and go back to her rich life. Because she was going to lose a lot more than her nose if she kept sticking it into his business.

15

Winslow woke, spent some time loving her cats, and then fed them as she ate yogurt for breakfast. She rarely turned the news on in the mornings, but she did now. She wasn't sure why; the hit-and-run hadn't been news for almost a week now. So she was surprised to hear the announcer say, "And after the break we have an update on the hit-and-run boating accident on Biscayne Bay that took the lives of two men and severely injured a young girl."

Winslow sat on the arm of the couch and waited through what seemed like endless commercials. Who cared about the embarrassment of body odor when all she wanted to know was had Elena taken a turn for the worse? No, she couldn't even think that. The girl's bandaged face came to mind and with it all the emotions Winslow had felt when she'd talked to Lidia at the hospital.

Finally the newscaster returned and recapped the accident. "Authorities have released new information that puts a deadly twist on the so-called accident. It now appears that Luis García, who was found in the water, was purposely run down after he'd apparently jumped out of the boat prior to impact."

Winslow didn't hear the wrap-up. Her brain was buzzing at the implication. Jayce had run down a man on purpose. But why? Had he known the men? Did he have a grudge

against them? Or had it started out as an accident, with Jayce
having to run down a witness who could identify him?

Salt, sensing her distress, jumped on her lap. "No, he
had to have known the brothers. He obviously has connections here in Miami, enough to find those two sleazebags.
Maybe he was staying with or near the Garcías. Maybe he
even had business dealings with them. This makes Jayce a
murderer. And he's going to marry my sister in four days.
No wonder she ran away from him, and no wonder he had
to grab her hard enough to put bruises on her. She must
have been terrified. How could she even think of marrying
him after that?"

She stroked Salt as she talked, her fingers leaving fur-
rows in the cat's silky fur. "What kind of hold does he have
on her?"

Urgency flooded her. What would Grant think once he
heard this? Jayce had probably given him some whopper of
a story. Would this revelation jive?

She dislodged Salt and took the phone from the hook.
Alex's card was sitting on her kitchen table, and she dialed
his home number. She listened to his Spanish-flavored voice
tell her that he wasn't there and to leave a message, and then
she dialed his work number.

"Did you hear the news about the hit-and-run?" she asked
when he answered.

"Yeah. No wonder Jayce or whoever is behind this wants
you to butt out. It's murder, Winslow. That means you've
been lucky up till now."

"It also means my sister is about to marry a murderer. I
can't let that happen. I have an idea."

"I was afraid you were going to say that. Tell me what
you're thinking."

"I'm wondering if Jayce didn't have a connection to the
Garcías. All this time I've been thinking it was an accident.
Now it looks as though he had a reason to run their boat
down. Jayce has connections in Miami. He lied about stay-

ing at the Astonia. Maybe he's been living here for years. He could be lying about the whole inheritance battle."

"Whoa, whoa, whoa."

"I can't *whoa*, Alex. I've got four days to save my sister from marrying a murderer. What we need to do is question the Garcías' business associates and friends, see if anyone recognizes Jayce's picture. If we can make that connection, I'll have something tangible to give to the authorities."

"At least you're saying 'we.' That makes me feel much better. Let's get together tonight and figure this out. I'll make you dinner at my place."

"All right."

"Should I pick you up?"

"I can meet you there." She tapped the card against her nails. "I've got the address."

"Come early. Don't do anything without me. No arguments."

She smiled. "Yes sir, Mr. Macho Cuban—"

"Damn straight. And don't you forget it."

Hearing the smile in his voice made her smile, too. "I won't."

When she hung up, she started investigating on the computer. That should be exempt from his orders. She found the name of the law firm representing some of the Bishop family. She then looked up the number on the Internet and spoke to the receptionist, who patched her through to Mr. Scruggins, the attorney.

"Hello, I'm Blythe Danner," she said, and then grimaced as she realized that was an actress's name. "I'm with the Danner and Portsmouth law firm here in Miami, Florida. Our client Jayce Bishop is involved in the Bishop inheritance dispute and he asked me to call and find out the status of the case."

"Jayce Bishop?" She could hear some shuffling in the background as perhaps the attorney pulled out a file.

"He's one of the Bishop grandchildren." *Isn't he?*

"I'm afraid I can't divulge any information about this case. I don't have you as the attorney of record for anyone involved."

"Please check again. Look under Jayce Bishop's name."

"Have your client contact me directly." And he hung up.

She made a face at the phone before pressing the off button. What she'd been hoping for was a, *Jayce who?*

She leaned back in the chair. "I'm going to find out your dirty little secrets, Jayce Bishop. Just wait and see."

When Winslow headed out late that afternoon, the air was beginning to chill, as the sun took its downward trek. She felt a hum in her veins. *From the new direction,* she told herself. *Nothing to do with seeing Alex.*

"Alejandro," she said, practicing. The name had become a mantra of sorts.

Just as she was about to get into Grant's Mercedes, that eerie feeling of being watched assailed her. She casually looked around as she sat in the driver's seat. Still nothing suspicious.

"Lord, protect me," she whispered as she backed out of her parking spot.

She drove from her familiar roads south to Coral Gables. Along the way, she stopped to purchase a bottle of dark rum to contribute to dinner. She rather liked the idea of having a Mojito again. She could still taste it—and Alex's kiss.

Ten minutes later, she pulled onto the side street and waited at the light. This wasn't the greatest area of town. Several of the storefronts across the way were abandoned, and there was evidence of the homeless who took up residence in the doorways. The side street didn't continue straight. Cardboard boxes filled the alley between the two shopping strips malls. When the light turned green, she followed the line of cars through, ready to turn left. The driver of the car two spaces ahead slammed on his brakes as a couple ran across the crosswalk. Tires screeched, brake lights flashed, and Winslow lurched to a stop an inch from the bumper in front of her.

The sounds of gunshots didn't fit the scene, nor did the screams as people dived to the asphalt. Glass shattered. Cars came to a standstill. She threw herself down on the front seat. How many shots were fired? She could only see blue sky and the tops of buildings from her position. A woman screamed nearby. Winslow waited. No more gunshots.

Please don't let there be another sniper running loose.

She heard voices. A siren wailed from the distance. She slowly lifted her head. People were beginning to get out of their cars. She opened her door and got out, searching for the source of the crying. A Spanish woman was sitting in the driver's seat of her car. Winslow ran over at the same time as two men did. One spoke Spanish, and he finally got out of the woman that she wasn't hit, only scared. She was staring at a bullet hole that was only inches from her face. Winslow understood the fear of seeing death so close.

Several people looked at a car that had been about to turn onto the side street that Winslow had been leaving. She could hear them talking about the bullet that had hit the side of the car. Another Spanish woman was now comforting the distraught driver.

Winslow only then realized she hadn't turned her engine off and started back toward her car to do so.

"Are you all right?" one man asked her.

She'd wrapped her arms around herself, only now understanding that she had been close to death herself. "I . . . Yeah, I'm okay."

One police car arrived, followed shortly by another. She walked to her car to grab her purse. Her first thought was to call Grant, but she halted it immediately. Of course he would be concerned, and he'd likely come right over. Then he would insinuate that this was a result of her snooping.

Was this a result of her investigation? Surely not. She had been driving somewhere, not asking questions. This was probably gang related or, even scarier, random violence.

She did punch in numbers and pressed the call key. Alex answered, and she felt a rush of relief at the sound of his voice.

"I'm going to be a little late," she said, hearing the tremble in her voice.

"What's wrong?"

"There was a shooting. No, nothing to do with the hit-and-run. The police are here. No one was hit. Someone shot about two or three times I'd guess. Sniper-type shootings."

"Where are you? I'll be right there."

"You don't have to—"

"Street names."

She would have kidded him about the macho Cuban male thing, but she couldn't find a speck of humor. Besides, she would be too grateful for his presence. She recited the street names from the signs.

"I'll be right there."

The police cars had increased threefold and officers were separating the witnesses. Two officers were redirecting backed-up traffic. Others were questioning those who had been in close proximity to the intersection. An ambulance pulled up. The couple who had raced across the road had skid marks on their legs where they'd hit the pavement. Blood dripped from the woman's knees, and her palms were scraped. They'd been particularly vulnerable.

"Ma'am, you all right?" an officer asked Winslow, his gaze assessing her.

She nodded.

"Where is your car?"

She mutely pointed, realizing she'd left the door open.

"We need you to stick around for a while. ID will be here soon with the Total Station to take note of the positions of the cars and bullet trajectories. We'll need your car to remain in position."

"Total Station?"

"It's a new investigative tool. We were the first to use it." He was obviously proud. "It won't take long once they're here."

Did she look as though she was about to faint? Possibly, because he guided her to a squad car and helped her inside. The officer knelt in front of her. "Tell me what happened."

Finally words came out, though they sounded hoarse. "I was turning. Someone hit their brakes and then there were gunshots."

He made her go over every detail twice. As she answered questions, ID arrived to assess the scene. They set up a tripod with what looked like a camera and small keypad on top, reminding her of the equipment surveyors used.

It was nice to focus on something else for a few minutes. "Is that the Total Station you mentioned?" she asked him.

"Yep. The techs use that laser beam to register measurements that will be downloaded to that laptop you see there. A program will draw the scene using animation. It's called forensic mapping."

She would have found it fascinating if her brain weren't half-functioning at the moment. Still, the writer part remembered seeing a newscast about lack of funding for CSI functions and wondered what publication would be interested in an in-depth article about it.

"If you start to feel light-headed, put your head between your legs. Is there someone you can call?"

"I've already called a friend. When can I leave?"

"Soon. I'll be right back."

She did feel a bit woozy, but she leaned her cheek against the seat instead and watched the techs work. A news crew arrived and filmed the scene from behind the barriers.

In that same distant way she heard a familiar voice. "I'm with the woman in the Volvo. She's sitting in that squad car."

"Hey, Stevens, the woman in your car been questioned yet?"

"Yeah, she's clear."

"Thanks."

Alex made his way to her, and she felt something lift in her chest. He knelt in front of her as the officer had done, though he took her limp hands in his. "Are you all right?"

She nodded, feeling detached like a balloon set free from the rest of the bunch. Alex kept her from flying away, with his firm hold on her hands.

"Tell me what happened," he said, his voice pulling her closer to earth.

Alex digested what she told him. "Will you be all right for a minute?" When she nodded, he waved one of the officers over and discussed something with him. When they pointed to the two cars directly in front of her, she saw the bullet hole and broken glass. An ID tech called out that he'd found one of the bullets. Her gaze went back to Alex and the officer. Alex was gesturing, trying to make a point. The officer didn't look convinced.

Stevens, the officer who had questioned her, walked over. "You're free to go, but we need to keep your car until we're done with all of the photographs and measurements."

Oh, brother, another car in police custody. "When do you think I'll be able to get it back?"

"If it wasn't hit, probably tomorrow. We'll let you know. Sounds like you have a ride home." He smiled. "Thank you for your cooperation." He returned to the scene.

Alex returned, and she said, "I can leave now, but my car can't." She explained the possible time line.

"That's all right. I don't want you driving anyway. You're still in shock."

She blinked, trying to pull herself together. She couldn't be in shock. She hadn't even been shot! "I'm okay. What were you talking to the officer about?"

"I'll tell you at the house."

"I don't know, Alex. I just need to—"

"Come to my house and let me take care of you." He'd

done it again, but she didn't have the heart to argue with him.

She pointed to her car. "I guess I won't be able to retrieve the rum I bought for dinner."

He smiled. "That's all right; I've got plenty."

The sun was getting ready to sink behind the cloudless horizon. As they walked past the barricades, cameras and microphones were shoved at her. Thankfully Alex steered her past them and to his Camaro. Within twenty minutes they were out of the traffic snarl and driving into a neighborhood of neatly kept Spanish-style homes. Yards were landscaped with lush foliage. Even in winter the hibiscus and bougainvillea bloomed wildly in their vibrant colors. Some of the houses looked ancient, with crumbling entrance gates and vine-covered walls. Old-fashioned streetlights, fountains, and arbors added to the overall elegance. The sunset added to the color.

"What?" she asked when she saw him looking at her for the fourth time.

"Just checking on you. You're smiling at least."

"I like the area."

Alex's house was white with a red tile roof. Lush vegetation grew right against the exterior walls. The overgrown look was likely on purpose, since the thick Saint Augustine grass was trimmed. Bright purple bougainvillea climbed up one corner of the house, its limbs sprawling like spider legs. It complemented the frangipani tree with pink blossoms. Fern fronds fluttered in the breeze. A passion vine was trying to take over a bush covered in red flowers. It all spoke to her soul.

He waited for the massive wooden garage door to open and pulled inside. She realized she was still staring through the windshield, though now it was at rows of shelving. *Get hold of yourself. You're all right. And you've got Alex.*

She opened the door before he could open it for her, and made a point of getting out on her own. She hadn't fooled him one bit. He was assessing her, seeing the shock still clinging to the edges.

"I'm okay. I've just never been involved in a shooting before." She turned to him. "Thanks for coming out."

"Anytime." He was standing in front of her, looking at her with compassion in his brown eyes. He tipped up her chin. "I have a feeling . . ."

"What?" she said on the breath she'd held waiting for his next words.

"I just have a feeling," he said, leaving it at that.

She'd made him cautious. She would have to accept that and his nonanswer. For now anyway. He steered her outside and closed the garage door by pressing a button. "I'd rather have you come in the front door than step over piles of laundry," he said. With his arm still around her shoulders, he led her toward the wood door that matched the one on the garage.

"I like the knocker," she said, reaching out and touching the wrought-iron lion's head. She lifted it and let it drop. It made a solid sound and left a pleasant ringing in her ears.

"I bought it when they tore down an old house around the corner. It came from a castle in Spain." He unlocked the door and guided her inside.

She instantly felt at home. "It's a bit like your restaurant," she said, touching the leaf of a potted palm near the front door. "Silk! A travesty!"

He caught her humor and smiled. "I cheat. What can I say? I'm not as good with plants as you are."

"I'll bet you don't even name them."

"Name them? The plants?"

Oops. Why had she said that? Because he was so easy to talk to. "Some people actually name their plants. Silly, huh?"

"You name them, don't you?"

She found she couldn't lie to him, not when he was giving her a teasing smile. "Maybe."

He surprised her by giving her a quick kiss. "You're adorable. Come on; I've got the table out by the pool set. I'll fix some drinks."

"And then you'll tell me what you and that officer were talking about. I'd like to look around if that's all right."

The floors were wood. The walls were off-white, with old-fashioned posters touting Cuba as a vacation spot. The wicker couch had plump, canvas cushions. The fan blades were wooden leaves that stirred the breeze coming in from the open sliders leading out to the lanai. He'd left so fast he hadn't even closed the sliders or turned off the Latin jazz pouring from the speakers.

She wandered over to the bar he'd fashioned in the corner of his living room. It was made of bamboo; the countertop was slices of bamboo in an acrylic slab. Everything was tropical, warm, even the red and blue macaw perched on a piece of driftwood on a large stand.

"Hello, pretty girl," he said, bobbing his head up and down.

Alex laughed softly. "He knows what he likes."

"You taught him to say that?"

He walked over with two glasses filled with rum, ice cubes, and mint leaves. "Yeah, to impress all my lady friends."

Of course he knew that's what she was getting at. "Does it work?"

"Actually, the guy I inherited the bird from thought he was a girl. With parrots, it's hard to tell."

"I'm not sure I even want to know how they tell."

"Luckily I was spared the details. My sister owns a pet shop, and she suspected that Girlie Bird wasn't a girl at all. She was right." He rolled his eyes. "She's so hard to live with when she's right. Anyway, I renamed him Havana. He was always crotchety. That's why I got him. My cousin Alberto married a woman who had a little girl. The parrot bit the girl and would dive-bomb the wife. Alberto begged me to take him. Ever since I renamed him and acknowledged his male status, he's been pleasant as can be."

"Ah, a Cuban macho male parrot."

"Bubble butt." Havana bobbed low and let out a whirring noise. His pupils shrank to pinpoints.

"None of his obnoxious vocabulary came from me." Alex offered the parrot his arm, and Havana stepped onto it. As was obviously their routine, Alex walked out onto the lanai and put him on an identical perch out there. "Unless you're hungry right now, I thought we'd sit and enjoy a drink before dinner."

"Sounds great." She wasn't hungry, even though something smelled absolutely delicious. A drink and some time would be just the thing to settle her stomach.

The day's light was nearly gone now. The lights hidden in the foliage made up for the impending darkness, giving the lanai a festive atmosphere. The pool was small and surrounded by brown tiles. A waterfall burbled gently at the far end. Back here, as in the yard, palms and other bushes grew in abundance. Like Alex, they were all just a little wild. He even had a banana tree in the far corner.

Once he had pushed in her chair, she said, "Okay, tell me what you and the officer were talking about."

"Drawing it will make more sense." He produced a notepad and pencil. "Here's the intersection. Here's your car as you're pulling through. The officer thinks the shots came from the alley here." He sketched the trajectory. "You said the guy two cars ahead slammed on his brakes for the pedestrians, right?" She nodded. "If he hadn't, your car would have been here." He drew a box around the car in the middle of the intersection. "That means that you were in the line of fire. Winslow, I think you were the target."

16

Grant, Jayce, and Ashlyn were eating sandwiches in the office. It seemed that most meals were eaten in the office anymore. And with the evening news on. Grant had always kept tabs on area events, but now it was his job to know what was happening in Miami. At least he hoped it *would be* his job.

Right now, though, they were going over Ashlyn and Jayce's wedding plans. His daughter was getting married that Saturday. It seemed unbelievable. Incredible. Fast.

Winslow's words floated through his mind. Whose idea was it to move it up so much? But Ashlyn seemed just as excited about moving it up as Jayce did. Grant felt guilty just thinking about Winslow's suspicions. He also felt empty without her around. He'd been sure that she would cave in when he gave her the ultimatum. Why was she so adamant about her suspicions? Could it be drugs? Jealousy? Both?

He hated to think that it could be either.

"Daddy, are you listening to me?" Ashlyn's voice cut through his thoughts like an ill-sharpened blade. She was hunched over a legal pad at his desk.

"Sorry, what did you say?"

"I was thinking that we'd have little fishbowls on each table filled with glass marbles, and with fresh flowers sprouting out of them. Surrounding the bowls would be colored candles of varying heights. Linen tablecloths with matching chair covers. Don't you think it'd be cute to . . ."

Her words were carried away by his much heavier thoughts. He didn't do trivial details well. He wanted Ashlyn to be happy, but his other daughter was very much on his mind.

"Daddy, you're a million miles away. Are you just not interested or . . . you're thinking about Winslow, aren't you?"

"It's hard not to. She should be involved. She could tell you if it would be cute to have . . . well, whatever it was you suggested. She's your sister."

Ashlyn usually chimed in with "stepsister" whenever he made that statement, but she surprised him this time. "She made the mess she's in. But yes, it would have been nice to have her around. It would . . ." Her voice had thickened, and she swallowed hard.

God, he hadn't even thought about how not having her mother around during this special time would affect Ashlyn. He reached over and gave her a hug. He'd never been good about discussing the heart-wrenching issues of her mother's death. The brain tumor had taken her two months after the diagnosis. It hurt to think about it still.

"Maybe it would be better to postpone the wedding. That way you'd have more time to get things set up, like all the table froufrous; maybe things will be smoothed out with Winslow by then."

Jayce put his arm around her. "Is that what you want, honey? You know I'd do anything for you. Do you need more time?"

She faltered but eventually shook her head. "No, this is already underway. Let's keep it on schedule."

Ashlyn *had* changed. It was for the better, wasn't it? And she wasn't as obsessed with fashion and adding little doohickeys to her clothing. She was smiling. And why not, the way Jayce doted on her. Grant shifted his thoughts away from Winslow's paranoid suspicions.

"I think about Winslow, too," Ashlyn said. "It feels wrong, the way things are."

Jayce said, "Winslow's got some issues to work through. Once she does, everything will be fine. I think the best thing to do is leave her alone for a bit. If she really needs us, she'll call."

The news anchor drew their attention when she announced a follow-up to that afternoon's breaking story. "As we reported earlier, shots were fired into traffic at five this afternoon." She gave the location, and a shot of the scene filled the screen. "No one was critically injured. Two pedestrians sustained scrapes when they hit the pavement. Bullets barely missed passengers but hit two vehicles. One woman cheated death by a mere inch."

Footage showed the aftermath, with investigators questioning witnesses. A woman was crying as she spoke with a police officer.

"Investigators won't speculate whether this was a random shooting or gang related. Right now they have no suspects."

When the camera panned across the intersection, Ashlyn said, "Oh my God," voicing Grant's thoughts as he saw his Mercedes and then Winslow sitting in a patrol car.

Both he and Ashlyn stood and walked closer to the television. Grant said, "They said no one got hurt, no one got shot. That must mean she's all right." He couldn't see her face because of the shadows, but she must have been terrified. And she hadn't called him.

That hurt, that she hadn't called her father in her time of need. Because he'd cut her off. Because he hadn't been there for her.

"It's Alex Díaz!" Ashlyn said, pointing to the Latino man who ran to Winslow just before the camera focused in on one of the officers for comments. "Was he there, too?"

Jayce was still sitting, his gaze glued to the television. It made Grant feel a little better knowing that Jayce was as concerned as they were.

"Is this because she's been poking into the hit-and-run?" Ashlyn asked.

Jayce blinked and focused on her. Then he looked at Grant. "It might be. And just that possibility is why it's important to keep her out of our lives. If she chooses to put herself in danger, that's one thing. But dragging us in is another. She was obviously snooping around again. Look what part of town she was in."

Grant kept looking at the television. They were wrapping up the story, promising updates as the police released information. "I should check on her."

Jayce walked over and planted himself in front of Grant. "Not a good idea, Dad. Didn't you hear what I just said? If we stay in touch with her, we put ourselves in danger. It's her choice to continue looking into the hit-and-run. We warned her time and again. Now she's on her own. We can't afford to let her back into our lives."

"But she doesn't know the truth."

"Winslow wouldn't believe the truth. She would keep trying to pin it on me."

Grant had never felt so conflicted before. He actually wanted to justify his reasons for checking on his daughter, and his next thought was to do it without telling Jayce. Somehow Jayce had become in charge not just of Ashlyn's life but even Grant's. Jayce had become that important in their lives, that integral. And he was right. Letting Winslow back into their lives could be dangerous. Not telling her the truth was dangerous, too. Because if she somehow managed to find out the truth on her own, she could be in more danger than she realized.

Winslow's fingers tightened on the cool, slick glass as Alex's words dropped into her stomach like lumps of uncooked dough. "But . . . how? I've never taken this route before. How would that person have known where I would be? Or more precisely, where I would head next?"

"You said you stopped at the liquor store. If he was following you, that gave him time to park behind this building and wait for you to come out. He would assume that you'd continue the same way. Except you hit your brakes unexpectedly and he missed. It's speculation on my part. Not a huge assumption considering what's happened to you so far."

She took a gulp of the drink but kept her eyes on Alex. "What did the officer say?"

"He took note of my suspicions, but he didn't seem to buy them. Maybe you should have those two detectives you dealt with talk to the investigators of this shooting."

"They think I'm nuts. My claims will be chalked up to my paranoia. Maybe you're getting paranoid, too."

"I hope so." He drew a line through his sketch. "So you think Jayce might have a connection to the Garcías? Or maybe someone who knew the Garcías?"

"It's a possibility. If we can tie Jayce to them . . ." The rum was slowing her thoughts as well as her blood flow. "Except that he has an alibi, the alibi provided by a respected businessman running for governor. But it'll be a start." She pushed the drink away. "I'd better eat something."

"Coming right up."

"Can I help?"

"I could probably find something for you to do. Do you cook a lot?"

"I make a mean spaghetti with meat sauce." After he put her to work pouring the black beans into a bowl, she said, "Or are you insinuating that I employ a cook?"

He shrugged. "I figured people like you have people who cook for them. And clean up afterward."

Guiltily she thought of Esme. "My father does. I'm sure he always has. He comes from money as far back as you can imagine. My biological father, Paul, came from middle class. He was a daring entrepreneur and made a lot of money. I remember the times when my mother tried to cook meals, and I remember her happiness when we could afford a maid and a cook." She smiled at the memory, but it faded. "And after the accident . . ."

"What happened then?"

She watched him chop onions as though he'd done it a million times. He wasn't even looking at the sharp blade as it sliced; he was looking at her.

"Everything changed," she said simply. She focused on scooping the rice from the machine that steamed it into the ceramic bowl. She had never been ashamed of being penniless, but her mother's shame had permeated the way she viewed that time. "Two years later my mother married Grant and everything changed again." She blinked and met Alex's gaze. "For the better."

He was studying her, and it seemed as though he could see right through her. "There's more to it than that, and you're not going to tell me what it is. But someday you will, Winslow. Someday you'll tell me everything that you keep hidden. You'll tell me about the mask you feel you wear. When you're ready"—he cupped her face—"you'll show me everything."

His soft-spoken words tingled through her veins. There was no question, no request, in his voice. Just knowledge, and that made her shiver. The music changed to a sultry song that matched his eyes and the mood. She swallowed hard, and he seemed to reluctantly release her. He turned away and took the chicken out of the oven. The aroma of roasted garlic filled the air. She shakily took the bowls of rice and beans and followed him out to the lanai. His words had charged the atmosphere with sensuality and made the rum-induced languidness dangerous, at least around Alex.

Alejandro.

The song ended as they started to eat, and the DJ probably identified the previous songs and artists. Probably, because she didn't understand Spanish. She didn't need to. The lilting sound of the language was enjoyable all its own.

"Just eat with your hands," Alex said, and made her realize she was cutting the chicken leg with knife and fork. He had picked his up. "We don't stand on formality at Casa Díaz."

Awkwardly she picked up the chicken leg. "I'm beginning to find this addicting. Cuban food, I mean."

His eyes were on hers. "It does have a way of getting into your blood. You'll find yourself craving it if you haven't had any in a while."

She cleared her throat. "Um, I can imagine." She wasn't about to admit that she *had* been craving . . . the food, the Mojitos . . . him. But maybe he knew that.

He'd panfried the plantains until they were crisp at the edges and tender inside. While she enjoyed one of those for dessert, he made two more drinks. "If you're finished, we can sit out by the pool," he said when he brought them to the table.

"We should probably clean this up. . . ."

"I've got someone who comes in to clean once a week. She'll be in tomorrow."

Winslow lifted an eyebrow, and he gave her a sheepish smile. "My aunt started a cleaning service a couple of years ago, so I helped her by becoming her first client. I got spoiled."

He indicated that she take the plump chaise longue out by the pool. He pulled up a chair next to it, sat down, and handed her a drink.

"You have a lot of family," she said. "And you're close to them. I saw all the pictures inside. There were several taken right here by the pool."

"We get together every Sunday. Family is important to Cubans."

She wondered how she would fit into his family, what they would think of her. Then she realized that such musings led her into treacherous territory.

"What are you thinking?" he asked, obviously studying her again.

"I'm not ready to tell you," she said.

He nodded. "At least you didn't say, 'Nothing.' Because I know it was something."

She turned away from him in pretense of looking around the lanai. The foliage pressing against the screen, as though trying to come in, made the area private enough for skinny-dipping. Or other activities. "You're good at reading people."

"You have to be when you're a writer."

"I guess I still have things to learn."

He shifted closer so that she had no choice but to look at him. "You can practice now. What am I thinking?"

The corner of her mouth twitched. "You want to kiss me, but you're not sure if I want to kiss you."

"You're half-right."

She flushed. "You don't want to kiss me?"

"Not that part."

Relief. "But then . . ."

"I know you want to kiss me, but you're not sure you want me to see you naked. And I don't mean physically. I bet you haven't been with many men."

Now he was probing her intimately. "Two." One had been the son of a friend of her father's, and the other had been a neighbor. Neither had lasted for more than a year.

"And they weren't one-night stands?" he said with only a hint of question.

"No."

His voice was low now. She found it hard to look away from his eyes. "Were you in love with them?"

"I *liked* one of them a lot. He asked me to marry him, but I didn't feel anything . . . passionate for him. I didn't think it was fair to marry him. The other, well, he had a real attitude about people with money. He didn't even try to get along with Grant. He assumed that anyone I associated with would look down on him, and he carried that chip on his shoulder. Every time I spent money, he made snide remarks."

"How did Grant feel about him?"

She had to admit, "He didn't much care for Jake, either. Probably because of the chip."

Alex touched her chin. "Let me pose a totally theoretical

situation. Say you fell madly in love with a Latino. What would Grant think of that?"

It was hard to think with his finger trailing small circles beneath her chin. "I . . . I'm not sure."

"But?"

"I don't think he'd like it. He'd rather I marry someone he knows."

"Someone in his own circle. He made your life different. Better, you said. How much do you owe him?"

She set her drink down on the small table. "I'm not sure Grant is even in my life anymore. But if you're asking would I not allow myself to get involved with someone he might disapprove of . . . I would. Wouldn't. I mean, I wouldn't let what he thought stand in my way of falling madly in love with someone. Latin," she added. "Have you ever dated a non-Cuban woman?"

He didn't even have to think about it, which she supposed was a good sign. "No. Not on purpose, but Cuban women are the ones in my social circle. Not that I date a lot, with my job."

She liked hearing that, both parts. "What about your family? Would they approve if you fell madly in love with—?"

"You?" he said before she could finish.

She tried to hold back her smile. "A woman who wasn't Cuban," she clarified.

"If I loved her, they would love her, too." He was stroking her jawline now, slow, sweeping movements that intoxicated her more than the Mojitos. The thought of being part of his family tingled through her. She thought of his father, the brother she'd seen at the office, the sister who owned a pet shop. So different from her family, from her world.

Now she knew that her world had been made of glass; when it had been jarred, it had shattered. Alex's world was real. It was sturdy, a bit rougher perhaps, but it wouldn't break. She knew that she wanted to taste that world; she wanted to taste Alex. She didn't want to think about what he'd said earlier about her showing him everything. Right now she wanted to show him how much she longed to be part of him and his world, even if for a short while. She could have died earlier. She wanted to feel life, to feel her blood pulsing through her veins. She wanted Alex to send her blood rushing.

She slid her hand behind his neck and pulled his mouth against hers. Their kiss was hungry and tasted of rum and mint. His fingers slid into her hair and held her while he devoured her. She hadn't realized how much she'd wanted this until the rush of feelings overwhelmed her. He had obviously wanted this for a long time, too, and now he'd unleashed all of the passion that had been waiting like a caged lion.

His mouth, hot and wet, moved down her throat. He touched her everywhere, arms, stomach, and then more intimately. She touched him, too, and all the while they kissed and sometimes murmured something soft and unintelligible. At the same moment, they both decided that their clothing was too much of a barrier. She started to unbutton his shirt, and he pulled her top over her head, and she couldn't remember even taking off the rest of their clothes. She thought he said something about going to the bedroom, but she wasn't sure and didn't care.

She was about to protest when he stopped kissing her, but then he slid lower on her body, kissing and licking and nibbling her skin as he went, and then he spread her legs and dipped his tongue between her soft folds of flesh, and her sounds of protest changed to soft groans. Those changed to short, shallow gulps of air and then long moans as he gave her a delicious orgasm.

As she rocked in the aftershocks, she thought he said, "Be right back," and a few seconds later he returned with a crinkly package. She could see enough of him in the dim light to see how gorgeous he was. It had been a while since she'd been with a man, but that wasn't what made a tingle of both exhilaration and apprehension electrify her. Somehow she knew that making love with Alex would be different, would change her somehow. She would have to show him everything, and that thought terrified her. But she also knew she couldn't stop now. Her body, her heart, wouldn't let her.

He was watching her, and she hoped he couldn't see her thoughts cross her expression. She was afraid he had, because he gently pushed her back on the lounge and started kissing her even more ardently than before. She could taste herself on his tongue. It was erotic somehow.

She pushed him back a few inches and slid the sheath over him. He leaned down over her and eased into her slickness before moving rhythmically in and out. She could hear his ragged breathing, could see the glaze in his eyes as he looked at her. It seemed so much more intimate, looking at each other while being physically connected. It felt good, right. So did Alex.

"Alejandro," she whispered as she felt the pressure building inside her.

She could see his face transform at the word, which meant she'd said it right. He smiled, and the passion in his eyes changed to something deeper.

"Mi amor te adoro con toda mi alma eres la mujer mas bella del mundo te deseo tanto eres mi vida cuanto te quiero."

She said his name again and again as they moved together and then she exploded. She felt him follow moments later, and he squeezed her tighter than she'd ever been held. Slowly she felt his body relax; hers had already turned to the consistency of maple syrup.

He leaned back and looked at her. "You're incredible."

"Mm, you, too."

She could see enough of him to know he was smiling. "You said my name in Spanish."

"I've been practicing. My cats are beginning to think I renamed them Alejandro."

He kissed her again, quick and spontaneous.

"What did you say to me? In Spanish," she asked.

"Stay with me. I want you here all night. Will Salt and Pepper be all right?"

It touched her that he'd remembered their names and especially that he'd thought of them at all. "They'll be fine." She wasn't about to admit she'd put extra food in their bowls . . . just in case. But she knew that wasn't what he'd said. She knew the word *amor,* and that had nothing to do with her cats.

He stood, helped her up, and then pulled her flush against his naked body. He kissed her again, as though he couldn't get enough of her. Without any notice, he swung her up into his arms and carried her into his bedroom. The room was as simple as the rest of the house, with bamboo furniture and wood floors. The bedspread and curtains were made of a blue canvas that reminded her of the tropics.

He set her on the soft bed and kissed her again. "Make yourself at home; use whatever you need in the bathroom— there's a new toothbrush in the upper cabinet. I'm going to close up the house and put Havana away. Be right back."

She watched him walk naked out of the room and realized that she was as naked as he. This kind of nudity didn't bother her as much. Baring her soul was another matter. She went into the bathroom and cleaned up, brushed her teeth, and looked at her reflection. Her hazel eyes looked heavy, still glazed with pleasure. She'd never seen that look on her face and allowed herself to absorb it for a minute before reality set in.

She needed to wash the makeup off her face. Later, just before she went to sleep. She would get up very early and reapply it before Alex woke.

She was happy to see that he didn't entertain overnight guests often. There was no sign of women's toiletries. He only had a few items on hand, all male: expensive shaving gel, razor, and the rest of the basics. She caught herself touching the razor's handle, picturing him standing there shaving in the mornings. When she glanced at her reflection again, she still wore that glow of contentment. That's what it was. She was content with Alex and here in this house.

More than content, Winslow. You're in love with him.

The words stunned her. In love? That was . . . well, it was huge. She'd never been in love before. The humming in her veins, the warmth in her heart, all seemed to confirm it. So did the fear she felt. Before she could think about making a commitment, she had to let him see her naked face. And she would have to show him her soul. She just wasn't sure she could do that.

Two men sat in a car across the street from Alex Díaz's house. The one with the binoculars said, "They've been in there a long time. What do you think they're doing?"

The man in the driver's seat rolled his eyes. "What do you *think* they're doing?"

"I can't see anything. Alex knows the Garcías. It's possible they could put it all together."

"Then we'll have to stop them before they can do that. Let's just hope they got permanently sidetracked by hormones."

"Stunning her was fun. The way her eyes rolled into her head and her whole body twitched and then just drooped as though her bones had turned to jelly." He laughed at the memory. "She hasn't been to the marina since."

"But that was only yesterday." He sat back in his seat. "We'll keep an eye on her."

"There was something strange the other day when we were watching her." He thought about it for a moment, trying to figure out if it was just his paranoia.

"What was that?"

A woman opened the door of the house they were parked in front of. She was obviously trying to find out what they were doing there. He started the engine.

"Ah, it was probably nothing. Let's get out of here."

17

Alex thought he'd heard Winslow stir early that morning, but he'd been in too deep of a sleep to rouse himself. He wasn't sure how much time had passed when he opened his eyes and found her side of the bed empty. Instantly awake, he threw on his sweatpants and wandered through the house looking for her. She'd slipped out early that morning. But why? And how? Had she called a cab?

He brushed his teeth and turned on the shower. He still had time to get to work without being late. But it wasn't the way he'd wanted to start the day. Winslow was unlike any other woman he'd ever met. She had made him careful, something he'd never been. He knew to take things slowly, at least on an emotional level. She would tell him everything when she trusted him completely. She would share all her inner secrets. But he was impatient.

Making love to her had been fantastic. Their bodies had come together naturally, effortlessly. They woke in the middle of the night, seemingly called by the same sensuous voice, and made love again. She'd also made him feel something he'd never felt before. He wasn't sure he could call it love, but he was pretty sure it was what came just before love.

Pretty sure? So what was that you told her last night? a voice taunted.

Thank goodness she didn't know Spanish. Those words had just come out. She was the woman he wanted in his life. *My love,* he'd called her. He wasn't positive because he'd never been in love before. But he was definitely willing to explore it.

Then he'd woken up to find her gone. Was she that timid, or did she regret what they'd done?

Steam wafted from the shower, and he started to strip out of his pants when he sensed someone standing in the open doorway. His heart did a funny bump-bump when he saw her holding two large cups and a bag.

She gave him a shy smile. "Sorry; you were so dead asleep, I didn't think you'd be awake for a while. I went out for *café con leche* and doughnuts. And a paper."

"How did you get there?"

"I usually walk the beach first thing in the morning. This time I walked around the block. I had a purpose."

He couldn't hide his smile as he turned off the water. "You actually got *café con leche*?" It made him feel the same way her saying his Cuban name had.

They walked out to the lanai, where the morning air was still crisp. She said, "Yep. I saw a café on the way here last night with a sign proclaiming they sold it."

"That was sweet of you." She'd run out for coffee for him. The thought did all kinds of strange things to his stomach. Even the coffee tasted sweeter because she had gotten it for him. The only thing he regretted was not seeing her sleepy face and tousled hair first thing. She was already made up, her brown hair brushed, body dressed.

She set the paper on the table. The shooting had made the front page. "I skimmed it on the way back. The police have no leads, though they made the usual speculations about drug activity. The bullets were .38-caliber, all fired from the same gun. They're trying to quell stirrings of sniper attacks, which was my first thought." She pointed to one of the pictures. "Luckily, I didn't make it in the picture. And more luckily, I'm not even named in the article."

"I asked the officer at the scene if they could keep your name out of what they released to the press. I said it was because of your father running for governor."

"Oh. Thanks. I'm sure he'll appreciate that, too." Her expression darkened as she probably thought of the man she'd considered a father for so long. Her hazel green eyes filled with sadness. "He left a message on my cell phone, saying he'd heard about the shooting and was glad I was all right. It was like he wanted to say more. He paused for a second, and I could hear his voice crack when he said good-bye."

Alex touched her arm. "Things will settle down once we get to the bottom of the hit-and-run. If Jayce is involved, Grant will come to realize that he wouldn't want that kind of man marrying his daughter, or running his campaign. It may just take some time."

"I don't know if it can ever be the same, though. I've lost respect for him. And maybe he's lost something for me, too." She took a pastry out of the bag and bit into it.

Alex felt for her, imagining if ties with his family were broken. "Do you have any close friends you can talk to?"

She shook her head. "I've never been all that close to anyone."

That would change, he thought, not letting her words stand as a warning. She would become close to him. But for now, she had no one. He remembered when she'd said she lost everyone and had probably lost him when she told him about her suspicions.

"You have me," he said, pulling her close.

Her smile wasn't convincing. "For now."

"For as long as you want." He'd thrown out the gauntlet, but she wasn't picking it up. "Talk to me. Tell me what you're afraid of."

She moved away and fiddled with the pastry, picking off chunks of sugar and sticking them in her mouth. "That if you were to know all of me . . . you wouldn't like what you see."

He was so relieved that her fears had nothing to do with him, especially his ethnicity, that he almost smiled. "Try me. I'll bet you're wrong." He wasn't about to say that he'd seen all of her and he liked every inch. That's not what she meant.

She shook her head. "I'm not ready. To be honest, I'm not sure I'll ever be ready. It's just not something I can think about right now."

That definitely did not make him smile. He could never have a relationship with her if she wouldn't reveal everything to him.

She changed the subject by saying, "The police called, too, while I was out. I can retrieve my car."

"Great; we'll get it today."

"What's our plan with the Garcías? I need to stop by my place and feed my cats."

"I'll call Lidia and set up a time to talk to her. Jose's cousins are running the garage, so we can show them the picture of Jayce. We'll take it as far as we can and see if there's any connection."

She smiled, but it disappeared far too fast. "But you need to work today."

He glanced at his watch. He was already a few minutes later than his usual arrival time. "I'll call Enrique, my brother, and let him know I'm taking some time off today. I can work tonight." He finished his coffee. "Let's feed your cats, and then we can take a shower at your place."

Her mouth quirked in a half smile. "Sounds like a plan."

At midmorning, Alex and Winslow spoke with the García cousins at the garage. Well, Alex did, anyway. She was irritated at having to stand by and listen to words she couldn't understand. If she and Alex could ever become more than they were—and she wasn't exactly sure what that was—she would have to learn Spanish.

The cousins seemed cooperative. Alex pointed at her as he spoke, and she wondered how he was explaining her part in all this. The obsessed woman who had embraced this tragedy because of one in her past? The slightly unbalanced woman who had thrown away her stepfather's money to sneak around old warehouses?

"Show them the picture," Alex said, tearing her from her thoughts.

She fumbled as she took the photograph from the front pouch of her purse. Both men studied it but shook their heads. Jayce was no one they had ever seen; even she could understand that.

"You don't look surprised," Winslow said when she and Alex walked back to the Camaro. Naturally the macho Cuban male had chosen to drive.

"I'm not sure you're on the right track. The Garcías had a close-knit circle of friends. I don't think they would associate with Jayce."

"He could have brought his car here," she suggested as Alex held the door open for her.

"Look around. See many *Americanos*?"

"Actually . . . no, I don't." She hadn't even noticed that everyone in the vicinity was Latino. "But this is the only way we can find the connection. I've got to try."

"I know." He gave her an understanding smile and closed the door before walking around to the driver's side.

He was doing this for her. And he probably hoped they found nothing so she would be forced to give up.

"Thanks for coming with me," she said when he got in.

"No thanks are necessary. I don't want you putting yourself in harm's way again. Not without me."

"Why?" She wasn't sure why the question had popped out, but now that it had, she was curious.

He started the engine and then looked at her. "I don't think you're ready to hear that yet."

Argh! He'd used her words against her. And how could she object? She merely nodded and faced forward. He was probably right. "Now where?"

"We can talk to the Garcías' neighbors, see if anyone ever saw Jayce at the house."

"Could the brothers have been involved in anything illegal? Say selling drugs? Maybe Jayce was a buyer."

"I asked the cousins that. I told them how important it was to be square with me, but they swore they'd never seen even a hint of anything like that going on. I believe them."

An hour later Alex and Winslow had talked to a few of the neighbors and came up with the same answers. Jayce just wasn't someone they'd seen around the house, and in the largely Latino neighborhood he would have stood out.

Alex and Winslow stopped at a diner for a quick lunch and then headed to the hospital.

"I can't wait to see Elena again," she said. "Do you know how she's doing?"

"Better. But she's got a long way to go."

"How's the benefit coming?"

"According to Lidia, they're getting a good response."

"Your article helped, I'm sure."

He waved that off, as though putting himself in a tight place to help someone he hardly knew was something he did every day. Then again, maybe it was.

"Did you get any backlash?"

"A couple of nasty phone calls. My dad stood behind me on this one, though, so that helped. I made it clear that it wasn't about politics but about innocent lives getting shattered."

They parked and walked into the hospital. Elena was still in the same room. Winslow peered around the door frame before stepping inside. Lidia was nowhere around, so she backed out again.

"She may be in the cafeteria. I'll get her," he said. "Stay here in case she returns."

Winslow meant to stay near the doorway. After all, the girl didn't know her; she'd slept through Winslow's visit. But she couldn't resist seeing Elena. She was at the center of the incident that had started everything.

To her surprise, Elena was awake. Huge brown eyes fringed with thick lashes held Winslow for a moment. Beautiful eyes that would be the only reminder of who she really was.

"Hello, Elena," she said, coming closer. "Can you understand English?"

The girl nodded. Her jaw was still bandaged, though her forehead was now revealed. The cuts there were shallower, but they still looked angry.

Winslow was afraid of what those bandages concealed. She knew that the propeller blade had sliced through Elena's face at about jaw level. She shivered at the thought and stepped closer, pasting on a smile.

"My name is Winslow Talbot. I was here with your mother last week. And I . . . when I was about your age, I was in an accident, too. I also spent a lot of time in the hospital. It's no fun, is it?"

The girl shook her head.

"I can remember how people would tell me it was going to be all right. But I didn't feel that way. Everything seemed scary and miserable."

The girl nodded.

Winslow sat in the chair Elena's mother usually occupied. "You're probably angry at the man who was driving the boat. I know I was spitting mad at the man who hit our car and then just stood there looking at us before he ran away."

Elena nodded harder, and her eyes glittered with unshed tears.

"It's okay to be mad. It's okay to cry about everything that's happened to you. I know you want to be brave. I did, too. I didn't want my mom to feel any worse than she already did. My dad died in that accident." Because she wasn't sure if Elena had been told, Winslow played it safe by not mentioning that her uncle and father were dead. "She was so sad about that and about me, I didn't want to cause her any more grief. I tried hard to hold back the tears." Her throat constricted, not only at the memory but also at the understanding she saw in Elena's eyes. "You don't have to hold back the tears. It's good to cry it all out, sweetheart."

She touched Elena's arm as the girl did cry. Her hands were not as heavily bandaged as they were before. The tips of her fingers showed, and with a stab at her chest, Winslow saw that someone had painted the fingernails purple.

When the tears started flowing, Winslow went into the bathroom to get some tissues. She looked at her reflection and a voice said, *Take off the makeup and show her your real face. Show her how you live with your scars, and how she can, too.*

She turned away and returned to Elena with the tissues, blotting her eyes. She could hardly tell Elena how she could live with scars when she hid hers. Alex would be back soon, and she just couldn't let him see her like that.

She stroked Elena's arm and spoke in soft tones. "You will be all right, though I know it's hard to believe now. It's not going to be easy. I won't lie to you. I had a lot of surgeries to fix my face." She glanced at the doorway to make sure Alex hadn't returned. "Believe it or not, you can kind of get used to being in the hospital. You become friends with the nurses and doctors, some of them at least, and the kids, too. You compare your injuries to see who's got the worst." That made Elena smile a little or at least made her eyes crinkle. Winslow swallowed the lump at the thought that Elena's mouth was so damaged.

"I remember sneaking a wheelchair out of a storage room and racing some of the kids who were in them permanently. They won most of the time. And I remember"—she studied Elena—"I remember wanting to see my face most of all. No one would let me see myself, because they were afraid that I would be scared of my own reflection. I couldn't wait to get out of bed and look in the mirror." Elena was nodding vigorously.

Winslow continued, feeling the pressure in her chest tighten. "I remember that first time I saw myself after the accident. I turned the light on and closed my eyes as I held on to the sink. My mother had covered the mirror with a pillowcase. She thought she was helping me. But nothing would keep me from seeing myself."

Elena was listening intently, her brown eyes riveted to Winslow.

"Some of the deeper cuts were still bandaged, but the rest of my face was left uncovered to allow for healing. It was shiny with the salve they put on. And I was . . . ugly. I looked like Frankenstein. I had stitches going from here, to here, to here," she said, drawing the edge of her nail across her face to demonstrate. "My cheekbone was crushed, so my cheek looked sunken in. It *was* scary to look at myself. But I knew I'd only get better. I might not look like myself anymore, like the girl I used to look like. But I would look better than this. That's what kept me going."

Elena was nodding again, and Winslow had to ask, "Do you want to see yourself? Are you sure? I can't help you to the bathroom. I'm afraid I'll hurt you. But I can give you a little look."

She pulled her compact out of her purse. Beige powder covered the small mirror that she rarely used. She wouldn't tell Elena how she still looked like a stranger to herself, how she hated looking in mirrors and only did so when she had to apply makeup. She wiped the mirror against her sleeve to clear the powder. Her hand was shaking when she held it up to Elena. The girl shifted to the left to see her reflection. She didn't like what she saw; that was evident by the expression in her eyes and the tears beginning to seep out again. But she kept searching that reflection for traces of the girl she'd been on that beautiful evening.

Winslow heard a woman speaking Spanish in the hallway and then Lidia rushed in. Her alarm turned to relief when she saw Winslow, but that expression disappeared when she saw Elena with the mirror—and her tears.

Lidia batted the mirror away and it fell to the floor. "What are you doing? Get out of here, now!"

Winslow fought with her own shame that she'd done something inappropriate as she tried to explain. Suddenly Alex was there, trying to calm Lidia by taking her waving arms into his hands. She screamed in Spanish, nodding toward Winslow.

Elena was shaking her head, her frustration at her inability to talk clear in her eyes. Winslow stepped in front of Lidia.

"I'm sorry. I didn't mean to upset you."

"Upset me? Look at Elena. You upset her!"

"She needed to see herself, Lidia. Do you know what it's like to not be able to see your face when you know it's been shattered? So you imagine it's much worse than it is. She can't even touch her face, can't feel the changes or the stitches or anything. All she has is her imagination. I know. I was in an accident, too, when I was twelve years old. My face was disfigured. And no one let me see myself. It made me feel even more helpless. When I saw myself, yes, I cried, too. But at least I knew. I asked Elena if she was sure, and she nodded." She turned to Elena. "Are you sad that I gave you the mirror?"

Elena shook her head.

"But you're sad at what you saw," Winslow said, rather than asking.

She nodded.

Lidia had calmed down enough that Alex released her. But he was looking at Winslow. She'd inadvertently revealed a part of herself. There was no choice.

"You had no right to do that," Lidia said, her voice still breathless.

"You're right; I overstepped my boundaries. But I knew that she needed to see herself. And I . . . I needed to help her."

Lidia walked over to Elena and asked her questions in Spanish. Elena alternately nodded and shook her head.

A few minutes later, Lidia turned back to Winslow. "She's all right. Maybe . . . maybe she's even better than she was. You were wrong to do that without asking me first, but I would have said no. So I thank you for helping my daughter." She sank into the chair and gathered her thoughts. "How did your article come out?"

"It's fantastic," Alex answered for her. "I'm publishing it in my newspaper."

Lidia gave Alex a look of gratitude, but her expression changed to a cynical one. "So the rich white people wouldn't print it?"

Winslow shook her head. "But frankly, it wasn't fair to expect them to. It's not even the type of magazine to run stories about rich *white* people in trouble. I'm afraid I jumped the gun or put the horse before the cart, or whatever you want to call it. Thanks to Alex, though, it found a home anyway."

Alex said, "The article is heart-wrenching. She captured yours and Elena's pain and courage perfectly." He looked at Winslow. "Now we know why."

And he wasn't happy that he'd heard her pain by accident.

Now that Lidia was past her confusion and anger, she looked at Winslow and Alex with hope. "Have you found anything?"

"Not for lack of trying," Winslow said, and ignored

Alex's huff of agreement. "We're looking at a new angle. Have you ever seen this man?"

Lidia studied the picture but shook her head. "He looks like that actor—Leonardo something. You think this is the man who was driving the boat? You heard"—she lowered her voice—"what the *policia* found?"

Alex nodded. "That's why we started wondering if the boat operator had done it on purpose."

"The *policia* called and asked if I knew anyone who might want to hurt Luis or Jose. He knew about the politics and didn't think it was *exiliados*. Other than them, I had no answers for him."

She looked at the picture again. "I don't think I've ever seen this man."

She started to hand back the picture when something clicked in Winslow's head. "Lidia, you said there was an *Americano* waiting to launch his boat while you debated letting Elena go with them. He was impatient, trying to rush you."

She shrugged. "Yes, why?"

"It wasn't this man, was it?"

"I don't remember him at all other than he was *Americano*. And rude."

"Could you tell if there was more than one person on the boat?"

She shrugged again. "Wait; I do remember him talking down into the cabin of the boat to someone."

Winslow turned to Alex. "I know; I'm grasping at straws. Jayce kept his boat in the water at the marina, and unless he'd taken it out for some reason, he wouldn't have been launching it."

"You are grasping at straws, but you may not be totally off on this one. Sometimes people pull their boats out of the water to launch closer to their destination. Especially small boats that might take a while to get to a particular fishing or diving spot. They can be put on a trailer. Maybe he'd done that and had returned the boat. Lidia, can you remember what the boat looked like?"

"I can remember exactly what Jose and Elena were wearing and how long I watched before I couldn't see them anymore." She shook her head. "All I can say is that it wasn't a big boat and it wasn't small."

"And it had a cabin," Winslow said.

"He had such bad words, too. There was a woman walking her dog by the ramp, and she told him to watch his language." A faint smile tinged Lidia's mouth. "I liked that woman."

"Was the dog an old golden retriever?"

Again Lidia searched her memory. "It could have been that kind of dog, but I don't know that it was old."

Winslow's gaze went back to Elena, who was intently listening to the conversation. She knew well that when you were deprived of having stimulating conversations with others, you absorbed every one that you could hear. And this conversation pertained to her.

Lidia looked at both Alex and Winslow. "Do you think you know who did this? Is it the man in the picture?"

"We don't know," Alex said. "We're exploring possibilities."

"You'll let me know?"

"Of course."

Lidia said, "Oh, there's something else; maybe it will help. Someone anonymously deposited three thousand dollars into Elena's benefit fund. Could it be the person responsible, maybe out of guilt?"

Winslow felt her face flush. "I'm sure it wasn't."

"How do you know?" Lidia asked.

"Because she did it," Alex answered for her, his eyes on Winslow.

For a moment Lidia looked deflated at the loss of a possible lead, but soon gratitude filled her expression. "Thank you."

After they said good-bye, Alex led Winslow down the hallway. "That was generous of you."

"I had to do it."

"Just as you had to show Elena her reflection," he said without judging.

She paused and turned to him. "Yes, just like that. Was I wrong?"

"Not at all. You were crying, too, you know."

"I was?" She found a metal door and saw her warped reflection. Her eyeliner was smudged. "You know, I didn't even realize it."

"You were so caught up in Elena's emotions. Your injuries were nearly as severe as hers."

"How do you know?" She'd told him about the accident but never the details.

"I pulled up old microfiche files. When I discovered you were lying to me I tried to figure out why you were so adamant about investigating the hit-and-run."

She felt violated somehow, even though the information was in the public domain.

"Your car fell off the overpass. You went through the windshield," he said. "You made it sound like you got a few cuts. You could have been killed."

"My father *was* killed."

"I know." He lightly stroked her cheek. "But I want to know a lot more. I want to know what you went through, why you were crying at the memory of it."

She swallowed hard.

"Not right now," he said. "But someday." Once they exited the hospital, he said, "You were asking Lidia about the dog."

"When I was questioning people at the marina I met a woman who was walking her old golden. She's the one who said that Ashlyn looked like she was being abused. I'm wondering if it's the same woman, and if so, maybe she can give us more on the guy."

"So you don't think Jayce has connections to the Garcías anymore?"

"Not so much. I'm back to the accidental theory, except that when one of the brothers survived, Jayce decided he didn't want any witnesses. And then he made it murder."

18

It was midafternoon when Winslow and Alex arrived at Boone's Marina. The sun warmed the wood planks of the dock and filled the air with the scent of tar. She tried to remember which boat belonged to the woman with the dog.

"It was a houseboat. She had a palm on the back deck," Winslow said. "And she'd installed a ramp for the old dog. That made me like her before I'd said a word to her."

He was shaking his head slightly, though smiling. "Does she name her plants, too?"

"We didn't discuss it, smarty-pants."

Much of what he knew about her he'd found out inadvertently or accidentally, like when she slipped about naming her plants. It struck her as unfair to him, and yet she wasn't sure she could remedy it.

"There it is," she said.

It was at the end of the slip where Jayce used to keep his boat and where the two men she'd talked to before kept their boats. The first man sat in the sun cutting fishing line with a sharp knife. Judging by the cold look in his eyes, he obviously recognized her. When they'd passed him and she glanced back, he was reaching for a cell phone.

Was he connected to Jayce or his repair guys? If only she could hear what he was saying. She had to admit to feeling safer with Alex here, especially after seeing that.

They stopped at the end of the dock. "Hello? Anyone home?"

A few seconds later the lady opened the small door. "Oh, hey. You're the one who was asking about your sister, right? Were you able to talk to her?"

Winslow shook her head, thinking of her desperation when she tore Ashlyn's shirt. "I have some more questions, though, if you have some time."

"Sure, come aboard."

The dog ambled out and sniffed them. A sudden sadness assailed Winslow at the thought that this dog was the woman's only companion and his years were waning. The shaggy blonde gestured to two chairs on the back deck, evidence of occasional company at least. Alex settled against the stern as Winslow took a seat.

"I'm Melanie, by the way," the lady said as she eased into a small metal chair that didn't look as though it could hold her weight. "This is Mudge."

"I'm Winslow, and this is Alex."

"Is this about your sister? Or the shelter?"

"Neither," Winslow said. She glanced at Alex, who was content to let her use the camaraderie she'd already established with Melanie. "Two weeks ago Friday afternoon, two Cuban men and a young girl were about to launch their small boat over at the ramp. There was a bit of commotion because the girl wanted to go, but her mother wasn't so sure. There was probably some crying and whining going on." Winslow watched Melanie's face.

She shrugged. "It sounds familiar."

"There was another boat waiting to launch, and the small boat was in the way. Apparently the guy on the boat, who was an *Americano,* started cussing at the Cubans. You were walking Mudge and told the guy to watch his language."

"Oh yeah, I remember. The Spanish people didn't realize

he was ready to leave, I guess. All he had to do was ask them to move, but he started cussing, calling them 'spics.' I told him to watch his mouth, and he flipped me off, called me a meddling such-and-such."

Winslow took out the photo again. "Could that guy have been the one here with my sister? And maybe she was there, too, in the cabin?"

Melanie hardly looked at it. "I didn't get a good look at his face; the cap he wore put it in shadow. He was about your age; young and cocky, that's the impression I got. I suppose it could have been him, but I'm not sure. For all I could tell, he was alone. Come to think of it, one of the guys who works in the warehouse knew him. He was laughing, the jerk, egging him on."

"Which guy?" Alex asked, obviously as eager for information as Winslow.

"You meet the guy in the office, slender man with red hair?" When Winslow nodded, she said, "It's his son, Frankie. Looks a lot like him, in his twenties. What's this about, anyway?"

"Did you hear about the boating hit-and-run where two men were killed?"

"Yeah, that was awful. The news said they launched from—wait a minute. That was the people I saw?"

"Yes, and we're trying to find out if my sister's fiancé had anything to do with it."

"Oh, wow. I didn't even realize. I hope you do find out it was your guy. He looked like the kind of person who'd do that."

And no one else could see that, Winslow thought in frustration. "Do you remember anything about the boat? Maybe a name."

Melanie gave them an apologetic smile. "I just don't pay much attention to detail. Unless it's something that touches me, like your sister's body language. The boat had a cabin, and it was about thirty feet long, I'd guess."

"You've been a big help. Thanks so much," Winslow said, coming to her feet.

Alex echoed her thanks, and they headed to the warehouses. Winslow spotted the gangly Frankie as he guided the boat-toting tractor to the river's edge. He was the only red-haired man in sight. The tractor's prongs lowered the boat into the water, where other workers secured it.

"Frankie!" Alex called as soon as the driver was finished and was about to climb down.

The young man sauntered over to the far corner of the large steel building where boats were kept like stacked cocoons. He swiped at his cap and rubbed the sweat off his forehead with his arm as he approached. "Yeah?"

Since the young man didn't look as though he'd be all that cooperative, Winslow decided to lie a little. "Your dad thought you could help us. We're working on some harassment charges for one of the marina residents."

"I didn't harass anyone," Frankie said, lifting his hands.

"They're against Melanie, the woman who owns the golden retriever." She could feel Alex's shock at that statement and purposely didn't look his way. Okay, that was a big lie. "I gather she's been giving people a hard time, telling them to curtail their language, lecturing them."

"Oh yeah. She's a pain in the ass. Someone filed a complaint against her?"

Frankie assumed she and Alex were someone of authority, though she'd purposely failed to mention what exactly.

"We're gathering statements to see if we have enough to press charges."

That seemed to delight Frankie, who showed filmy teeth in a wide smile. "That'd serve that bitch right. Well, she's never said nothing to me, but I know others she's given a hard time to. Pat Jones in slip A-Eight and Jenny Cartwright in L-Twelve also got told what's what by her. Jenny can cuss like no man I ever knew." He said this with pride.

"What about people using the boat ramp?" she asked.

"Oh yeah, she walks that lame old dog over there. You should see her picking up turds with her little Baggies. Pitiful!"

It was all Winslow could do not to deck the guy. And considering that she'd never decked anyone in her life, that was saying something. "Let's stick to the facts, why don't we?"

"I've heard her giving folks a hard time a few times. Hell, when you pinch your fingers between the dock and the boat or when the boat gets away from you, you're entitled to a cussword or two, don'cha think? But the folks that use the ramp aren't residents, so I wouldn't know 'em."

Damn. "Are you sure there aren't any ramp users you'd know? See, that would really strengthen our case. Otherwise it might look like a personal vendetta."

"Oh, I see." He scratched his head in such a typical thinking gesture Winslow had to keep from smirking. She could almost see the lightbulb when his eyes widened. "My friend was there a couple of weeks ago; she was laying into him. I bet he'd be glad to tell you about her."

Winslow pulled out her little notepad, her chest tightening at the possibility of hearing Jayce's name. She'd even started to write the *J* when Frankie said, "Mike. Mike Stevens. He lives over on One-hundred-and-eightieth Court, not far from here. House is a god-awful pink color, thanks to that snippy wife of his. He runs some hellacious poker games from— hey, y'all aren't cops or anything, are you?"

"No, we're not," Winslow said, adding the *anything* in her mind. "Thanks so much for your help."

"Nail that self-righteous bitch," he said as he turned away, adding a holler for good measure.

She shuddered. "Yuck! What a creep."

"It was all I could do not to deck him," Alex said.

"Hey—"

"Don't worry; I rarely resort to violence," he quickly assured her.

"No, I was going to say that's exactly what I was thinking. I wanted to deck him bad."

He slid his arm around her shoulders as they walked toward the parking lot. "First that grandiose lie—very smart, by the way—and then this revelation. You're just one surprise after another."

"To myself, too," she had to admit.

He grinned. "I like it."

She smiled. "Me, too."

"Though I have to amend my admiration to include only when you're not lying to me."

"I won't lie to you again. But it doesn't sound like this guy is Jayce. Unless this is Jayce's real name. He lied about staying at the Astonia. He could be lying about his name, too."

"Let's see who's home."

"Hey, Frankie!" Pete Stamper waved the string bean over when he got his attention. "Who were those people?"

"Lawyers, I think. Someone here's trying to nail that Melanie for harassing us guys just 'cause we want to express ourselves. Can you believe it?"

"No. I can't. What'd they ask?"

"Just who Melanie's been harassing. I asked if they was cops and they said no. They gotta tell me, right?"

"They're not cops. But they might be even bigger trouble. Did you give them any names?"

"Pat and Jenny. Oh, and Mike. You remember how she was laying into him a couple of weeks ago—what's wrong?"

"What did you tell them?"

"His name and what street he lives on. Oh, and I might have mentioned the color of the house, though 'god-awful pink' could mean different things to different people. That's all, I swear. What'd I do?"

"Keep your big mouth shut from now on. Shit." He stomped away and pulled out his cell phone. Thankfully his buddy had alerted Pete to Winslow's presence. Now Pete knew just how much trouble the woman was going to be. He made a call. "Yeah, guess what? . . . That Winslow woman just got your name and where you live. She's with the Cuban. I imagine they're going to pay you a visit anytime now. . . . Yep, I know what to do. And maybe this'll all be over soon."

Winslow and Alex drove past Mike Stevens's house, and yes, it was a god-awful pink. "The creep was right about that, anyway," Winslow said. It actually hurt her eyes to look at the house in the bright sunshine. "There's a wife, Frankie said. If Jayce is Mike, then Ashlyn can't marry him this Saturday." She searched the dirt-and-weed yard for any sign of Jayce but saw only a broken tricycle, a car that hadn't run in more than a year, and beer cans stacked in the shape of a house. "He might even have a child. What a sad place to raise children."

The street was as run-down as the houses on it. At least the pink paint was new, perhaps a vain attempt to brighten up their lives. Behind the house was a handmade shed that looked like a barn. It was big enough for a boat. Ruts in the dirt led from the back of the house to where the old car sat in the driveway. Maybe it had been in the barn once. Maybe they'd needed the space for something else.

Alex continued cruising by, and the house fell behind them. She didn't want to be too obvious, but she turned slightly to keep the shed in view.

"We should come back at night," he said as he found a place to turn around.

"I agree. Checking things out during the day didn't help me last time."

He gave her a look that told her how horrified he was that she'd been sneaking around warehouses by herself. "Well, I didn't know you then, not really. And I survived."

"You still have nightmares about being locked in the

trunk, don't you?" At her surprised look, he said, "You were calling out in the night, 'Let me out of here! God, please get me out of here.' I tried to wake you, but you seemed to drift into another dream and quieted down after that."

She studied the house as they passed it again. "I have nightmares sometimes. I'm sorry if I woke you up."

"I'm glad I was there."

She gave him a grateful look even though she was embarrassed at having called out in her sleep.

He stopped at the beginning of the street. "Let's get your car, eat dinner, and then you need to change into darker clothes. By the time we're back we can move around without detection." He shifted so that he faced her. "But I want you to promise me something, Winslow. That this will be the last time you do anything to investigate the hit-and-run. If this doesn't pan out, it's over. You're down to grasping wild threads, but this is the last thread. Promise me."

"All right," she said reluctantly. But he was right. She was out of leads after this.

"That was too easy."

She lifted her fingers in scout's honor. "I promise."

But she hadn't promised anything about Jayce.

Night had fallen by the time Alex and Winslow returned to the gaudy pink house. At least they couldn't see the color in the darkness. The moon was just a sliver, barely enough for them to see by. Winslow had used her tan foundation to make her pale face a little darker without being obvious if they were spotted. Alex, of course, was already a beautiful olive color.

He pulled into the driveway of a vacant house sporting a faded For Sale sign in the front yard. A group milled about in the garage of a house two lots down working on a car. Two people sat in the dark on their front porch smoking. All Winslow could see was the cherry bouncing back and forth between shadows. Music floated from somewhere.

Alex said, "We're just a couple strolling down the street. If anyone approaches us, let me do the talking. And no, it's not a macho Cuban male thing. All right, maybe it is. I don't want trouble."

"Don't you know that Trouble's my middle name?" she said, trying to lighten the mood.

"I do know." He leaned forward, tipped up her chin, and kissed her. "That's why I'm here. Let's get this over with. Our goal is simple: see if Mike Stevens is Jayce."

"And get a peek at whatever's in that shed."

"Winslow . . ."

"While we're here."

They walked casually, holding hands, down the side of the street.

"Hey!" one of the guys in the garage hollered to them.

Her fingers tightened on Alex's.

"Keep walking," he said softly.

Alex made a noncommittal sound and waved back.

The guy lifted his beer bottle up in a gesture of hello. Or maybe he thought he knew them. Winslow hoped he would think they were busy on their romantic stroll.

The pink house looked dark inside, but the occupants could be back anytime. The house to the right looked unoccupied, too; the undulating light of a television moved behind curtains in the one on the left.

She glanced back at the crew in the garage. No one was watching as she and Alex ducked between the houses. Behind this row of houses were the backs of the houses on the next street. The shed structure hid them from view for the most part. The aromas of fried food scented the air along with a distant barbecue grill's charcoal. Their shoes crackled on the dry weeds. She wore pink sneakers, the darkest practical shoes she owned.

Alex paused, his hand tightening on her arm. He was listening to something, but she hadn't heard anything but distant sounds. The door was slightly open, and inside, the barn smelled of must and engine oil. The door creaked when they opened it, and it sounded like an alarm to her ears.

They slipped inside and closed the door before Alex aimed his penlight in front of them. They were standing only inches in front of the bow of a boat. For the first time, Winslow allowed herself to get excited, to hope that justice would finally be done. Alex trailed the light down the hull, which was torn apart. Someone had been trying to fix it. It amazed her that it hadn't sunk. *Lucky the devil,* her grandmother used to say. Winslow hated when it was true.

"Let's get out of here and call the police," Alex said. "Now we have probable cause." Except that this wasn't the boat she'd seen at the warehouse. And—

Winslow was bombarded by sensations, the first of which was fear, followed by a cold metal cylinder pressed against her forehead; she heard a click, and a man's rusty voice said, "No, you don't. You got nothing, not even your life."

Alex's tiny light flashed over the man's face long enough for them to see that he was holding a rifle on her—and that he wasn't Jayce.

"Pete, back the truck up. We're going for a little ride to the Everglades." He turned to them. "My uncle's got a hunting cabin out there, and I know just where to put your bodies so no one will ever find 'em." When Alex started to move, the guy—Mike, she had to guess—shoved the rifle harder into her temple. "Make another move like that and I blow her head apart right here. You want a chance to escape, don't you?" He cackled.

Alex still held the penlight, casting an eerie glow but not giving them a real sense of their surroundings. She did get a good sense of how terrified he was for her. But he was also calculating. She wished she could read his mind.

"You ran over those people," Winslow said, feeling the muscles in her temple move against the cold steel as she talked.

"Spics," he said. "Just like your boyfriend here. I told

them to move out of the way, and they took their damned time while my own time for catching fish was running out. Do you know what I gotta go through to get out of this house? Old bag gave me two hours to get my fishing in."

"That was no reason to kill them," Winslow said, her anger overpowering her fear. "You ran over a little girl!"

"Like I care. Just more of them breeding, taking over my city, hell, the whole damned state. I saw them out fishing a while later, and you know what that spic son of a bitch does? He gives me the finger. It's my country, dammit! You spics gotta learn respect. Comprende, amigo? That's what you all get for trying to make me learn your language. Everywhere I go, Spanish!"

He was literally spitting angry, and she had to quell her instinct to wipe it off her cheek. His hatred was vile. She'd never seen anything like it before and had no idea how to counteract it. With the venom of it, though, she knew that this man would kill them without compunction . . . especially Alex.

A truck engine rattled on the other side of the door, and she saw a slice of brake lights before they were extinguished.

"And then you had to butt in, you and your spic friend here."

The door opened and Pete walked back inside.

She said, "You shot me with the Taser gun."

Pete smiled. "Yep. That was fun. Never used one of them before."

"You broke into my apartment; you were on my balcony."

"Nope, we just parked outside your building and watched you."

"You shot at me, didn't you? At that intersection by the liquor store."

Mike gave Pete an amused look. "You've just been one unlucky lady." His face went back to an all-business expression. "Tie him up first. He won't try anything with the gun on his girlfriend here."

As Pete reached for Alex, she dropped to the floor. Alex shoved Pete into the gaping hole in the hull of the boat. The penlight skittered across the floor, casting vague light near the trailer the boat was sitting on. Alex and Winslow were nearly blind, but they had desperation on their side.

Unfortunately, so did Mike and Pete. And they were blocking the only exit she knew about.

"Shit, now it's going to be messy," Mike said, and suddenly lights came on. He was already aiming the rifle at her. "Pete! You all right?"

Pete climbed out of the hole. The jagged edge of fiberglass had scratched the side of his face. "I'll get the spic," he said.

She was standing next to the warped propeller. She couldn't see Alex, though she could hear his feet shuffling on the other side of the boat. Then she couldn't hear anything as a shot deafened her. Fiberglass exploded next to her, and she ducked down by the props and breathlessly searched for another way out. She could see no exit other than through the two men.

More shots rang out, pumping fear into her. Sweat covered her face and dampened her armpits. *Alex! Where are you?*

"Good shot! Pete, go around the other side and we'll trap her at the back."

She dared a look beneath the trailer and saw Alex lying on the floor, blood flowing onto the concrete. She couldn't help the cry that escaped her mouth.

Oh, God, Alex, I'm sorry! It's all my fault.

She only had one weapon, she realized, and she had to use it. She started screaming. A couple of gunshots might be ignored in this neighborhood, but she hoped screams to go along with them wouldn't. As she screamed, she climbed up on the boat and dived to the deck when Pete shot at her again. The bullet hit the steering wheel. She climbed down into the damaged cabin and then out the hole in the front.

"Pete, she's going out the front! Get her; get her; get her!"

She was already outside, tearing through the night trailing a now-hoarse scream behind her. "Call the police! Rape! Fire!"

Front porch lights came on; doors opened. She ran to the house across the street where a balding man was standing in the open doorway. "Call the police and an ambulance. They shot a man!"

Her legs would barely hold her up, but the sound of screeching tires made her turn around. The brown truck meant to take them to the Everglades now tore down the street. She took a deep breath and ran back to the barn, back to Alex. She hadn't heard any more shots, so the two men had been more concerned with saving themselves than making sure Alex was dead.

When she ran into the barn, she collapsed at his side.

19

Ashlyn slipped into her Cosabella Tangier chemise, in black, and studied her reflection in the bathroom mirror. She'd been excited about the chemise when she bought it two months ago, but now she just let out a soft sigh. It was made in Italy for Pete's sake. Italy! She loved Italian clothes, food, and before Jayce, she used to say, *Italian men, too!*

Jayce was already lying in bed, naked, watching television. He did that a lot, and she was trying hard not to be annoyed. She hardly ever watched the boob tube. He glanced up at her and gave her a wolf whistle. Before the whistle was even over, though, he'd switched his focus back to the television. It was like they were already married. She didn't like this living together thing, and quite honestly, she wasn't sure how it had come about. But here they were, for better or for worse.

Ashlyn, you're getting married in three days!

Even that did little to pep up her spirit. Without looking up at her, Jayce reached over and yanked her arm so that she had to lean down. He gave her a wet, sloppy kiss.

"What's wrong, baby?"

She rubbed her arm where he'd nearly wrenched it out of the socket. But how could she complain when he'd done it to pull her close?

"I dunno."

"You're not getting cold feet, are you?" He actually looked right at her, waiting for her answer.

"Of course not."

"Good, because I don't know how I could live without you."

He settled back in place, his black-stockinged feet crossed at the ankles. With him being otherwise naked, it wasn't a pretty sight, not even on Jayce. She focused instead on his body, on the contours of his muscles . . . except they had softened in the last month or so. Of course, he'd been so busy working on her father's campaign he had no time for workouts.

Something was missing, though she couldn't pinpoint it. She was fairly, nearly positively sure that it wasn't Winslow. She ought to be glad her stepsister was out of their lives. My God, she'd nearly attacked Ashlyn! That refreshed her ire until she remembered the concern in Winslow's eyes. She'd only attacked because she was desperate to find bruises to prove Jayce was hitting Ashlyn. That was ridiculous, of course. He'd never do that again.

He pressed his hand against her back. "Baby, you make a better door than a window."

"What?"

He waved her out of the way.

She crossed her arms in front of her. "What's so damned important on that thing?"

"The news is coming on in a few minutes. I think they're going to have an update on the shooting."

"Oh." Well, at least that was important. She tried to forget that he was always glued to that thing anyway. And she did want to know more about the shooting that Winslow had been caught in. She moved to her side of the bed—it used to be on the side closest to the bathroom until Jayce took it over—and fiddled with the lacy hem of her chemise. Red satin roses, just tiny ones, would look nice sewn at intervals of about five inches. She wondered if she had any in her boxes of adornments but wasn't motivated enough to go look.

"Have you talked to Grant yet about this place?" Jayce asked.

"No."

"What are you afraid of? He'll give you anything you want."

"I've never asked for a million-dollar condo before. In fact, I don't ask him for much of anything. I just tell him I want it and he gets it for me. Or I charge it to the card."

She thought of Winslow not having the card that Grant had given her. She was independent. She had her own money. She was probably doing fine. That sent a pang of envy through Ashlyn. She was plain tired of envying that woman. For a while, she thought Winslow would envy her for a change, after she'd hooked up with Jayce. Boy, had that backfired.

"Ashlyn, did you hear me?"

She blinked and looked at him. "Sorry, what did you say?"

"The solution is simple. Just tell Grant how much you'd love to have a place of your very own, with just your and your new husband's names on the deed. He'll probably give it to us as a wedding present."

She didn't like how much Jayce was hounding her about this condo. Okay, she had led him to believe that it was hers to begin with, and he'd been surprised when she'd admitted it wasn't. He talked about her financial security and what would happen if Grant lost everything. She knew how Winslow's father's death had left them poor; Jayce probably had a point. Still, Ashlyn wasn't comfortable taking that much from Daddy. Damn, Winslow had rubbed off on her.

"Winslow bought her own place," she said. "Daddy gave her a loan on the down payment, and she makes the payments. She said she wanted a home that was totally hers. We could do that, ask Grant for a loan. Then you could make the payments. And when your money comes in, we'd pay it off."

"Sweet pea, my money could be a long time coming. Cal just told me today that my cousin Bertha has filed yet another petition. It's getting frustrating, but I've got to hang in there. Until then . . ."

"We can live here. It's free. You can hardly beat that."

He settled back on the pillow with a thud, his mouth set in a hard line. "I'll talk to him."

She didn't argue. That's what they were doing, she supposed. At least it wouldn't be her doing the hinting.

The news anchor came on. "Stay tuned for *News at Eleven*. We've got a shocking update on the hit-and-run boating accident that claimed two lives and injured a young girl on November fourth."

Jayce shot up, and Ashlyn scrambled to the foot of the bed. They looked at each other, but neither said a word. When the news began, she impatiently waited through the staff introductions.

"November fourth was a tragic day for the García family," the woman finally said. "Jose García, his brother Luis, and Jose's ten-year-old daughter, Elena, set out on an evening fishing trip out on Biscayne Bay. Events took a horrific turn when their small boat was hit by another boat at a high rate of speed. Both men were pronounced dead at the scene, and Elena suffered terrible injuries. For almost two weeks investigators have been trying to track down the boat. Then authorities released a chilling update: Luis García, the man found in the water, had been purposely run down.

"Two Miami citizens cracked the case tonight amid a blaze of bullets and a near kidnapping at a Miami residence. All we've learned so far is that an unknown man and woman found the boat sought in the hit-and-run. The man was injured in the shooting, but we don't yet have details on his condition. Mike Stevens, the Miami man who resides at the house where the shooting took place, is the registered owner of the boat suspected in the accident. He and Pete Stamper, also of Miami, were allegedly on the boat at the time and both are implicated in the events tonight. They led police on an eight-mile chase but were apprehended without incident.

It looks as though the accident wasn't an accident at all but a case of boat rage and racist brutality. We'll tell you more as we learn it. Now, on to other news."

Ashlyn was already scrambling to the phone on the nightstand. "Daddy, did you see the news?" she asked as soon as he answered. "It has to be Winslow and Alex. . . . Yes, we'll be ready. We'll meet you out front." She hung up. "Daddy's calling his friends at the police station to see what's going on and find out for sure if it's Winslow. We'll head down together. Maybe this will finally be over."

Winslow had been waiting at the police station for what seemed like days, though she knew it was actually a couple of hours. She wanted to see Alex, to be at the hospital even though she knew he was in surgery. They wouldn't tell her much beyond that, just that he'd been hit in the thigh and that he'd be fine. Platitudes. She'd seen how much blood he'd lost.

Detective Ramey, the older of the men who had interviewed her after her false imprisonment ordeal, had been called in after she'd told the detectives on the scene the whole story. Detective Capperson was with him.

"So your future brother-in-law had nothing to do with the hit-and-run, then," Ramey confirmed.

"I guess not. Can I go to the hospital yet?"

"In just a few minutes. Tell me again why you thought it was him."

She told him and then asked, "Can I go now?"

Ramey took a call on his cell phone, and then said to Capperson, "We have some witnesses coming into the station. She ought to be here."

"I'm going to the hospital to see Alex. Take the witnesses there."

She figured they were probably neighbors or maybe even people from the marina. She didn't care. The two detectives looked at each other, then shrugged. "All right. We've got your cell number if we need you," Ramey said.

She didn't respond, just walked out of the station with a huge sigh of relief and headed straight to the hospital in Alex's Camaro.

He was out of surgery, the nurse said thirty minutes later. Stabilized. Yes, Winslow could see him, but he'd be under sedation. She didn't care; she needed to see him, to make sure he was all right.

"His family should see him first. You're the girlfriend, right?"

"Right," she said without even thinking about it. At least until a few moments later.

"I'm afraid family takes precedence. They've been waiting here for the last two hours."

As though she'd been out having her nails done! But she didn't want to get into all of that, so she gritted her teeth. She didn't want to see his family, didn't want to feel their anger at her for dragging Alex into her mess. Still, she walked to the waiting room while they all crowded into his room, whispering, crying, and shushing one another. Their unity stabbed at her, reminding her of everything she didn't have. The Díazes would stand by one another no matter what. They'd never let an outsider come between them.

She realized that she was the outsider here. But she would never come between him and his family. She wasn't sure he would want to be with her now. Worse, she wasn't sure she even deserved to be with Alex.

Lazaro was the first to return to the waiting room. Guilt reddened her face when he saw her sitting in the far corner. "Winslow, what happened? The hospital, the police, they won't tell us anything."

"It was me," she said. "It was my fault." And she dissolved into tears.

Thirty minutes later she'd told the Díaz family the whole story. She searched their faces for blame and anger and was surprised when she saw none. Horror, of course, and worry. But not blame.

"Alex would do something like that," his sister, Elizabet, said. "He puts himself on the line all the time for justice. Add a pretty woman with a mission, along with what happened to the Garcías, and it's all over."

A pretty woman. It was the first time Winslow thought about her makeup or perhaps the lack of it. She needed to touch up. "Excuse me," she said, feeling low about her compulsion to cover her imperfections at this time. Her eyes were puffy red, and she splashed water on them several times before washing her face and reapplying her makeup.

"I'd like to see him now, if it's all right with you," she said to the gathered group when she returned. "Just for a few minutes. You have to let the nurse know it's all right."

Lazaro wrapped his arm around hers and guided her to the nurses' station. "She's okay to see Alex Díaz, anytime she wants."

She turned and hugged Lazaro, out of need or gratitude, she didn't know. He didn't seem to think anything of it, holding her close and patting her back.

With a ragged sigh she pulled away and walked to Alex's room. It was a private one. She stepped to the edge of the bed, hating how pale he looked and the huge bandages swathing his thigh. He was deep in slumber, breathing steadily—breathing at least. She thanked God for that.

She reached out and touched his hand. "I'm sorry I got you into this. But we did it. We got justice for Elena and Lidia. I promise I'll behave from now on. And . . . I'll try to show you everything."

Winslow didn't want to leave the hospital until Alex woke, so she sat in the waiting area with some of the Díaz family. Lazaro warned her that reporters were gathered outside. He'd given them a brief statement, but they wanted to interview her.

"Do they know I'm here?" she asked.

"They do not know who you are yet, only Alex. I told them the mystery woman was still at the police station."

"Thank you for that." She was surprised that the media knew Alex's name and not hers yet.

She thought she was imagining things when she saw Ashlyn, Grant, and Jayce walk in. Especially when even Ashlyn looked concerned as she rushed toward Winslow.

"We saw the news!" Ashlyn said, tucking herself into the seat beside Winslow. "What happened?"

"Are you all right?" Grant said, kneeling in front of her.

She could only nod; words jammed in her throat.

"We've been down to the police station. We need to talk to you in private. There are things you should know . . . now that it's over."

Her eyebrows furrowed, but she wordlessly stood and followed them outside. The air was chilled, and she instinctively hunched her shoulders. She'd been cold since the shooting, unable to shake the chills. Just as Grant shrugged out of his light jacket and slipped it over her shoulders, they spotted a group of reporters hovering outside the entrance.

Grant said, "Let's go back inside. I've asked that your name be withheld for as long as possible."

She would have thanked him, but she suspected it was as much to protect himself as her. Since there were no children in the playroom, they closed themselves in the cheery room filled with toys.

"You could have gotten yourself killed," Grant said in the way of a parent who'd discovered his child was in a dangerous situation. "I'm not happy about that or how obsessed you became over this. But in the end, you did a good thing. I'm proud of you for it, so long as you never do it again."

She was still focused on what they needed to tell her but said, "I'm not about to take up the cause of every hit-and-run accident victim, if that's what you mean."

"Not even the ones where the victim is a little girl. We can't go through this again."

Promise me, Alex's voice echoed in her head.

"I won't; I promise. The only reason I became involved was because I thought Jayce had hit that boat. The way Ashlyn was acting, that his boat was suddenly missing . . . it looked suspicious."

Jayce spoke for the first time since they had arrived. "We *were* involved in the hit-and-run. I didn't want to drag in Grant or you, but you made it necessary to bring him in. Then you wouldn't leave it alone, even after he asked you to drop it. To trust him."

She ignored Jayce's subtle castigation, too caught up in his first sentence. "You were involved." Her head was spinning. Pete and Mike had confessed; it was definitely Mike's boat in the barn. How . . .

Jayce pulled Ashlyn so close he seemed to crush her. "We saw those guys hit the Garcías' boat. It was intentional. I grabbed the binoculars to get a better look. We were idling a short distance away, and—"

"We heard the boat engine and looked up. And saw the crash," Ashlyn said on a sob.

"I watched through the binoculars, hoping they would leave so we could go over and help, but"—Ashlyn sobbed again, and he squeezed her closer—"that's when he came back and ran over the guy who'd jumped into the water. I wanted to radio the Coast Guard, but I knew those guys would hear it and know we were there. They must have seen the flash of the binoculars, because they spotted us and took pursuit. They shot at us, but we managed to outrun them.

"I was able to get in touch with some guys who do repair work . . . on the side. I couldn't take the boat to a regular repair shop to fix bullet holes, after all. They usually deal with drug runners, that sort, but we were desperate. That's what you saw getting repaired when you were sneaking around: the bullet holes."

"You had them put me in the trunk!"

"They did that on their own. They were protecting themselves, not me. I knew they wouldn't hurt you."

Sure he did. "Why didn't you go to the police?" she asked.

"I was afraid for Ashlyn. Those guys meant business, and if they found out we were the witnesses, I had no doubt they would come after us. I was right, wasn't I? Besides, we really didn't see any identifying clues. Two guys on a boat, that was about it. So Ashlyn and I decided we would keep quiet."

Winslow crossed her arms. "Except that Ashlyn was afraid, and maybe she even felt guilty about not going to the police. That's when you tried to convince her to stick to the plan, and put those bruises on her."

Grant grimaced. "Winslow, it was a desperate situation. Ashlyn has a tendency to panic, and he had to shake some sense into her. That bad feeling you had about Jayce, your suspicions, they were all because of this. You were astute enough to pick up on it, and though you could have gotten yourself killed, you went ahead and solved the case." He placed his hands on her shoulders. "But it's all over now. Time for us to move ahead, together, as a family."

She wanted that, especially after seeing the Díazes uniting in their time of need. "All right. Yes, of course you're right. Shouldn't we tell the police—"

"Already done," Grant said. "That's what took us so long to get here. Once those two Neanderthals were in custody it was safe to come forward. Jayce and Ashlyn told them everything."

So they'd been the witnesses who were on their way in.

"What did they think of you making up an alibi for Jayce?" she asked.

He had the decency to look shamed. "They're considering what to do about it. That was the hardest thing I'd ever had to do, and I'll pay whatever penalty is necessary."

At least he didn't say that she had forced him to do it. She was sure they were all thinking it, though.

"I'm sorry for everything I put you all through," she said. "If you'd just told me the truth—"

"You would have still tried to find the culprits," Ashlyn said.

"Or you wouldn't have believed us," Jayce said.

He was probably right.

"Okay, we move ahead then," Winslow said. "There's someone I'd like you to see, though. So you'll understand why it was so important to me."

She led them upstairs to Elena's room. Lidia was asleep, and so was Elena. Winslow beckoned Grant inside; Ashlyn came, too, but Jayce stayed outside the room.

When they stepped back into the hallway, Winslow said, "The day you asked me to drop the investigation, I came here. I saw Elena for the first time. And I knew I couldn't drop it. Yes, it had everything to do with my accident and the justice I never got. And it had everything to do with that little girl. I'm hoping that when Mike and Pete get convicted, there will be some financial restitution."

"I doubt it," Grant said, his gaze still lingering on the foot of the bed inside the room. "Sounds like they don't have much."

"I know." She pictured the crummy house. "There's going to be a benefit at the end of the month. But for political reasons the Garcías are not popular. I don't know how successful it will be."

Grant was again looking into the room, even though he couldn't see Elena. "I'll see what I can do."

As noncommittal as the words were, they gave Winslow hope. "Thanks, Dad."

"You put your life on the line. The least I can do is pull strings, get her surgeries done at a reduced cost."

Winslow felt her eyes well up with tears. She hugged him, which gave her time to compose herself.

"Winslow!" a female voice called from down the hall. When she turned, she saw Elizabet just outside the elevators. "Alex is awake! He's asking for you."

They rode the elevator to Alex's floor together as Winslow made introductions. It was still hard to say the words *future brother-in-law* when introducing Jayce. She had to get past that. He and Ashlyn would get married, and Winslow hoped everything she, and Melanie, thought they'd seen was only a misunderstanding. With Elena's surgeries on the line, as well as family reconciliation, Winslow had to believe that everything was tied into the subconscious knowledge that Jayce had been involved in the hit-and-run.

At the sight of Alex, her heart nearly burst with guilt, relief, and a feeling that surpassed them both: love. She rushed to the bed and then didn't know whether to take his hand—the IV embedded in it dissuaded her of that—or hug him or just stand there. When he smiled, she leaned down and kissed his dry lips.

"How are you feeling?"

"Okay now that I know you're all right," he said in a raspy voice. His eyes still looked sleepy from the anesthesia. "I had to see for myself."

The fact that he wasn't angry with her nearly made her cry. Her voice broke when she said, "I'm sorry I dragged you into this."

He reached out with his free hand, and she gently squeezed it. "I went along willingly. I wanted to see justice done, too. Getting shot was worth those two getting nailed."

The bullet had cut an artery, and surgeons had spent hours doing microsurgery to repair it. He would have to stay in the hospital a few days while doctors made sure the surgery was successful. She knew that much from his family.

"You didn't say how you were feeling," she said.

"Groggy, a little nauseated from the anesthesia. I'll survive. I'm just glad this is all over. Now we can move forward."

Did he mean the two of them? Did she dare hope? Old

doubts surfaced, but she pushed them aside for now. She was too fragile, too vulnerable, to think about them now.

"Yes," she said. "Your family's been great."

"They like you. They like your passion."

She smiled at that. "Do you know that the two men are in custody now? I'm sure one of the detectives will be in soon to take your statement, but the two have confessed to boat rage. They'll be put away for a long time. And I was right about Jayce and Ashlyn being there when it happened." She filled him in on that and told him that things were smoothing out with her family.

"Good. Did you tell them about us?"

Us. She liked the sound of that. That was when she remembered that they were there. She glanced back to confirm that. They were standing outside the doorway, turned away to give her and Alex privacy. "I think they already know."

They took her glance as an invitation, though, and came into the room. Grant started to instinctively shake Alex's hand, then saw the IV and tucked his hands at his sides. "Nice to see you again, Alex. Thanks for standing by Winslow when I didn't. Couldn't."

Winslow could see that he felt bad about that; she wasn't sure she could forget that he'd taken Ashlyn and Jayce's side . . . that he hadn't confided in her. She stepped a few feet back so the two men could talk.

Ashlyn stepped into Winslow's vacated spot beside the bed. "I hope you understand why we couldn't tell Winslow the truth. We just didn't know what she'd do. We didn't plan for any of this to happen." She looked at the IV bag and monitors. "I still can't believe it did happen."

Winslow felt Jayce move up beside her. His arms were crossed in front of him, and his left arm brushed hers. She turned to him, expecting to find some of the compassion and regret that tainted Ashlyn's and Grant's faces as they talked to Alex. Jayce's cold blue eyes reflected nothing.

Neither did the low voice that whispered, "See what

happens when you stick your nose where it shouldn't be."

The threat—and she was sure that's what it was—took her breath away. She stumbled as she took a step away from him.

"What's wrong?" Alex asked, making Grant and Ashlyn turn to her.

She wanted to reveal what Jayce had said, but he put his arm around her shoulders and said, "She's just tired. You can imagine how this has taken a toll on her." He gave Alex a compassionate look now. "And you, too." He turned to her. "Isn't that right?"

Winslow moved out of his embrace. Jayce was challenging her to repeat what he'd said. Now that her family was coming together, he was daring her to upset everything again. She would look like the paranoid one, and Jayce would no doubt say she'd misunderstood him. Grant and Ashlyn would believe him.

She'd promised to stay within the lines now that the hit-and-run was over.

"Yes, that's right," she said, her words sounding wooden.

Jayce gave her a smug look, so subtle no one but her would see it. "We should go, let Alex here have some quiet time to recuperate."

She met Alex's eyes. He sensed that something was off; he knew her that well already. She couldn't tell him, not now or anytime soon. He needed time to recover, and the last thing he needed was her suspicions about Jayce or knowing that she was still digging into his past. She gave Alex a brilliant smile as she walked over to him.

"I'm just worried about you," she whispered as she kissed him. "Take it easy. I want you back to one hundred percent so we can take up where we left off."

She had to convince him that everything was fine. If he knew it wasn't, he'd make her promise to back off, at least until he was on his feet again. She couldn't do that, not now when, more than ever, she was sure Ashlyn was in danger. Not with the wedding days away. She glanced at the doorway where Ashlyn, Grant, and Jayce were waiting. Jayce especially was watching her, his eyes slightly narrowed as he studied their exchange. She shivered but kept that smile pasted on her face for Alex. She wouldn't drag him into her investigation. This time she would do it alone.

"I'll be by tomorrow," she said, feeling a weight in her chest. "Sleep well."

She paused in front of Jayce as she left the room. Lifted her chin. Met his gaze. Then she walked away. He was playing her, but he wouldn't cow her as he had Ashlyn. She was determined to find the truth . . . no matter what.

20

Winslow dreamed of drowning. She had learned to scuba dive when she attended the University of Miami, along with a group of friends she'd long ago lost touch with. In her dream, she heard the hollow sound of her breathing and the bubbles as they escaped to the surface. She was watching a parrot fish nibbling on the coral when her air disappeared. Frantic, she felt for the tube from her regulator to the tank, following it to . . . a cut end.

She turned around and saw Jayce floating in front of her, waving good-bye. And in the reflection of his mask she saw not her face but Ashlyn's.

She woke with a start, heart pounding, drawing heavy breaths as though she really had been holding them in her tightened chest. Salt and Pepper, jarred from sleep, walked over to see if she was all right, or maybe they thought it was time to get up.

They were right; no way was she going back to sleep. She didn't see the dream as a portent. She knew exactly where it had come from: the dark recesses of her imagination where her fears for Ashlyn grew. She felt it in her bones, that Jayce had wooed his way into her family for the sole intent of marrying Ashlyn for her money. But if he intended to kill her, he'd be unpleasantly surprised to find that Ashlyn had very little in the way of assets.

Jayce needed to know that.

Winslow fed the cats and filled their water bowl, then watered her plants. She had showered early that morning when she'd gotten home, but she jumped in again just to feel the hot prickles against her skin. To feel alive. The beach called to her, and she swore she could hear seagulls squawking and smell the salty breeze. She had too much to do to indulge in that luxury today.

She called Alex at the hospital first, hoping that he hadn't come to his senses and blamed her for his wound. "How are you feeling this morning?"

His voice sounded tight. "I'm fine."

She could hear voices in the background and assumed his family was there. "Are you in pain?"

"A bit."

It amazed her that he'd admitted to being in pain at all. Most of the men she knew would hardly do that. Alex might be a Cuban macho male, or so she'd teased him, but he was down-to-earth enough to admit his weaknesses.

"I'll be by later today."

"Can't wait."

She sighed as she hung up. She couldn't wait, either. Except she'd be hiding something from him once again, and she hated that. She could excuse her subterfuge the first time, when she hardly knew him. Now it was much harder to justify.

After breakfast she called Detective Capperson's cell phone. Though both detectives were still unsure of her, Capperson seemed the most cooperative. "This is Winslow Talbot. I'm sorry to bother you so early, but I wanted to know—"

"We found no .38-caliber guns at either the Stamper or Stevens residence, nor were there any licenses for such issued to them or anyone related to the parties. They deny having anything to do with the shooting. Since they copped to the Taser and the hit-and-run, I'd say they're telling the truth. The shooting was a coincidence."

She wasn't sure whether to be relieved or not.

He said, "I'm afraid the press know who you are now. They've been hounding us for your contact info."

"They haven't found me yet. And I'd rather they didn't."

"We'll do our best. If anyone harasses you, just let me know."

"Thanks. Can you please do me a favor? Run a check on Jayce Bishop. He may have been a resident of San Francisco, though he told us he's from Chicago."

"You nearly got yourself killed doing exactly what we asked you not to do—sticking your neck into an official investigation. Yes, it turned out all right, and I'd venture to say you're a bit of a hero, and yes, you were even right about Jayce and your sister being at the scene. Everything's been resolved but the paperwork. Why do you want me to do a check on Jayce?"

Capperson would hardly perceive Jayce's words as a threat. "I still have reason to believe he isn't who he portrays himself to be. It would ease my mind a great deal to verify that he is. My sister is marrying him the day after tomorrow. He's in a big hurry to marry her. It worries me."

"I probably shouldn't tell you this, so I'll ask you to keep it confidential. Someone here already ran a check on him. He's clean."

"Somebody ran a check? Why?"

"I can't say any more than that. So will you be a good girl and occupy yourself with charity balls and the like?"

She bristled at his insinuation. "Thank you, Detective."

Maybe someone had believed her after all, at least enough to have Jayce checked out. Knowing he was "clean" didn't ease the feeling that knotted her chest, though.

Everyone wanted her to be good. Not that she could blame them after everything she'd been through. All she had to do was conjure up that scuba-diving nightmare, though, and her resolve strengthened.

She went to her computer and did another search on the

Bishop family dispute. Nothing new there. Then she tried
something else: a general search for Jayce Bishop. Nothing
relevant. Then on a lark she typed in *Jason Bishop*. Two
thousand, one hundred, and thirty matches came up.

Daunting as it was, she was glad to have something to
check. For the next hour she hopped from link to link, from
silly diaries of a high school track star, to an ego page high-
lighting some Joe Schmo's minor accomplishments, to the
Jason Bishop who had dedicated an entire Web site to a relatively unknown actor named Bill Fredd.

She honed in on an AP article dated December 2003 because of the location: San Francisco. Jason Bishop's wife of
one year, Amber Mills Bishop, and his stepdaughter, two-
year-old Paige Mills Bishop, were murdered in their upscale
home. The accompanying photograph of the young blond
woman and her daughter broke Winslow's heart. This was
the kind of story she used to shy away from, especially when
a child was the victim.

She focused on the article, though her gaze kept stray-
ing to the picture. Amber had been a single mother and belonged to the old-money Mills family in San Francisco,
owners of the largest bread and bakery company on the West
Coast. She and Jason had married after a whirlwind romance,
and by all accounts he was a doting husband and loving father to Amber's child. He was having dinner with Amber's
parents at the time of the murders; Amber and Paige had
stayed home because they both were sick with colds. Time of
death and the fact that a Kleenex had unidentified DNA on it
cleared Jason of direct involvement. Amber's parents stood
behind his claim of innocence. Nothing was found that connected Jason to the crime indirectly, and the case was listed
as an unsolved murder, likely a break-in gone bad.

Winslow's pulse quickened as she read the article and
then reread it. Unfortunately, there were no pictures of Jason. She did another search for any more articles on the
murder. There were two short follow-ups on a lead involving

cat burglars who had been infiltrating exclusive gated communities. One had been arrested for another burglary but couldn't be connected to the murders.

While the articles printed, Winslow phoned her travel agent. "Mary Pat, I need a flight to San Francisco tonight. Bring me back the following night, though I may change that."

Bless Mary Pat's heart, she didn't complain at having to finagle a last-minute flight. It wasn't cheap, but she managed a direct flight, coach on the way out, first class on the return. Winslow had never flown coach, but she'd fly in cargo if it meant getting out there by tonight.

As she dressed she considered whether to call the Millses and arrange a meeting but decided against doing so until she arrived. She could then tell them she'd flown all the way out just to talk to them; if she called now, they could easily put her off.

An hour later she walked into Alex's hospital room. His mother was there, and she smiled at Winslow as she stood. "I thought you might come this morning. You should cheer him up more than me."

"No one can take the place of his mom," Winslow said, touched by the woman's warmth.

She said something to Alex in Spanish and then, "I will leave you alone."

Winslow made noises about her not having to leave, but Estela Díaz insisted, closing the door behind her.

"She's nice. I like her," Winslow said as she settled against the side of the bed. The chair was too far away. She wanted to touch him, even if only on his arm.

"She likes you, too."

"Even though I almost got her son killed?"

He waved that away as though getting shot was nothing. "She's happy that Elena is getting justice."

Winslow doubted there were no hard feelings about her

involvement. She could sense a reserve beneath the pleasantness. At least they *were* pleasant, though. She'd take the reserve any day. She deserved that and more.

"What are you up to?" he asked, giving her a jolt. Not in an accusing way, she realized.

She had thought about how to explain her absence. More lies, but the truth would only cause dissension. "I'm working on an article for *Dazzle*." Every word scratched her throat as it came out. "Sebastian asked me to tackle an assignment in California, so I'm going out tonight. I'll keep in touch with you, of course, and I should be back late tomorrow night."

"I thought you didn't want your job back."

"I don't, but I'll take freelance assignments until I find something I like." She tilted her head and finally spoke an absolute truth: "I hate leaving you, though."

"I've got my family around. Don't worry about me."

"Impossible," she said in a thick voice.

They talked for a while longer, thankfully about things other than the hit-and-run. It hurt more that he believed her story; she was betraying him. Maybe she was only chasing another wild goose, but something felt right that Jason Bishop was Jayce.

"I've got to go home and pack, load the cats up on food, and all that. I'm taking the five-forty flight; I arrive at nine tonight." She kissed him softly on the mouth. "I'll miss you."

"Come right here after your flight gets in. As long as you're up for it." He squeezed her hand.

That he wanted to see her so badly warmed her. Everything between them felt so tenuous, and she knew that was her fault. How could she think of opening up when she had to keep important information from him?

She said good-bye and went to the children's floor, realizing that she kept herself from looking anywhere but at Elena's door. When she peered into the room, she couldn't have been more surprised. Jayce was talking to Elena and Lidia.

"What are you doing here?" Winslow asked before she could take back the clipped words.

He gave her a smile. "I'm getting information about the benefit and the fund set up for Elena's expenses. For Grant, of course." He was enjoying this, not only surprising her but making her uneasy as well. Elena was vulnerable. Lidia would trust Jayce as Grant's representative.

Jayce placed his hand on Elena's shoulder. "We're going to get this little girl the surgeries she'll need to be beautiful. Just like you had, Winslow."

She shivered, at his touching Elena, at his knowledge of her surgeries and the slow, sticky way he said her name. Still she forced herself to walk into the room and greet Lidia and Elena. Jayce's presence spoiled any good feelings she had about Elena's progress or even Grant's offer of help.

"We're very grateful to your father," Lidia said. "And to you, too, Jayce."

He gave her a warm smile. "I'll do my very best, Lidia."

Winslow stayed for only a few minutes before leaving them to their business. That was her excuse, anyway. She couldn't stand to be in the room with Jayce for longer than that.

Winslow got little sleep on the plane or in the hotel room that night. Early Friday morning she turned on her cell phone. The words *Message Waiting* filled her display. She dialed in and retrieved a message from Alex. His voice sounded subdued, the message a simple, "It's Alex. Call me as soon as you can." He left the number at the hospital but didn't even say good-bye. Strange. Or maybe something was wrong. Maybe he'd been given a bad prognosis or something had happened to Elena.

She called Alex's room. He still didn't sound like himself when he answered.

"Hold on," he said, and then to someone else, "Can you give me a few minutes alone please? Close the door. Thanks."

She was starting to feel uneasy. He was sending his

family out of the room, and she got the distinct impression it wasn't because he wanted to talk sweet.

"You there?" he said a moment later. When she said she was, he said, "You lied again. You're not on an assignment. I should have known that was a lie. It didn't sound right. You're not the kind of writer to cover mushroom festivals anymore. What the hell are you doing, Winslow?"

She felt her insides crumble. "I didn't want to worry you."

"Well, thanks for being so considerate. You told me you weren't going to do this anymore. What the hell could you be—oh, I know. It's Jayce, isn't it? You're still digging into his past."

"I wasn't going to do anything; I swear. But he said something to me when we were in your room yesterday. He whispered it so no one else could hear, and he knew I wouldn't repeat it. He said, 'See what happens when you stick your nose where it shouldn't be.'"

"That's when I saw a strange look on your face. I asked you what was wrong."

"I couldn't tell you, of course, not then."

"Or apparently not even later. Dammit, Winslow, I can't trust you. You're a woman obsessed and you're taking chances again. What are you doing out there?"

She couldn't deny any of that. "You'd do the same if you thought your sister might be in danger. Alex, I found an article on the Internet about a Jason Bishop whose wife and stepdaughter were murdered in their home. The wife came from big money. And they live in San Francisco, the origin of the person Jayce has been calling."

"The one he might be calling in to solve a problem."

"But Jayce doesn't know I'm out here. It's perfectly safe. I never told anyone—wait a minute. How did you know I was lying?"

"I called Grant to find out where you were staying so I could send flowers. You don't know me well enough yet, but I'm a sentimental guy when I care about someone. Grant knew nothing about your so-called assignment, so he called your ex-editor and found out it didn't exist. He knows what you're up to."

Her mind sorted the facts. Alex was going to send her flowers. Guilt. Grant knew she was in California, that she'd lied about why she was going. He would likely mention it to Jayce. Crazy Winslow is at it again. Jayce would know she was here. And he might know why.

"Oh."

"Yeah, *oh*. So it's not perfectly safe. Would he guess what you'd be doing?"

"Only if he's got something to hide out here. I'm going to talk to the wife's family; first I have to ascertain that it's Jayce. I'm hoping to get some ammo to give to Ashlyn. The murders were never solved. Jayce was with her parents when it happened, but that doesn't exonerate him. He could have had someone else do the deed to set up a perfect alibi for himself. The police couldn't really consider him a suspect, especially when her parents stood by him."

"Maybe because he didn't do it."

"I can feel that something's not right. I've always felt that way about Jayce. And now I may have the reason why."

"I'm checking out and coming there."

"No, you need to recover." From the last time he'd helped her. "I'm not dragging you into this. Not after what just happened. I'm not sneaking around abandoned warehouses in the wrong part of town. These people live in an exclusive gated community. And now that Jayce may know I'm out here, I'll be doubly careful."

"Dammit, Winslow. You have a lot of nerve making me care about you and then throwing yourself in danger again."

"I care about you, too. But this is something I have to do. I've got a flight scheduled home tonight; that part is true. And I will come by the hospital . . . if you still want me to."

"Just call and let me know you're back."

When he hung up, the sound put a dent in her heart. *Alejandro*. He cared about her, but he wasn't going to let himself care anymore. He couldn't afford to. She understood, but it didn't make it any less painful. But she was already committed to finding out the truth here. She had to follow through. She half-hoped that Amber's husband wouldn't be the same man and that she'd find nothing else to incriminate Jayce.

She phoned the Millses sometime later and spoke first with their butler and then with Mrs. Mills.

"My name is Winslow Talbot. You don't know me, but my sister is about to marry Jayce Bishop down in Miami, Florida. I think her fiancé may be the same Jason Bishop who was married to your daughter. I'm so sorry to bring up such a painful time in your lives, but I need to talk to you about Jason. I flew here from Florida last night just to see you."

The woman seemed to digest this. "I'm not sure how I can help you."

"Just help me verify whether the men are the same."

"But to what purpose are you investigating? I'm not sure I understand."

"Please, let me meet you and I'll explain everything." When the woman hesitated, Winslow said, "Jayce Bishop wooed my sister and has now pushed up the wedding to this weekend. If he's the same person, he never told her about his wife and stepdaughter. And I think she needs to know."

"Well, all right. You may come here then." She gave her directions and they set up a time of eleven that morning.

"Thank you so much."

She hung up and looked at the clock. She had two hours to kill. If Jayce wasn't Jason she could breathe a little easier. But she'd still keep digging into Jayce's past.

Because that feeling wasn't going to go away until she found out what was causing it. She knew she was risking everything to find a truth that might be nothing at all. She could lose her family again, Alex, and, at the furthest extreme, even her life. But she knew she couldn't let this go.

Grant was staring out the window when Jayce's voice pulled him from disturbing thoughts.

"Hey, Dad, you okay?"

He tried to put on a happier face but couldn't. Just when the whole hit-and-run ordeal was finally behind them, when he could once again focus on his political aspirations, Winslow seemed to have gone off the deep end again. This time, though, it had nothing to do with the hit-and-run. So it could only be about one other thing—or person, as the case was.

"Jayce, do you have any connections in California?"

His eyebrows furrowed. "Why do you ask?"

"Just tell me first."

"Yeah, I lived in San Francisco for a few years."

He was waiting patiently for Grant to elaborate. Should he? Jayce ought to know his future sister-in-law was still gunning for him, Grant supposed. He had had a friend at the city police department run a check on Jayce just to make sure he didn't have any convictions on-record. Winslow's insistence on her bad feelings had prompted the action, and he'd been ashamed of having done it when Jayce came back clean other than a speeding ticket two months ago. The only evidence of subterfuge was that Jayce's real name was Jason, hardly incriminating.

"Dad, what's going on?" Jayce sat down in front of Grant's desk.

"I'm afraid Winslow seems to be at it again."

"What? But she knows everything about the hit-and-run."

"I don't think it has anything to do with that. I guess we've got to accept that she has it in for you, just as you suspected. I don't know exactly what she's up to, but I got a call from Alex Díaz yesterday. He said that Sebastian had Winslow flying to California to write a freelance article. Alex wanted to send her flowers. I didn't know anything about it, but I had to admit she and I haven't quite reconnected yet. So I called Sebastian and discovered he hasn't spoken to her since she quit. Because she lied to Alex and didn't mention the trip to me, I have to conclude she's up to something. And that something concerns you."

Jayce was now staring out the window. He muttered, "It's my fault."

"What?"

He blinked, perhaps surprised he'd said his thoughts aloud. "I said something to her at the hospital. I don't remember the exact words, but something to the effect of, 'Now that this is behind us, maybe you'll see that I'm good for this family.' She got this funny look on her face and moved away from me. I thought it was pretty obvious that I was trying to mend fences. It seemed to set her off instead."

Jayce stood and glanced at his watch. "This is upsetting. Ashlyn's going to be upset, too. She was really hoping that Winslow could be part of the wedding." He ran his hand through his hair in an agitated manner. "I should probably let Ashlyn know. Winslow may call her, and Ashlyn wouldn't suspect that the purpose of the call might be to intimidate her. Do you mind if I talk to her in private?"

"No, of course not."

Jayce grabbed his cell phone and walked out to the pool deck. Grant turned back to the forms he was filling out. Just when things had started to get back on-track. Who knew what trouble Winslow would get into this time?

Cal Driscoll was in the middle of a dream and at the edge of his hangover when the phone rang. He jolted out of bed as his groggy brain tried to remember where his cell phone was. Clipped to the belt on the jeans he'd shucked last night—no, earlier that morning. He moved toward the chair where the jeans were draped, and his feet got caught in the tangled sheets, sending him hurtling to the floor. He grabbed the leg of his jeans and yanked them closer, pressing the button a second before the call would go to voice mail. His cousin hated when that happened.

"Yeah?"

"We got trouble, and I'll bet she's right there in San Fran."

Cal glanced at the clock on his nightstand. "Dude, it's six thirty in the morning!"

"Listen to me. Winslow's there. I'll guarantee you that she found an article somewhere about the murders and is now checking into it. I want you positioned at Portsmouth Landing's entrance watching everyone who goes through the gates. She'll be in a rental car. I'm going to e-mail you a picture of her so you'll know what to look for."

"And if she shows? What do you want me to do?"

"Call me immediately. If she's found the Millses, I'll need a game plan."

The phone disconnected and then rang again. He pressed the button. "Yeah?"

"Don't go back to sleep!" It disconnected again.

He mimicked Jayce's order, and though it sounded juvenile, it made him feel better. His older cousin had always been the order giver, like one year's difference gave him authority. Still, those five years Jayce had lived with Cal's family had changed his life. He had to admit that Jayce had instilled discipline and focus in him.

Cal had hated Jayce at first. He'd never known his cousin before his dad, Bonner, had offered to give him a home. While Cal and his father had always been at odds with each other, with Cal bucking his disciplinary techniques and strictness, Jayce had hit it right off with Bonner. He'd even taken up that sucky game of golf that Cal's dad loved. Bonner worked at one of the area country clubs as head of golf course maintenance. Jayce went with him and helped, making Cal sure he was just sucking up to the old man. Then the son of a bitch, as it turned out, had a knack for golf.

When Cal was snooping around in Jayce's things, he found a stash of cash. In return for his silence, Jayce told him how he'd earned it—betting on golf with the snobby country clubbers. He'd called the rich folks suckers, and Cal had liked his attitude.

Jayce began having Cal do errands for him and paid him well. That was when Cal had started to like him. Not only for the money but also for all the things Jayce taught him. And for all the dreams he'd instilled in him.

So Cal popped open a beer—hair of the dog—and pulled on the jeans and a clean shirt. He'd watch the entrance. He'd do just about anything for Jayce.

21

Winslow was relieved that Mrs. Mills had remembered to alert the man at the Portsmouth's Landing guardhouse that she be allowed in. She'd been worried that the woman had changed her mind.

The home at 1441 Langley Drive was in the Tudor style, the lawn immaculately kept. It reminded Winslow of Grant's parents' home in Connecticut, where they sometimes went for Christmas holidays. Everything was so formal and stuffy. Servants cooked, served, and cleaned up after the big meal, and Winslow always felt sorry that they couldn't spend Christmas with their own families.

She parked on rust-colored pavers in the circular drive and walked up the stone steps to the massive arched door. A maid led her through a foyer larger than Grant's, then through a formal living room. Winslow needn't have been concerned about resurrecting painful memories of Amber. A huge portrait over the stone fireplace depicted the beautiful blonde and her baby girl, who was a near mirror image of her mother. Framed pictures were everywhere, formal family gatherings and a few candid shots. Winslow got her answer in a studio portrait set off to the side. Amber's husband posed elegantly next to his wife, his arm draped over her shoulder, his fingers brushing the baby's arm.

Her heart was thudding now. *Jayce.*

"Ma'am?" the maid said.

Winslow had come to a halt in front of the picture. "They were a lovely family."

"Yes, they were," she said in a soft voice, obviously uneasy. "We should continue."

Winslow was led to a sunroom, where one could pretend to be outside without the nuisance of fresh air. Mrs. Mills sat at a small table in a pool of sunshine.

"Thank you so much for seeing me." Winslow shook the woman's hand and then took the padded iron chair across from her.

The maid brought a silver tray with tea and cookies. Winslow felt strange being served as though she were a guest. She went through the ritual of preparing her tea and taking a bite of a lemon cookie while observing Mrs. Mills. The woman had aged significantly since those portraits in the living room were taken.

Mrs. Mills set half of her cookie down on a delicate plate. "I'm not sure how I can help you, as I said on the phone."

"You already have, in a way. The man who married your daughter is indeed the man who is about to marry my sister, Ashlyn."

"You said he hasn't mentioned Amber to your family." The thought obviously hurt, that her daughter had become an unmentionable. Or even worse, forgotten.

"And since it only happened two years ago, I find it strange."

Mrs. Mills sighed. "I suppose he's able to go on. It's enviable."

"I'm not sure how anyone could go on after such a horrible tragedy. Your daughter and granddaughter were beautiful."

"They were. Jason positively doted on them. They were married for a year before . . ."

"The newspaper said he courted her in a whirlwind style."

"He did indeed. They'd only known each other for a few months when she announced they were getting married. He even asked our permission in a gallant, old-fashioned gesture. We, of course, objected to the time line. We had hoped for a yearlong engagement in which they could get better acquainted, but they wanted to marry within the month. Amber was a single mother. She'd become involved with the wrong sort of man, who impregnated her and then left town. It hurt her immensely. How could we object when she'd found a man who would love her and another man's child? We scrambled to put the event together—four hundred guests, an orchestra. It worked out wonderfully."

It sounded exactly like her sister's situation. "Who was pushing for the quick wedding? Was it Jayce—Jason?"

"They both wanted it. They were so excited."

He had probably persuaded her that she wanted a fast wedding, too, just as Winslow was sure Jayce had done with Ashlyn.

"You liked Jason," she confirmed.

"Tremendously. He was so kind to Amber and Paige. They deserved a good man. He was in the process of adopting Paige, and that made us all so happy. She was too young to understand not having a father's last name, but it wouldn't be long before she would. We were pleased that she wouldn't have that stigma. Even after . . . we made sure the papers ran Paige's last name as Bishop."

"What was Jason's background?"

She gave that some thought. "His family was from Nevada. I gathered there were bad feelings, because he didn't talk about them or his past much. No one on his side came to the wedding. Naturally we suspected he might be after our money, at least at first. He had money of his own, but he didn't seem to come from money. But he wasn't interested in material things. Nevertheless, we kept them on a tight leash. Jason had nothing to gain financially by marrying into our family. Everything was set up to benefit Amber and Paige. And Charles, my husband, put Jason to work at the company. He had to earn his keep."

"Jason told us he's from a wealthy family in Chicago. He's supposedly mired in an inheritance dispute. I was unable to verify if he is, indeed, part of that Bishop family."

"That is strange. Perhaps it's another branch of the same family."

"Perhaps," Winslow echoed. "How did your family come to know Jason?"

"He was a new member of our country club. Though Charles wouldn't admit it, I suspect the two were betting on the game. Jason is a phenomenal golf player. It's a wonder he didn't pursue that professionally. Charles invited him to a couple of social events, and that's where Jason met Amber."

"That's how he met my sister, too. It looks like a pattern."

"Well, dear, if he plays golf, he's bound to make friends. Meeting the daughter of one of the club members would be quite normal."

Winslow and Mrs. Mills were dancing around Jayce's intentions. She suspected the worst, and Mrs. Mills believed the best.

"I understand that Jason was here when . . . when the murders happened."

"Yes, we had a standing Sunday dinner, something we'd been doing since Amber moved out on her own. She and Paige had come down with a bug, but Jason came anyway. We had a lovely dinner, as usual. He even called Amber to check on her. I spoke to her, too." Her voice softened. "The last time I ever did. She sounded miserable. Then he got back on the phone and told her he loved her and that he'd be home soon. She told him to take his time, as she was going to sleep. The police asked me if she sounded different. But aside from being congested, she sounded normal. They said it happened . . . soon after that call. Jason enjoyed an after-dinner drink with us and updated us on his plans to adopt Paige."

Cementing his alibi, Winslow's suspicious mind added.

"He left here at ten o'clock and . . . found them."

Both had been murdered in Paige's room. Amber had apparently lain down on a bed she kept in there.

Mrs. Mills composed herself after a moment. "He called nine-one-one and then us. He was in complete shock. We rushed right over; their home was only a couple of blocks from here. No one could pretend to be that grief stricken. The news stations played the nine-one-one tape. Anything to get a reaction," she added bitterly. "You could hear the emotion in his voice."

"Was he a suspect?"

"The investigators looked at him, of course. They always do in these kinds of cases. He was quickly eliminated. When time of death was determined, he couldn't possibly have been there. They found a tissue with DNA that couldn't be matched to anyone in the house. The police thought it might belong to the murderer. We were behind Jason one hundred percent. There wasn't one person who could say that they'd seen him be anything but loving to both of them."

Either Jayce was innocent or he was an Oscar-quality actor. "It sounds as though he really did love her." That was what Mrs. Mills needed to believe. "Do you still keep in touch with him?"

"Oh no. Things got, well, a little ugly. You see, we had given them the home as a wedding present. Jason was surprised to learn that the house was in the family trust. He couldn't touch it. As soon as the investigators were finished, we put it on the market. It hurt us a great deal that he fought us for that house. We battled for months over it, but eventually he lost. It soured our relationship with him. All he got was the money from the insurance policy he'd taken on Amber."

"Insurance policy? Wouldn't that be considered motive?"

"Naturally the police checked into it. The policy was only for two hundred thousand dollars, not really big enough to drive a man to murder. He had one on himself, too, in the same amount, to take care of Paige should something happen to either of them."

But Paige was killed, too. "The article I read said it was probably a home invasion gone bad."

"Several items had been taken; drawers had been rifled through. They thought that these burglars knew about the Sunday dinners, that maybe they'd been casing the home for a few weeks. They were surprised to find my daughter and granddaughter there. Maybe they panicked or didn't want to be identified. We'll never know."

Why kill a baby? Paige wasn't old enough to identify them. But if Jayce wanted all the money and no child to take care of, he would have her killed, too. The thought sickened Winslow.

"Did the police ever consider that Jason had someone break into the house? You have to admit that his being with you gave him an ironclad alibi. He could have set it up that way."

"Yes, they did explore that horrible theory. There was no evidence of it."

"Didn't it make you wonder, though, when he fought you for the house?"

Doubt shadowed her face. "It made Charles wonder. But it just didn't make sense. Jason could live in the house as long as he was married at no cost. He had a good job. He loved my daughter and granddaughter. Why would he throw all that away for a house worth only one-point-eight million dollars, even less with the stigma of the murders?"

Greed, Winslow thought. One-point-eight million wasn't a lot to people like them. It was a heck of a lot to someone who had no money of his own. Especially if he was only pretending to love Amber and Paige. Especially if he hated having to work.

"Can you remember . . . did he isolate Amber from her friends? Or rather, did he want her all to himself?"

"Amber didn't have any good friends. Being a single mother, an unwed mother, didn't exactly make her popular with her peers. I think we were her closest friends."

A vulnerable young woman in need of friendship and acceptance. Winslow kept the words inside.

"I'm sorry to dredge up all of this, Mrs. Mills, and I really do appreciate your time. The only reason I would ever do that is because I'm concerned about my sister's safety. I want to make sure nothing terrible happens to her, too."

Mrs. Mills grasped the handle of the delicate teacup, though she didn't lift it. "We all want to protect our loved ones. But I don't think Jason will hurt her. She's probably a lucky girl if he loves her as much as he loved Amber."

Winslow couldn't help shuddering at that. She imagined how he always touched Ashlyn, how he doted on her. Was it real? She had seen evidence of his acting ability, when he was cold to her and then in front of others eager to make her a sister figure in his life. Was he so good that he'd fooled this couple? The possibility chilled her to the bone.

She stood. "Thank you so much. Please, don't get up; I can let myself out."

Before she left, she drove past the house that Jason and Amber had lived in so happily. It was probably worth a lot more now, even with the taint of murder. It was nearly as big as the Millses' house and situated on a lake. This house and a two-hundred-thousand-dollar life insurance policy were definitely motive for murder.

She stopped at the end of the road and called Mary Pat. "Hey, it's Winslow. Can you get me an earlier flight home? Yep, call me when you find something."

Despite Mrs. Mills's naive beliefs, Winslow was afraid for Ashlyn's life. Now more than ever, she was sure that Ashlyn would not be coming back from her honeymoon.

Cal called Jayce as soon as Winslow's car passed through the gated entry of the snooty community. "You called it, dude. She's going in now."

There was a lapse as Jayce obviously walked out of the father's office to talk in private. "Okay, here's what you're going to do. She's supposed to be flying back to Miami tonight. Make sure you're on that flight. Get a rental car with a GPS. I'll be there to meet you. Until then, tail her."

"You got it."

Cal wished he'd brought something to eat. And a bottle to piss in. He was parked on the other side of the highway across from the entrance. He maneuvered to the passenger side of the BMW Jayce had bought him, cracked open the door, and aimed for the opening. After that, he had only his hunger to focus on. And the guardhouse.

Winslow drove through the exit gate a short while later. Long enough to have had a nice little chat with Mrs. Mills. He wondered what the old bag had told her. Winslow asked the guard something, and the man pointed west. Cal pulled onto the highway, turned around, and followed her. Thankfully she turned into a shopping center and walked into a small café. He watched from the McDonald's parking lot.

She spent enough time in there to eat lunch and then headed west again. She pulled into a library's parking lot a few minutes later and went inside. He parked near her car and followed her, keeping out of sight while she scanned the rolls of old microfiche. When he saw the headlines about the murders he knew what she was doing. She printed out several articles and paid the librarian.

Winslow's cell phone rang just as she walked outside, and she stepped to the side and answered it. He walked out and lit a cigarette, facing away from her.

"Mary Pat, I love you! Wait; let me write this down. . . . Flight Twelve-fourteen, Alaskan Airlines, at three-oh-five." She checked her watch. "I can make it. I'm sending you a bonus. Talk to you later." She disconnected and nearly ran to her rental car.

He called Alaskan Airlines while he drove. "I want to book a flight. Flight Twelve-fourteen, at three today. Do you have anything in first class? . . . Great. I'll take it."

Ashlyn knew something was up when Jayce asked her to come to the house for lunch. She could hear it in his voice.

During the drive over she drowned in the fear that he had changed his mind about marrying her tomorrow. He sounded that ominous. No, it was probably about whatever Winslow was up to.

"What's going on?" she asked as soon as Esme had delivered their sandwiches and closed the door behind her.

She, Grant, and Jayce sat at a small table by the pool. The sunlight reflected off the water and splashed reflections across the deck and table.

"We all hoped that once Winslow knew the truth, she'd return to her normal self, maybe even come to the wedding," Jayce said. "But she's still up to her tricks trying to find something incriminating against me. She's in California now." He rubbed his hand over his mouth. "The thing is, I lived there for a while. I think I know what Winslow's looking into. There's something I haven't told either of you, not because it's a secret, but because . . ." He looked away and took a deep breath. It was going to be painful; she could see it in his eyes.

"Because it's very painful," he said, confirming her thoughts and making her feel as though she knew him so well.

"What is it?" Grant asked when Jayce once again lapsed into what must be an awful memory.

"I was married once."

The revelation was painful for her, too, not only because she'd believed she would be his first wife, indeed, his first real love, but also because he'd lied to her. "When?"

"November of 2002. Amber and I were married for just over a year. She had a little girl by a boyfriend who had abandoned her." Jayce pulled Ashlyn's hands into his. "It wasn't the kind of love I feel for you. I liked Amber, but mostly I felt sorry for her. She had no friends and lived with parents who were older. I felt a need to protect her and her daughter. I cared about her. So we married."

Ashlyn wanted to pull her hands free, but he was gripping

them. He hadn't loved that woman as much as he loved her. She held on to those words. "What happened? Did you get a divorce?"

"I wish it had been something like that." He cleared his throat and stared at his shoes for a moment. "She and her daughter were murdered in our home." He looked up, and Ashlyn saw agony in his eyes. "I found them. I'd been at her parents' home for our usual Sunday dinner. Amber and Paige were home with the flu, and she insisted that I go ahead without them." His voice cracked when he said, "I wish to God I had stayed. Someone broke into the house. I think Amber surprised them."

"Oh my God." Now Ashlyn squeezed his hands back. "And you found them?"

He nodded. "It was horrible. Paige still in her crib. So much blood. I couldn't believe it; it was like a nightmare. The killer or killers were never caught."

Grant asked, "Did they suspect you?"

"Only because it's standard procedure. I was with her parents when it happened. I had no real motive, other than an insurance policy, and I sure as hell wouldn't have killed two innocent people for two hundred thousand dollars. Especially not a baby." He took several deep breaths and then looked at Grant. "So you see, I had no reason to keep this from you other than to spare myself, and you, a painful story. That's really why I came to Miami, to get away from the memories."

"You lived in California?" Ashlyn asked, trying to understand the logistics.

"For a couple of years. I wanted a break from the Midwest. So there, that's my big secret that Winslow has finally dredged up. I hope she's happy." He broke down then, burying his face in his hands.

Ashlyn looked helplessly at her dad and then put her arms around Jayce. "Damn her. Damn her to hell."

• • •

Dallis Jordan felt even more depressed than usual. She sprawled on her black velvet bedspread and let Bob-the-snake slither around her. Ashlyn was getting married tomorrow. Dallis read the announcement in the paper and felt angry, empty, and . . . depressed. It would be a small ceremony, mostly for friends and family. She and Ashlyn had been best friends once.

Dallis had written a song that morning about a man coming between two women friends. Later she would play it for her dad and see what he thought.

Though it was in the middle of the day and the sun was shining brightly, the black drapes made it look like twilight in her room. She liked twilight, that eerie time of day that wasn't light and wasn't dark but somewhere in between.

Her room was the only place in the house that was truly her own. For as long as she could remember, there had been a steady stream of friends and strangers coming and going in whatever house they lived in, staying in whatever room they found handy. Doing things other than sleeping in them, too. She kept her door locked.

Her mother had died of a drug overdose when Dallis was seven. She'd found her in the bathroom, her vomit all over the white tile floor. Since then, Dallis's dad had had a steady stream of women, too. Some had the mistaken notion of wanting to be a mother to her. Others didn't give a crap. Either way, Dallis wanted nothing to do with being mothered.

She brooded some more, and then anger grew as bright as the tip of her cigarette. She pulled herself up and started digging through her drawers filled with DVDs from her video camera. She'd labeled most of them: *Ashlyn and me at the music festival; Ashlyn and me at Dad's benefit concert, 2001.*

"Ass. Bitch." She continued down the alphabet, finding disgusting words to describe Ashlyn. As she recited the words, she dumped disk after disk into the garbage. Most of the videos were on her computer, and as mad as she was, she still recognized the act as more symbolic than destructive.

She stopped when she came across a disk titled *Ashlyn, Jace, and me on his boat, 2005*. Now she knew she'd mis-spelled his name after reading the stupid wedding announce-ment. She started reciting names for him instead. "Arrogant. Butthead. Cocky." But she held on to the disk. It was the last time she'd been with Ashlyn.

Since self-torture appealed to her, she put the disk into her computer and waited for the movie software to automat-ically start up. The beginning of the disk was Ashlyn trying on bathing suits in preparation for their boat date with Jayce. She was positively giddy, something that Dallis was pretty sure she'd never been. Ashlyn's slender body barely filled in most of the bathing suit tops, a frequent lament.

"I asked him if he had a friend for you, but he doesn't know many people in town," Ashlyn said before disappear-ing into the dressing room again.

"Puhlease, don't set me up with anyone." She'd dated lit-tle, though she had a slew of male friends.

Ashlyn had brought fancy little pins and she nipped and tucked a dark purple suit and checked the results in the mir-ror. "Perfect. You think?"

"Divine, dahling!"

Ashlyn beamed, but her joy was short-lived as she eyed Dallis. "What about you? Do you have a new bathing suit?"

"I'm not wearing a bathing suit. But my shorts are new." With her square body, she hated wearing suits. Ashlyn al-ways seemed to forget that.

Dallis watched the video for a while longer, feeling a longing that cut right through her. No one had ever liked her as much as Ashlyn had. She had been one of those pretty, rich girls who usually looked down on Dallis. But Ashlyn hadn't looked down. Dallis loved her because of that, be-cause of a lot of things. And now this guy she hated—and who disliked her—was marrying Ashlyn.

The clip ended with a fancy fade-out as Ashlyn posed with her altered suit. A moment later a new clip showed them out on Jayce's boat. Dallis panned the surrounding communities and big houses perched on the water's edge of the bay. Jayce always seemed to turn away when she aimed at him. Maybe he had the same problem she did, though she doubted it. Her last therapist—Dr. Cruella, as Dallis had dubbed her—had decided that Dallis hid behind the camera. It was a kind of security blanket. The witch had a point. Whenever someone wanted to take the camera, Dallis wouldn't let it go. But heck, she didn't want to see herself on the videos.

Finally Jayce said, "Turn that thing off. It might get blown off the boat."

At the time, she thought he'd been concerned about her camera flying overboard. Now . . . now it almost sounded like a threat. She could tell that she'd set the camera in the bag, but the screen never faded out. She obviously thought she'd hit the button. For the most part, she couldn't see or hear much over the engine noise. The sky passed by; a hand fluttered in front of the lens.

Fifteen minutes later the boat slowed to an idle, and then the engine cut off. They'd brought wine and sandwiches. Jayce dropped the anchor using the windlass; she heard the grinding sound of chain being released into the water. The camera bag shifted, probably while they cleared space for food. The camera ended up at a tilted angle showing the back portion of the boat.

She heard herself announce that she was going to the head and rolled her eyes. She hated, absolutely *hated,* her voice on tape. Once the cabin door slid shut, she heard Ashlyn asking where they should set up the condiments.

Jayce said, "I'm not sure what it says about you that your best, and from what I can tell only, friend is a demented cow."

"Jayce, that's a horrible thing to say!"

It didn't surprise Dallis, but it hurt just the same. At least Ashlyn had stood up for her. She was almost afraid to keep listening, but what could he say that would hurt her more than that?

"I'm just kidding," he said, but didn't mean it.

She saw Ashlyn's shoulder in the corner of the screen and then heard the cabin door slide open and closed again. Dallis remembered Ashlyn being down in the cabin when she'd gotten out of the head, and she'd looked a bit upset. She'd said it was hot out there and she was feeling cranky. Probably her period coming on. They'd talked for a few minutes.

But the camera was taping what was going on up on the deck. Dallis felt dizzy as she heard what Jayce was saying, obviously to someone on a cell phone. He abruptly ended the call at the sound of the cabin door sliding open.

"Oh my God." She leaped off the bed and grabbed the Scooby-Doo phone. Winslow had left her home number, and with shaky fingers Dallis dialed it. The machine picked up and Winslow's cheery voice asked the caller to leave a message.

"Winslow, it's Dallis. I just found a video from the last time I was with Ashlyn. Jayce had taken us out on his boat. Oh, jeez, you were right about him. And I've got proof. The camera was taping and . . . I'll let you watch it. Come right over to the house as soon as you get this."

She thought about calling Ashlyn, but what if Jayce was with her? Knowing him, he would come, too. No, she'd wait for Winslow. And she'd hope it wasn't too late.

"Here, kitty, kitty. Come out and play."

The black cat peered out from beneath the foliage around the fountain, but it wouldn't come out. The white cat had run off as soon as he'd come into the condo using Ashlyn's key. Jayce hated cats.

He hated Winslow more.

He walked around the condo looking in her files and on her computer, trying to find out what she knew. She'd done a search on his name, both versions of his first name. That was how she'd found out about Amber. Well, he supposed Winslow *was* a journalist of sorts. It was in her blood to sniff things out. What he couldn't figure out was why she'd had it in for him from the beginning. He'd been charming from minute one. He'd actually thought that she might have wanted him for herself, that maybe she was jealous that he'd honed in on Ashlyn instead. While that had boosted his ego for a while, he now knew it wasn't true. Winslow saw something in him that most people didn't. That made her a threat.

The phone rang four times before the answering machine picked up. He'd checked the messages when he'd come in and found one call from some chick who wanted to go shopping in Palm Beach.

He was surprised to hear Dallis's voice on the machine. He'd had no idea they were friends. When he heard the message, though, he understood perfectly. So Dallis had something of interest.

Cal had informed him that Winslow was taking an earlier flight. Still, she wouldn't arrive until one thirty that morning, so it would be after two by the time she got home. He pressed the erase button on the machine with the tip of a pen.

"Here, kitty, kitty," he chanted as he peered out the window to make sure no one was lingering about. No cats lingered, either. Maybe they also sensed something in him.

He locked the door and headed to his car as though he had every right to be in the building. That was the trick: look as though you belong.

Salt and Pepper eased out of their hiding places moments after the intruder had gone. The phone rang again, four times, and then the machine picked up.

"Hey, it's Dallis again. Forgot to mention that my dad's having one of his parties tonight, so just come in and up the stairs like last time. Don't worry about knocking; no one will hear you anyway. I don't care how late it is. There's no way I can go to sleep now. Just get here as soon as you can."

The phone disconnected.

22

Dallis was used to falling asleep to the sounds of laughter, loud music, and the occasional scream of joy. She never wanted to know what caused those, though sometimes a groan from the bedroom next to hers told her anyway. The bass wasn't always the only thing pounding at the walls.

She had set the camera on the dresser loaded with the disk, ready to take to the police. The air in the room was thick with the pack of cigarettes she'd polished off waiting for Winslow's call. It was after midnight. She called again, but the answering machine picked up, and she hung up. She hoped Winslow was all right. Dallis supposed she could go to the police on her own, but she needed Winslow's credibility—and her knowledge of Jayce.

After waiting another thirty minutes and calling one more time, she flopped back in bed and closed her eyes. The noise in the house fused into one hum that lulled her to sleep. She dreamed of Ashlyn and her dad and even Mom. Her mom smiled in her dream, something Dallis had rarely seen her do.

Dallis felt Bob-the-snake slithering around her arm, tightening ever so slightly. Then she felt a prick, as though he'd sunk a fang into her skin. Before she could put together that her snake had no fangs, she felt a rush of liquid joy and warmth. Bells tinkled in the distance. She dreamed that Bob-the-snake was injecting her with sunshine; she could feel the golden aura traveling through her veins.

Her eyes snapped open. When she saw Jayce standing beside her bed she thought she was still asleep, having a nightmare. Especially since he was smiling at her. No, not at her. Just smiling in a smug way.

That's when she came fully awake, when she realized that he was really in her room and that she couldn't move. Her breathing came in heavy gasps and it was hard to focus. But she did, forcing her gaze to the arm where the snake had bit her. She saw a snake, but it wasn't Bob. It was flesh colored, and in that instant Jayce released the snake, and it fell to the floor.

Not a snake. Rubber tubing. She knew exactly what it was: standard equipment for shooting up.

Her father's raucous laughter filtered from downstairs. They were playing a track from his comeback album that hadn't helped him to come back.

"What. . . . what?" she tried to ask, but her mouth wouldn't form the words.

Jayce had picked up her camera and was aiming it at her. The little red light was blinking. He was filming her! There was some significance to that camera, but she couldn't figure it out. All she knew was she didn't want him filming her. She hated to be on-camera.

"Speedball," Jayce said, and it took her a few seconds to realize he'd answered her unfinished question.

Cocaine and heroin, the deadly mix that had killed John Belushi and Chris Farley. She knew others, personally knew them, but couldn't come up with their names. She'd never mixed the two before, though she had shot up cocaine a couple of times. She hadn't liked it. One of the reasons was the bells she heard, as though angels were summoning her. Bells, angels . . . death.

"How do you feel, Dallis? Do you feel *high*?"

She didn't know if he was drawing out the words in a high pitch of voice or if she were just hearing it that way. That earlier joy turned to hatred and fear. *He was planning to overdose her. He knew about . . .*

About what?

She heard more laughter from downstairs and Cammie's high-pitched giggle. So close, just down a flight of stairs. If only she could move. In the background, Dad's song about how drugs weren't the only way of getting high. Album too clean, he said. That's why it tanked.

Jayce sat at her computer desk and tapped on the keyboard with one hand while keeping the camera aimed on her with the other. The drawer holding all of her DVDs was open.

The DVD. It was in the camera. Something about Ashlyn. Danger.

He was fiddling with her computer, and then he said, "Ah," and started a video on the screen. She couldn't focus on it. All she could hear was the whining sound of an engine and then voices above the sound. Ashlyn. Jayce.

She rolled to her side, feeling nauseated. He'd shot her up. That meant she couldn't even throw it up to get it out of her system. She was going to die. Her heart was already racing from the cocaine. Her bones felt as though they'd melted.

Ashlyn laughed. Not real. On the tape.

Dallis tried to focus on the screen. It took a few minutes. Just sky. Then Ashlyn yelling at him, going down to the cabin.

"This is what you had, isn't it? This is why you called Winslow."

He turned up the volume, but she already knew what he was going to say. Or said. Past tense. God, her brain was muzzy. Her stomach lurched, and she dry-heaved. She saw Bob-the-snake in his aquarium, sliding up against the glass.

Jayce's voice on the computer. "Hey, Cal. You used to be chubby. I just screwed up and called Ashlyn's friend a demented cow. . . . No, not to her face. But Ash is pissed at me.

I want to say something to the cow to redeem myself. So
Ash will know I was just kidding. I'm still in the perfect
boyfriend phase; I can't mess it up now. . . . Oh yeah, I've
got her hooked. I've only got a few seconds. Give me some
help here."

Then the sound of her and Ashlyn's voices. Jayce's comment that Dallis should wear a bathing suit next time. He bet
she looked great in a bikini.

She heard her dad's laugh again, and it made a tear fill
her right eye. Jayce tapped on the keyboard again. Erasing
video. Evidence. She dry-heaved again; a string of saliva felt
cold against her chin. The panic at the sight of blood-tinged
saliva made it hard to breathe. Not good; not good at all.

Jayce broke the DVD in half. Tucked it in his pocket. He
was wearing gloves. No fingerprints.

He turned in the chair, camera to his eye. "How ya feeling, Dallis? Flying high yet?"

She felt numb. Couldn't move. Couldn't even hate him
anymore. Still couldn't breathe. Her chest hurt, as though an
elephant were sitting on her.

"Winslow's not going to get your message, by the way. I
was there when you called. I erased it."

She wanted to call him a bastard, but her mouth wouldn't
move. Her lips were tingling. Her eyes burned and her lungs
felt as though they were going to explode.

He seemed to be watching her from a great distance. He
lifted her hand and said, "Wave bye-bye, Dallis. Yeah, it's
been real nice. Bye-bye."

She couldn't think. Cammie laughed downstairs. Someone else shouted. Music got louder. *Dad's laugh one more
time . . . please, let it be the last thing I hear.*

Her vision blurred. She couldn't see Jayce anymore,
though she knew he was still there. She felt light-headed
as she sucked in shallow breaths. Then, finally, her dad
laughed, almost drowned out by the music. She slid into
oblivion.

• • •

Ashlyn opened her eyes to find Jayce kissing her neck. "We're not supposed to see each other before our wedding day." She looked at the clock; it was just after midnight.

He was staying in the guest room at her dad's place. Or at least that was the idea.

"I missed you," Jayce said, and took her protests away with a deep, lunging kiss. "I can't sleep. I'm used to having my baby snuggled up beside me."

He wasn't a snuggler, but she could hardly argue at the moment. He was snuggling now, and she hadn't realized how much she wanted that. He cupped her breast beneath her pajama top and stroked her nipple.

"We really shouldn't," she managed, already breathless. "The wedding . . ."

He stopped abruptly. "Are you going to send me away? When I want you so much, when I need you? I just want to make love to you and then I'll go back home."

He needed her. That's all he had to say. She kissed him hard and forgot about her request for a night apart. He had never been so loving, so gentle, and at the same time so passionate. He had never said he'd needed her before. And so she gave in as she always did, because she loved him so.

At two in the morning, Winslow dropped her overnight bag just inside her doorway and called her cats. They didn't come out.

"Come on, guys, I know you're mad that I left, but you had plenty of food and water."

It was still another few minutes before they inched out from hiding places. Strange.

"I missed my boys," she said as she scratched behind their ears and rubbed their tummies. The blinking light on her machine caught her eye. *Alex?* Her heart jumped at the thought. She was supposed to call, just to let him know she was back safe. It hurt that he hadn't wanted to see her. Not that she blamed him.

A reporter had found her phone number and left a message offering her a chance to tell her story, as though it would be the most exciting thing she'd ever done. Dallis's voice on the machine was a surprise. Dallis *again,* she said. Winslow listened to the message several times, but it didn't quite make sense. She was anxious, and whatever it was about was urgent. "I don't care how late it is. There's no way I can go to sleep now. Just get here as soon as you can."

She first called Alex. His sleepy voice sounded thick and sweet. It reminded her of the night she'd spent with him when they'd woken in the darkness and reached for each other. It made her ache that she wouldn't have another night like that.

"It's me, Winslow. You wanted me to let you know when I got back."

He cleared his throat. "You're home?"

"Yes. But I've got to go over to Dallis's house. She left an urgent message for me."

"Are you sure it's her?"

"Yes. It sounds important. Then I'll crash for several hours. I'm sorry I woke you."

"I told you to call. What did you find out in San Francisco?"

She felt relieved that he asked, that he still cared about her investigation at least. She told him what she'd found. "I know it doesn't prove anything, especially since he was hardly a suspect. But it's another piece."

"I'm getting out of the hospital tomorrow."

"Already? I thought they wanted you to stay a few more days."

"They do. But I can't let you run all over the place poking your nose into rattlesnake nests."

"I'm not poking my nose into any nests. I'm going to get Ashlyn alone before the wedding and tell her what I found. That's all I can do. If she chooses to marry him anyway, there's nothing I can do about it. So stay in the hospital."

"You're lying again."

She wasn't sure if she was lying. That was her next step, but after that . . . no, she couldn't give up. Even if they did marry, she was going to do everything in her power to dig up something that would convince Grant to look further. *If* Ashlyn survived the honeymoon. But she couldn't tell Alex that.

"Look, this is my problem, my sister, and my investigation. I . . . I don't want you involved. Just stay out of my life."

She hung up, feeling the impact of what she'd just done. "You had to do it. Now that it's personal, it's not fair to drag him into it."

The phone rang, but she grabbed her purse and walked out the door. After she'd closed it, she could hear Alex's voice. "Dammit, Winslow!"

She drove through Dallis's neighborhood a short while later. Most of the houses were dark or lit only with outside lights. The Slitherhouse was alive with lights and sound. She wondered how he got away with it, though the houses on either side looked unoccupied.

"No wonder."

Cars were parked everywhere, leaving her a tiny spot between two palms to tuck her car. She opened the front door and walked in. The music wasn't loud, though it was heavy rock and roll. A few people were sprawled on the sofa and floor in the family room toward the back, but they didn't even see her come in. The air smelled of cigarette smoke and some other smell she didn't care to identify. She went right to the staircase, not wanting to engage anyone in conversation. She tried to remember which room was Dallis's and then knocked on the door. No answer. The girl was probably asleep. It was almost three in the morning.

She opened the door and discovered she'd guessed right. Dallis was lying on the rumpled bed facing away from the door. Winslow was startled to hear Ashlyn's laughter and discovered it was from a video playing on the computer. She was trying on shoes, teasing Dallis about her big clunkers. Winslow walked over to the bed.

"Dallis. I'm here. I got your message."

The girl looked preternaturally still. Her skin was even paler than usual. Winslow reached out and shook her arm, then yelped and stumbled backward when it felt cold and stiff. A frothy, bloody substance had leaked from Dallis's nose and mouth.

Winslow looked on the black carpet and saw a length of rubber tubing. Her gaze went to the needle lying nearby. She didn't want to move Dallis, but she could see a bruise on the inside of her elbow.

"God, no. This can't be." She searched for the phone and found the Scooby-Doo one on the desk. When the 911 operator answered, Winslow said, "Please get an ambulance and the police out to 118 Westwood Place. A girl has . . . I think she's overdosed."

But it couldn't be. Dallis had something important to say. Winslow ran down the stairs and into the family room. "Where's Dallis's father?"

A skinny man with black hair and deep grooves in his face said, "And who are you?"

"A . . . well, a friend of hers. She asked me to come over and—she's dead. I'm so sorry. I've called an ambulance and the police."

Johnny went from lethargic to a streak as he flew past her and up the stairs. Others followed, but she couldn't do anything but sink to the black and red tile steps leading down into the family room and cover her face.

An hour later Winslow had told her story four times. Yes, it was odd that she was here at the house when she and Dallis barely knew each other. Yes, she'd been told to go inside and up to Dallis's room. She'd tried to tell them that the girl had something to tell her.

"She wouldn't have killed herself."

"It's not the first time she's tried," Detective Adams said. "Her father told us that she's overdosed twice before."

A caterwaul sent both their gazes to the top of the stairs. Johnny Slither followed Dallis's sheathed body as two officers carried her down on a platform.

"I'm a terrible father," he wailed. "I didn't pay enough attention to her. I didn't see the signs."

Winslow turned to Adams. "I know she didn't do this to herself."

His expression went from sympathetic at the father's anguish to stern when he focused on her. "What are you saying?"

How could she suggest Jayce had anything to do with this? He hardly knew Dallis and probably hadn't seen her in weeks. Most important, why would he kill her? He would have had to have been in her condo, heard her message . . .

"Dallis left a message for me tonight. It sounded like a second message." She tried to recite as much as she could remember. " 'Again,' she said. It didn't sound right. Maybe . . . maybe someone heard the first message and came here. Could you listen to the message? You could take the tape and see what's been erased recently, couldn't you?"

"I could listen. We'll be checking her phone records to see what her last calls were anyway. Was Dallis involved in something?"

"It's not Dallis. It's . . . just listen to the tape first. Then we can talk."

Once the scene was being processed, Adams followed her home. She felt a little better having him with her, especially after suspecting that someone had been in her home. The message light was blinking, and she was a bit embarrassed to have Adams hear Alex's message. She planned to press Skip immediately.

Except that nothing played on the tape.

She kept forwarding, rewinding, and even took it out and replaced it again. "Everything is gone. Dallis's message, a new message someone left as I was leaving. It's all gone."

"Ms. Talbot, we're going to need you to stay close to town in the next few days. Just in case the investigation shows any foul play in regard to Ms. Jordan's death. Especially if you were the last person she called before her death."

After he left, she sank onto her sofa. Not even Salt and Pepper could bring her out of her despondent confusion. Only the thought of someone still being in the condo got her off the sofa and checking every room, even the kitchen cabinets.

"Ashlyn has a key to my place." The revelation startled her. She'd given Ashlyn a key in case she needed the plant-watering favor returned. That meant Jayce could get hold of it. She checked the door and found no sign of jimmying or forced entry. "He could have walked right in." When Salt rubbed against her ankle, her stomach turned. Oh, God. The cats had been spooked. Because someone had been in here.

She called a locksmith and arranged for emergency service, then sat staring at the door while warm dawn light filled the living room. When the man arrived, she had him rekey her front door and install an extra security lock on the doors to the balcony.

After he left, she played the messages again. Still nothing. Had someone replaced the tape altogether? She ran into her room and looked at everything and then went into her office. The only thing that seemed strange was that her monitor was on, though the computer was off. She never left her monitor on.

When Jayce learned she'd gone to San Francisco, he'd come here to search her things. He'd heard Dallis's message.

And he'd killed her.

It was a ridiculous plan; even Winslow had to admit it. But it was all that she had. She had picked up the bunny costume at Masquerades, along with a bouquet of silver helium balloons and a business card for a singing telegram company that she could present as her employer. Coming up with a wedding wishes song she could perform to Ashlyn was the hard part.

"I wish you all the best on your happy day, and hope your new husband doesn't kill you" just didn't have the right ring to it.

Of course she'd have to sing something sappy. She would hand her the printouts she'd gotten at the San Francisco library branch before Ashlyn could call security. She'd bet everything left in her savings account that Jayce had made sure she wasn't welcome in the building. It hurt to think that her father might have called with the orders.

And thus her desperate, ridiculous plan.

As she weaved through traffic, though, that eerie watched feeling returned. She kept checking the mirror—while pushing the balloons out of the way—looking for Jayce's Ferrari. Just to be safe, she took several out-of-the-way turns. A white convertible Mustang fell in behind her after each maneuver. She tried to see who was driving at the next light. It wasn't Jayce, though it was a man about his age.

"He's having me followed!" Had he hired a private detective? Or was it whoever belonged to that California phone number? "Well, let's see what you've got in that little thing. I've got about three hundred and fifty horses under my hood." She'd heard Grant talk about it enough to know.

At the green light, she gunned the engine and zipped around a corner. The balloons floated into the driver's side, and she batted them away. She knew this area better than her pursuer might. He knew she'd gone to a costume shop, and she suspected he'd be reporting that to Jayce. What would he make of it? Luckily the shop also sold party supplies, so that might throw him off.

Her tail gave himself away in his desperation to keep up with her. She blew through the red light; traffic kept him from doing the same. She pulled into a parking lot and around the back of the building. A small alley led to another street; she took that north and then weaved from side street to side street until she reached a road that led back to A1A.

After only a short distance on that road, she turned into Talbot Tower's parking lot. She was relieved to find that the card that allowed her into the parking garage still worked. That meant she could go right to Ashlyn's apartment and by-pass the security guard. She tucked the car behind a van, knowing that Jayce and anyone he might know could have access to the garage as well.

She felt angry and triumphant all at once. And afraid. There could be two of them now. She knew that Jayce had killed Dallis. He wouldn't hesitate to kill her at the first opportunity. In fact, he was probably looking forward to it.

"All right, catch your breath. You've just got to be smarter than they are. And faster." She gave herself a few minutes to process everything, to work through the fear. There was no going back now, anyway. She couldn't just pretend that everything was great and that she was now crazy about her brother-in-law. Jayce knew too much, and so did she. This could only end two ways: he would kill her or she would find proof of his plans to kill Ashlyn. She just hoped that she'd find that proof in time.

"Now, to get into this thing."

She wriggled into the pink furry costume, bumping her steering wheel and even hitting the horn once. She was hot already, and the importance of how she handled this was making her sweat even more. The bouquet of balloons scattered everywhere as soon as she maneuvered out of the car, though she clutched the squishy blob that held them together.

Once she caught her breath again, she started toward the elevators. The rabbit's head hung behind her like a hood; she'd pull it on when she got to Ashlyn's floor.

Once the door slid shut she thought of something else: what if someone called for an elevator at Level 1 where the security guards were? Her fears were borne out when the car stopped at the next floor. She tucked herself into the corner when the door opened, though she could hardly hide.

A woman carrying her Yorkshire terrier stepped on, pausing when she saw Winslow. She tried to smile, but she could hardly breathe. Making matters worse, the dog started barking at the balloons. What if the woman said something to security? What if the guard saw her?

"Singing telegram," Winslow offered as the door closed.

The woman said nothing, just openly watched her for a moment before realizing she hadn't chosen a floor. The dog kept barking. She pressed the eighth-floor button just as they passed it. Her eyes narrowed. "Did you come from the garage?"

Winslow tried not to look taken off-guard. "I came through the lobby, of course, but the car went down to the garage for some reason."

She nodded but didn't look totally convinced. Thankfully, the car reached Ashlyn's floor and she quickly departed. With her stomach already clenched tight, she readied herself for the plan. Except that it was thrown into disarray as she stood outside the condo door and heard crying.

Not the kind of crying that accompanied being beaten or scared. This was plaintive, with low mewls that grabbed Winslow's heart. Did Ashlyn know about Dallis's death? Probably not. They had managed to keep it out of the news so far, though Winslow wasn't sure how newsworthy Dallis's death would be.

Was Ashlyn having doubts about her wedding, then? Winslow kept listening and making sure she heard no one else. Hearing the crying was hard, especially when she heard, "Mom, why aren't you here? A bride should have her mom on her wedding day."

Winslow leaned against the door for a moment, closing her eyes. Through all of this, she hadn't thought how Ashlyn would miss her mom on this important day.

Even Winslow hadn't been there for Ashlyn, though she

had good reason for that. She'd been too busy trying to prove Jayce was the wrong man to marry. Hardly maid-of-honor material.

Now, though, she felt the need to do something. Her heart ached for the younger sister she'd never been close to. She knocked on the door.

A few moments later Ashlyn cracked the door open. Even through the crack, her eyes looked puffy, her nose red. Her throat was raw when she said, "Winslow?"

"I'm not your mom, and I'm hardly your sister. But I want to help you get ready."

The door opened a little more, and Ashlyn looked a bit chagrined. "But you're not even invited to the wedding. Jayce wouldn't have it, not after you went to California to check on him. He told us about his wife and stepdaughter, how they were murdered. He didn't do it, Winslow. So if that's why you're really here—"

"I'm not. Aside from my giving you copies of the newspaper articles—don't you want to know the details?—I won't say a word about Jayce. I promise."

Ashlyn hesitated, but her need for comfort was bigger than her skepticism and she opened the door. As soon as Winslow walked in, Ashlyn said, "What in the heck are you wearing?"

"Oops. I forgot about this when I heard you crying. I wanted to sing you a wedding greeting." She shoved the balloons at her. "I really do want you to be happy."

Ashlyn struggled with them as she set them on the coffee table.

Winslow climbed out of the furry costume. "You've washed your hair. Let's see what we can do with it for the ceremony. It's supposed to be windy tonight, so we're going to need a lot of hairspray." She waited for a response. It was a request of sorts. Would Ashlyn let her help?

Ashlyn obviously couldn't believe that Winslow was there, but she smiled. "I've got some that'll hold it against a hurricane."

Not only did Winslow feel relief, she felt something else: a warmth inside her, a need to connect to her stepsister.

The phone rang. Damn. Winslow said, "That'll be Jayce, wanting to know if I'm here." She held back the words *since he had me followed.*

Ashlyn picked up. "Hi, honey. Just getting ready for our big date. . . . Hm? . . . No, I haven't seen Winslow. . . . Sure, I will." She hung up. "You were right. But he's only trying to protect me. You've been acting so weird."

And he doesn't want me to tell you what I've found.

Winslow released a soft sigh of relief as Ashlyn nodded toward the bedroom. She'd lied to Jayce. It was a good sign.

When they went into the master bathroom, Winslow handed her the folded copies of the articles. "I printed them out in California. As you probably know, I spoke with Amber's mother. I needed to know that you were safe. When I found out about his last wife, I got scared for you." She hurried on, aware that she'd already broken her promise not to discuss Jayce. "Her parents don't believe that he had anything to do with their deaths."

Ashlyn relaxed a little. "That's what he told us."

"Which is especially significant considering he fought them for the house. There was a discrepancy in Jayce's history—but that was probably a misunderstanding. I wrote notes about all that on the backs of the printouts. But you know what? It doesn't matter. Jayce knows you have little in the way of assets, right? So there's no reason for me to think he'd try to do you in for money." She stuffed the folded pages into the wastebasket beneath the vanity. "Shall we get to work?"

For two hours they tried different hairstyles, experimenting with the beautiful veil. Ashlyn's gaze would sometimes fall to the pearl wastebasket, but she always quickly looked up again. Winslow hoped her plan would work. It was her last chance.

"Remember when we played dress up?" Winslow asked.

"Dad bought us that huge trunk of vintage clothing. That was fun." It was one of the few times they'd really connected as preteens. "Then you dismantled all the lace and buttons and glued them to your regular clothes."

Ashlyn smiled at the memory. "Dad was pretty mad about that. I guess he'd paid a lot for that clothing."

They shared a laugh, both obviously remembering Grant's suppressed anger when he found the tattered dresses.

Ashlyn turned toward the large mirror, Winslow behind her, both inspecting hair and makeup. Winslow said, "Where is the wedding going to be?"

Ashlyn hesitated, though she smiled when she said, "You're not going to run in objecting, are you?"

Winslow had to smile, too, because of her earlier thoughts about doing just that. "No."

"It's going to be downstairs by the pool at sunset."

"That'll be nice." And awful. That was nothing like the wedding Ashlyn had dreamed of. Winslow took a deep breath. "We're ready for the dress."

"It's in my closet. I'll get it."

Winslow looked for telltale adjustments and additions as Ashlyn pulled off the plastic. "You didn't modify the dress," she said.

It was an ivory color, floor-length, with a straight skirt and beading along the collar. Plain boring. Nothing like the ones Ashlyn had designed.

"No."

"You could have made it so much nicer. Are you going to stop designing?"

Ashlyn shrugged. "It's just a silly pastime."

That sounded like something Jayce had said.

"I used to think it was. Wouldn't it figure that as soon as I realize how talented you are, you stop?"

"I'm not talented," Ashlyn said, though Winslow could tell she wanted to hear a refute.

"Yes, you are, and anyone who tells you otherwise is lying."

Ashlyn smiled, probably not getting the Jayce inference. As Winslow helped Ashlyn into the dress, she said, "You could make something of your talent, like get into fashion design. You could work with one of the big designers even. Look at the Hale Bob tops, with the lace and sequins attached here and there. That's what you do. You could be part of all that excitement you only see from the outside when you attend the New York fashion shows."

Ashlyn was staring at Winslow in wonderment. Her blue eyes glistened. "Do you really mean that?"

"Yes. I'm sorry I didn't see it sooner." Her eyes started watering, too. Not only at this tenuous thread between them but because of her fears that she might not have a chance to strengthen that thread before Jayce took Ashlyn away. Winslow turned Ashlyn toward the mirror and situated the veil on her head. And took a breath. "Wow, you are beautiful."

"Am I?" She stared at her reflection, looking for what Winslow saw. It hurt that she had to look so hard. She turned first one way and then the other. "I always imagined this day differently. I thought Dallis would be here . . . and that it would be a big, fairy-tale wedding."

"Me, too," Winslow said. This rushed wedding wasn't right, but she held the words, just as she held the words about Dallis's death. She couldn't tell Ashlyn, not right before her wedding.

Ashlyn gave a sad laugh. "I was always worried that you would look more beautiful than me. I didn't want you as a bridesmaid because I didn't want you to upstage me."

Winslow put her hands on Ashlyn's shoulders, looking at their reflections. Her perfect face stared back, that face she'd never accepted. She should show Ashlyn what was beneath the makeup. But she couldn't trust that Ashlyn wouldn't throw it back at her later.

"I would never have upstaged you."

Ashlyn smiled, but it was a sad one. "I'm sorry that you can't be there."

"I'll be there." At her sister's conflicted expression—
Jayce would cause her grief if Winslow showed up—she
clarified. "I'll be on the beach. Just during the ceremony. No
one will know I'm there. Except you."

Ashlyn dabbed delicately at her eyes. "Thank you for
coming here. For helping. For everything."

"It was something I needed to do."

Winslow hugged her, careful of her hair and makeup.
"When do you leave on your honeymoon?"

"Tonight. He's got it set up that I'll take scuba lessons tomorrow and get what they call a vacation certification. Then
he arranged to rent a boat and we'll go out on our own." She
couldn't have looked less enthusiastic about it.

This was part of why Winslow had come. "I know you're
uncomfortable scuba diving. If you still feel that way, don't
do it. Trust your gut instincts. If Jayce truly loves you, he
won't make you do it. He'll respect your fear."

Ashlyn gave a shaky nod. Would she have the guts to
stand up to him?

Winslow couldn't think about that. She was afraid she
knew the answer. "I'd better get going, just in case Jayce
comes by to check on you."

"He's not supposed to. I told him I didn't want to see him
the day before our wedding. But he already broke that."

Winslow crept into dangerous territory. "Was he here . . .
last night?"

"For a while. But I didn't mind that he was disregarding
my request. If you could have seen him . . . you'd know how
much he loves me, Winslow. He said he needed to hold me,
to make love to me. He needed me."

And that was so very important to her; Winslow could see
that. "Was he here long?"

"For a couple of hours. He woke me up to tell me that."

Winslow played her hand very carefully. "Woke you up?
Goodness, what time did he get here?"

"It was just after midnight. He was staying at Daddy's

house in one of the guest rooms. He couldn't sleep, so he came over."

After midnight. A little earlier than the time Dallis probably overdosed.

Ashlyn tilted her head. "Come to think of it, it couldn't have been midnight. I watched some of David Letterman before I dropped off." She waved that away. "Well, whatever."

"You looked at the clock?"

"Yeah. It's a habit, whenever I wake up in the night."

So Jayce could have changed the time to make Ashlyn think it was earlier. To set his alibi. How Winslow wanted to tell Ashlyn about Dallis and her suspicions, but she just couldn't. Ashlyn would never believe that Jayce caused her former friend to die. Winslow needed to keep things open between her and Ashlyn. She couldn't afford to alienate her right now.

"I'm glad you're happy," Winslow said instead of all those other things she desperately wanted to tell her. "That's all I want for you, Ashlyn. To be happy. You deserve that."

She gave her another hug, squeezing her eyes shut as she hoped it wouldn't be the last time. "I'll see you tonight."

I'll see you, but you won't see me.

"Dammit, Cal, how could you have lost her?"

"First of all, she was deliberately trying to ditch me. And do you know how many damned Mercedes there are in this frickin' town? Plus she's got a fast one."

Jayce rubbed his forehead, feeling annoyance tighten his muscles into knots. "Did she get a good look at you?"

"Only in the rearview mirror."

"All right, trade the car in on something else. Go to her apartment building and wait for her. Get better at tailing. She's not at the condo; I just called Ashlyn."

"You sure she wouldn't lie to you?"

"I'm sure. I've got her under my thumb. It makes me real uneasy, wondering what the bitch is up to, though. Frankly, there isn't much she could find or do at this point. Everything is in place, the plan is in action, and you're poised and ready. Right?"

"Right-o. You still leave on your honeymoon tonight?"

"Yep."

"By next week, you'll be a rich man."

And it was about damned time.

23

Winslow pulled into her parking spot in front of her building, feeling sad and scared but also feeling good about her interaction with Ashlyn. She now had to hope that her sister's curiosity would win out and she'd look at those printouts. They weren't enough, in and of themselves, to stop the wedding, but Winslow hoped they'd stir some suspicion and make Ashlyn cautious. Hopefully it would keep her from scuba diving.

Winslow could too clearly see Jayce holding Ashlyn down after he'd turned off her air tank. Then he would turn it on again and play dumb as to how she'd drowned. He wouldn't cut the line; that would be too obvious. Winslow wasn't sure how he would manage to make the murder look like an accident, how he would explain why he wasn't present to help Ashlyn. They'd be alone on a boat for much of the week. He would have plenty of opportunity to stage it just the way he wanted.

Winslow stepped out of the car, hating her dark thoughts. The feeling of being watched hit her again. Now she knew it was entirely possible that someone *was* watching her. She walked inside the building's courtyard and nodded to one of her neighbors who was heading to his truck. She pretended to admire a bush full of peach hibiscus blossoms, all the while peering from the shadows. She saw no one obvious. But she knew he was out there.

Ashlyn looked at the clock again. Daddy would be here soon to escort her downstairs. She finished her glass of champagne and walked into the bathroom for a last check. Her gaze went to the pearl wastebasket where Winslow had tucked those articles. She should get rid of them; what if Jayce saw them?

She pulled them out, folded them again, and started to head to the kitchen. No, he could find them in there, too. She needed to dispose of them elsewhere. She tucked them into a hardcover book, which she returned to the purple bag.

Did she have time for another glass of champagne? Maybe half a glass. Why was she so nervous? It was a simple wedding, with only a few acquaintances and friends of her daddy's.

The question was why wasn't she excited? She was marrying the man of her dreams. A gorgeous, charming, smart man who needed her. Things were beginning to mend with Winslow. She hadn't realized until earlier that day how much their huge rift had bothered her. And how much she wanted a sister.

But could she trust Winslow's outreach? How could one woman be so obsessed with finding fault with her fiancé and then be as sweet as she was today? It didn't make any sense.

Ashlyn downed the half glass and was about to refill it when the doorbell rang.

Alex hated not knowing what Winslow was up to. He knew she'd cut him out of her life "for his own good." Luckily she hadn't used those words; he probably would have broken something.

Unluckily his mother had caught him trying to check out of the hospital against doctor's orders. His family was now keeping vigils on him to make sure he stayed for the rest of his sentence. Just a couple more days. Then he'd talk some sense into Winslow. What scared him most was that he might not have the chance. If Jayce had killed a woman and her baby for money, he wasn't about to let a nosy sister keep him from succeeding.

Winslow didn't see the white Mustang when she left her apartment that evening. Its absence didn't comfort her. Jayce wouldn't give up that easily. Still, she saw no one following her as she drove to the beach access and parked. She wore a floppy hat and shades as she walked down the beach. The wind played havoc with the hat and her hair, but she held on to both as she neared the back deck for Talbot Tower.

The sun had just set; it had taken her longer to reach the building than she'd thought. The eastern sky was an indigo blue, though to the west pink and purples splashed the horizon. Lanterns blazed around the pool deck, and flowers had been strung to the smooth trunks of royal palms. It looked cozy and tropical, even with a cool breeze. She meant to look like just anyone out for her evening walk. People often stopped and watched public weddings—ah, so sentimental, and all that dreck!

So she paused, holding on to her hat with one hand, her other arm wrapped around her waist, and watched her sister exchange vows with Jayce from a distance that felt like miles. Winslow didn't feel sad that she hadn't been included. She certainly didn't feel sentimental. All she felt was scared.

It was nearly dark when she made the trek back to the car. Couples wandered close to shore, holding hands. She walked fast, wanting to get back as soon as possible. Jayce's cohort could well be lingering in the shadows of the sea grape bushes, waiting for a chance to dispatch her. It didn't occur to her that she could check on that cohort until she reached the parking lot. It was full dark now, though the lot was lit in a sodium haze. She watched shadowy figures coming through the narrow beach access and wandering to their different vehicles.

She took out her cell phone, while standing next to her car, and played the San Francisco number she'd repeated on her recorder. She then initiated a call.

Across the parking lot, a cell phone rang. Once, twice, and then it stopped as a man said, "Yeah?"

"Sorry, wrong number," she mumbled as she tried to pinpoint where the ringing had come from.

She pressed redial and heard it ring again. No doubt now; Jayce's cohort was definitely here in Miami. To take care of a problem. And that problem was her.

She was startled by the ringing of her own phone when she got into her car. The number on the display was the cohort's. Of course he had seen the Miami number when she'd called him.

"Who is this?" a man's voice said.

She hung up and started her car. It didn't ring again. He'd probably figured it out.

Winslow went home, fixed dinner, and fed her cats. She was too restless to relax, though, too antsy knowing that he was out there. So she got into her car and drove to the hospital. It was hard to tell if someone was following; if he was, he stayed a good distance behind her. What could he do? Shoot her?

She felt a chill. Yes, he could do exactly that. Someone *had* shot at her. She was now sure that she was the intended victim. The thought had her changing lanes often, just in case.

She parked directly beneath a light at the hospital and walked inside with a group of people. She was officially paranoid.

Lazaro was sitting beside Alex's bed, his chin to his chest, snoring softly; Alex was also asleep, his face turned slightly to the side.

His father's presence alarmed her, and she walked quietly

inside and took all of Alex in with worried eyes. He looked
fine, sleeping peacefully. His color had returned. She could
see his form beneath the sheet, his body intact.

Lazaro opened bloodshot eyes and took her in with a
start. She wondered how much they knew about her, if they
knew she'd lied to Alex. Still, she smiled as Lazaro walked
to where she stood at the doorway.

"How's he doing?" she asked. "Looks like you're standing guard."

He grunted. "He's fine, but too stubborn for his own
good. He's in pain but won't admit it. Doesn't want to be
given something that makes him sleepy, so the nurse has to
pretend it's for infection. And I *am* doing guard duty. He
wants to check himself out because of you. We have to make
sure he doesn't. He thinks you're doing things to put yourself in danger. Are you?"

She swallowed hard. The family was guarding him because of her? "My sister is marrying a man I think intends to
kill her for her money. I have to do everything I can to find
proof of that. I don't want to involve Alex. I told him to butt
out, for his own good. I don't want him hurt again."

Lazaro seemed to assess her. "You love my son." It
wasn't quite a question.

She saw it was no use lying. "I . . . think I might. He's
mad that I lied to him."

"Lying is bad. Putting yourself in danger is *muy* bad."

"I know. But it's too late now. I have to find some resolu-
tion. Until then, I'm not seeing Alex."

"He's very worried about you."

She leaned against the door opening. "I'm sorry that he
is. Tell him that I stopped by. No, tell him I went back to
California. That way he won't try to get out early."

Lazaro stretched; his back obviously ached, and that made
her feel terribly guilty. "I will tell him this. But you be careful. It's not for a pretty woman to solve crimes by herself."

She nodded as he ambled to the restroom, and then shook

her head. The police wouldn't get involved unless she had proof. Until then, she sounded like a paranoid schizophrenic. She couldn't help but walk back into Alex's room and then to his bed. He must be furious at her, for putting him here, for making his family guard him, and for her lies.

She kissed him softly on his cheek. "Alejandro, forgive me."

To her surprise, he opened his eyes. They looked glazed. "Winslow?" he slurred.

"Go back to sleep. You're dreaming."

His eyes drifted shut. When he got out of here, he was going to be a force to be reckoned with. She only hoped he still wanted to reckon with her.

"Jayce, I don't think I want to do this," Ashlyn said after panicking for the third time that afternoon when the dive instructor removed her mask under the water. Even though she had the regulator in her mouth, she still breathed through her nose and shot to the surface. He'd admonished her for that.

"Honey, you're doing fine," Jayce said. "You just have to get past this little problem."

"You're not the first person to have trouble with this part," the instructor said. "But you've got to pass it before I can give you a license."

Jayce had, in fact, suggested they skip this course and he would teach her. Then he'd get the equipment using his license. She hadn't liked that idea at all.

The knot in her chest was getting tighter. "Jayce, let's forget this. You go diving and I'll stay on the boat."

"Not a good idea," the instructor chimed in. "You've got to have a buddy with you at all times."

Because awful things could happen.

"I don't want to scuba dive. I'm sorry, but I'm just not comfortable with it. You should respect that."

She saw irritation cross Jayce's expression. "Do I have to find some other woman willing to learn to dive for me?"

She bristled. "That would be a nice thing to do on our honeymoon."

He circled her with his arms. "I was just kidding. But like you said, this is our honeymoon, and we should do this together. Come on; you'll get over this and you'll love it. Do it for me."

He didn't respect her discomfort. He'd been pushing this on her since they'd moved up the wedding. *Which he'd instigated.*

Oh, God, she was now hearing Winslow's warnings. Jayce was *not* planning to harm her. He had nothing to gain. He loved her.

She put the mask on, stuck the regulator back in her mouth, and sank to the bottom of the pool. The instructor swam down and knocked the mask off her face. She started breathing fast but stayed down, and then her breathing became normal. She saw Jayce in front of her, clapping.

When she came to the surface he hugged her. "That's my baby. You make me so proud."

Those were the words that always filled her with warmth. And trust. She pushed away her doubts and looked to the instructor for the next part of the course.

Winslow was surprised—and, she had to admit, happy—to hear from Grant on Sunday afternoon.

After they got over somewhat stiff greetings he said, "I want you back in our lives. I just don't know how to do that, what with your bad feelings about Jayce and your problems with Ashlyn."

"Ashlyn and I have come to terms, but I'll never come to terms with Jayce." There was no point in mentioning that he was having her followed or that he'd probably had Dallis killed. Those would sound like paranoid observations.

Grant let out a sigh. "I'm sorry to hear that. But I don't want to lose touch with you. I'd like to get back into a routine again. You know, breakfast, and then maybe we could come back here. I'd like your opinion on a few things. We've been brainstorming campaign slogans and 'You *can't* lose with *Grant'* is the best we've come up with. Pretty pitiful."

"I'd love that," she said, a smile breaking on her face. "Wednesday?"

"Jayce has me scheduled for something Wednesday morning, but how about tomorrow? We could have a new day. A new start."

"Sounds wonderful."

"I'll pick you up at nine."

She hadn't let herself see how much she missed her father. Even though she'd lost some respect for him, she still loved him.

Her cell phone rang a few minutes later, and she was just as surprised to hear Alex's voice.

"My dad said you stopped by last night."

"I wanted to see how you were doing."

"He said you're going to California."

She got to her feet, as though that would help substantiate the lie. "Yes, I'm in Atlanta right now actually. Layover and all." She turned on the television to simulate the sounds of the airport. "It's just another lead I'm checking out. Nobody knows I'm going this time. Jayce is on his honeymoon."

"I know what you're doing."

Her face flushed. "What?"

"You're trying to shut me out to protect me. What you don't realize is that I happen to care about you, even though you're making it harder than hell to do so."

Her mouth quirked in a smile at that, and she forced it away. "I don't want you to care about me. Not right now. I'm trouble. You're right; I *am* protecting you. I feel terrible that I got you shot. Worse than terrible. So I'm going to handle this on my own."

"Handle what?"

"Finding something that will prove Jayce is after Ashlyn's money. He beat me to the punch and told Grant and

Ashlyn about his wife's and stepdaughter's murders. Naturally they believe he had nothing to do with it."

"Are you sure that you're not fabricating all this? Conspiracy theories, murder, greed—it sounds like a movie of the week! You were right about the hit-and-run, but I think you may be off-base about this."

"I used to wonder that myself. I don't anymore."

"What's convinced you?"

She stopped just short of telling him about Jayce's cohort. "I just know."

He made a sound of frustration. "Winslow—"

"I'll call you later. They announced my flight."

She hung up, feeling guilty for the lie. It was for a good cause, though. She stroked Salt, who was sprawled on the couch with her. Pepper was at her feet benefiting from a toe rub.

"This is my game now. I intend to finish it on my own."

Monday morning Ashlyn had woken up nauseated at the prospect of diving. Yes, she'd passed the tests; she also knew all the terrible things that could happen, including bumping into fire coral, sharks, and jellyfish. Her air could run out. Her foot could get stuck in a crevice. She could lose her mind due to nitrogen narcosis.

Again, Jayce had coerced her into going out on their boat despite her concerns. Getting up at six in the morning hadn't been her idea of fun, either. She didn't quite understand why they needed to spend so much time between morning and evening dives. But he had been right about one thing: once she was floating in crystal-clear water watching an array of fish swim past, some of her fears disappeared. They were alone, at least for the time being. Jayce had heard about this special place from another diver at a bar the night before. It featured caverns and formations divers could swim through. The thought had captivated him.

Jayce had talked about making love beneath the water, but

she wasn't ready for that yet. Maybe she'd get comfortable with this diving thing. It helped that he kept reaching over and squeezing her arm, giving her reassurance.

A short while later everything got dark. Startled, she searched around them. In the far distance she could see brilliant cerulean water; the sun must have gone behind some clouds. All of the beautiful colors were gone. She glanced toward the surface and saw three long fish hovering above them. Not sharks, she assured herself, but nearly as bad: barracuda. Ugly fish with teeth. Not aggressive, the instructor said, but they sometimes thought fingers and jewelry were food. She curled her hands into fists. Then she realized that the surface was a long way away. She looked at her depth gauge. They were at sixty-five feet! Jayce had promised they'd go no deeper than thirty.

She waved frantically to get his attention, but he was too busy watching a parrot fish. She grabbed his arm, startling him, and pointed up to the barracuda and then jabbed her depth gauge. Her heartbeat was pounding. She needed to get away from the nasty fish, needed to go back to the top. The diving instructor had warned her about getting panicked. She knew she was doing exactly that but couldn't help it. She *had* to get out of the water. She started to swim up, but Jayce grabbed her arm and violently shook his head.

She tried to free herself, feeling the panic balloon in her chest. He'd taken them to the deep area on purpose! He was going to drown her! The more she struggled, the tighter he held on. The wet suit hampered her movements, made her feel smothered. She screamed, and her regulator popped out of her mouth. The current swept it behind her.

She had no air! She was going to die! Jayce grabbed the regulator with one hand and stuffed it back into her mouth. Then he took both arms and shook her hard. His eyes were stern behind the fogged glass. She knew hers were wide.

Still holding on to her arms, he started to swim upward. After what seemed like twenty minutes they broke the surface.

She threw off the regulator and gulped air. The tank weighed her down; the fins seemed to keep her from being able to kick.

"What the *hell* were you doing?" he yelled.

"Get me out of the water!"

The boat looked miles away. They'd drifted along the bottom of the ocean, going deeper all along. The sun came out again, lifting her spirits somewhat as they swam end-lessly to safety. Finally they reached the boat, and Jayce climbed up the ladder to the platform before reaching out for her. His face was taut with anger.

"You almost killed yourself out there!" he said as soon as they got back on the boat.

She dropped to the bench and ripped off the fins. "You said we would stay in the shallow areas!"

"You were doing fine, enjoying the scenery."

She threw the mask at him. "So you tricked me!"

He ducked, and it dropped to the deck. "I didn't trick you. I saw that you were comfortable and there were a lot more interesting things as we went deeper. You were fine until you freaked." He ran his fingers through his wet hair, spiking it. "You know better than to shoot to the surface like that."

"You held me down!"

"To keep you from hurting yourself. You were being completely stupid down there."

She held in her words, hating that he'd called her stupid. If he'd been in her shoes, or fins, he would have done the same thing. It was her first real dive. And he'd never once respected her fear.

"Let's relax on the boat for a while, have lunch, and then we'll try it again. In twenty feet of water," he ground out in disgust.

"Take me back to the hotel. I'm not diving again."

His voice softened. "Ashlyn, you panicked. It happens to a lot of new divers."

"No, I was being *stupid*. And stupid people shouldn't

dive. I want to be alone for the afternoon. Go find someone else to take with you as a buddy."

She wasn't going to let him use that threat against her again. She was done diving, and nothing he could say or do would convince her otherwise. He could dive; she would lounge by the pool. They'd spend the evenings together.

Jayce was quiet during the ride back, and after dropping her off he took the boat out, against the rules, to dive alone. That was his last-ditch effort, she realized. His last way to guilt her into going with him.

She'd stood up to him. It felt good. No, it felt wonderful. Other than lying to him about Winslow's presence at the condo, this was the first time she'd stood up for herself in . . . heck, she couldn't even remember.

Winslow was right; she was a completely different person now. Maybe that Ashlyn whose pictures were on the bulletin board was a bit too flaky and flighty; maybe she partied too much. But she enjoyed life. And she wasn't such a pushover.

It was startling to realize she didn't like herself anymore. Not that she'd ever loved herself like those magazines told her to do. She'd always been insecure. Now she was . . . nothing.

She slid off the bed and peered out the window that faced the water. Their boat was nowhere in sight. She pulled out the purple bag and removed the hardcover mystery she'd brought with her. It wasn't the book that held her interest, though. She unfolded the printed articles about Jayce's slain family and started reading.

She felt some relief that Jayce had only been a cursory suspect. As Winslow had said, even the parents stood behind him. She followed an arrow that Winslow had drawn and read her notes on the back:

> *The Millses didn't suspect Jayce because they didn't think the $200,000 life insurance policy he had taken out on her was enough motive. The*

*police did, however, but could not crack his iron-
clad alibi. They tried to find an accomplice, but
none was found. The case is still unsolved.*

*There was something that weakened the
Millses' confidence. Amber had told Jayce that the
house given to them as a wedding present was in
their names. He was furious to discover that the
$1.8 million home was locked in the family trust.
He, in fact, fought the grieving parents in a pro-
tracted legal battle that he lost.*

*The number I saw on Jayce's cell phone be-
longed to someone in the San Francisco area. The
accomplice? $1.8 million home? Plenty of motive!*

Ashlyn felt a chill snake through her veins. Winslow
couldn't possibly know how Jayce was hounding her to put
the condo in both their names or, at the least, in her name.
He'd even mentioned it on their wedding night! He'd been
trying to manipulate her, saying how he didn't want to live
there if it wasn't *theirs*. She'd been uncomfortable asking
her father for the condo, just as she'd been with diving.

She scrambled off the bed and searched for Jayce's cell
phone. He'd taken it with him, of course. Though she wasn't
sure what she was looking for, she searched his suitcase. She
found nothing incriminating, but her suspicions throbbed
throughout her entire body. She'd been blinded by Jayce, by
his charms, by the very fact that he loved her. Now she
wasn't so sure. Fresh from the panic episode sixty feet under, she could believe the worst. After all, her loving husband hadn't been so loving or understanding, only angry.
Because he wanted her to keep diving with him. But why?

She knew he'd be hounding her to do it again. She
couldn't bear the thought of the whole week stretching out in
front of her, with his hounding, with her suspicions. She
dressed, scribbled a note to Jayce, and hauled her bag to the
car. He could arrange for a rental car. For now she wanted to

put some space between them. Now that she had fully opened that door, urgency pushed her forward . . . almost as if her life depended on it.

Cal made the most out of the hour he had, along with the alarm code and key, to wire everything. Personally, he preferred the hands-on type of killing he'd performed on Amber, but orders were orders. He hadn't enjoyed killing the baby, though. Again, orders were orders. This time plans had changed a little; at least he had been prepared for that.

He settled in to watch the fireworks. He did, after all, deserve to see the fruits of his labor. And it was going to be beautiful.

24

Because of an unscheduled meeting with the current governor, Winslow and Grant were having lunch instead of breakfast. Conversation was a bit awkward. They had a lot of bad feelings to overcome. She was grateful that she had the chance.

They'd spent most of their first hour talking about safe subjects, like his campaign. Every time he mentioned Jayce, though, Grant paused, she looked away, and then he had to restart. He had purposely avoided mentioning the wedding altogether, so she brought it up.

"The wedding was nice. I watched from the beach," she added at his surprised expression. "I felt I should be there." She decided not to mention her time with Ashlyn, though, just in case he mentioned it to Jayce. Ashlyn had taken a stand by lying; Winslow didn't want her to get in trouble for it. "She is my sister, after all."

"I'm glad to hear that. I keep hoping things will smooth out. I realize that it will take time for you to trust Jayce. I'm willing to give you whatever you need. Just know that I miss having you around."

Jayce had taken a year last time to have his family killed, but she held those words in. Grant's words about missing her halted any thoughts of voicing her suspicions. "I miss you, too. I wish things were different." Winslow would never trust Jayce.

When Grant had earlier walked to another table and talked to someone he knew for a few minutes, she had dialed the California number to see if the cohort was in the elegant restaurant somewhere. She was relieved not to hear a corresponding ringing.

She gathered the nerve to ask the question that had been bothering her for some time. "Dad, why did you stop calling me Winnie?"

His eyebrows furrowed. "You don't like the nickname."

"I admit that it doesn't thrill me, but I didn't mind when *you* called me that. How did you know I didn't like it?"

"Jayce said you mentioned it to him."

She nodded, understanding now. "Jayce called me Winnie, and I told him not to call me that. I think he just likes causing trouble."

"Now, Win. He thought he was doing you a favor. No harm done, right?"

She forced a smile. Jayce was good, very good. She could see how he'd charmed the Millses so thoroughly. He was a master manipulator.

Grant said, "Someday you'll see that he's not a bad guy. In fact, it was his suggestion that we resume our traditional weekly get-together. He felt bad that things were off between us. I only wish I'd thought of it myself."

"Jayce suggested this?"

Grant gave her a *see* look. "He's been trying to befriend you from the beginning. Even now, he wants harmony in the family."

She stemmed her frustration and helplessness at ever getting Grant to see the real Jayce. After he had nudged her and Grant apart, though, she had to wonder what Jayce was up to now.

"He told you about his wife and stepdaughter being murdered," she said. "He only told you because he knew I was in San Francisco."

This time she saw disappointment in Grant's face. "It wasn't easy for him to tell us, either. Naturally he wanted to put that painful part of his past behind him. You forced him to dredge it up again. He would have told us eventually. When he was ready emotionally."

"Did he cry?" she asked. "Was he all broken up when he told you?"

He'd picked up on her sarcasm, even though she'd tried to mask it. "Yes, and it was real."

"Did he tell you that he was furious when he found out that the house Amber's parents had given them as a wedding present wasn't in his or Amber's name? He thought it was, but it was locked in the family trust. He fought them for it, dragging the grieving parents into a legal battle that he eventually lost."

Grant stuck his thumb in his mouth, chewing on an already ragged nail. He was uptight about something. Was it her statement? Or the fact that she was still bringing up Jayce's dirty laundry?

"He didn't get into the details. And frankly, I don't want to discuss him anymore. Let's consider Jayce off-limits as far as topics go. Oddly enough, politics is a much safer subject to discuss."

Disappointment washed over her. She took a sip of wine as he asked her opinion about some of his campaign slogans. Jayce still hovered at the edge of the conversation, particularly since Grant was so obviously avoiding mentioning him. All the while, the uneasy feeling kept growing.

Something terrible was going to happen, and she was helpless to do a thing about it.

Cal was bored to death as he waited in the car across from the family mansion. He was surprised he hadn't heard from Jayce. Though Cal knew it would be hard to make calls during his honeymoon, Jayce always found a way to sneak one in here and there. When Cal glanced at his cell phone, his stomach dropped. The thing was dead.

"Damn it!" He fished through the glove box and plugged the cord into the lighter. Oh yeah, there were messages all right. From a pissed Jayce who had managed to find a minute away from his blushing bride and then couldn't reach Cal. Instead of retrieving the messages, he called Jayce directly.

"It's about damn time," he answered.

"I didn't realize the phone went dead. But worry not; everything's ready. Just as you said, the maid's off today. Winslow and Grant are having lunch—it apparently got moved back—and I suspect will be returning anytime. And then . . . boom."

Obviously Jayce wasn't with his bride, as he said, "The trigger's set?"

"As soon as they walk into the office, with a backup wire, just in case. Nothing should go wrong."

"As long as Winslow is with him. We've got to get rid of her, and if she's not with Grant, it's going to look damned suspicious if something happens to her separately. That's the one variable I'm not comfortable with. I told Grant he should run some of our slogans by her, even get her to look at the charts. Since I'm not there, Winslow won't mind going to the office. You know, I actually like Grant. He's a good guy."

"You're not getting soft on me, I hope. 'Cause it's too late now."

"I don't like Grant more than I like his money. This time my pretty wife is going to be rich, guaranteed. Winslow may get some money, if she's alive. But the majority should go to Ashlyn."

"Have you talked to her about that? Last time Amber lied about the house being in her name, just to make you happy."

"I've been bugging Ashlyn to get him to put the condo in her or our names, but she's resisting. I was willing to give her some time, but Winslow's moved up the time line.

Besides, with the Cubans' hit-and-run in the news, this is a good time for retaliation. Did you leave newspapers in the office?"

"Yep, four different articles, so at least one should survive. I've been practicing my Cuban accent, too." In his accent he said, "Talbot's daughter should have left the García case alone. They're traitors. They didn't deserve justice."

"Not bad. Keep working on it, though. You need to sound more Spanish."

He bristled at the criticism. But Jayce knew what he was doing. He was going to make Cal a rich man. He would get a hefty payment as well as a top position in Grant's development company that Jayce would oversee.

"Do you know where Winslow and Grant went?"

"Nope. Grant picked her up and they headed east. Then I went to work."

"Okay, sounds like you've got it covered. I'm having a bit of a problem on my end, but nothing that can be handled. Ashlyn freaked on our first dive this morning. I went out for the second dive by myself, and when I came back to the room she left a note that she'd gone for a drive. She's not answering her cell phone, probably trying to punish me like last time. She's been gone for about three hours according to the front desk clerk. Maybe she took off to Key West to do some shopping. She's gotten a little too independent, obviously. Her daddy's death will incapacitate her, though. I'll be all she has in the world."

At least he was getting some. Cal couldn't wait until he had his Lamborghini and the money to draw in the rich chicks. He was as good-looking as Jayce, and if he worked on it, he could be just as charming. Maybe he'd even get his own rich girl to add to his funds.

"Sounds like we're almost there," Cal said. "I'm keeping an eye on the house until they arrive. Then I'll take off. Don't worry, I'm parked at a construction site, so anyone who sees the car won't think anything of it. Nobody's working at the house today. They'll think I'm a solitary construction worker."

"All right, but be careful."

He knew Jayce wouldn't like his car sitting there for someone to take notice of. "The car's stolen. I wouldn't risk being here in the rental car."

"Good thinking. Let me know when it happens. If I can't talk, I'll do what I always do. Just say, *It's done,* and hang up."

"Got it. And hey, don't forget I want my brass knuckles back, dude. I got those from a real movie set."

"It was a B movie. Even a C movie, if there is such a thing."

"*Killer Ninjas from the Sewers* was one of the best movies I ever saw. I want those knuckles."

"Uh, about those . . . they're gone."

"Wha—"

"Stop whining. I tried to break into Winslow's place and do some more plastic surgery on her face. She woke up, and I had to take a leap from her balcony. They fell out and when I went back the next day they were gone. I'll get you another set on eBay. I gotta go."

Damned Jayce. He owed him an even better set. From an A movie even. Cal settled in to continue to wait.

When the garage door started opening, he scooted up in his seat. They were back. Except that a yellow Porsche pulled in with the roof down and Ashlyn driving.

"Oh, jeez! She's not supposed to be here. What if she—"

He thought of calling Jayce, but the *what if* shot him into action. He couldn't let her walk into that office. He scrambled out of the car and ran across the street toward the house. Ashlyn couldn't die; Jayce would kill him! He left behind a string of expletives as he ran up the steps and fumbled with his key. What was he going to do now? She might not go into the office, but he couldn't take that chance, so he'd have to blow his cover. Maybe he'd knock her out, put her in the car, and drive her somewhere? Maybe he'd even get lucky and she wouldn't remember his face. He could use the trick that Jayce had used on Winslow, putting Ashlyn into her own trunk. Once he had her out of there, he'd call Jayce and get instructions.

He opened the door and couldn't believe it. Ashlyn was walking straight to the office. She was going to open the door!

"Hey! Don't touch that!" he yelled as he ran toward her.

Her eyes widened and she pushed the door open, probably intending to run into the office and lock him out. He watched the door swing in, every inch bringing it closer to the trigger. He threw himself at her. She pushed at him and screamed as they fell to the side.

The room exploded. The force threw them. He could feel a blast of heat roar up behind him and a thousand shards of glass prick his back. He heard nothing beyond the deafening thunder. As they hit the hard marble floor, he felt a piercing pain in his back. He grunted as they slid several feet across the floor.

The smell of burnt flesh stung his nose. It felt as though his back were on fire. The piercing pain got worse, and he tried to reach behind him to remove the object that was causing it. Things were still falling to the floor around them. He kept reaching, stretching, and then he felt the sharp edge of a large piece of glass. He followed it with his finger, feeling the sting of the edge cutting him, until the piece disappeared deep into his flesh.

Even worse, he felt the charred surface of his shirt—and his burnt skin that was sticking to it. A fire alarm went off, and water sprayed down, cooling his skin. From the corner of his eye he saw flames shooting up near the office door, and he heard the sizzle as the sprinklers extinguished them.

Each breath became shallower and more painful. He looked at Ashlyn lying next to him. She was breathing, though unconscious. He had covered her body with his, taking the brunt of the shrapnel for her. Oh, jeez, her face . . . it was blistered bad. She must have twisted to the side, though, leaving her face exposed. Her eyebrows and lashes were singed completely away. Her arms were cut, too. But she was alive. He'd saved her. He hadn't totally screwed this up. Jayce would be pleased.

He fell to his side, unable to hold himself up any longer. The glass pressed deeper into him. He coughed and felt blood trickle from his mouth. He needed to get out of there. He couldn't be found at the scene.

But first he needed a few seconds of rest. He closed his eyes. Then he'd escape. Just a few seconds. . . .

When Jayce's cell phone rang, he was sure that it was Ashlyn telling him she was coming back. She'd have some groveling to do. He simply couldn't let her get away with this crap. He doubted she'd give him much trouble when he initially took over Talbot Development—he would, after all, play the hero and keep Grant's considerable wealth safe—but he needed her completely under his control so she wouldn't get any ideas about stepping in later. The only thing he would have to ensure was that she didn't get pregnant. The last thing he needed was some kid to deal with again. Or the media attention of yet another missing pregnant wife.

"Ashlyn?" he answered, trying to sound worried.

Grant's shaky voice totally threw him. "There's been . . . an explosion. At the house."

Why the hell was he alive? Jayce hoped Winslow had been killed, at least. "Dad, what do you mean, an explosion at the house? That sounds crazy."

Grant was nearly breathless. A siren pierced the air in the background, and he waited until it faded before he spoke again. "I don't know; I don't know," he said, sounding disoriented. "Ashlyn—"

Another siren drowned out his words. He probably wanted to talk to Ashlyn, hopefully to tell her that her sister was dead.

Jayce said, "I don't know where Ashlyn is. We had an argument and she took off."

"She was in the house . . . they're taking her to the hospital right now."

His stomach clenched. "Ashlyn? Hospital? She can't be there! She's in Key West shopping."

"We couldn't understand it, either. We weren't even sure if you were here somewhere, too."

The phone slipped from his hand when his fingers went numb. He fumbled to pick it up. "I'll be right there. I'll catch a flight, do whatever I have to do to be there. Is Ashlyn all right? Can you tell me that much?"

"She's alive. She suffered a lot of superficial cuts. We couldn't see anything worse, but they"—his voice broke, and he regained control—"have to check for internal damage from the force of the explosion. And there's more. Her face was badly burned. Her eyes are all right, thankfully. God, who would do this?"

"We're going to find out, Dad. I promise you that."

If Ashlyn died, he'd have to adjust his whole plan. Hell, he wasn't sure he would even have a plan. "Is Winslow all right?"

"She's fine. We arrived a few minutes after it happened."

Minutes. He'd been minutes from success.

"There's something else," Grant said. "A man was found in the rubble, next to Ashlyn. We don't know who he is."

Jayce's throat tightened. "A man?" Cal. It had to be Cal, who had probably tried to keep Ashlyn from going into the house. Dumb flighty bitch. How badly was he hurt? Jayce couldn't ask without giving away his concern.

"They think it might be the guy who set the explosion. He doesn't have any ID on him."

Jayce's mind scrambled through the facts. No ID. Had Cal ever been fingerprinted? He didn't think so. But what about the cell phone? It would lead right to Jayce's cell number. If

Cal was hurt, he'd be under guard at the hospital, a suspect.

Grant said, "Just come right away. Take a cab from the airport. We'll be at the hospital. I've got to go."

"The man. Has he said anything?"

"He's dead."

The phone disconnected. Jayce fell to the bed, his legs boneless. Cal was dead. Everything was falling apart. He could be convicted if they had the cell phone. But he wouldn't know until he got there. And if he disappeared, he'd be suspect one.

He would go—and figure out his next steps when he got there.

An hour later, Jayce settled on the small airplane that would take him into a potentially dangerous situation. Once again things had gotten screwed up. Was he destined to be that poor, unwanted boy of his youth? He had tried hard to shed his past, to reach for a better life. He should have pursued professional golf, as friends had suggested over the years. He'd been afraid that being a celebrity would open his past to the press. It was bad enough that *he* knew that scrawny boy; he wanted no one else to know him. He would kill to keep his past buried.

His mother, Paula, had gotten pregnant at seventeen; when Jayce's father wouldn't acknowledge her baby she'd shot him. Having survived the wound, Jayce's father disappeared after Paula's trial. She received parole after one year in prison. During that year, his grandmother, Mollie, had gotten "stuck" with him. That's what she'd considered it anyway. When Paula was released, she moved in with her mother, too, creating a tense situation full of resentment and criticism that spilled over onto him. The trailer was too small for all of them.

Their one amicable activity was the thing that shamed Jayce most—Dumpster diving, as Paula called it. They would scout the "good" Dumpsters in Las Vegas and make

Jayce climb inside to retrieve anything that could be resold.

Even that "family bonding time" couldn't save them. When Jayce was ten, Paula started staying out all night. Mollie's long, stinging lectures didn't deter her one bit. In retaliation, Paula stayed away all weekend. And in retaliation, Mollie left for the weekend, too. When Paula returned, she discovered Jayce alone and the kitchen a mess from his trying to cook what he'd found. She'd worked herself up into a lather by the time Mollie came back.

Jayce was sent to his room while the two women fought, and it wasn't until he heard no more shouting, only crying, that he dared come back out. Paula was lying on the kitchen floor with a bloody knife in her hand. Mollie was dead from twenty-two stab wounds to the face and chest. This time Paula would not be getting paroled anytime soon, and Jayce was sent from relative to relative until he landed at his uncle Bonner and aunt Susie's place in Hendersonville.

Bonner was the first real father figure Jayce ever had. Cal was like a malleable younger brother. They lived in a small house in a poor neighborhood, but at least it was a home. Bonner worked at a prestigious golf course as grounds manager and sometimes took Cal and Jayce with him. There Jayce got a glimpse of not only golf but also the rich life. They started playing golf and he got good at it. But he hated the way the rich people treated him. He wanted to be one of them. The more he saw their fast cars and extravagances, the more determined he got. As soon as he graduated, he moved to California. He worked as a caddie, got friendly with some of the members, and started playing with them. Betting. Charming them. Trying to ignore the way they still looked down on him.

So he got an idea. Old Seymour Phillips bragged about not only his upcoming sojourn to Italy but also his multiple country club memberships. Jayce called one of those clubs as Seymour and paved the way for his *close family friend* to play golf. Suddenly Jayce wasn't a caddie. He wasn't trailer trash.

He was the guest of a powerful, rich man and was treated the same way. After the first day Jayce knew he would never go back.

That was when he met Amber Mills, the insecure daughter of the old-money Mills family. An idea came to life. Find a rich woman in need of someone to feed her ego, give her affection, and fulfill her life. Amber was perfect, but she was also in need of a father for her daughter. Jayce watched *Leave It to Beaver* reruns before he approached Amber, learning what a good father was like. Charming Charles Mills hadn't been so easy, but Jayce appealed to his ego in a different way. He let Charlie win at golf a few times.

Once Jayce was invited to a couple of social events and a few dinners at the Millses', he had Amber where he wanted her—in love with him. Jayce had worked carefully to win her parents over by being polite, doting on Amber and Paige, and never being dazzled by their money. Within a few months, he and Amber were married and set up in a beautiful home that her family bought them. He had control of Amber, but he didn't have control of her money. Her family kept a tight leash on them. Her father *generously* got Jayce a job at the company where he worked ten hours a day at a desk. The kid was getting on his nerves. So was Amber. She tried too hard to be a good wife.

He played along, though. Worked at his boring job, lavished affection on his wife and stepdaughter. Even talked about adopting her. He knew that marrying a rich woman with the intent to kill her for her money wasn't anything original. But he also knew what mistakes many of the others had made that put them in the police crosshairs. Being greedy was one of the biggest, second only to mistreating the wife. All Jayce wanted was the house. He'd planned to stay there long enough for the stain of murder to fade and then cash it in.

He had his cousin Cal on call, ready for action. The timing was important. And then fate handed Jayce the perfect opportunity when Amber and the baby were both down with a cold for their standing dinner invitation on Sunday nights with her parents, something else he hated. It was another way to keep tabs on him and Amber.

When Jayce discovered his wife and stepdaughter slashed in Paige's bedroom, he played the part with precision. That was another big mistake the morons had made, acting too cool or odd in the aftermath and especially lying to the police. He called 911 first, and anyone who heard that tape would cry at his fear and shock and disbelief. He cooperated fully in the investigation, never once requesting a lawyer. Funny how Amber's parents were his alibi. Time of death saved him. He'd dragged out the evening long enough to make a difference. He'd even volunteered to take a lie detector test and passed. Those things depended on having emotions and reactions.

Then Jayce got his nasty surprise. Amber had nothing in her own name. The house was locked in the Millses' family trust. All he'd gotten was the $200,000 from the life insurance policy. He'd kept it moderate, with one in his own name, so it wouldn't be an obvious motive. Just a small policy on Paige.

He was furious. Compared to what he thought he was getting, the policy was a pittance. Amateur mistake on his part, believing Amber. So he fought the Millses for the house. He'd walked away from the battle with less than $100,000 and the Millses' anger. He didn't care if they hated him. They couldn't take their alibi back.

As he began infiltrating Miami society using someone's name as a family friend, though, he took that valuable lesson with him: Find a vulnerable woman who stood to inherit a fortune. But don't kill the woman. No, kill the parents. Then she'd inherit, and he'd have total control of her and her money. When he met Ashlyn, he knew she was perfect. Bonus: no kids. Big bonus: single father. This time it needed to look like an accident, in case anyone caught a whiff of his past. He would play it just as he had last time. Get in with the family, be the perfect son-in-law, and give Ashlyn no doubt that he loved her and not her money. There would be no friends talking about how unhappy the wife was, no whispers of divorce. Who would suspect him of offing his father-in-law when he was so devoted to Grant?

It was unfortunate that he actually liked Grant. But Jayce would have his money this time. Conscience wouldn't play into it.

Everything had gone perfectly—until Winslow had poked her nose into his past. If only those stupid Cubans hadn't died. Now he didn't know if his wife was even going to live. Or if he was walking into a trap. But he knew two things: he would not go to prison, and Winslow would pay for her part in screwing up his plans.

25

Winslow was going to make Jayce pay for this. If there was a scrap of justice in this world, he would go to prison for the rest of his life. She wanted to imagine all kinds of terrible things would happen to him there, being so pretty and all. Unfortunately, she was realistic enough to know that he'd use his manipulative powers to stay safe.

She stood near Ashlyn's bed, feeling anger pulsate outside a core of numbness. Grant felt the same way, she guessed by the pale way he looked, the disbelief and shock in his eyes.

Luckily Ashlyn's face was the only part of her that was badly burned. It was unlucky, though, that it *was* her face. A burn specialist was called in, and it was deemed that Ashlyn wouldn't have to be transferred to a burn unit. At least not for now.

Lightweight dressings treated with medication covered her face. Her eyelids were swollen shut. Doctors had examined her eyes before the swelling started, and her corneas were undamaged. Only a portion of her right cheek had survived the funnel of fire that had apparently reached out for her. The doctors still had to determine how deep the burns went, though so far it appeared that they were second-degree. She was under sedation for now. She'd suffered several cuts on her face, neck, and arms. The mystery man had shielded her from much of the blast.

Jayce knew who he was. Too bad Grant had already told him the guy was dead. Then again, Jayce was just cold enough not to be affected by the news. The metro police had arrived at the house first, then Miami-Dade police, and finally ATF. Winslow had gone through all three levels to tell them to find the man's cell phone, knowing it would lead to Jayce. Unfortunately, it had been on the dead man and was now in pieces. The car that he'd probably used to keep an eye on the house had been stolen.

The most disturbing evidence wasn't even real. The bomber left newspaper articles about the arrest of the two men who had run over the Garcías' boat in the office. Bombs, one investigator had said, were the trademark of terrorists. Though Winslow had protested that the papers were meant to lead them astray, they told her that they had to follow up all leads.

She could *feel* Jayce's hatred of her as he came in the room behind her.

He ran straight to Ashlyn's bedside. His voice was breathless when he turned to Grant. "How is she? I was going crazy on the flight home. There's a crowd of reporters out front. It's on the news. But no one said a damned thing about how she's doing." He turned back to her. "Why is her face covered?"

He was so good it chilled Winslow. The emotion in his voice evoked pain and frustration. It sounded so real.

Grant said, "The burns I told you about."

"Oh, baby, I'm so sorry. I wish we hadn't had a fight."

That had been the overriding question once the chaos had settled down. Winslow couldn't figure out how Jayce had gotten Ashlyn to race home during her honeymoon.

"That's why she came home?" Winslow asked. "You had a fight?"

He nodded, though he didn't look at Winslow. "She had a

scare on our first dive. When you're underwater marveling at all the sea life, you lose track of where you're going. We went deeper than she wanted to go, though she was doing fine until she saw some barracuda and freaked. She wanted to shoot to the surface, but if she'd held her breath, she could have had an aneurysm. So I held her, tried to get her to calm down. I made her ascend slowly, safely."

His voice cracked, and he cleared his throat. "Afterward she didn't want to dive anymore. I was mad at her for being so timid. We'd gone through the lessons and I was really looking forward to a week's worth of diving together. So I took the boat out by myself. When I came back, she was . . . gone."

Maybe his story was true, or maybe he'd tried to drown Ashlyn and she fled. Either way, there was no reason for him to arrange an explosion at Grant's office. It didn't make sense.

Jayce turned to her, and his face was rigid with anger. "I heard that they think the anti-Castro terrorists were responsible for this. That they were punishing you"—he turned to Grant—"for her actions. She did this to us." He pointed to Winslow, his finger shaking. "She did this by going against your request, Dad. By involving you—and Ashlyn—in terrorist politics. She had to find justice for that Cuban girl. But it was at the cost of her sister's safety."

With her doubts so fresh in her mind, Winslow couldn't think of a rebuttal. And accusing Jayce would only make matters worse for her. All she could say was, "We don't know that the exiles had anything to do with this. Why would they target Grant? I was the one who found the two men."

"Maybe they couldn't find you. Grant is accessible. In the public eye. They made it more than clear that this was because of you. The guy on the radio said terrorists left behind newspapers about the hit-and-run. They wanted you to know that they'd done this because of you."

She couldn't look at that bitter face anymore, so she

looked at Grant. And she saw the same accusation in his grief-stricken face. "Dad, you don't believe that, do you? Why would they punish me? So what if I found the men who hit those people? The *duros* didn't do it. They weren't implicated."

Grant said, "But they hated the García brothers, hated their political views. They would have liked their murders to have gone unpunished."

He believed! Jayce had already poisoned him. And now the snake walked over to Grant and put his arm around his shoulders. "I'm sorry, Dad. I shouldn't be bringing this up now. We need to stand together for Ashlyn."

She bristled whenever he called Grant *Dad*. And at his lies. He didn't want them standing together. He wanted her out.

She gave him what he wanted, at least for now. She left to get some fresh air. Instead of going outside, though, she went to Alex's room. He was walking, with the assistance of his brother Enrique. Just as she had sensed when Jayce had entered the room, Alex sensed when she did, and looked up. That simple thing melted her stomach.

"Winslow!" He made his slow way toward the door, but she saved him some steps and met him halfway. "I've been trying to call you all evening. I heard about the explosion. Your sister—is she all right? No one would tell me anything here."

"Her face is burned pretty badly and she has some cuts, but otherwise she's all right." Except that she would never be all right, not if her face was scarred. Winslow couldn't think about that. She realized her manners and nodded in greeting to Enrique.

He nodded back and said something in Spanish to Alex. "I'll leave you two alone," he said to her, and left.

Winslow took his place, putting her arm around Alex's shoulder to give him support. She felt a stabbing pain at the realization that she had been responsible for Alex's injury. Maybe she'd also inadvertently caused Ashlyn's. Had Ashlyn read the newspaper clippings and, more important, Winslow's notes on the back? Was that why she'd fled, after the warnings Winslow had given Ashlyn about Jayce forcing her to dive?

"Are you all right?" Alex asked, watching her face.

Her arm tightened on his shoulders as she felt a wash of gratitude that he didn't hate her. "I need you to find something out for me. The investigators think that the exiles may have set the explosion in retaliation for our solving the Garcías' hit-and-run. Jayce is using this to once again put a wedge between my family and me. I think he's going to succeed this time unless I can prove that his cohort was behind the explosion."

"His cohort?"

Oh boy. "I found a California number on Jayce's cell phone. It was a cell number, too. When I returned from California, I think the cohort came, too. He followed me once, but I managed to lose him. I didn't tell you all this because—"

"You didn't want to worry me," he said without humor. "But how do you know—"

"That it was Jayce's cohort? Because I dialed the number and heard a phone ring nearby. Twice. This guy was here setting up the explosion while Jayce was on his honeymoon." Her eyes widened. "Jayce had an alibi. He was on his honeymoon. Just like he was with Amber's parents the night of the murders. His cohort killed them."

"Winslow . . ."

"And now he's dead. Jayce blames me; I could tell by the look on his face just now. Can you talk to your father, find out if he's heard anything at all about anger toward me?"

He was searching her face. "If you believe that Jayce is that dangerous, you need to back away from him."

"I know he's going to kill my sister. I know that he somehow planned for her to run home. We won't know the whole story until she wakes from the sedatives. She's my sister. I never realized how much she meant to me until all of this happened. I can't let Jayce destroy her."

"All right." He started toward the bed, and she helped him. "But I'm working with you."

"Alex, look at you. You're almost pale with pain. You can hardly walk." *Her fault, her fault.* "You can help by finding out if there's even a chance that the exiles did this."

"And if they did?"

"Then . . . then I'll need to rethink everything. And I'll have to back away from my family. I won't endanger them—or you."

He picked up the phone and made a call. She only understood a word here and there. A few minutes later he hung up. "He's heard about the newspapers left behind, but at this point no one has taken credit for it. He's going to ask around, see if there's been any talk about you at all. Do you know if the man found in the rubble was Latino?"

She shook her head. "I'll try to find out."

He was leaning against the bed, trying to conquer the pain. "I know you want to spare me from getting hurt again. You're even willing to cut me out of your life to do so. But it's not going to work, Winslow. Promise me you won't shut me out." Despite his pain, he gave her a stern look.

"I'm here now, aren't I?" She forced a smile. "I'm going to talk to the police this time, convince them to look into Jayce. I won't have anything to do with him."

But she knew she was lying. She was on her own until she figured out just what was going on. And though that thought terrified her, she wouldn't involve Alex again.

"I've got to go home, check on the cats," she said.

"Be careful," he said. "Live as though you're under fire."

She shivered. He was right. Because someone wanted to hurt her and right now she wasn't sure who that was.

Jayce and Grant sat side by side next to Ashlyn's bed. Once again Grant was torn in two. He'd seen the hostility sparking between Winslow and Jayce. He knew she still suspected him of foul play. Maybe she couldn't face the fact that she

ad brought this on them. If investigators could figure out
ho the dead man was, they could probably make headway
n the case.

How could Winslow doubt Jayce's devotion to Ashlyn,
hough? If she could see him now, talking softly to her, try-
ng to draw her out of her sedated sleep, Winslow would
now that he was madly in love with Ashlyn.

Jayce turned to Grant and said in a soft voice, "This
oesn't change anything, Dad. I mean . . . if she's scarred, it
on't change how I feel about her. I don't want that to be a
uestion in your mind. I'm here, no matter what."

It hadn't occurred to him yet, but he appreciated Jayce
aking it clear. "I know," he said.

"What are you going to do about Winslow? I have a sug-
estion, though I know you won't want to hear it. Cut her out."

Grant rubbed the bridge of his nose. Looking at his
aughter, her face covered in gauze, enormous pain and sur-
eries ahead of her . . . yes, he knew what to do. Winslow
ad to go.

t two o'clock that morning, Winslow slipped into the hos-
ital. She couldn't sleep. She peered into Alex's room,
appy to see him sound asleep. His sister was sleeping in a
hair nearby. The sight of her devotion both touched
Vinslow and made her sad, and she moved on to Ashlyn's
oom. She could hear Jayce's voice as she approached the
pen doorway, and she stopped just out of view.

"I'll take care of you, baby. I'll take care of everything; I
romise."

Though the words spoke of devotion, there was some-
ing sinister in the way he said them. She couldn't pinpoint
hy. And then his next words iced her over:

"Winslow made this happen by making you doubt me. I
und the articles in your car along with her notes. Look
hat trusting her got you. I'm going to take care of her, too."

She didn't know if Ashlyn was awake; she couldn't hear

any response. Quietly she backed away, found the stairs, and used them instead of waiting for the elevator.

Jayce was going to take care of her. She had to be very careful from now on. And somehow she needed to talk to Ashlyn before Jayce could brainwash her once again.

Winslow got her chance at lunchtime the next day. She watched Jayce and Grant pull out of the hospital parking lot as she pulled in. She took a deep breath as she walked into Ashlyn's room a few minutes later. The girl's eyes were closed; Winslow wasn't sure if she was still under sedation.

Her heart broke when she saw the singed eyelashes barely a fringe left. She choked back a sob, and Ashlyn's swollen eyes opened a sliver.

Winslow covered her mouth as she tried to get her emotions under control. "How are you doing?" she whispered a few seconds later.

Ashlyn's voice was muffled. "Jayce said the bomb was because of you."

Had she heard Jayce's threat to take care of her? "That's what he wants you to think. The truth is, we just don't know. I'm trying to find out." She took in her sister, as much as she could see of her. "I'm so sorry this happened. But why did you come back to Miami?"

"I didn't want to dive anymore. We had a fight." Ashlyn swallowed. Her words were soft, as though her lips couldn't part enough. "I read your notes. And . . ."

"And what?" Winslow was leaning toward Ashlyn, riveted for the reason she fled the Keys. "Tell me."

She shook her head. "I have to believe that he'd never hurt me. He told me he loved me, that he'd never leave me even if I'm ugly." Her eyes welled up. "They can't fix burn scars like they fixed your face. How am I ever going to look in the mirror? Jayce still loves me. Don't you see that I have to believe that?"

Oh, God, she could see. Poor insecure Ashlyn facing

future of being uglier than she ever perceived herself to be. Winslow remembered Ashlyn's admission about being worried that Winslow would overshadow her on her wedding day.

Ashlyn closed her eyes. "Go away."

Winslow couldn't move. This was the time. She had to tell Ashlyn the truth about her face. No, more than that, she had to show her. Her chest tightened at the thought. If she hoped to reach Ashlyn, she had to reveal everything.

She made herself walk into the bathroom. She didn't turn on the light at first, just turned on the water and squirted a rail of pink soap into the palm of her hand. She scrubbed at her face with a damp paper towel. She even rubbed away her eye makeup. Only after she'd rinsed off the soap did she turn on the light and look at her damp face in the mirror. The fluorescent light made the fine red lines even more prominent. She squeezed her eyes shut. No, she could do this.

She turned off the light and walked back to Ashlyn's bedside. Ashlyn cracked open one eye before shutting it again. She was going to ignore Winslow.

"After every one of those plastic surgeries I underwent, Dad and Mom would make a big fuss at how beautiful I was as I healed. But I looked in the mirror and saw the ugly scars the incisions left behind. I saw a face that I didn't even recognize."

Winslow's words sounded as tight as Ashlyn's had. "But I wanted to please Dad so much, especially Dad, because he had gone to all the trouble and expense to make me beautiful. To make me perfect. It sounds silly now, but I felt as though I'd failed him by not healing perfectly. Mom started putting heavy cover makeup on me so I'd be perfect. The more fuss she made, the more I had to keep putting on the makeup, until I couldn't go back. It was like a big lie; the more I perpetuated it, the harder it was to show my true self. That face you've been jealous of all this time isn't even mine."

That finally got Ashlyn's attention. She opened her eyes.

Winslow gestured to her face. "This is me. See, I'm not perfect." She felt as though a great weight had been lifted from her chest.

Ashlyn studied her face, taking in every inch of it.

"That's right. I've been wearing a mask all this time. That's what it felt like. And . . . well, I couldn't trust you enough to tell you. I thought you'd throw it back at me. I knew it would be because of your insecurity about your looks, and that always puzzled me. You're a beautiful girl."

"You're still beautiful," Ashlyn said. "But you look different."

"I feel ugly. But you know what? I feel more like me. I've been hiding behind my mask. That's why it felt like a mask to begin with. I'm not perfect; I'm not even beautiful. And it's okay. You're going to be okay, too. Dad will do everything he can to restore your skin. But promise me that you won't let him alter your face. Perfection isn't what it's cracked up to be."

Ashlyn didn't promise, but she was still looking at Winslow's face. "You're not ugly."

Winslow smiled at the statement. "You're not ugly, either."

That got a little smile out of Ashlyn, but it faded. "The reason I came home . . . it wasn't the articles. It wasn't even so much that Jayce was making me dive when I didn't want to."

"He said you panicked and he held you down."

"I realize now that he was doing what was best. I was stupid to panic. But I wasn't going to dive anymore. I stood up to him, and it felt good. It made me realize what you'd been saying was true. I was a different person, and I didn't like who I'd become. So I pulled out the articles and read them. It was something in your notes that made me run. You said that Jayce was mad when he found out the house wasn't in his name." She closed her eyes for a moment; either because of emotional or physical pain, Winslow wasn't sure. "Jayce has been bugging me to get the condo put in our names. Or at least in mine. I didn't want to ask Daddy to do that, so he

vas going to. Your note made me wonder. I panicked again.
thought I was safe in coming home."

Winslow winced. "I know. You should have been. The
nan they found in the house . . ."

"The police asked me about him this morning. But I don't
emember much right before the explosion. Only that I went
nto the house and nothing until I woke up in the middle of
he night." She swallowed hard. "Winslow, you should know
omething. Daddy is at the attorney's right now. He's writ-
ng you out of his will . . . out of our lives. He said you en-
langered us all. Jayce had no idea that I'd be coming home,
o he couldn't have had anything to do with the explosion.
3esides, he was in the Keys."

"He has a friend—the man found at the house probably.
he one he called in California. That man followed me when
went to your condo on your wedding day. I lost him, so he
lidn't know where I'd gone. But I'm sure he called Jayce
nd told him. That's why Jayce called to make sure I hadn't
ome there."

"But you're forgetting something important. I'm not
vorth anything. It's Daddy's money, not mine. Jayce knows
hat, so he has nothing to gain if I die."

"Are you absolutely sure he knows?"

"Yes."

What was Jayce after? Then the pieces came together,
nd Winslow had to hold on to the side of the bed with the
orce of the realization. "Oh, my God. He never had any in-
ention of killing you. That bomb wasn't meant for you; of
ourse it wasn't. It was meant for me and Dad." Her legs
uckled, and she had to brace herself against the bed now.
Dad called and wanted to resume our weekly breakfast. But
t got put off until lunch. We always go back to the office af-
er our meal. Jayce knew that. And Dad said it was Jayce's
lea that we resume our routine. Jayce knew we'd be at the
ouse together. He had his friend wire the office."

Though fear and uncertainty tainted Ashlyn's eyes, she

said, "No. No, that's a horrible thing to say. He loves Daddy."

"What if it's true?" She leaned closer to Ashlyn. "Can you afford to take that chance? Gambling with your life is one thing, but gambling with Dad's is another. And Jayce wants me out of the picture, too. I'm pretty sure he had his friend shoot at me. Those two creeps didn't have any .38 caliber weapons. Were you awake last night when Jayce told you that he was going to take care of me?"

The denial in her eyes was real. "No. You were here?"

"I couldn't sleep and I was worried about you. Jayce was saying how he was going to take care of you. Of *everything*. He said he'd take care of me, too, but he didn't mean it the same way."

"Winslow, I just don't know . . ."

"You don't have to know anything. Let me search your condo."

She said, "I don't think Jayce knew you were at the condo that day, but he had security cancel your garage key card."

"Fine, tell security to let me in. We could be saving Dad's life."

That clearly worried her. "All right."

"And remember that Jayce loved his little stepdaughter, too. He was even talking about adopting her. But someone broke in and viciously stole their lives. We know that Jayce wasn't that person. We can't be sure that it wasn't the same guy who was found dead at the house. He probably saw you go in and tried to stop you. You weren't supposed to die—Dad and I were."

"I'll call the building," she said in a rush. "Just don't get caught."

Winslow saw fear in her eyes. She was afraid of Jayce's wrath if he found out. "I won't."

Ashlyn was already on the phone when Winslow walked out of the room. She stopped when she saw Alex coming slowly down the hallway without anyone's help. She ducked back inside the room. He was coming here; she was sure of it. Was she ready for him to see her like this? And could she quickly leave without giving away that she was up to something?

She took a deep breath and stepped into the hallway. After pretending to be surprised to see him, she gave him a kiss and stepped back so he could see her. She waited for him to register something—surprise, disgust, even confusion as to what was different.

"How's Ashlyn?" he asked instead.

"Better. She's resting now."

But he could hear her voice wafting into the hallway. Luckily her words weren't clear.

"Sounds like she's talking to someone."

Winslow edged around him, still trying to seem casual.

"You look different," he said finally. "You're not wearing makeup." But he still didn't look disgusted.

"This is the real me. Behind the mask."

"I know."

Now it was she who looked surprised. "You do?"

"The night you spent at the house. I woke up in the middle of the night and watched you sleep for a while. The moonlight was coming in through the window, bright as day. You were beautiful." He reached out and stroked her cheek. "I like you better this way. I was disappointed that you were made up when you came back with the *café con leche*."

He'd seen her without makeup. It stunned her, that and that he actually liked her better without it. She loved this man. Oh yes, she loved him more than almost anything.

And she had to lie to him again. "I'll tell you more about it. I'll show you everything. Right now I have an appointment. And I'm late."

His warm expression cooled to a skeptical one. "Winslow . . ."

"It's nothing." She gave him another quick kiss and waved good-bye as she walked down the hall. "I'll talk to you later."

She ran down the stairs and out to her car. Once she realized she might be in sight of windows above, she slowed her pace. As soon as she got out of the parking lot, though, she gunned the engine and flew toward the condo.

Alex watched Winslow disappear down the fire stairway. "Dammit." She was up to something. Lying to him again. He'd never be able to catch up to her, and he had no vehicle in which to follow her anyway.

He strained to hear Ashlyn's voice, but she was quiet now. Winslow had just come from her room. That meant Ashlyn would likely know what had sent her running. He knocked on the open doorway and smiled. Winslow wasn't the only one who was investigating. And he knew exactly how he would extract the information from Ashlyn.

26

Grant sat in the conference room while the secretary prepared the new will. Jayce was out in the waiting area. He'd started to come in with him, and Grant had asked him to wait. Jayce had been a little surprised, and maybe even put out, but this was personal.

The coffee that the secretary brought in tasted bitter, and Grant was pretty sure it had nothing to do with the quality of his lawyer's coffee. This whole thing left a bad taste in his mouth and in his heart. He was angry that Winslow had introduced so much havoc and danger into their lives, but she was still his daughter. He had been in a fog when Jayce had suggested doing something proactive about Winslow.

Jayce had told him that changing the will now would ease his anger and pain and would make it official in his mind. Grant had liked getting some power back over his family situation. But now that his head was clearer, he could see that this wasn't going to solve anything. He walked out of the room to find the secretary.

Jayce sat in the posh waiting room. This was what his office would look like. Dark and masculine, with lots of leather. He loved the smell of it. When Grant was gone, he'd probably suggest they sell the house. Memories and all. He'd had his eye on a place on Fisher Island, but it would probably be sold by the time he was ready. Since he had to wait awhile for things to die down, he would have to plan Grant's death carefully. This would be his last chance. And he was damned well going to make it work.

His cell phone rang, and he felt a pang of emptiness when he realized it wouldn't be Cal. He was alone now. It was all up to him.

On the upside, he wouldn't have to share the fortune, either. "Yes?"

"This is Fred over at Talbot Tower. Winslow Talbot just came in. Apparently Ashlyn notified security that she was to be allowed up to the condominium. Sorry, but she's the owner. Had to follow orders."

She wasn't the owner, but Jayce held back those bitter words. "Thanks for letting me know. You get a bonus the next time I see you."

Damn it to hell! What was she doing there, and why was Ashlyn letting her in? He sprang up from the cushy leather couch but froze as he realized he couldn't ditch Grant. They'd ridden together, even if Grant had shut him out of the proceedings.

What did this all mean? Was Ashlyn suspicious? Was everything falling apart just when he'd sewn it back together again?

He heard Grant's voice in the hallway. "Ms. Fleming, tell Ted to put a hold on the paperwork. I need to think on it a while longer."

Jayce wanted to explode. He could feel blood rushing to his face, sweat popping out of his pores. He had to get to the condo, but what would he do about Grant?

He told the receptionist, "Tell Grant that something urgent came up and I had to run. Would you call him a cab?"

He would have to take the chance that Grant might go to the hospital, where Ashlyn would tell him whatever it was that she now suspected. And he'd have to come up with a cover story as to why he'd left Grant without wheels.

He tore out of the office and down the stairs to the car. He had to stop Winslow from finding anything.

Winslow felt the urgency as she searched through dresser drawers. Jayce had plenty of clothing but nothing incriminating. "Where would he put his personal papers?" She was hoping to find drugs, too, to prove that he'd overdosed Dallis. God, Ashlyn probably didn't even know her former best friend was dead yet. Winslow couldn't bring herself to tell her, not now.

What she did find was a small key tucked way in the back of his sock drawer. She palmed it and looked for whatever the key belonged to. The dresser in the bathroom was jammed with men's grooming products. He had more than Ashlyn did. Winslow went through all the drawers in the bathroom and even climbed into the lower cabinets while searching the far corners.

The closet was meticulously organized, except for one corner. Jayce had moved into one side of the closet; that was about all he could fit into with all of Ashlyn's clothing. She riffled through the hanging clothes and then started in on the shelves in the far corner. She found several boxes filled with personal items such as an old 35mm camera and a key ring stacked with various car and house keys. A box was filled with maps, including one of San Francisco and one of Miami.

In the back of the lowest shelf she found the metal box that the key belonged to. She pulled it out, turned the key, and opened the lid. Why did he have a video camera in here when he kept his 35mm out in the open? She set that aside and looked through the paperwork.

His birth certificate was inside, verifying that he was, indeed, Jason Bishop. But he hadn't been born in Illinois or even California. His place of birth was Las Vegas. He had three different driver's licenses, all in his name.

"Dammit, there has to be something in here!"

She went still. Had she heard a noise? After a few moments of intent listening, she dismissed it and continued looking. There were several old photographs, probably dating back to the eighties. Most were of him and his family. A couple posed on a front porch in one. In several others two boys were often pictured together. They were close in age and looked somewhat similar. One was Jayce. She would recognize those eyes anywhere. The other . . .

She tried to recall the face of the man who'd tailed her but hadn't seen him clearly enough. Still, if the police could match this boy to the man found at the house, they would then have a connection to Jayce. She stuck a picture in her pants pocket and kept picking through the paperwork.

Beneath more papers was a plastic bag containing two Baggies of substances that looked a lot like drugs. Both were a fine white powder. Two syringes and a metal measuring cup, lighter, and curled length of rubber tubing were all the evidence she needed that it was indeed drugs. She pulled out the bag. Maybe they could tie it to the same formula in Dallis's system, if that was possible. Nothing else looked promising, so she turned to the camera. Was there a reason it had been locked away so that Ashlyn would never see it?

She had to plug it in, since the batteries were dead, and she did so at the bathroom counter. She pressed Play and watched a video of Ashlyn trying on bathing suits at a store. Why was Jayce in the dressing room area with her? She put the speaker up to her ear and listened. Dallis's voice sent chills down her spine.

Winslow searched for a label identifying the camera as belonging to Dallis. Residue on the bottom indicated that a label had once been there.

She fast-forwarded through the DVD. They were out on a boat. She saw Ashlyn and Jayce moving around, and then the camera faced the sky for a while. She fast-forwarded again and recognized Dallis's room. And then Dallis herself on her bed looking dazed and scared. Winslow held the speaker up to her ear again.

"Speedball," she heard Jayce say. "How do you feel, Dallis? Do you feel *high*?"

His voice was taunting. Dallis did look high. She looked sick, too. Off to the side Bob-the-snake slid up against the glass in his aquarium.

"This is what you had, isn't it? This is why you called Winslow."

Her stomach lurched as she realized what she was watching. Now he showed the computer screen and she saw the same video she'd watched prior to this one. He turned up the volume.

She could barely hear Jayce's voice. "Hey, Cal. You used to be chubby. I just screwed up and called Ashlyn's friend a demented cow. . . . No, not to her face. But Ash is pissed at me. I want to say something to the cow to redeem myself. So Ash will know I was just kidding. I'm still in the perfect boyfriend phase; I can't mess it up now. . . . Oh yeah, I've got her hooked. I've only got a few seconds. Give me some help here."

Her eyes watered as she watched the small screen. Dallis leaned over the side of her bed and dry-heaved. Jayce took a DVD and broke it in half. Obviously not this DVD. But from the look on Dallis's face, she thought he had destroyed the evidence she'd found to nail Jayce. And they would have, if only he hadn't intercepted Dallis's message. Anger and fear roiled inside her.

The camera focused on Dallis. "How ya feeling, Dallis? Flying high yet? Winslow's not going to get your message, by the way. I was there when you called. I erased it."

Dallis was trying hard to focus, but anger burned in her eyes. Her mouth was hanging slightly open, but she looked unable to speak. He had drugged her. That must be what a speedball was.

He lifted her hand and said, "Wave bye-bye, Dallis. Yeah, it's been real nice. Bye-bye."

Now Winslow gagged and turned off the camera. But she still heard Jayce's voice saying, "Enjoy the movie?" For a moment it was disorienting. Until she saw his reflection behind her in the mirror.

He looked so calm, as though she'd just watched a Disney movie. Her fingers tightened on the camera. She could feel perspiration on her palms. Her options played through her mind: scream; throw the camera at him; bolt at him, push him aside.

They all evaporated when he pulled a gun. A .38-caliber, she guessed.

"Forget whatever it is you're thinking. I should have taken you out long ago."

"It wasn't for lack of trying."

"No, it wasn't. You got lucky at that intersection. And you keep getting lucky again and again. Well, guess what? Your luck just ran out."

She heard a distant cell phone and realized it was hers, stuffed into her purse out in the living room. While that distracted her, he moved so fast she didn't have a chance to counteract him. Within seconds he had her pinned to the floor with a washcloth in her mouth. He rolled her over so that her face was pressed into the plush white carpet.

"Look at you, bringing your stash of drugs into my condo. I told Grant you were on drugs; he hated to think it, but he had to wonder. Now he'll know for sure. You came here to end your pathetic, delusional life. Did you see how much fun Dallis had before she died? It's a nice way to go."

Winslow struggled, but his strength easily overcame hers. She could hardly breathe. Did Grant think she was using drugs? Oh, Jayce had probably laid the groundwork. Maybe he'd been planning to do her in this way for a while now. She couldn't let him inject her with that stuff. He was going to make it look like she was a drug addict! Like she'd over-dosed! She bucked but hardly budged him.

She heard him open the bag. He wrapped the rubber tubing around her arm. It hurt when he cinched it tight. She heard him messing with the drugs, doing what she didn't even know.

His cell phone rang. "Dammit." She felt him maneuver as he set the measuring cup on the counter. "Yeah?"

She could hear a man's voice say, "It's Fred again, down-stairs. Ashlyn just called to give an Alex Díaz permission to go to her condominium."

Winslow tried to make noises through the towel, but Jayce shoved her face farther into the carpet. "Fred, do whatever you can to stall him. The guy's a reporter and a trouble-maker. Tell him you didn't get the message and make him wait while you call Ashlyn to verify her permission. You want to be careful, don't you?"

"You got it."

She heard a beep as Jayce disconnected and tossed the phone on the floor next to her. "We've got to move things up. Your boyfriend's on his way. I wouldn't want to have to hurt him, too. If you cooperate, he'll arrive just as you're ex-piring. I'll tell him how I walked in to find you about to shoot up and tried to talk you out of it. You confessed to do-ing drugs, but this was your first time shooting up. It looks like suicide. After all, your family has shunned you. And there's your guilt. This would be an appropriate place to fin-ish yourself."

No, he couldn't hurt Alex! She stopped moving. Alex would know that she didn't take drugs, but it would seem a plausible explanation for her behavior lately. If they looked hard enough, they would find no evidence of previous drug use. Maybe they'd find towel fibers in her mouth. But she knew that Jayce would likely get away with her murder. Then he'd kill Grant.

He pulled her to her feet and guided her to the living room. Sunshine poured through the doors facing the ocean. He shoved her to the floor again and pinned her down by straddling her.

"Say good-bye, Winnie."

Ashlyn couldn't stand it any longer. First she called Winslow's phone, but it went to voice mail.

She then called her daddy. "Don't write Winslow out of the will," she said without preamble. "It's not right. And don't write Jayce in."

"I didn't write Winslow out. I told the attorney I'd have to think about it more. And as far as Jayce goes . . . I'm rather annoyed at him at the moment. He ditched me at the attorney's office. The receptionist said he got a call and told her he had to leave, that it was an emergency. I'm in a cab, which he did have the decency to send for. Hey, why are you calling about this? You sound shaky. Are you all right?"

She burst into tears.

Winslow watched Jayce mix the two powders with some liquid he'd gotten from the kitchen and heat them in the cup with the lighter. He blew on the resulting substance. Her arm was now aching from the blood being cut off.

"This is all going to work," he muttered. Clearly he was trying to assure himself. "As long as your boyfriend doesn't burst in here." He looked at the front door. The dead bolt wasn't thrown. Apparently Jayce hadn't wanted to give away his presence with the sound.

"If he does, I'll have to shoot him. Then I'll shoot you and tell everyone you shot Alex and yourself. I'll leave to get Grant, supposedly, while Fred calls an ambulance. I'll have to ditch the Ferrari, of course. That'll really piss me off. But as a backup plan, it's not all bad." He gave her a smile. "It means I get away. And you die."

She was torn between trying to fight and saving Alex's

life. She felt no relief that he was on his way. But *why* was he on his way? She couldn't fathom how that had come about unless Alex had charmed Ashlyn into telling him what Winslow was up to.

Jayce drew the liquid into the syringe and pressed the plunger to remove the air. "Let's do it."

She squirmed as the needle aimed for the plumped vein. His mouth tightened as he stilled her arm.

They both heard the sound of the elevator swishing open. Jayce reached for the gun on the coffee table and aimed it at the door. She tried to make warning sounds, but they came out as grunts.

The door swung open. The gun went off, and the man she loved stood in the doorway for a moment, as shocked as they were. Blood spurted out of a hole in his white shirt and dribbled down his stomach. Then he crumpled to the floor.

She took advantage of Jayce's shock to shove him off her and race to the door. God, please don't let it be too late! She jerked the towel from her mouth and pressed it against his wound. "No, no, no. Please don't die. We have so much to talk about." She started screaming, "Please, somebody, call the police! Help!"

Then she turned to Jayce, who stood with the gun in his hands staring at them. He didn't have a backup plan for this.

The second elevator swished open and she nearly collapsed in relief. The security guard and doorman rushed out of the car, guns drawn. And behind them Alex raced out and fell to his knees beside her.

She turned to Grant, whose face was pale. "Dad, hang in here." She looked up at the doorman. "Call an ambulance!"

He nodded, but his attention was riveted to the guard who was ordering Jayce to drop the gun. Jayce held it at his side, his fingers white where he clutched the handle. He was shaking his head so subtly it was hardly detectable.

Then Jayce aimed the gun at his head and squeezed the trigger.

Alex shielded her as the gun exploded. She kept her han
pressed hard against her dad's chest but looked away fro
the living room.

"Oh, jeez, oh, jeez," the doorman said, covering his fac
with his hands. He rushed out the door and threw up.

Alex pulled out his cell phone and called 911. The gua
wasn't taking any chances. He approached Jayce's body an
even checked his pulse. It was hardly necessary with h
brains splattered all over the carpet and walls.

"Fred, get downstairs and escort the paramedics and p
lice up here. Tell them the scene is cleared." The gua
rushed over to Grant and checked his pulse, too. "Shallo
but steady. Keep the pressure on, just like you're doing. M
Talbot, we're going to get you to the hospital in just a fe
minutes. Can you hold on for us?"

Grant managed to nod.

"Dad, what are you doing here?" Winslow asked, hopin
to keep him talking and awake.

"Ashlyn," was all he could manage to say.

She looked at Alex. "And how did you manage to com
here?"

"Ashlyn. I convinced her to tell me where you were going

"But . . . how?"

"I'll tell you later."

It seemed like an hour passed before Fred radioed fro
the lobby that the paramedics were there. A minute later th
elevators opened and blessed help arrived. She watche
them work with precision as they strapped Grant to a gurne
and rolled him back into the elevator that Fred was holdin
for them. The second elevator opened to spill out four poli
officers. Winslow collapsed against Alex as the doors to th
elevator taking Grant away closed.

One of the officers approached them. "What's going o
here?" His gaze went to the living room and he grimaced.

Alex slid his arm around her, helping her to her feet an
giving her support. She didn't know where the words cam

om, but she said, "Allow me. I'm getting good at explain-
g."

inslow was surprised to find that she'd fallen asleep in the
aiting area. Her head was pressed against Alex's chest.
ie'd been careful not to lean against his leg and hoped she
idn't done so while she'd dozed.

"There hasn't been—"

Alex pulled her back down to his chest. "No, nothing
:w. He's still stable."

Grant had undergone four hours of surgery. The bullet
id missed his heart and lungs, but he'd suffered heavy in-
rnal bleeding. She'd gone in to see him in recovery, just
ng enough to see for herself that he was alive. She meant
hat she'd said. They had a lot to talk about. First, she was
dering him to call her Winnie again. Everything else would
ow from there.

"I just realized something," she said, rubbing her eyes.
Everyone I love is in the hospital right now."

Then she realized exactly what she'd said. When she
ipped Alex a look, she saw that he recognized the signifi-
nce of that little statement.

"Is that so?"

Well, there wasn't any point in denying it. "It's so."

He traced his finger across the curves of her face. "Are
ιu sure you can handle loving a journalist?"

She had to laugh. "If you'd even consider"—he hadn't
id he loved her yet—"being with me, I could definitely
it up with your career and its hazards." Her smile faded. "I
ot you shot. I nearly got you killed again, if you'd walked
rough that doorway first. This wasn't even your problem."

"It was your problem, so it was my problem."

That probably meant that he loved her. She started to set-
e against him again but stopped. "You never told me how
ιu convinced Ashlyn to tell you what I was up to."

His mouth twitched in a smile. "It was actually a little by

accident. I knew you were lying to me—again. And I was scared that you were going to get yourself killed this time. Which, as you'll recall, almost happened."

"Yeah, yeah, go on."

He lazily curled a strand of her hair around his finger. "I told her how much you meant to me. That if something happened to you I would wither away and die. I told her how much I love you."

She smiled. "Is that so?"

"It's so." He gave her a sweet kiss. "The sad thing was, she compared my proclamations to the ones Jayce had been making, and she saw the real thing. It convinced her that he'd been laying it on her. So she called security in the building and told them to let me up."

"And then that bubble brain doorman alerted Jayce. He felt so bad, though, that I almost feel sorry for him getting fired."

The highlight was having Detectives Capperson and Ramey apologize for thinking she was crazy. Ramey even said, "I know, so you don't have to say it. In fact, I'll say it for you: I told you so."

A nurse opened the door and said, "Your father is awake and asking for you."

Winslow leaped up and then turned to Alex. "Come on."

"I'll leave you two alone. It's a family thing."

She tugged on his hand. "If I have anything to say about it, you'll be a part of our family soon. Come."

After not knowing where she fit in for so long, she'd now found just the right place. It wasn't even far from where she'd always been. But now she belonged there.

EPILOGUE

THREE MONTHS LATER . . .

Ashlyn, Grant, Winslow, and Alex sat by the pool on a beautiful spring night finishing Mojitos after a fabulous Cuban dinner prepared by Esme, who was indeed Cuban. Though it shamed Winslow that she'd never thought to inquire, it also irked her that they'd been missing out on eating Esme's Cuban cooking all this time.

Ashlyn sucked the rum off her mint leaf and nibbled the leaf. "Winslow, I think you're wrong." Her face was healing nicely, thanks to dermabrasion treatments that sanded down the scar tissue. Like Winslow, she would always have scars, to remind her of her misplaced trust. But also like Winslow, they would be minimal. "Have a big wedding. I know you're planning something more subdued because of me . . . to protect me. But I don't want you to do that. When I gave up my big fairy-tale wedding—though I'm glad I did now—I regretted it. You will, too."

"Maybe." Winslow had never dreamed of a big wedding, but heck, she did dream of lace and tulle and traditional vows. She already knew it would be big, though; Alex's family would ensure that. Alex's mother had already taken her to lunch to discuss the wedding. Winslow discovered that she liked her; and she had some great ideas, too. She had learned that Cuban women were very attached to their children, and his mother was already looking at Winslow as a daughter. When Estela Díaz had invited Winslow to call her *mima,* her eyes had got all teary. "Are you sure, Ashlyn? I don't mind—"

"I'm sure." She waved away the lingering question in Winslow's eyes.

Grant still looked worn down by guilt. He'd withdrawn from the governor's race, though Winslow had made him promise that he'd run next term. The house was the only victim that had healed without any scars. That would never be true for any of them. Winslow hated that most of all, that Jayce had left aches in all of them. She was determined to eradicate most of them.

Maybe this would help. "Detective Capperson called me today. They finally positively identified the man found in the rubble as Cal Driscoll, Jayce's cousin. They were able to match his DNA with the mucus found on the tissue at Amber Mills's house, too. Jayce went to live with Cal and his family when his mother killed his grandmother. I think he was a pretty messed-up boy who turned into an evil man. Don't blame yourselves for what happened. He was a master manipulator. He duped the Millses and even the police in San Francisco."

"He didn't fool you," Grant said, and she saw a spark of admiration in his eyes. "You were on to him from the beginning. If only I had—"

"Stop it, Dad. He was good." She reached over and took his hand.

He squeezed hers and gave her the first smile she'd seen since the explosion. "I think a big fancy wedding is what we all need. And I won't hear of anyone but me footing the bill, got it?"

She couldn't deny him that, couldn't risk losing his smile. "All right." She turned to Ashlyn. "And it would honor me you would be my maid of honor."

It wasn't quite the first smile she'd seen on Ashlyn's face, but she was glad to see it just the same. "Really?"

"I couldn't think of anyone else I'd rather have by my
de. But on one condition."

Ashlyn looked skeptical. "What's that?"

"That you bring Dr. Kane as your date."

He was the reason Ashlyn had smiled at all, especially af-
r learning of Dallis's death. That had been harder than
ything else for her to handle. She was seeing a therapist to
ork through her guilt. "I don't know . . ."

"I do. I see the way that man looks at you. And you look
him the same way. You don't have to rush into anything.
st invite him as a friend and take it slow. I know it's going
take time to trust a man again. But I'm betting he's a good
sk."

"I believe you," she said. "I'll always trust your opin-
n, Sis."

The endearment warmed her, and so did Alex's fingers
rabbling along her arm. Just one of his many gestures of
fection.

"All right, I'll invite him, but only on one condition,"
shlyn said. She tilted her head and looked at Winslow.
've got the perfect design for your wedding dress."